Jo,

To one of my
dearest friends.
Love and hugs,
Marilyn

I'm only the author's

# What Readers Are Saying About
## *Polished Arrows...*

"I couldn't put it down!"
—David Teitelbaum, electrical contractor

"It's a cross between *Woman, Thou Art Loosed* meets *Desperate Housewives.*"
—Danielle Greenberg, Rebbetzin, New Beth Israel

"I have brought so many books home from the library in the last several months. This is the first one I have found interesting enough to finish."
—Peg Kowalski, M.D.

"Simply amazing. You describe everything so perfectly!"
—Lea Rimon, Ginot Shomron, Israeli settler

"After reading the Devorah sections, I really felt encouraged to get closer to God."
—Pat Groff, NY

"This book is fantastic!"
—Margaret Lowinger, Rebbetzin, Congregation Brit Hadashah

"That's it? I want to keep reading! When is book two coming out?"
—Sharon Grubner, wife and mother, after reading the final page of *Polished Arrows*

# POLISHED ARROWS

## DEBORAH GALILEY

CAPSTONE FICTION

WATERFORD, VIRGINIA

*Polished Arrows*

Published in the U.S. by:

**Capstone Publishing Group LLC,**
P.O. Box 8
Waterford, VA 20197.

*Visit Capstone Fiction at*
**www.capstonefiction.com**

Cover design by JNC Studios
Map © 2007 by Esther Galiley. All rights reserved.
Author photo © 2007 by Robert Jeff

ISBN: 978-1-60290-005-9

*This book is lovingly dedicated to*

**Steve Galiley,**

*the Lappidot in my life.*

# Acknowledgments

I wish to acknowledge the following people for standing alongside me and helping to make *Polished Arrows* a reality.

Peggy Kowalski, for your untiring encouragement and vital prayer support. I value our friendship immensely;

Danielle Greenberg, for your insightful comments and fabulous enthusiasm. Your faith in this project boosted my faith;

Lisa Schell, for the initial edit of the manuscript. You put a "polish" on *Polished Arrows*. Thanks for being a great friend and letting God use you;

Wendy Christian, for wonderful counsel. You never fail to find time in your busy schedule for my e-mails and phone calls. You are a true friend;

Margaret Lowinger, for the right words at the right time;

Natalie Heretz, for your prayerful belief that this book was from God;

Carleen, Debbie, Eliza, and Mary Jean, my prayer group, for your faith, encouragement, and prayer support;

The people at Beit Shalom Messianic Jewish Congregation, Utica, NY, for your love and faithfulness;

Ramona Tucker and Jeff Nesbit, of Capstone Fiction, for having the vision to publish *Polished Arrows*. Ours is a divinely ordained partnership;

Leonard & Esther Galiley, my in-laws, for raising such a great son and passing on a godly legacy to future generations. A special thank you to my mother-in-law for drawing the map of ancient Israel on such short notice;

Robert Jeff, for your generous photographic help;

Harry Teitelbaum, my dad, the English professor. For good or ill you passed on to me the ability to spot a typo at 20 yards! I thank you for doing an early read-through of the manuscript with your trusty red felt pen. I have to admit I didn't know what to expect and was blown away when you proclaimed it "excellent";

Marilyn Teitelbaum, the world's greatest mom. I wouldn't be surprised if you single-handedly spread the word about this book from Los Angeles to Tel Aviv and all points in-between;

My brother, Mark, for invaluable advice;

Dave & Lynda, Sarah, Irving & Susan, for adding to the richness of my life;

Josh, Shimon, Yael, Noa, and Ellie. You are incredible kids, and I love you all so much! Thanks for giving me the space to write this book and not complaining (even when I had to kick one of you off the computer because I had an extra half hour and wanted to write NOW!);

Last, but not least, my husband, Steve. I shamelessly stole from both our life together and your anointed sermons. This book would not have been possible without you.

And to everyone whose name I didn't mention due to space constraints, my gratitude and love for your part in my life.

*Listen to me, you islands;*

*hear this, you distant nations:*

*Before I was born the Lord called me;*

*from my birth He has made*

*mention of my name.*

*He made my mouth like a*

*sharpened sword,*

*in the shadow of His hand He hid me;*

*He made me into a polished arrow*

*and concealed me in His quiver.*

—ISAIAH 49:1-2

# PROLOGUE

## *Jericho, 1308 BC*

Sweat ran down the back of the young man as he waited in the king's antechamber. Nervously, he raked his fingers through thick, black hair and pushed it out of his eyes. To him had fallen the thankless and dangerous task of bringing this year's tribute to the greedy and dreaded conqueror of Israel. For eighteen years Israel had been plundered by the loathsome Moavite king, Eglon. All over the land, people cried out to God for deliverance from the onerous burden exacted on them by the required tribute. The young man had cried out to God as well, and now he had a plan.

The door to the antechamber swung open, and the captain of the king's guard emerged. Perhaps this man had been a warrior to be reckoned with years ago, but now he was merely another overfed, indulged middle-aged man. He snapped his fingers, and several guards deliberately walked forward. They patted down each of the men in the delegation in a sloppy and routine check for weapons. The young man prayed silently to Adonai when the guard assigned to search him pushed him against the wall. The guard felt under his arms, front, back, and then ran his hands up only the left leg, skipping the right. He didn't consider that the young man might be left-handed.

After the security check ended, the young man and his caravan were escorted into the king's presence. The sight of the king shocked the young man. Once a fit and formidable military man, Eglon had indulged his every carnal appetite until, at well over 300 pounds, he had become a mountain of flesh. Impatiently, his labored breathing audible to all, his small, sharp eyes greedily watched as the Israelites set up the piles of gold and silver.

The young man cleared his throat. Hiding his disgust, he knelt before the king. "There is also the sheep and grain, Your Majesty. They are outside."

The king scowled. Standing up, shaking with rage, he screamed, "It's

not enough! Not enough, do you hear me? I know there's more gold to be had. You have one week to double this amount or Israel will pay in blood!" The delegation was dismissed by the king in a fury.

It was time to follow the plan. The young man quickly led the caravan out of Jericho and into the countryside so they could safely get away. He then said to his second-in-command, "Release the runners and send the message." Turning on his heels, the young man headed back into the city and toward the great room. Passing through the same sloppy security as before, the young man stepped into the king's presence declaring: "I have a secret message for you, O King!"

Eglon broke into a broad and crafty smile. Expecting a bribe, he dismissed his court and led the young man into an upper room that had access to his hidden personal safe. The walk had winded Eglon, so he sat down.

"I have a message from Elohim for you," the young man said.

Eglon stood up.

The young man reached left-handed to his right thigh and drew a double-edged sword. He thrust it upward through Eglon's stomach, cutting through intestines and lungs. In order to be certain the sword had done its job, the young man drove it even deeper until the handle was covered by fat. Looking into the shocked eyes of the king already glazing over with death, he whispered, "Elohim has ended your reign of terror."

Moving quickly, the young man escaped out the porch and locked the doors of the upper room. Then he ran. And ran. Making it to safety in Seirah, he blew the shofar with a battle cry! The yoke of bondage was broken.

So a new chapter of freedom started. . . .

# PART I

# DEVORAH

## 1232 BC

*Celebrate the Feast of Tabernacles*

*for seven days*

*after you have gathered*

*the produce of your threshing floor*

*and your winepress.*

*Be joyful at your Feast—*

*you, your sons and daughters,*

*your menservants and maidservants,*

*and the Levites, the aliens, the fatherless and the widows*

*who live in your towns.*

*For seven days*

*celebrate the Feast*

*to the Lord your God*

*at the place the Lord will choose.*

*For the Lord your God will bless you*

*in all your harvest and in all the work of your hands,*

*and your joy will be complete.*

—DEUTERONOMY 16:13-15

# ONE

"But I just can't miss Sukkot!" The little girl hopped restlessly from foot to foot. "I've been looking forward to it all summer. Please, Ema. Let me go this year!"

Her mother didn't even pause as she busily swept the clay floor of their little home. "Devorah, you know I can't travel this year. And I don't think it's a good idea for you to go without me."

The naturally high-pitched voice of the seven-year-old went up an octave. "Oh, please, please! I'll be with Abba." The hopping accelerated.

Before her mother could answer, the front door opened and Avraham ben Yosef strode cheerfully into the house. "Did I hear my name?"

"Abba!" Devorah squealed and ran to her father. "Tell Ema that I can go with you to Shiloh for the Feast. Can I, please?"

Avraham looked over the top of their daughter's head at his wife.

"What do you think?" she said.

"Go outside so Ema and I can talk about this," he told the child.

"And here." Her mother handed her a hand-sewn bag. "Go into the garden and pick some beans for dinner while you're waiting."

Devorah took the bag from her mother and walked outside slowly, reluctant to miss this important conversation. Once the door closed behind her, the parents discussed in earnest what to do.

"Why don't you want Devorah to go to Shiloh?" Avraham asked.

"I'm worried." She stroked her swollen belly unconsciously. "We've lost so many babies, I couldn't bear it if anything happened to her. Or to you."

"Miryam." Avraham took his wife in his arms and held her close, breathing in the familiar earthy smell of her. "To go to Shiloh for Sukkot is an act of obedience to the Lord. God will protect us."

"I'm sure you're right. But Devorah's not a baby anymore." Miryam put her arms around Avraham's neck and looked up at him. "You would have to make sure you keep her with you and away from anyone we can't trust. Like the lovers of Canaan."

Avraham frowned. "I don't think we'll see too many of them on this trip. Most of them don't even pretend to worship the one true God as they did when Ehud was in his full strength." He pulled thoughtfully at his beard. "To tell you the truth, I'm very concerned about the direction Israel is taking. I think it's important for Devorah to come with me so she can worship the Lord with her fellow Israelites."

After fifteen years of marriage and seven stillbirths, both Avraham and Miryam doted on Devorah, their only child. Mature and joyful, Devorah reflected the best of both her parents. On the outside, Devorah was unmistakably Miryam's. Her curly, red-blonde hair, carelessly pulled back from her face, fell in loose tendrils that framed wide-set green eyes and a face covered with freckles, while sturdy brown legs carried her on endless explorations of the fields and pastures on Avraham's farm. From her father, she had gained an intelligent curiosity and an exceptional understanding of Torah that amazed many.

"Miryam, you're right—Devorah's not a baby anymore, which is why she should come to Sukkot," Avraham said. "I believe God has great things in store for our daughter."

Miryam sighed. "All right. Take her with you. But come home safely."

"Always," promised Avraham.

It was early fall, and all over Israel people prepared to travel to the Feast of Sukkot—the Israelites' annual pilgrimage to the Tent of Meeting in Shiloh. There the Israelites would build small booths, or huts, called *sukkot*, which served as a reminder of the flimsy desert huts that had provided shelter for the Israelites when the Lord brought them out of slavery in the days of Moshe. Once they reached the Tent of Meeting, the pilgrims would offer the firstfruits of their crops and animal sacrifices to the Lord in celebration of the way He had protected their ancestors in the harsh desert so many years ago. Throughout Ramah, men, women, and children worked hard to bring in the harvest and the new wine in time to bring their gift offerings to the feast.

When the day finally arrived, Avraham and Devorah joined a group of fellow pilgrims from Ramah for the twenty-mile journey to Shiloh. At the end of a long, tiring day, they stopped to make camp for the night. Men fed the animals and tethered them for the night, children gathered kindling, and the women prepared meals over open campfires. Once supper had been cleared, the pilgrims wrapped themselves in warm goatskin blankets, settled around a fire, and listened in fascination as their elders recounted tales of Israel's heroes.

"Tell us the story of Ehud," Avraham said to Kenaz, the oldest of their company. "The children need to know about the hero they are going to meet at Sukkot."

"Who is Ehud?" Devorah said.

Kenaz smiled at her. "Ehud is the judge of Israel, little one. He led us to victory against our enemies, the Moavites."

Devorah sat mesmerized as the old man's voice carried through the dark night, while firelight reflected off the faces of his audience. "The story begins almost eighty years ago, when Ehud, the son of Gera the Benjamite, went to pay tribute to Eglon, king of Moav."

"What's tribute?" a small boy said.

"Tribute is what the Moavites stole from our hard labors," one of the men said.

"That's correct," Kenaz said. "Now Ehud, who is left-handed, had made himself a special sword—a double-edged sword about a foot and a half long—and he had strapped this to his right thigh under his clothing." Kenaz stopped briefly and took a drink of water from the leather pouch at his side. "He brought the tribute to Eglon, king of Moav at Jericho. Eglon was a very fat man." Kenaz stood up and stretched his cloak as far as possible away from his narrow frame. "So fat, in fact, that two grown men could stand next to each other behind him and you couldn't see either one of them."

The children giggled.

Kenaz grew serious. "Everyone was afraid of King Eglon because he was as mean as he was fat. He would send his men to raid the Israelite villages—to kill, loot, and destroy. And Eglon would give extra plunder to the men who killed the most Israelites in the raids. Those were terrible times."

"Ehud must have been brave to go visit the king," Devorah said.

"Indeed. Very brave. After Ehud had presented the tribute to the king, he dismissed the men who had carried it for him and sent them to their homes. But at the idols near Gilgal"—Kenaz spat at the mention of idols—

"Ehud himself turned back toward the palace. He returned to the king and said, 'I have a secret message for you, O king.'

"The greedy king thought that Ehud had a special bribe for him, so he snapped his fingers and shouted, 'Quiet!' And his frightened attendants ran out as fast as they could. No one wanted to cross old King Eglon.

"Ehud approached the king where he sat alone in the upper room of his summer palace. He walked right up to him and said, 'I have a message from God for you.' As the king rose from his seat, Ehud reached with his left hand, drew the sword from his right thigh, and plunged it into the king's belly.

"Even the handle sank in after the blade, which came out of the king's back. Ehud did not pull the sword out, and the fat closed in over it." Kenaz paused dramatically and allowed the image of the fat-covered sword to sink in, much as the sword itself had sunk into the unfortunate king years before.

"*Yofee!*" a boy shouted.

Devorah sat bright-eyed and silent.

Kenaz went on. "Now Ehud was a remarkable man with nerves as strong as iron. After he killed Eglon, he calmly walked out of the upper room, shut the doors behind him and locked them, and left the palace. A little later, the servants came and found the doors of the upper room locked. They said, 'The king must be relieving himself in his inner chamber.' They waited to the point of embarrassment, but when the king did not open the doors of the room, they took a key and unlocked them. And what do you think they found?"

Devorah's little voice spoke up. "They found the uncircumcised body of one who dared to defy the Living God!"

The crowd erupted in cheers and shouts of laughter.

"This little maiden is a warrior!" Kenaz said.

Avraham nodded. *This daughter of mine is in the hand of God Himself*, he thought.

"You are right!" Kenaz said to Devorah. "The servants saw their king fallen to the floor, dead. And while they waited, Ehud got away."

More cheers went up around the fire.

"He passed by the idols"—here Kenaz spat again—"and escaped to Seirah. When he arrived, he blew a shofar here, in the hill country of Ephraim. 'Follow me!' he ordered, 'for the Lord has given Moav, your enemy, into your hands!' So we followed him down and took possession of the fords of the Jordan that led to Moav. We allowed no one to cross over. I was twenty years old that day, and it was the most momentous day of my life."

Kenaz paused, suddenly lost in thought as he stared into the fire.

"How many Moavites did Israel kill that day?" someone asked.

"Ten thousand," Kenaz said. "Ten thousand, all vigorous and strong. Not one man escaped! And I"—the old man stood up and his voice quivered as he looked around at all the faces—"I struck down five of them myself, and I would do it again today to free Israel!"

Staring at the fire, he recalled the decisive battle of almost seventy-five years ago—a day of fury, blood, and vengeance. Kenaz had been plowing his father's field when he heard the blast of the shofar echoing through the hills. Excitement had surged through him, for he knew immediately what was happening. "This is the day," he had shouted to the startled oxen. "This is the day we will lose the stench of the Moavites from our land!" He had run with all his strength to the house, where his parents waited. They had heard the shofar as well, and they knew where he was going. He hugged them good-bye, pulled his sword from its hiding place, kissed the tears on his mother's cheeks, and laughed aloud. "Ema, Ema," he had said, "don't cry. Today is the day the Lord has given our enemies into our hands!"

He'd had just enough time to pack a loaf of bread, a cake of raisins, and a skin of water before racing to meet up with Ehud. Along the way, he was joined by men from his village, then others from neighboring villages. More and more men ran toward the sound of the shofar. The very air pulsated with the promise of the victory of God. By nightfall, the first of them had reached the banks of the Jordan River, which led into Moav. Clan after clan took up position, allowing no one to cross over....

"Kenaz?" The voice of Avraham broke in on the flood of memories. "Kenaz, why don't you lie down now? It's very late."

Kenaz shook himself out of his reverie as he turned to look at Avraham. At first glance, there was nothing very compelling about Avraham. He was of average stature, and had pleasant, though not extraordinary, features. He shared the olive skin, brown hair, and brown eyes that characterized so many of his countrymen. But even the briefest interaction with Avraham revealed a godliness and humility that set him apart and brought him great respect in the village. Indeed, many people came to him instead of their local Levite with questions about the Torah. Many found it odd that a man so beloved by the Lord should be married to a woman who had stillborn after stillborn baby. Yet Avraham steadfastly refused to take a second wife.

He claimed that his love for Miryam did not allow for him to lie with another. His patience had been rewarded seven years ago, when Miryam had at last given birth to Devorah.

Kenaz looked at little Devorah's sleeping form. *Ah.* He smiled to himself. *Here is a daughter equal to any son!*

"All right, Avraham," he said. "You're right. It is very late. But I'm glad I was able to tell the children who Ehud is and how the Lord God used him. When we get to Shiloh and they see a frail, blind, old man, they need to realize that he was not always this way. That once"—Kenaz grew misty-eyed—"he was a powerful warrior filled with the Spirit of God!"

Avraham shook his head. "I'm concerned that as Ehud ages, faith among the Israelites gets weaker. So many of our people have fallen into the way of the Canaanites. I fear for our nation, Kenaz."

"We must pray, Avraham. We must ask the Lord to raise up a judge after Ehud."

Avraham clasped Kenaz's hands. Together they prayed fervently to the Lord for the salvation of Israel.

Two days later, the company of pilgrims from Ramah wearily climbed the last little hill to the west of Shiloh. When they reached the top, they stopped to look down into the town.

"Ohhh," Devorah gasped. "Abba, look!"

Sukkot dotted the valley below as far as the eye could see. Wooden poles laced together with cords of flax formed tiny, temporary dwellings. Palm fronds, leafy branches, and poplars decorated the sides and occasionally the roofs, according to the owner's tribe. Clusters of grapes and pomegranates hung from doorways and side poles. Women cooked over makeshift stone ovens while young children ran around, yelled, and explored from booth to booth. Men ate and talked in small groups. Even the sheep and goats socialized, bleating and *maaahing* among themselves. It was a scene fraught with energy, color, and excitement. Devorah smiled widely.

Avraham nodded with satisfaction. "Look, my daughter. Look carefully and remember this sight all of your life. Here are the Children of Israel, obeying the word of the Lord and coming together to worship Him at the Festival of Sukkot."

Father and daughter stood together in silence. Avraham serenely watched the crowds, his eyes half-closed in prayer. Devorah's eyes scanned the valley, not wanting to miss a single detail. Suddenly she observed a sukkah that stood alone in the middle of all the others, but with much more space around it. As she squinted, she could just barely see a man sitting in front of the doorway, with long lines of people in front of him.

"Abba!" Devorah tugged at her father's sleeve.

"Yes?"

"Look! Is that Ehud's sukkah?"

Avraham squinted. "Ah! Yes, my little one. That is the sukkah of the judge of Israel. That is Ehud, and the people are lining up to speak with him about different things."

A voice interrupted. "Come on, let's go!"

Avraham and Devorah turned to see Moshe, the scout of their group, waving them on. One would never know from looking at Moshe's round, friendly face that here was a man who could find his way through every ravine and crevice in the hill country of Ephraim. He often joked and played with the younger children, who all adored him. Now, however, he spoke brusquely.

"Let's get going, you two!" he shouted. "We need to stake out a place and build our sukkot before evening prayers."

Avraham and Devorah turned and dutifully followed Moshe and their fellow townspeople down the hill to Shiloh.

Three hours later, their sukkah built and decorated, Avraham and Devorah went with Kenaz to wait for their chance to meet Ehud.

Avraham mopped sweat from his brow as they stood in the late afternoon sun. He had offered to share their sukkah with Kenaz, and the older man had gratefully accepted and tried to help with the construction. But as Avraham ruefully contemplated, no matter how strong and energetic, a ninety-five-year-old is not a newborn lamb. Devorah's high spirits, though charming at first, had become more and more annoying until Kenaz had sent her off to find decorations for the walls. She had returned with an armload of wildflowers and, in complete concentration, had woven the flowers throughout the palm branches, turning their simple sukkah into a vibrant masterpiece. Now all three of them stood in line to pay their respects to Ehud before they assembled for evening prayers.

Suddenly, out of the corner of his eye, Avraham caught sight of a boy moving toward them so quickly it looked like a blur. Before Avraham had time to react, the boy crashed into Devorah, who fell to the ground with a thump.

"Hey!" Avraham shouted.

A man's voice in the background yelled angrily. "Lappidot!"

Avraham bent down to Devorah. "Are you okay, *motek*?"

Devorah's eyes filled with tears, but she nodded bravely. "I...I think so, Abba."

"I'm really sorry—I didn't see her!" the boy exclaimed as he struggled to stand.

"Lappidot!" A tall man strode forward angrily and grabbed the boy by the shoulder. "What are you doing?"

"I'm sorry, Abba," Lappidot said. He shook himself free of his father's grasp. "Yehudah was chasing me and I didn't look where I was going." He peered sheepishly at Devorah who, hurts already forgotten, stared in wonderment at him.

Avraham stepped in. "No harm done. My little girl seems to be fine and the boy was just being a boy. Don't worry about it." He put his hand out. "My name is Avraham ben Yosef, and this is my daughter, Devorah."

The man shook hands stiffly. "Ammon ben Binyamin. From Beit El."

"Ah!" Avraham exclaimed. "Then we're neighbors! We live in Ramah."

Ammon's face loosened into a smile. "Fellow Ephraimites! It's good to meet up with a brother. Are you here with your whole family?"

"This is my family." Avraham gestured toward Devorah, who had begun chatting with Lappidot. "My wife is expecting a baby next month and stayed behind. Devorah is our only child. How about you?"

"I am the opposite," Ammon said. "I am here with two wives, eight children, assorted relatives, and several goats. They're all making me *meshugga*, but he"—and here he pointed to Lappidot—"is ahead of all the others!"

"Is he the oldest?"

"Yes, yes, the oldest. He is bursting with energy. I am glad that your daughter was not harmed by his poor behavior."

Avraham studied his new acquaintance. *Eight children*, he thought. *Eight children and he understands nothing! Perhaps Adonai wants me to teach this fellow.* "You know, Ammon, I see from his eyes that your boy is a good boy at heart. If you would like, I would be honored to pray with you and seek the Lord's guidance on the best way to train him up into manhood."

Ammon raised his eyebrows at this suggestion. "Uh, thank you. Let me think about that." His eyes strayed to Devorah and Lappidot sitting on the dusty ground. "They seem to be getting along just fine now, don't they?"

10

They certainly did. Devorah giggled as Lappidot entertained her with wild stories accompanied by exaggerated gestures. Feeling his father's eyes on him, Lappidot stopped talking and stood up. "Is everything okay, Abba?"

"Yes, son. Come! Say shalom to our new friends so we can return to the sukkah before we miss dinner."

Lappidot turned to Avraham and Devorah. "Shalom!" he said enthusiastically. "I hope to see you again."

Avraham shook the boy's hand warmly. "I hope so, too. Shalom, Ammon. Good to have met you."

"Bye, bye, bye!" Devorah waved happily to her new friend. "We'll see you later!"

"Good-bye." Ammon stopped and looked Avraham in the eye. "I will consider your offer of prayer. Come on, son." He put his arm on Lappidot's young shoulders, and they headed off into the crowd.

"Abba, where's Kenaz?" Devorah asked. Avraham spun around, remembering the long line to meet Ehud. To his great relief, the line had moved rapidly, and Kenaz had doggedly held their place. Now he gestured to Avraham and Devorah. "Let's go!" he yelled. "We're next!"

Avraham and Devorah stood by quietly while Kenaz and Ehud hugged each other.

"It is always good to see you, Kenaz." Ehud spoke softly and with difficulty. He was an extremely old man, well over a hundred years. Deep lines crisscrossed his brown face. Judging the pain and suffering of an entire nation for more than seventy-five years had weighed heavily on him. Devorah stared intensely at him and attempted in her young mind to imagine how the strong hero who killed King Eglon could be the same person as the old man before her now.

"You know, of course, Avraham ben Yosef of Ramah." Kenaz drew his friend into the conversation. "And this," he said as he put his arm around Devorah, "is his daughter, Devorah."

"The Lord's blessings on you both, Avraham and Devorah." Ehud smiled.

Devorah shyly spoke up. "May I ask you something, sir?"

"But of course, *yaldah*."

"Was God in the room with you when you stabbed Eglon and saved

Israel?"

Kenaz and Avraham stared at Devorah, surprised.

Ehud broke out in laughter. "Here's a true Israelite maiden!"

"But was He?" Devorah said.

Ehud grew serious. "The Hand of the Lord came upon me heavily that day, child. It was His Spirit that drove me and prepared me and made it possible to accomplish His purposes. Yes, He was in the room with me when I subdued Eglon." He turned his head in the direction of Devorah, his unseeing eyes still shrewd. "Now tell me why such a tiny thing is asking this question."

Avraham interrupted. "Please excuse my daughter, sir. She can be outspoken."

Ehud waved him away. "Let her answer me. Why the question, little one?"

Devorah eyed her father tentatively, a little frightened now at all of this attention. But Ehud's kind voice gave her courage to respond. "I know I'm just a girl, sir," she said in a voice barely above a whisper, "but I love the Lord God with all of my heart, like Moshe said to do, and I want to lead Israel to victory one day just like you did."

Ehud reached out and felt Avraham's arm. "I would like to pray for your daughter," he said.

"Of course, sir."

Ehud put his hand on Devorah's head. "*Baruch Atah Adonai Eloheinu Melech ha olam,*" he boomed, his voice strengthened by the power of the Spirit of God. "Blessed are You, O Lord our God, King of the Universe, who sustains us and has allowed us to reach this season of Sukkot. O Lord! We ask that Your hand would be on this child of Yours. You have taken a young girl, O Lord our God, and have put in her the heart of a warrior! I ask that You mold her and mature her and bring to bear all that You have desired to accomplish through this, Your maidservant, Devorah. In the blessed Name of Adonai, Amen."

"Amen," Avraham and Kenaz echoed.

"Amen," Devorah said, her eyes shining.

Many hours later, Devorah slept soundly in one corner of the sukkah, wrapped in a goatskin.

Avraham, too excited to sleep, lay on his back, arms behind his head, and gazed through the palm fronds up into the clear, starry night. "What a day!"

"Amen to that!" Kenaz said. "What did you think of the conversation between Devorah and Ehud?"

Avraham remained silent for several moments before he answered. "On the one hand, I've been noticing a special anointing on Devorah more and more as she gets older." He sighed heavily. "On the other hand, I want to be very careful before I encourage her to move in a direction that could cause her to be prideful, or to make choices that could harm her."

"Do not take Ehud's words lightly," Kenaz said. "I am absolutely confident that he hears clearly from the Lord."

"Well, my friend, I trust that you will give Miryam and me good counsel as we raise this child."

"Pray for me to have a long life, Avraham. I am very curious to see what happens to our little Devorah, and I want to be around when it does."

"You have my prayers."

"Thank you. And now I'm going to sleep. *Lilah tov.*"

"*Lilah tov.*"

Soon Avraham heard the labored sounds of Kenaz's breathing mingled with the soft breaths of Devorah. He alone lay sleepless in their temporary shelter. Dimly, by the light of the moon, he could discern some of the flower decorations Devorah had made earlier that day. Sweet, tender love for his daughter flooded his heart. "O Lord," he entreated. "Keep her safe, protect her. I know that she's Yours, but her mother and I love her so...." Words failed him as he struggled to release ownership of his daughter into the hands of the One who created her.

# TWO

Avraham stood, legs apart, arms folded, and gazed in satisfaction at his land. Broad fields of green, unripe barley undulated in the breeze as far as the eye could see. Rows of meticulously cultivated grapevines made an intricate pattern off to the left side of the fields. Far off in the distance grazed his growing flock of sheep. From where Avraham stood, with the spring breezes blowing just the right way, he could make out a faint *baa* here and there. Avraham sighed contentedly. *God is good.*

The house of Avraham ben Yosef had prospered these last five years. Miryam had given birth to three healthy sons in a row, and the land had showered forth its fertility accordingly. Never before had harvests been so plentiful. Between the barley, the wool, and the new wine, there had been enough money to hire two servants—one for the house and one for the fields. In addition, Ammon's son Lappidot, now sixteen, had temporarily come from Beit El to live with the family, acting as shepherd for Avraham's flocks.

"You're a rich man's wife now," Avraham had proudly told Miryam, to which she responded in mock exasperation, "Yes, I have six times the work I used to have and twice the help!" But she laughed as she said it. Laughter came frequently these days, the childlessness of their early marriage all but forgotten.

"Abba?"

Turning, he saw Devorah climbing the hill to meet him. She had changed considerably in the past several years. At age twelve she already stood as tall as her mother. Her curly red-blonde hair was wound demurely in a bun. Her face reflected a new seriousness toward life.

Avraham adored her. "What is it, *motek?*"

"Um." Devorah paused and pushed an imaginary stone on the ground with her toe. She looked up at her father and blushed slightly. "Can I catch up with Lappidot and help him with the sheep today?"

*Oh no,* Avraham groaned inwardly. *It's happening too soon.* To Devorah he said mildly, "Do you think the Lord would approve?"

"What do you mean?"

"I mean that you're getting to be a young lady and it doesn't look right to have you spend the day all alone with a young man. Remember, we're to avoid even the appearance of evil."

"Abba!" Devorah cried. "How can you say that? You know that Lappidot is like a brother to me!"

"Is he really? Is he the same to you as Yitzhak, Yaakov, or Yosef?"

Devorah blushed again. "Of course not! They're just babies."

Her father pointed his finger in the air. "My point exactly. Lappidot is a young man, and I don't want you running off alone with him anymore." He ignored his daughter's look of frustration. "Have you noticed what's been happening on the high places lately?"

Devorah seemed perplexed at the change of subject. "You mean the Canaanite altars?"

Avraham shook his head. "Not just Canaanite, *motek.* Israelite, as well. It used to be that only a few would sneak off and sacrifice to the pagan gods. Now we're seeing more and more of our own people worshipping these nasty idols." Avraham sat down on the ground and motioned for Devorah to join him. "You know, Devorah, when people run after these other gods, two things happen. First, and most importantly, it angers Adonai."

Devorah nodded.

"Second, these gods attract sin the way a beehive attracts bears. False gods are from *hasatan,* the adversary." Distaste passed over Avraham's features as he pronounced the hated name. "And as such, they will always demand more and more evil."

Devorah looked down at her feet. "You mean, like the terrible things they do to babies?"

Avraham's face grew gentle. "You've heard of that?"

Devorah nodded and tears formed in her eyes. "Marta told me," she said, referring to an older girl in the village. "She said that the Canaanites take their newborn babies and burn them to death as an offering to their gods." She shuddered. "Oh, Abba, it's so awful!"

Avraham put his arm around Devorah and drew her close to him. "Never forget, Devorah, that what the evil one seeks is death. All sin leads to death. Sexual sin takes longer, but it will bring death too, in the end." He kissed the top of her strawberry blond head. "Our God, Adonai, brings life. I know what a good girl you are, but as the darkness around us increases, our righteousness must increase all the more. Which is why I don't want any opportunity for gossip where you are concerned. You'll see Lappidot in the company of others."

"All right, Abba, I understand." Devorah gazed longingly at the hill in the north. "But I did want to be outdoors on such a glorious day."

"Go check with Ema. I'm sure she can find some outdoor chores for you today." As Devorah turned to go, Avraham added, "Oh, and Devorah..."

"Yes, Abba?"

"I like Lappidot, too."

Devorah flashed a smile, then skipped toward the house.

"Hey, Devi, wait up!"

Devorah turned toward her brother Yitzhak's voice. True to Avraham's prediction, Miryam had given Devorah a long list of outdoor jobs, including a trip to the communal well. Fetching water for the household was Devorah's favorite chore. Although the two goatskin water buckets were heavy to carry, she loved taking the walk at the end of the day when the heat lessened and the sky began to change colors. It was a time for her to catch her breath from the seemingly endless list of things Ema had for her to do and to think her own thoughts. She also loved the conversations that went on at the well. She had learned many interesting things while drawing water.

Devorah smiled at her brother affectionately. "What is it, Yitzie?" He was the oldest of the three boys and seemed very grown up by comparison. Almost six years old, Yitzhak had earned the nickname "the Shepherd" for the gentle and responsible way in which he protected his younger brothers. Serious, with deep brown eyes and a sweet smile, he was Devorah's favorite.

As he gazed up at her with big, brown eyes, a lock of brown hair fell across his forehead. "Can I come with you?"

Devorah sighed. She had looked forward to taking a walk and pondering all that she and Abba had discussed this morning. Her thoughts had tugged at her heart throughout the day, but with one chore after another, she had been continually distracted. *But how can I resist this little motek? Besides, some company might be nice.* "Sure you can come."

"Yay!" Yitzhak yelled. "I'll carry the buckets for you."

"How about you take one and I'll take one?"

"Okay." He grabbed one of the buckets and immediately began swinging it as he walked alongside her. Yitzhak seemed content to kick along a succession of stones as they traveled the rocky, dirt path to the well. Soon, though, he became more talkative.

"Guess what?"

Devorah, lost in thought, didn't answer.

He tried again, louder. "GUESS WHAT?"

"Yitzie! Don't yell! What?"

"Lappidot told me something about you."

Devorah swung around. "What did he say?"

The little boy smiled and puffed out his chest. "He said that I need to watch out for you because you're the sweetest and prettiest girl in all of Ramah."

Devorah's heart did a flip. "What else did he say?"

"That's it."

"Is that why you wanted to come with me to the well? To protect me?"

Yitzhak nodded solemnly. "Yes."

Devorah stopped and set her bucket on the path and pulled her brother into a big bear hug. She planted kisses all over his face.

"Hey! Stop that!" he cried, offended.

Joyously, she released him. "I think you're the best brother in the world." She grabbed his hand and together they skipped, laughing, the rest of the way to the well.

The town well was a natural gathering place for the people of Ramah. Women and girls like Devorah came to the well daily to fetch water for their households. When Devorah and Yitzhak arrived, the place was bustling with activity. A long line of women stretched around the circular well, each waiting her turn. Devorah was pleased to see their friend Leah at the end of the line with her six-year-old son, Shmulie. Leah, six months pregnant, looked exhausted and pale as she absently tolerated her son, who tugged at her and demanded continual attention. Leah smiled with relief when Devorah and Yitzhak stepped up behind them.

"Shalom!" Leah said. "Look, Shmulie! Yitzie is here. Why don't you go play with him?" As an afterthought she turned to Devorah. "Is that okay with you?"

Devorah felt pleased that a young woman would treat her as an equal by asking her permission. "Of course, Leah. Yitzie, go play with Shmulie."

Yitzhak hesitated, not wanting to leave his post as bodyguard. "Will you be okay?"

"I'll be fine," she said. "Go and have fun. Just please be where I can find you."

"Okay." He waved at her, then chased after Shmulie, who was happy as a frog now that he didn't have to stand in line with his mother.

"Whew!" Leah wiped her brow with the edge of her sleeve. "*Baruch ha Shem* you came along. He was driving me crazy!"

Devorah laughed. "Adonai works all things out for the good of those who love Him. I was on my way here alone when Yitzie joined me unexpectedly, and now look at the helpful purpose he's served!"

Leah and her husband, Amos, had been close friends of the family for as long as Devorah could remember. Leah was not so much older than Devorah that she couldn't recall what it had been like to be twelve years old, but at the same time she was an adult. Devorah had a genuine fondness for Leah, borne of much time spent together.

Now Leah studied her closely. "Why are you so happy?" she asked suspiciously.

"Happy? Do I seem happy?"

"I'd say," Leah said carefully, "that if you were any happier, none of us could stand you."

Devorah giggled. "Somebody said something nice about me, that's all."

Leah's eyes narrowed. "Would this somebody be a sixteen-year-old shepherd boy with the sweetest smile and reddest hair in all of Ramah?"

"Maybe." Devorah grinned.

Leah's face softened. "Want some advice, Devi?"

"Sure."

"Don't be in such a rush to pair off and get married."

Devorah opened her mouth to object, but Leah kept talking.

"Enjoy these carefree, wonderful years. You'll never reclaim them."

"Carefree?" Devorah, eyes wide, dangled the water buckets in front of Leah. "Ema has me working from dawn to dark!"

Leah snorted. "That's not work! Motherhood is work."

Devorah started to reply when a loud chatter arose from the large crowd of women around them. Devorah turned to see a strange man running at full speed into the village square. He was small and slender, with powerful legs. Dust mixed with sweat covered his head, and his clothes were torn. His chest heaved as he gasped for breath.

"Water, he needs water!" someone shouted. One of the women raced over to the well, pushing aside a startled old woman. She hurriedly lowered her bucket, filled it to the brim, and brought it out of the well and over to the man. He gratefully put the bucket to his lips and drank it down in long, deep gulps.

"Thank you, thank you," he gasped, bending over as he regained his breath.

They all waited expectantly. Obviously this man was a "runner," a messenger sent from town to town to spread critical news. The women eyed one another fearfully as they waited for the man to speak.

"I am Asa ben Naphtali," he said. "I deeply regret to inform you that Ehud has gone to be with his fathers. May God have mercy on Israel!"

A shocked silence muted the crowd. Then one woman moaned. Another joined her. Soon all the women were lamenting loudly and bitterly, their voices weaving together as one. Devorah fell to her knees, scooped dust into her cupped hands, and sprinkled it on her head. Tears ran down her cheeks. "Today one of the great princes of Israel is no more. Dear Lord, protect us!"

Shmulie and Yitzie returned in the middle of a great cacophony. The boys stared at each other.

"What do you think it is?" Yitzie said.

Shmulie shrugged. "I don't know. Someone must have died." His little brown eyes brightened. "Let's find out. Race you to the well!" Shmulie zipped off like a hare. Yitzie proceeded more cautiously. His concern for his big sister overrode his desire to play.

He found Devorah sitting with her back to the well with her eyes closed. Her lips moved silently in prayer. Quietly he went to her and climbed in her lap. Devorah hugged him closely. "Oh, Yitzie," she said in a torrent of tears, "Ehud is dead!"

Yitzie knew he should be upset about Ehud, but he felt more worried about his sister. He was not used to seeing her like this, and it bothered him. He frowned and patted her on the back in an attempt to comfort her.

A thought came to Devorah suddenly: *What would Abba do right now?*

She looked up and saw Asa, the runner, sitting by himself amidst the sea of wailing women. *Of course!*

Devorah stood up. "Come on, Yitzie." She held out her hand. The little boy took it, and the two of them worked their way through prostrate bodies until they reached Asa.

"Hello," she said. "I'm Devorah, daughter of Avraham, and this is my brother Yitzhak."

Asa gazed at them blankly.

Devorah plunged on. "Would you be willing to come to our home for the night? I know my parents would be most honored, were you to accept their hospitality."

Asa scratched his beard and broke into a brilliant, toothy smile, a sharp contrast from his torn clothes and dusty head. "I would be thrilled, young miss. Please lead the way."

Devorah was about to lead him away, then halted abruptly when she realized that, regardless of the national crisis that had befallen them, Ema would be furious if they returned home without water. "I have to fill these buckets," she said and took advantage of the temporary lack of line to do just that. Buckets brimming, Asa graciously insisted on carrying them both, and the two children ran ahead of him through the dusky evening toward their home.

Miryam started pacing nervously when there was still no sign of Devorah and Yitzhak at sunset. "Why are they taking so long? Do you think they're all right?"

Normally Avraham would have chided his wife, but the hour was much later than Devorah generally returned from the well. Concerned, he put on his cloak, took down a torch, and headed for the door. "I'll go to the well and see if I can find them. Be back as soon as I can." He kissed Miryam on the cheek and hurried out into the night.

As Avraham strode quickly down the path to the well, a knot formed in his stomach. "Devorah! Yitzie! Come to Abba!"

At the edge of the path, he saw three shadowy figures outlined against the trees off in the distance. He held up the torch. "Who goes there?" he shouted.

One of the three figures broke away from the other two and ran straight toward him. "Abba, Abba! It's us!"

Relief swept over Avraham as he recognized his son's voice. "Yitzie! Devorah!" he called sternly. "Where have you been?"

"We're sorry, Abba," Devorah called to him.

Yitzie reached his father first and, unable to contain himself, flung his arms around his father's waist. "Abba, Abba! Ehud is dead!"

"What?"

"It's true, sir," a young man said as he and Devorah caught up to them.

"And who might you be?"

Asa bowed. "Asa ben Naphtali, at your service. I'm a messenger sent to the hill country of Ephraim to inform people of the passing of Ehud. Your daughter most graciously invited me to your home for the night. I am very grateful."

"Of course," said Avraham. "Come, come. Ema—Miryam—is anxious to see the children safely home. Let's go. We'll discuss this news at dinner."

Quickly they made their way through the dark shadows to the ben Yosef home.

Later that evening, Avraham ben Yosef and Asa ben Naphtali sat across from one another at the scarred wood table, while Miryam and Devorah cleared away the dinner dishes. Well fed and rested, Asa was ready to talk, and Avraham eager to listen.

Avraham leaned forward and selected a fig from the bowl of dried fruit Devorah silently set on the table. "Tell me about Ehud."

Asa frowned. "Well, as you know, Ehud has lived one hundred and ten years and was not in the best of health."

"Yes, yes, I remember. We had the honor of speaking with him six Sukkot seasons ago."

"Oh? Well, Ehud passed on in his sleep. He has already been buried in his hometown in the territory of Benjamin." Asa paused to pluck a date from the bowl.

All eyes in the room watched him as he chewed.

"And...?" Avraham prodded.

"That's really it. I am one of twelve messengers sent to each of the tribes of Israel. For the past week, I have worked my way through the hill country here. Ramah is the fifth town I have entered today alone." He pointed his finger, sticky with date, at Devorah, who sat quietly behind her father. "*Baruch ha Shem* for the hospitality your daughter offered, my friend. I had reached the limit of my endurance."

Avraham wanted to know more. "What about a successor to Ehud? Is there someone in line to take over as judge of Israel?"

Asa wrinkled his brow thoughtfully. "No, not really. His sons are nice enough, but"—and here he tapped the side of his temple next to his eye—"no vision. And they've never caught onto their father's vision. No, I don't see anyone who is able to step into Ehud's sandals." He yawned.

Miryam gestured to her husband with a look that said, "Let him go to bed!"

Avraham got the hint. He stood up and clapped his hands. "Miryam, it's late and our guest is tired. Have Avdah show Asa to our room."

"Oh, no," Asa protested. "I can sleep on the floor by the door. You shouldn't give me your own bed."

"Nonsense!" retorted Avraham. "You're our honored guest. And who knows," he added, with a twinkle in his eye, "but that you may be an angel in disguise?"

The following afternoon, Lappidot headed back to Avraham's home behind a large flock of sheep. He had spent the night outside at a pasture several miles away.

It was a beautiful day. The sun shone, a soft breeze blew, the birds sang, and wildflowers dotted the hills like glittering jewels as they reflected the light of the sun. He breathed deeply. How he loved Ramah! And how he looked forward to seeing Avraham and his family. Avraham had become more of a father to him than his own father. A dark cloud passed over his happy mood as he thought about his father, but he shook it aside.

Then the image of Devorah popped in front of him. He smiled. Devorah had enchanted him from the moment he ran into her at the Feast of Sukkot so long ago. She was so unlike anyone he had encountered. Her lively intelligence, her joy and her precocious wisdom made her beautiful in his eyes. And her all-consuming love for God was nothing short of extraordinary in a day when so many were turning their backs on Him.

Lappidot was grateful to be with a family that held the Lord in such high esteem. His great-grandmother had fled Egypt with the Children of Israel as a young girl and had regaled him with countless tales of life during the great Exodus. Lappidot could still picture her bent, gray head, brown, wizened face lined with hundreds of fine wrinkles, and angry eyes as she bewailed the fact that people's hearts had grown cold. Her words still echoed in his head:

*"You don't lose your love for God when you depend on Him for everything in your life. From the manna we collected daily and the water He gave us in the midst of a dry and barren land, to the fact that our sandals never wore out and our clothes didn't disintegrate on our bodies, not to mention the wonderful miracles like the parting of the Red Sea, He was always there. We only had to open our eyes to see in front of us the pillar of cloud by day and the pillar of fire by night; our ears to hear the thundering voice of the Lord rolling down from Mount Sinai. We saw the Glory of the Lord reflecting off the face of Moshe so intensely that he had to put a veil over his face so we would not melt in fear. You never forget the Holy One of Israel when you see His strength and His might!"*

Lappidot wished now with regret that he had spent more time with Savta. Her stories had fascinated him, but he had also often chosen to run off when his friends came to play. He had grieved deeply when she died four years earlier, leaving him bereft in his parents' home. Then Avraham had stepped in.

Now that Lappidot roamed the hills each day with Avraham's ever-multiplying flock of sheep, he had plenty of time to sing, pray, praise, and worship the Lord. And Avraham always made himself available to discuss the things of God. Avraham loved the Lord in a deeper, more meaningful way than anyone Lappidot had known in Beit El, with the exception of Savta…and now Devorah.

Lappidot's thoughts came full circle back to Devorah. She had an un-canny knack for always being around when he and Avraham talked about Adonai. Her sharp mind had an exceedingly legal quality to it. She could see the flaw in any argument! Lappidot had to work harder and harder to win debates with her, and she was only twelve.

*Only twelve*, he mused. He stooped down to pick a few scarlet wildflow-ers, then tossed them away absently. A sheep bleated as Lappidot took his shepherd's staff and poked the animal's rear. "Move along."

As he descended the hill toward the sheep pen, he paused to gaze at the valley below. Lappidot loved this view. Fields, vineyards, and olive groves formed a patchwork of browns, greens, and, purples, while the sun reflecting off the white roofs of the houses added a sparkling intensity to the scene. He narrowed his gaze to the area surrounding Avraham's house to look for signs of activity. Someone was sitting in the courtyard grinding grain. Was it Devorah? Or Avdah, Miryam's servant? He couldn't tell for sure from this distance. Only one way to find out.

"Come on!" he yelled at the sheep. "Let's go, my fine wooly friends!"

Devorah sat in the courtyard under the shade of the large oak tree grinding barley into flour for Ema's bread-baking. It was hard work, and Devorah concentrated intently on both her grinding and her thoughts of Ehud. She did not notice Lappidot until he arrived in the courtyard and called her name.

Devorah, startled, glanced up from her task. "Lappidot! I didn't hear you come in!"

"I know. You seemed lost in thought."

"I am. I mean, I was."

His eyes twinkled. "Were you reciting the 613 laws in Torah in your head?"

Devorah stuck her tongue out at him. "I was thinking of our guest last night."

"Guest?" Lappidot's eyebrows rose. "What guest?"

"Asa ben Naphtali, a messenger sent throughout the hill country of Ephraim."

"Why was he here?" He grabbed a chair and sat down next to her.

"Oh, Lappidot!" Tears formed in Devorah's eyes as she drew in her breath and prepared to share her big news. "Ehud has died, and Israel is without a judge!" She waited expectantly for his reaction.

"Oh."

Devorah watched Lappidot's face for signs of grief, shock, or even concern. She expected him to fall to his knees and throw dust on his head. Instead, he did nothing. Her heart began to pound and her temper rose. "'Oh?' Is that all you can say?"

"Well, I'm sorry he's dead, but he was over a hundred years old. Nobody lives forever."

"But aren't you going to do something?" she shouted.

"Do something?" Lappidot stared at her. "I'm not the coming Messiah, Devi. I can't raise the dead."

She stood up, realizing the foolishness of her actions but unable to stop herself. She snatched the basket with the ground flour and put it under her arm. "I'll see you later!" And she stalked off.

Lappidot scratched his head as he watched Devorah leave. *What was that all about? Better find Avraham and tell him I'm back.* And he left the courtyard in search of Avraham.

News of Ehud's death spread rapidly throughout the countryside. Mixed reactions followed the news. Some, like Avraham and his family, mourned deeply for the loss of this godly leader who had devoted eighty years of his life to leading the people of the House of Israel. Others, like Amos and Leah, felt only a brief nostalgia, overshadowed by their excitement at the prospect of a younger judge. Those who had turned from the faith and engaged in idol worship received the news gladly, perceiving a new opening for their pagan lifestyle.

One week after Asa ben Naphtali had come, Avraham assembled in his home several of his most trusted friends in Ramah. Besides Lappidot, who lived under his protection, he invited Kenaz, Amram the Levite, Amram's grown son, Aharon, and Micah, the carpenter. He debated asking Leah's husband, Amos, but a check in his spirit told him not to.

Devorah desperately wanted to be included as well, but Miryam absolutely would not hear of it.

"Please, Ema, please let me listen!" Devorah sank down on her knees for added effect.

"No!" Miryam refused, exasperated. "I wish you understood that you are not a man, but a young girl. You should remember to keep your place."

Devorah jumped up. "I know I'm a girl. Everyone knows me. They won't mind if I'm there. I can even"—she flew around the central room in the house where the men were going to meet later that night and stopped in front of a small table—"sit under this table and hide!"

A playful smile tugged at Miryam's mouth. "And you think that no one will notice the red hair?" She reached out and affectionately pulled one of Devorah's many curls. "Or the table shaking?"

Devorah shook her head. "I don't think so. They will be too busy talking. So can I? Please, please?"

Miryam studied her daughter's sweet face. How she loved this child! But she gave the only response acceptable under the circumstances. "Definitely not," she said and crossed her arms.

Devorah's face fell. After all these years as her mother's daughter, she knew better than to keep pushing. Dejected, she turned to go.

Miryam offered a small consolation. "Look, Devi, you know that Abba will tell you all about the meeting after everyone has gone home. If you're still awake, you may know what happened even before I do."

Devorah stared at the floor silently.

Miryam tried again. "You know, even though you feel like one of the men and are quite capable of adding to their conversation, the fact that you're a twelve-year-old girl causes them to speak differently than they would if you weren't there." Devorah opened her mouth to protest, but Miryam put out her hand to stop her. "Trust me, you're very noticeable these days. You're no longer the little girl they can ignore while you hide in your father's arms." Miryam looked appreciatively at her daughter. "You're a beautiful young lady now, and no table is going to conceal you."

Devorah blushed and put up her hands in surrender. "Okay, Ema, okay, you win. I'll wait and find out from Abba after the meeting." She allowed her mother to give her a kiss on the cheek, then headed to the kitchen to punch down some bread dough she had kneaded earlier in the day for tonight's supper.

Later that evening, after the three little boys had been tucked into bed, there came an assertive knock on the door. Devorah ran and opened it, finding Kenaz standing outside, hand raised in mid-air, on the verge of another sharp rap. Devorah stifled a giggle at the contrast between the ancient little man and his bold knocking. Before she even had time to usher Kenaz inside, Amram and his son Aharon approached from the street. Behind them was Micah.

"Shalom, shalom, come in everyone," Devorah welcomed them.

Her mother emerged behind her and greeted each man as he entered. "Kenaz, so wonderful to see you. Amram, how well you look. Aharon, welcome. Micah, always a pleasure!" She led them to the family living quarters where Avraham and Lappidot awaited them. Devorah followed, too, but Miryam turned her aside at the entrance and shook her head.

"Gentlemen, if there is anything I can get you, please let me know," she said sweetly as she ushered her daughter away from the meeting.

"Friends," Avraham said. "Thank you for coming out tonight. I won't waste any time but will tell you why I've called this gathering." He stood and paced up and down the room, hands clasped behind his back. "As you know, we've been slipping toward idolatry here in Ramah for a few years now."

A murmur of assent rippled through the room.

"Now that Ehud has passed on and has not left a suitable successor, I fear the situation will deteriorate rapidly. What I propose"—Avraham caught the eye of each person in the room—"is that we formulate a plan of action to protect the worship of Adonai in our town."

"Excellent idea," Kenaz said. "What do you suggest?"

"The Law of Moshe says we should stone to death any man or woman found worshipping other gods and purge the evil from among us," Micah said.

"Well, yes…that's true," Avraham said. "But the point to this meeting is that there aren't enough of us. We would have to stone most of Ramah." He smiled wryly.

"May I speak?" Amram asked from where he sat in a corner of the room. A short, stocky man with white hair and a beard that reached part-way down his chest, Amram radiated piety like heat from a stove.

Avraham bowed his head in deference. "Of course, Amram. Go ahead."

"We live in an adulterous and perverse generation that has forgotten God's promises. I do not believe that any one of us apart from God can fight this rising tide of paganism." Amram stopped and looked around. "What I propose is that we live the holy lifestyle God called us to through Moshe, and let God Himself establish us as a bulwark in Ramah."

Aharon leaned forward. He was a thin, young man of thirty, with a narrow face, strong mouth, and a close-cropped dark beard. He had recently married, and he and his wife were expecting their first child. A nervous energy that had characterized him as a small child now manifested itself in a foot that hadn't stopped tapping since he sat down. Black eyes snapping, he spoke up. "What my father proposes to do on a practical basis is, at all costs, to maintain the structure of a Mosaic lifestyle. That means that we keep Shabbat, obey the Law of Moshe, raise our children in a godly fashion, observe the seventh year of rest for our fields, support the Levites who live among us…." Aharon glared as Lappidot chuckled good-naturedly at that last suggestion of a Levite seeking support for Levites. "…and never set up an altar on the high places. I think we all know what's expected."

"Young man," Kenaz said, "that's all very well and good. But we're going to need more force if we expect to do more than wind up as a small splinter group in the midst of a sea of"—here he spat discreetly into the sleeve of his robe—"idol worshippers."

Everyone but Lappidot joined in the heavy debate that ensued. Lappidot listened intently but did not at first feel he had anything worthwhile to add, and if Avraham had pounded it into his head once, he had pounded it in a thousand times: Don't speak when you have nothing to say.

After a while, though, he sensed the Spirit of the Lord pressing him. During a brief pause, he timidly raised his hand and caught Avraham's eye. "Uh…"

"Go ahead, Lappidot," Avraham said, pleased to see his young charge enter in.

Lappidot began talking nervously but gained confidence as he proceeded. "I've been listening to everyone's ideas, and excellent ones they are, too. But I believe the Lord has said the only way we're going to win this is through prayer. It's been said that the prayers of righteous men are effective, and that's us, right?" He flashed his young, toothy smile at each of them.

Amram stared stonily back at him.

Lappidot gulped and continued. "Why don't we join together in prayer right now and get God's direction?"

Avraham stood up and walked over to Lappidot. He placed his hand tenderly on the boy's neck. "That's an excellent idea, son. Why don't you begin?"

"Okay, sir." Lappidot closed his eyes and started praying in the style and manner he had witnessed in Avraham many, many times. He paused and breathed deeply. "O God, and God of our fathers," he began quietly, "we, Your humble servants, come before You to repent of any intentional or unintentional sin we may have committed in Your sight." His voice strengthened. "You know, Lord, that our hearts are heavy over the condition that Israel is in. You know that Ehud's death has opened the door for all sorts of wickedness to come forth. We ask now that You would take this time to give us direction so Israel may be saved from her sin."

Avraham joined in. "Thank you, Lord, thank you for Your Presence with us in this place. I thank You also for this faithful young man whom

You have given me the privilege of knowing." He smiled as he squeezed the back of Lappidot's neck affectionately. "Adonai Elohim, You know that many things have been discussed here tonight, but we do not have a clear consensus on which road to take. Please speak to us now, Adonai."

Silence reigned over the men for several minutes as each one of them sought to hear the still, small voice of God.

Finally, Micah spoke. "I have a sense that we need to pray for a leader to be raised up in the spirit of Ehud," he said, his eyes closed and still in an attitude of prayer.

Again the men murmured their assent. Amram prayed, "Adonai, Holy and Righteous One of Israel, we ask that You bring forth a leader from Your people who will lead us into an era of righteousness and peace. Someone after Your own heart. Praise You, Adonai."

After several more prayers, silence ensued for close to half an hour. At the end of this period of time, Avraham wrapped things up. "Adonai," he prayed, "we thank You for the opportunity to come before You with our needs and concerns. We now lay at Your feet the discernment that each of us, separately and together, need to keep praying for the person You would have to shepherd Your people, Israel. In the meantime, keep us strong and steadfast and focused on You. In Your holy Name, Amen."

"Amen," they solemnly repeated.

Over the course of the next several months, Avraham met with Lappidot and the four other men on a weekly basis to pray for Israel's next leader. No one received specific direction, but an odd thing happened. Each of the men involved in the prayer developed a deeper interest in Devorah. Avraham began to include her more often in spiritual discussions; Lappidot sought her out as often as he could without causing trouble in the household; Kenaz came to the house and asked for Devorah to sit with him in the courtyard, where he recounted story after story from the early days of Ehud to her eager ears; Amram said, "I know this is unusual, but I would like Devorah to join our Torah discussion group even though she will be the only girl." Even Aharon made several halting attempts at conversation; and Micah showed up at the house from time to time with little intricately carved animal figurines, which he had whittled in his spare time as gifts for Devorah.

Devorah did not ponder the changes in behavior of the men around her. In this time of life when relationships were in flux everywhere—parents, brothers, friends, neighbors, Lappidot—she simply held fast to her relationship with God.

Devorah couldn't remember a time in her young life when she had not felt the presence of God. As a three-year-old, running in the fields gathering armloads of flowers for Ema, she felt Him there, watching over her with the protective love of a father. Later, when she was old enough to pray on her own, she kept up a running dialogue with the Lord, chattering incessantly into His ever-patient ear. The last two years, she had daily intense talks with Him as her emotions bounced up and down with the changes in her body. Since last fall, however, Devorah found stirring inside of herself an intense longing to know God intimately, on a par equivalent to what Moshe had experienced. In every way, she felt utterly compelled to press forward toward the goal of knowing God.

She seldom spoke of these things, and then only to her father. His was a kindred spirit, and they understood one another with a rare compatibility of souls.

One day later that spring, as the rains pelted the earth, Lappidot led the sheep to shelter and took refuge in the house. Miraculously, he found Devorah sitting alone—a rare opportunity in a home with three young boys. Devorah sat on her favorite stool in the kitchen and sewed a piece of embroidery with agile fingers. She wore a shawl to protect her from the unusually cold, damp weather but still shivered.

Lappidot peered over her shoulder at her work. "That's pretty."

"Thanks," she said, dimpling at him before she lowered her eyes to focus on her work. Ever since last year when Abba had cautioned her against being alone with Lappidot, she had avoided what she considered to be "dangerous situations." In the house, though, one could count on being interrupted relatively quickly. So she felt comfortable right now.

Lappidot pulled up another stool and sat across from her quietly, watching her sew. He loved her sweet, serious face and her keen mind. He actually found her quite brilliant and rejoiced within himself whenever she made an especially insightful point. Now, however, it pleased him to relish the charming domestic picture she presented. He sighed contentedly.

"What's wrong?" Devorah asked.

"Must you know everything?" He smiled.

Devorah stuck her tongue out at him. For a few minutes they sat together in companionable silence—she sewing, he gazing.

"So," he said, "what do you think about all the attention you've been receiving lately?"

"What attention?" She bit off a piece of thread.

"From your father's prayer group."

"You mean Kenaz and the rest of them?"

"Exactly."

Devorah dropped her sewing into her lap and stared at Lappidot. He stared back. "I haven't really thought very much about it at all," she said. "But I guess the old men have been really nice to me."

"Not just old men. There's me, too." His voice was suddenly husky.

Devorah blushed and looked down at her hands. "It's been a strange time since Ehud died," she said shyly.

"In what way?"

"Well," she said hesitantly, not sure if she should expose her heart to Lappidot.

As she wavered, God's voice spoke within her spirit. *Tell him.*

*It's all right for me to talk to Lappidot, Lord?*

*Tell him,* the Voice said again.

Lappidot waited patiently, watching the expressions that flitted across Devorah's face as she debated within herself what she should say.

"My relationship with the Lord has changed. I—" She groped for the right words. "I want to see God face to face like Moshe did."

"Don't we all."

Devorah raised her hand in the air for a few seconds, then let it fall to her lap. "I don't think we all do," she said slowly. "I think most people are content with their own mental image of God and are afraid to let Him get too close. He can be awfully terrifying, you know."

"Yes," Lappidot said, chastened.

Devorah smiled self-consciously. "I don't want to sound proud, but I believe that the Lord has a big plan for me, and I think that I'm supposed to prepare myself by drawing as close to Him as I possibly can. Does that make sense to you?"

Lappidot reached out and took Devorah's small, graceful hand and held it tenderly between his two calloused, rough ones. They smiled at each other.

"You know," he said, "there's nothing I'd like more than to be in the center of God's will for my life with you by my side." He held her gaze as she held her breath. "May I speak to your parents about becoming betrothed to you?"

Numbly, Devorah shook her head yes. Lappidot grinned broadly as he leaned over and kissed her tenderly on the cheek. A gentle, sweet spirit permeated the room.

Silence reigned until banging footsteps brought little Yaakov to the doorway. "Hey!" he shouted curiously. "What's happening here?"

# THREE

*Praise the Lord...*

*praise Him with the harp and the lyre...*

*Let everything that has breath praise the Lord.*

—FROM PSALM 150

The next two years before their marriage were full, tumultuous ones for Devorah and Lappidot. Avraham and Miryam readily gave their blessing to the young couple but insisted that they wait until Devorah was at least fifteen years old before getting married. *And you,* Avraham said kindly but firmly to Lappidot, *you are in no position to support a family. Wait! Wait! God will provide!* Deliriously happy, Lappidot and Devorah agreed to everything as they fixed their eyes on the goal of building their life together.

Lappidot wrestled with the decision of where to live and what to do and eventually concluded God had called him to remain in Ramah after the marriage. Consequently, he spent much time traveling back and forth to Beit El, arranging for a portion of his inheritance so he could establish his own household. At first his father had argued with him, but Lappidot stood firm in his belief that God had called him to Ramah. Eventually Ammon capitulated and agreed that perhaps his son should keep his new bride in her own town after all.

Meanwhile, Miryam joyfully went about the task of preparing Devorah for her new role as wife. "You've already learned much of what it takes to keep a house up by helping me all these years," Miryam said one day as they prepared the evening meal together. "But the secret to being the best wife you can be is to have a strong relationship with Adonai."

"I do want that, Ema," Devorah said. "I have always felt close to Adonai, but I want to know Him even better. How do you find time to spend with Him, when from sunup to sundown there is always something else to do?"

"I make the time, Devi," Miryam answered gently.

The next morning, Devorah began what would become a lifelong practice of rising from her bed an hour before dawn and meeting with God. Sitting in the chair next to her bed, she would speak to God about her day and the concerns of her heart, and then would sit in quiet expectancy as she learned to recognize His voice.

Often as she lay warm and cozy under her blankets in the cold pre-dawn morning, she would desperately want to stay huddled in her bed. But her heart tugged, and she knew God was calling her to come and be with Him. Sometimes she failed and went back to sleep. Those were the days when, later, her heart would break and she would stand meek and contrite before the Lord. "Forgive me, Lord," she would pray. "I have wasted time that could have been Yours." As the weeks and months passed, however, more and more frequently Devorah managed to slip out of bed, wrap herself in a blanket, and sit before the Lord.

Devorah soon discovered that these times spent with God caused her to have a heightened awareness of spiritual things as she went about her daily business. Gradually she noticed that, during conversations, she could easily see beyond other people's words...and right into their very souls. She could discern true motives and hidden agendas. Eventually God began to speak to her concerning her future as well.

"Oh, Ema," she said one morning as they cleaned up after breakfast, "Adonai always amazes me. I can get through an entire boring day of chores, just knowing what wonderful things He has in store for my life. Sometimes His words are so sharp and clear it's as though I were talking to you or Abba!"

Miryam smiled. "Always stay close to Him, my daughter. His words satisfy more than the choicest meat and drink. He will give you a hope and a future."

Devorah spoke of these things to Lappidot as well, and he matched her enthusiasm with his own ever-increasing hunger for the things of God. Often as he walked alone with the sheep, he would suddenly feel compelled to drop to his knees in prayer and worship. On one such occasion, a very exciting thing happened.

Lappidot had in his possession a small harp that he had inherited from his great-grandmother. Years earlier, she had taught him how to play a few simple songs, and he had taken to it naturally. On occasion, he still pulled it out and strummed it, though never often enough to satisfy Yitzie, Yaakov, and Yosef, who clamored for songs far more regularly than Lappidot indulged them.

One day at the end of the summer, just before the Feast of Trumpets, Lappidot was roaming the hills with the sheep and praising God when a melody line to a song he had never heard before flashed into his mind. Quite unconsciously, he sang words of praise with this melody. They went together perfectly!

*Not bad*, he thought. *Did I just write a song?* He sang it through again, changed a word here, and added a word there. He worked with the song all afternoon as he walked through fields and herded recalcitrant sheep with his long shepherd's crook. Deep in his spirit, he knew this song had come as a gift from God. All that afternoon, and into the evening, he sang it over and over to burn it into his memory. He couldn't wait to get back to Avraham's house and share the news with Devorah.

By the time he penned up the sheep for the night and walked to the house, the family had eaten dinner and the boys were back outside playing. When they saw him, they all came running. Yosef reached him first. "Lappi, Lappi!"

"Hey, Yossi!" He grabbed the little boy and held him upside down. Yosef's delighted screams attracted the attention of his brothers, who both begged to be next. Laughing, Lappidot held a boy under each arm as a third jumped on his back. He looked up just in time to see Devorah coming quickly toward him, her face all smiles.

"Boys! Leave Lappidot alone!"

Her brothers unanimously ignored her and continued to climb on Lappidot as he tried to have a conversation with Devorah.

"I've got something exciting to tell you." Lappidot reached up to tickle an already squealing Yosef, who hung over his shoulders like a pet snake.

"You must be starving," she interrupted and flashed a "get down now" look at her noisy brother. "Ema has food prepared for you, so come inside and talk to me as you eat." She turned and lightly ran over to the house.

He obediently followed her, shaking off the boys as he went.

Seated at the table with the rest of the family, Lappidot couldn't wait another moment. "God gave me a song today!"

Devorah smiled curiously. "A song, Lappi?"

He finished his last bite and wiped his mouth. "Yes, a song. I'll sing it for you." He stood up to sing for his expectant audience, and then, just as quickly, he froze.

"What's wrong, son?" Avraham said.

Lappidot scratched his head. "You know," he said, a trifle sheepishly, "Something's missing. Would everyone mind waiting while I run and get my harp? I feel like I'm supposed to have it right now."

"Go ahead," Miryam said with a soft smile. She grew more and more pleased with her daughter's intended every day.

It only took Lappidot a minute to pull the harp off its spot from the table in the tiny room he occupied off the family's living quarters. Tenderly, he wiped dust off the top of it with the edge of his sleeve. He tucked it under his arm and headed back to the family.

"Okay, here goes." He took a deep breath and strummed the harp as he sang:

*"We praise Your name, O Adonai,*

*We praise Your name, Blessed One,*

*We praise Your name, King of kings,*

*We praise Your name, Lord of lords.*

*Alone anointed, is the Father,*

*Coming to Israel—rule forever!"*

By the end of the song, the boys had begun to clap and soon everyone joined him in the song. Devorah beamed with pride. Avraham stroked his beard thoughtfully. Miryam dabbed at her eyes with a handkerchief.

Avraham spoke first. "That was beautiful, son. Did you say that the Lord gave you this song?"

Lappidot nodded vigorously. "Yes, sir. He kind of"—he searched for the right word—"dropped it into my spirit. Nothing like this has ever happened to me before."

"Well, I think that it's the first of many," Devorah said. "It's a wonderful song, Lappi."

Lappidot grinned broadly. "I don't know if I should say 'thank you' or not. I really didn't write it myself."

Avraham leaned back in his chair. He was not one to let a teaching opportunity pass by unused. "Tell me," he said pointedly, "why do you think Adonai gave you this song today?"

Lappidot didn't answer immediately. Avraham had taught him to think through his answers. "I believe it's a gift," he finally said slowly, feeling his words as he went along. "You know that lately both Devorah and I have sought after the Lord more intensely than ever before. I believe it's a reward, of sorts, and an encouragement to persevere toward knowing Him more fully." Lappidot stopped.

Avraham nodded in agreement. "Yes, yes. All that is true. But there is more." He cleared his throat.

Miryam, Devorah, and Lappidot all looked at him questioningly.

Avraham raised his finger in the air. "This is how I see it. You seek God, you show Him your love, He responds with a sign of His favor. In this case, the favor is a special gift, a song-writing anointing, if you will." He paused for emphasis. "But what's always the greatest purpose in our relationship with God?"

Lappidot and Miryam hesitated. Devorah answered first. "To give Him glory?"

"Excellent!" Avraham nodded approvingly. "To give Him glory! So, how does this special ability to write worship songs give Him glory?"

"It came from Him?" Miryam said timidly.

"Yes. There's more, though."

"It came from Him, and it will be used by the people who sing the songs to bring more glory to Him through their worship!" Lappidot said confidently.

Avraham pounded the table with his fist. "That's it! So what's your next step?"

"I need to be open to the possibility that the Lord will use me to write more songs, and I need to pray about what to do with the song He's already given me."

Avraham raised both hands in the air, palms facing out. "I couldn't have said it better myself."

Devorah's eyes shined brightly and one dimple showed. "So, Lappi, does this mean you'll be playing your harp more often?"

Lappidot looked down at the little stringed instrument he had been holding in his lap. "I need to learn to play this a lot better than I do now."

"Can I learn it with you?"

"Sure," he said.

Miryam raised her eyebrows. "Just make sure you're not alone."

"You can be in our harp class and learn too, Ema," Devorah told her mother demurely.

Miryam waved at them dismissively as she stood up from the table. "Like I have time to sit and learn a musical instrument." But she smiled as if the offer pleased her.

"All right, everyone." Avraham stood up and clapped his hands. "Evening chores and get to bed. Tomorrow is another full day!"

Devorah and Lappidot bade each other good night as all scattered to obey Avraham's command, humming as they went. Joy rose up from the household that evening as strains of "Alone Anointed" wafted into the night sky.

All told, Adonai gave Lappidot three more songs as gifts before making him work for them. But by that time, Lappidot was so taken by the idea of writing songs, he was virtually unstoppable. He made it a discipline to carry his harp out into the fields and practice playing it for at least one hour a day. Except for the days when rain forced him to leave the harp at home, or days when the sheep demanded extra attention, Lappidot held faithful.

Just about the time he wrote his third song, word got out in Ramah. Soon all sorts of folks were dropping by, asking Lappidot to play "those songs he wrote." Thrilled at the chance to glorify God by singing for an audience, Lappidot always complied. The songs caught on rapidly. Women sang "Alone Anointed" at the village well. Boys whistled "When Israel Was a Child" as they led sheep and goats to pasture. Aharon even introduced a song into the Saturday morning weekly Shabbat service in the central square. He encouraged Lappidot to lead the congregation in worship by playing harp and singing. The first time Lappidot performed, he turned bright red and looked as nervous as a new baby bird. But eventually he grew in confidence and greatly enjoyed the position.

When the songs ceased to present themselves full-blown into his head, Lappidot took to studying the Torah of Moshe diligently, waiting on the Lord to illuminate those passages that would make a good song. Ironically enough, the story he chose first was one set in his hometown of Beit El. Lappidot had a special fondness for the account of the Patriarch Yaakov, in which he received a promise from God in a dream:

"I am the Lord, the God of your father Avraham and God of Yitzhak. I will give you and your descendants the land on which you are lying. Your descendants will be like the dust of the earth, and you will spread out to the west and to the east, to the north and to the south. All peoples on earth will be blessed through you and your offspring. I am with you and will watch over you wherever you go, and I will bring you back to this land. I will not leave you until I have done what I have promised you."

When Yaakov awoke, he named the place where he'd slept Beit El, "the house of God."

The song Lappidot composed from this story took him several weeks to perfect. When he finished, he sang it privately for Devorah. She listened with her eyes closed, her hands folded in her lap, and the hint of a smile played at the corners of her mouth. When the last note had died away, she opened her eyes.

"Well?" he said. "What do you think?"

Devorah's eyes sparkled. "It's perfect. I could really feel what Yaakov must have felt when God gave him the promise…reverence, excitement, and awe, all at the same time." She clapped her hands together delightedly. "Oh, Lappi! I'm so excited, thinking about what the Lord's going to do with these songs!"

Lappidot reached over and quickly kissed Devorah on the cheek. "I just adore you. I can't wait to get married."

"That makes two of us."

Lappidot and Devorah married in the spring of her sixteenth year. Avraham felt close to bursting with emotion as he watched his daughter and son-in-law take the vows that would join them together as man and wife. Once the solemnity of the ceremony ended, the bride and groom worked their way through the crowd and greeted and kissed just about everyone as Avraham and Miryam began to welcome their many guests.

All of Ramah, plus a significant entourage from Lappidot's hometown of Beit El, turned out for the joyous occasion—at least two hundred, Miryam guessed, as she and Avdah cooked and replenished tables to the point of exhaustion. Three of Avraham's choice lambs served as the main course of the wedding feast.

"They are well matched, these two," Kenaz observed as Avraham went to greet him. "It isn't often one sees a family who loves their son-in-law almost as much as their daughter."

Even Lappidot's family, much less familiar with their new daughter-in-law, and much more reserved than the ben Yosefs by nature, treated Devorah with exceptional warmth.

"I don't know what to say to your father," Devorah whispered to Lappidot.

"Why should you be any different from me?" he whispered back. His new bride giggled. He grabbed her hand. "Come on, let's go eat."

He led her through the crowd and toward the food tables, where the cheerful guests ushered them up to the front of the line. Lappidot piled his plate high with roast lamb, bread, raw vegetables, and handfuls of dates, and encouraged Devorah to do the same. Then, gripping their loaded plates, they sank down on the first available blanket they could find. Instantly, family members, friends, and neighbors gathered around to congratulate them. Lappidot swallowed enormous quantities of food in between conversations, while Devorah merely picked at a few bites of lamb.

"What's wrong?" he asked when he noticed her lack of appetite.

Devorah shook her head. She looked down shyly. "I'm just so excited!" she whispered.

Lappidot laughed. "Me, too, but I'm still hungry!"

"Can anything affect your appetite?"

"I doubt it." He grinned and popped another date into his mouth before he was pulled into another conversation.

Finally the time came for the newlyweds to retire to the bridal chamber. Lappidot had spent every spare minute building a house in Ramah. The tiny home consisted of one room, plus a small kitchen area enclosed and roofed. Lappidot planned to build additional rooms on throughout the years as they needed more space. Devorah, her mother, and several close women friends from the village had gone through cleaning, decorating, and stocking it with the couple's personal possessions, as well as the items they would need for everyday living and housekeeping. On a little table Avraham had made, in a place of special honor, stood Lappidot's harp.

Now they held hands tightly as the crowd escorted them to their new house. Devorah kissed both of Lappidot's parents and her own mother and father before entering the house.

"My prayer for you is that your marriage brings you the same joy mine has brought me," Miryam whispered to her daughter, "and that you may be blessed with children as worthy as yourself."

"Should I have one-tenth of the love I see between you and Abba, I shall consider myself blessed." Devorah and her mother hugged each other fiercely.

Devorah watched over her mother's shoulder as Avraham embraced Lappidot and quietly said something to him that brought tears to both men's eyes.

Next Avraham came to her and gently extricated her from her mother's arms. "Let go, Miryam," he teased. "She's not bringing her mother in with her."

Miryam gave her daughter a final kiss and wiped her eyes. "Go hug your father, the funny man," she said, half-laughing, half-crying. "I'm going to give Lappidot a few more instructions while I still have time." And with that threat, she went and hugged her new son-in-law.

Avraham held his daughter by the shoulders and gazed into her eyes. "Devorah," he said, emotion rising up in him as he struggled to keep his voice steady, "I don't have the words to tell you how much I love you, but I want you to know that I am always here for you and that you're the best daughter a man could have. I also want you to know that I believe Adonai is in this marriage and that if you and Lappidot stay close to Him, He will bless you mightily." And with those words, he kissed her glowing face and held her to himself until Lappidot came to take his bride into her new home.

"Shalom, shalom!" They waved at all the well-wishers before disappearing into the cool, dark interior of their home. Lappidot shut the door firmly and then, for added measure, bolted it from the inside.

"There!" he said, turning to Devorah. "We're alone!"

"Kind of." They laughed at the sounds of merriment, partying, and shouted helpful hints that penetrated the timber walls of their home.

The two grew quiet. For the first time, they were indeed truly alone. They had kept themselves pure out of obedience to Adonai, but that didn't mean it hadn't been a struggle. Now it was not only okay, but *good* to do what they had put so much energy into not doing for so long! Suddenly they felt shy.

Lappidot broke the silence. "It was a great wedding."

"It was a beautiful wedding," Devorah said, her cheeks flushed pink.

The sight of her sweet face filled Lappidot with such love that he forgot to be awkward. He gathered her up in his arms and buried his face in her hair. Her scent intoxicated like wine, more fragrant than the finest of spices. "I love you so much," he whispered.

Devorah responded to his touch with a passion that made her tremble.

She wrapped her arms around his neck and pulled him close. "I love you so much too."

He kissed her softly, and the kiss was sweeter than honey. He gazed into her sparkling green eyes. "You are so beautiful, Devorah," he murmured. "Like a rose of Sharon…or a lily of the valley." He drew her down onto the bed with him. "You have stolen my heart, my bride."

Devorah's heart beat fast as she lay with the man whom she loved so dearly and now belonged to. His left arm lay beneath her head and his right arm embraced her. She looked deeply into his eyes. How handsome he was! She longed for him with an intensity unlike anything she had ever known. "You are altogether lovely," she breathed. "You are sweetness itself."

Then they consummated their marriage in the sight of God.

Afterwards, they knelt down hand in hand and thanked Him for His goodness to them.

The weeks and months that followed were exceedingly happy for the new couple. They settled into their home and played house together. They luxuriated in one another's bodies. Devorah strived to please Lappidot with her cooking and couldn't help but be gratified when he declared each successive meal "the best he ever had." Lappidot strummed his harp and sang for Devorah, writing several new songs in a burst of creative energy. Devorah sang with him and learned to be proficient on the harp herself.

They had little contact with family and friends during this early period. At first Devorah felt guilty. "Shouldn't we go to my parent's house tonight and play with the boys?" she asked anxiously, not sure if one human should feel this much happiness.

Lappidot walked over to her and kissed her neck. "What does Moshe say?"

"Moshe?" Devorah looked up, momentarily confused. "What does he have to do with this? I don't even remember seeing him at the wedding!"

Lappidot threw back his head and laughed. "Not Moshe from our village. Moshe the prophet!"

"Oh!" Devorah giggled as she realized her mistake. "I don't know. What does he say?"

Lappidot recited from memory. "If a man has recently married, he must not be sent to war or have any other duty laid on him. For one year he is to be free to stay at home and bring happiness to the wife he has married."

"Well," said Devorah, beaming, "if Moshe commands you to stay at home and bring happiness to me, then obviously it would be sin for you to do otherwise."

"Obviously," Lappidot agreed as he took her in his arms.

# FOUR

*In those days, Israel had no king;*

*everyone did as he saw fit.*

—JUDGES 21:25

Despite all the joy of their first year of marriage, Lappidot and Devorah were troubled. Even as their love for one another and their faith in God grew, it seemed that Israel's unity continued to break down. They, like Avraham, feared for their nation's future.

Israel desperately needed a leader. In the three years since Ehud's death, no one had succeeded him as judge; his sons fought amongst themselves, but no one capable came forward. Distant rumblings of trouble with the Philistines, long-time enemies of the Israelites, filtered in from along the coastlands. Ramah and Beit El saw declines in the number of people who came out for Shabbat services, and each year, fewer and fewer pilgrims made the yearly trek to Shiloh for the Feast. Worst of all, altars to foreign gods rose up in unexpected places, and people who once followed Adonai were drawn to the false gods in alarming numbers.

In the days of Yehoshua son of Nun, Ramah and the surrounding areas had been completely occupied by the Tribe of Ephraim. Now, however, Canaanites had migrated from the west and intermingled with the Ephraimite towns to the east. Pagan temples—makeshift, mud-brick affairs hastily thrown together—proliferated at the edges of the population centers. Devorah felt sick when she thought of the atrocities that routinely took place on those altars. *How much more of this can Adonai stand before His wrath comes down?* she thought. *O Lord, have mercy on us. What can I do to help? Use me, Lord.*

One day, it seemed to Devorah that everything reminded her of Leah and Amos. She had not seen Leah since her wedding, as they kept missing each other at the well.

She mentioned it to Lappidot at dinner that night. "I've had Leah and Amos on my mind all day today. I keep thinking about how tired and sad she looked the last time we saw them. I can't seem to get her off my mind."

"Well, you know why, don't you?" he said.

"Why she's unhappy?"

"No. Why you keep thinking about them. The Lord is bringing them to mind, which means one of two things. Either He's telling you to pray for them, or He wants you to go see them. Which do you think it is?"

Devorah pursed her lips. She closed her eyes and silently prayed while Lappidot finished eating. Finally, she opened her eyes and met his gaze. "I think it's both. Let's pray for them together, and tomorrow I'll stop by and see how Leah is doing. Okay?"

"Okay." He held his arms open. "Come here."

Devorah got up and walked around the table. She sat on his lap and snuggled against his chest. He put one arm around her and with the other he held her hand.

"Adonai," he prayed, "we come before You to lift up Amos and Leah and their children. I thank You that You've quickened Devorah's spirit regarding them and now I ask that You prepare Leah for Devorah's visit tomorrow. We ask that she be receptive to Your will in her life."

"And, Adonai," prayed Devorah, "please use me to be a blessing for Leah. Help me to not say or do anything rashly but to listen carefully to Your Spirit as I meet with her."

They sat in silence for several minutes with their eyes closed. Then Lappidot squeezed Devorah's hand. "Amen," they said.

The next day dawned bright and clear. After Devorah made Lappidot breakfast and got him off to work, she ran around the house doing all of her morning chores. When she had finished cleaning and had set the bread dough to rise, she washed her face and combed her hair. Then, leaving the house, she gathered a basketful of flowers and headed to Leah's home.

As Devorah approached the modest, one-story dwelling, she heard children fighting. Leah's oldest, Shmulie, now a big boy of ten, argued with his little sister about a toy that she held tightly in her arms. Devorah watched, aghast, while he yanked one of her long braids and grabbed the toy from her as she started to cry.

"Shmulie! Stop that right now!" Devorah yelled. Startled, the two children stared at her, and the little one momentarily forgot her tears.

"What do you want?" Shmulie asked sullenly.

"I want to know why you're acting unkindly."

Shmulie curled his lip in a sneer. "I don't have to tell you anything."

Devorah began to respond when the front door of the house banged open and Leah, a baby on her hip, walked out into the sunshine. She raised a hand to her eyes to shade the sun. "Shmulie, Naomi! What's going on here?"

Devorah's heart sank at the sight of Leah's uncombed hair and filthy dress. She stepped into her line of vision. "Hello, Leah. I've come to pay you a surprise visit."

"Devorah!" Leah eyed Devorah as though she were an unwelcome intruder.

Undaunted, Devorah plunged on. "Look!" She brandished her basket. "I brought you some flowers. I remember how much you like blue, so there are lots of those."

Leah smiled tightly. "Thank you, Devorah. How kind of you to think of me."

"Do you have a few minutes to visit?"

Leah laughed mirthlessly. "Do I look like I have any spare time?" Devorah didn't turn away but continued to look expectantly at her until Leah ungraciously relented. "Why don't you come in and have a cup of water?"

"Thanks, I will."

Devorah followed Leah into the dark interior of the house. Broken toys and articles of clothing littered the dusty floor. Dirty dishes were stacked in a bucket of murky water. The stench of unwashed bodies assailed Devorah's nostrils. She resisted the urge to crinkle her nose. *When did Leah get so slovenly?* she wondered. *What's happened to her?*

Devorah seated herself on a chair and waited while Leah fetched some water. She forced herself not to examine the cup and maintained a pleasant expression while drinking. Setting the cup down on the little table between them, she smiled at Leah. "How's the new baby?"

"He cries a lot at night." Leah's face looked haggard. She glanced down at the baby. He was sleeping peacefully. She shook her head ruefully. "I'm getting a little crazy from not sleeping."

"Why don't we pray together and ask Adonai to change the baby's sleep patterns?"

"Oh, it's not that bad," Leah said quickly. "Don't worry about it."

Devorah kept silent.

"How's married life?" Leah said.

"It's great. I love it." Devorah wanted to continue but realized that it would be like licking honeycomb in front of a starving man to describe her marriage in too much detail.

Leah, however, did not appear to be envious. "Wait until you have kids. It'll change."

"I hope not."

The sounds of the children yelling at each other drifted into the house. Devorah turned in the direction of the noise while Leah steadfastly ignored them.

"Are they okay?"

Leah waved a hand in the air. "They're fine. They always fight like this."

*They don't sound fine to me,* Devorah thought. *Maybe you should step in and discipline these kids!* But aloud she merely said, "Do you want me to go and see if there's a problem I can help them with?"

"No!" Leah spoke sharply, then appeared to force herself to speak more gently. "It's all right. Don't worry about them."

Devorah tried another topic. "How's Amos doing these days?"

"Who knows? I hardly ever see him."

"Why not? What's the matter?"

Leah sighed. "Look, Devorah. I appreciate you coming over to visit, but I don't think there's a lot we have in common anymore. It would probably be better if we just said good-bye and let it go at that."

Leah's abrupt attitude unnerved Devorah. *Lord,* she silently prayed, *I know that You sent me here today. Is there anything I can do for this woman, or have I accomplished Your purposes?* She didn't hear anything, so she stood stiffly and held out her hand to Leah. "Well, I guess I'll be going then. Please feel free to come and visit me any time, Leah. You're in my prayers."

Leah nodded, staring at Devorah with distrustful eyes. Devorah turned to go and, as she did, caught sight of something propped in a corner of the room. She peered more closely. It was a statue of a Canaanite fertility goddess.

Devorah shuddered with revulsion. "Leah! You have an idol in your house!"

Leah's face reddened, but she met the charge head-on. "What about it?"

Righteous indignation rushed through Devorah, and she forgot her usual manners. "You're an Israelite! What do you have that contemptible thing for?"

"That's none of your business!" Leah shouted. "Just get out of here! Leave me alone!"

Devorah ran outside into the bright sunshine. Shmulie and his sister stopped fighting long enough to stare at her. Blinking back tears, she walked quickly in the direction of her home.

"Oh, Lappidot, I still can't believe it!" Deborah said later that evening, after she had recounted to her husband the meeting with Leah.

Several times that day she had resisted the temptation to run to her parents' house as she waited impatiently for Lappidot to return from work. Every time that she started to leave, though, an irresistible tug kept her firmly planted in her own home. *I need to talk to Lappidot first. It would be disrespectful if I were to go to my parents before him.* After he finally arrived, she launched into a detailed version of her time with Leah. She waited for him to say something. Though she knew that he processed information slowly, still, she couldn't help urging him along.

"This is really awful, Devi." Lappidot's tone was grave. "I suspected that Amos and Leah were falling away from Adonai, but I really didn't think they had given themselves over to idol worship." He stared thoughtfully at the wall.

Devorah fidgeted and tried not to say anything while he considered what she had just told him.

"You know, it's interesting that the Lord told you to go over there today. Why do you think that is?"

"Because there should be a witness before we stone them?"

Lappidot laughed grimly. "Close. Try again."

"Hmmm. Because they desperately need someone to reach out to them and pray for them?"

"Closer, I think," he replied. "Moshe said to purge the evil from among you. I also think it is the Lord's heart to see people restored whenever possible. I'm going to let your father know about this and see what he thinks the next step should be."

Devorah's heart overflowed with love for this godly man the Lord had given her. She put her arms around his waist and hugged him, hard. He returned the embrace and for a while they put the difficulty about Amos and Leah to the side.

Micah pounded his fist on the table. "We cannot stand for this wickedness in our own town!"

"We agree, we agree, but we must talk about it rationally," Avraham said.

In response to the information from Lappidot and Devorah, the faithful had gathered at Avraham's home for an emergency meeting. Everyone was present, including Kenaz, who, at well over one hundred years old, kept dozing off. Now he blinked, mumbled, "Yes, rationally, that's right," and slipped back into unconsciousness. Devorah, who had been allowed to attend this meeting, unlike the first one five years before, smiled at him fondly.

Avraham stroked his graying beard. "What do we know about Amos?"

There was silence as everyone pondered this question. The Amos they had all known was big, burly, shy, soft-spoken, ever-present at Shabbat services, always willing to help someone move their possessions or recover a stray animal. He was the type of man who instantly came to mind when something needed to be done and more manpower was required. He never really got involved in heavy spiritual discussions, but neither was he a source of conflict. After he married Leah, he had grown a bit more abrupt and moody; his firstborn son, Shmulie, nudged everyone with his unruly behavior, but even that did not seem like a problem that would require intervention in Amos' life.

Over the last three years, Amos and his family had drifted more and more onto the fringes of believing society in Ramah. Their occasional absences from celebrations of Adonai always carried an excuse: a sick child, extra work in the fields, a lost sheep. Lately, though, they had ceased to bother with excuses. Not until Devorah saw the idol in their home with her own eyes did anyone realize the extent of their falling away.

Now Aharon hesitatingly raised his hand. Avraham nodded at him. "I have something to say, but I'm not sure that it's for all ears here," he said. He looked meaningfully in the direction of Devorah, who lowered her eyes and tried to look invisible.

"I think we're all in agreement that Devorah has been specifically used by the Lord to break open this situation and that she has a right to be present. You can speak freely in front of her," Avraham said.

Aharon consented. "Okay. A few months ago my wife came back from the well and shared with me some shocking news that she had overheard two of the other women discussing. I chided her about passing on gossip, she apologized for even repeating it to me, and we put it behind us." He paused and wiped his brow nervously. "Now I think Rachel was right to let me know what she heard, and I should have done more with this information."

He sighed heavily. "It seems that the husband of one of these two women was in the vicinity of the Canaanite temple, and he saw Amos coming from one of the inner rooms with a temple prostitute. It was obvious that they had just slept together." His face flushed beet red as he studiously avoided looking in the direction of Devorah, the only woman present. "That's not all. There's talk that Amos has fathered a child with this prostitute."

"Has the baby been born yet?" Avraham asked.

Aharon shook his head. "Not that I'm aware of. But you know what happens to these temple babies."

They all knew. The pagan temples had altars that would be used for the sacrifice of babies—often, but not always, babies born from contact between temple prostitutes and "worshippers." Some Israelite families, to prove their devotion to their new idol, went so far as to sacrifice children born of husband and wife, thereby offering "the best" to their bloodthirsty gods.

Occasionally, righteous men banded together, burned these temples to the ground, and drove the inhabitants off. But like poison mushrooms, altars to foreign gods tended to spring up faster than they could be yanked out. These places were a magnet for prostitution. Men who showed up at the temples had the sense to be ashamed at first but eventually grew bolder as they became more and more entangled in the society of people who participated in the deviant behavior.

Devorah spoke up. "Why do you think Leah was protecting the fertility goddess in her house? Shouldn't she have been praying to Adonai to set Amos free from his adultery?"

"Not necessarily," Amram said. "Leah was never the most fervent believer in Adonai to begin with. She has always had a tendency to worship her husband far more passionately than her God. It's likely she let herself be drawn into temple worship to hold onto her connection with Amos. And once you bow down to these statues of wood and stone, it becomes a matter of pride. It can be hard to repent and turn back to the one true God."

Devorah jumped up in her agitation. "But her life is awful!"

Lappidot put a restraining hand on her back.

She sat back down but leaned forward, her green eyes flashing with urgency. "Her house is a wreck, her kids are nasty and fighting, her husband is steeped in sexual sin...why would she hang on to something that is destroying her family?"

Amram shrugged. "The human heart is desperately wicked. Who can know it?"

"You know, Devi," Avraham said, "perhaps deep down in her heart, Leah doesn't believe that she deserves any better."

"Poor Leah," Deborah said softly.

Micah had been impatiently drumming his fingers on the table during this exchange. Now he burst in. "Enough with the sentimental stuff. When do we stone them and burn their house to the ground?"

"Let's see if we can win them back to the Lord first, before we do anything irrevocable," Avraham said. "How about if you, Amram, and I pay Amos a visit and try to talk some sense into him?" He looked at Lappidot and Aharon. "It's probably best for us to start with men older than Amos. It may make it easier for him to humble himself." Nobody mentioned taking Kenaz, who was contentedly snoring in his chair.

"All right," Micah said. "When?"

"Tomorrow, an hour before sundown. Meet me here."

That next night, Devorah could hardly sleep, so anxious was she to find out what had happened in the meeting with Amos. In the morning, as soon as she had given Lappidot his breakfast and he left for the fields, she rushed over to her parents' house. To her disappointment, her father had already gone out.

Miryam blinked when she saw her daughter. "Why are you here so early? Is everything all right?"

"Fine, Ema, fine. I came to find out what happened last night with Abba. Do you know?"

Miryam put down the bowl she had been carrying. "Not all the details. It was late when your father came home, and I was half asleep. He did seem pleased, though."

"Really?" Devorah's face lit up. "Where's Abba now?"

"He's training the boys to handle the sheep. Haven't you noticed how quiet the house is?" Now that her mother mentioned it, it was unusually quiet. Miryam pointed up toward the hills. "They could be anywhere by now."

Frustrated, Devorah slumped down into a chair. Her mother laughed. "Relax, *beeti*. You and Lappi come and eat dinner with us tonight. Abba will surely be home by then." She kissed the top of her daughter's head.

"Can I help you with anything, Ema?"

"No, no." Her mother bustled about. "I have Avdah to help me. You go and make a nice home for that sweet husband of yours."

Devorah grinned at her mother conspiratorially. "There's certainly no end of things to do, is there?"

"Wait until you have children. This will seem like the life of a princess in comparison!" She smiled affectionately at her daughter, kissed her good-bye, and the two women parted company for the day.

"So, tell us how things went?" Devorah asked her father that evening. Avraham had just spoken the blessing over their food and bowls were being passed around the table.

Avraham smeared oil on a huge chunk of bread, starved after his day of chasing sheep and boys. He nodded at her with his mouth full. "Good, good."

Devorah sighed impatiently and waited for him to say more. Lappidot put his hand over hers. "Let your father eat," he whispered. "You'll find out what happened."

"Okay." She sighed and scooped marinated beans onto her plate. *Help me, Lord*, she prayed silently, *not to be so impatient.* She sighed again.

Avraham laughed at her, and his eyes twinkled. "We'll talk after dinner." He gestured to the three boys, who ate as quickly as their father. "Not in front of them."

Yitzhak looked up indignantly. "Why can't I be part of things? I'm ten already!"

"And a very mature ten you are, too," Avraham said. "But this concerns things that are not for your ears yet."

"C'mon, Abba!"

Avraham held his finger up in the air. "First, you take responsibility for the sheep all by yourself. Then maybe you can find out more about the human sheep." He resumed eating.

From his expression, clearly Yitzie knew it was useless to argue any-more. He grabbed another hunk of bread from the loaf on the middle of the table and doused it with olive oil.

"Enough, Yitzie, enough!" Miryam cried. "Don't use it all up!"

Finally, dinner was over and Avraham, Lappidot, and Devorah walked to the edge of the garden to talk privately.

"Amos was very agreeable," Avraham said. "More so than I would have expected, given the circumstances. He apologized about the idol and told us that he would get rid of it."

"When?" Devorah interrupted.

"Shhh!" Lappidot's hand touched her arm. She glared at him briefly but closed her mouth.

Avraham pretended not to notice their little interchange. "He denied sleeping with temple prostitutes. He seemed shocked at the idea."

"So what do you think?" Lappidot asked.

Avraham scratched his bearded chin. "I think that this was either a lot easier than I thought it would be or..." He paused.

"Or what?" Devorah prodded.

"Or Amos is a much better liar than I ever would have given him credit for."

A week later, Micah paid a casual visit to Amos.

Leah met him at the door. Hostility dripped off of her like rain off a roof. "What do you want?"

"And a hearty shalom to you as well. Is Amos in?"

"Come in," Amos called from inside the house.

Leah put her head down and moved to the side so Micah could get past her and enter the house.

Inside, the place was still cluttered and unkempt, but the corner where the idol had been was now vacant. Micah sighed with relief. "Shalom, Amos. How are you tonight?"

"Fine, fine. You?"

"Fine as well." Micah sat down heavily on a chair close to Amos. "I see that you have gotten rid of the *pesel*, idol," he said approvingly.

"Yes," Amos said, his gaze shifting ever so slightly.

"What did you do with it?"

"Tossed it somewhere."

*Uh oh*, thought Micah. *This doesn't sound good.* Aloud he said, "Show me."

Amos stood up and clenched his fists. His face turned red and the cords at the side of his neck stood out like knotty wood. He glared at Micah. "I told you that I got rid of it. It's none of your business, anyway. I haven't done anything to you."

Micah stood up as well. He was shorter than Amos and not as muscular, but zeal for the Lord blotted out any sense of inferiority in size. "Oh, yes, you have."

"How?"

"When you, an Israelite, turn from Adonai and take on the *detestable* practices of our Canaanite neighbors," he said, breathing scorn into the very word, "it harms the entire society. All of us will suffer when God's wrath comes down from heaven."

"He's a god of destruction!" Amos said. "I'd rather worship a god of love!"

"You mean a god of sex, don't you?" Micah stared boldly at the younger man.

Amos's face turned even brighter red. "I've always respected you, Micah. Go now, before I break your teeth."

"Try it."

There was a moment of indecision before Amos threw the first punch, sending Micah stumbling backwards into a table. Spurred on by sheer adrenaline, Micah got to his feet, ran at Amos with all his strength, and knocked him off balance. The two men started pounding each other, toppling furniture as they rolled across the floor.

Leah raced into the room. "Stop it!" she shrieked. "Get out, get out!" She yanked at her husband's robe.

Micah took advantage of the distraction and headed for the door. "We're not done!"

Fury propelled him along the path from the house and out onto the street. Instinctively, he turned his feet in the direction of Avraham's home. But by the time he arrived there, the blows he'd suffered at the hands of Amos had made themselves known. Blood dripped off of his face and every part of him ached. When he was within a few yards of Avraham's door, weakness overcame him and he crawled the rest of the way. Unsteadily, he knocked at the bottom of the door.

Avdah, the house servant, opened the door and screamed when she saw him. Avraham, Miryam, and the boys all rushed over. Avraham took Micah by the arms and draped him over his shoulders, carrying him to a low couch much as he would have carried a lame sheep.

Miryam clucked her tongue. "Micah, Micah. What happened?"

"I had a little chat with Amos," Micah whispered feebly. He winced as he tried to smile.

Miryam and Avraham exchanged glances. "Tell us about it later," Avraham said as he and Miryam deftly set about cleaning Micah's wounds.

Micah did tell them about it later, and another meeting of the faithful was called. Everyone spoke at once. They didn't notice Amram, who waved his hands for silence. When the group quieted down, he said, "This Shabbat, I will make it known to everyone present that Amos and Leah are to be treated as foreigners. They have lost their standing in Israel." Everyone solemnly agreed, and the meeting was adjourned.

That night, when the house was quiet and dark, Avraham held Miryam in his arms in their bed and recounted to her the outcome of the meeting.

"Casting them out? Isn't that a bit harsh?" she said.

"Harsh?" he repeated, puzzled. "Harsh is stoning them and burning down their house."

Miryam ignored him. "Putting them outside the community will crush them."

"Miryam, Miryam," Avraham whispered tenderly, gathering her tighter against his chest, "we're thinking of the whole community with this decision. What did Moshe say?"

"Purge the evil from among you," she murmured.

"That's right. We're not currently in a position to purge the way Moshe did in the desert, but idol worship is a cancer which, if left unchecked, will spread throughout the body, causing devastation and death. God is merciful. If Amos and Leah are truly repentant, He will restore them."

Miryam considered his words carefully. "Okay," she said finally. "You're right about everything, so no doubt you're right about this, too."

Avraham laughed. "It's a blessing for a man to have a wife who thinks so highly of him." He kissed her neck. Smiling, she kissed him back.

# PART II

# YAEL

## SPRING, 1215 BC

*The descendants of Moshe's father-in-law,*

*the Kenite,*

*went up from the City of Palms*

*with the men of Judah*

*to live among the people*

*of the Desert of Judah*

*in the Negev near Arad.*

—JUDGES 1:16

# FIVE

"Yael, Yael, wait for me!"

The late afternoon sun flooded the desert from an angle, casting long shadows against the hard, rutted edges of the many *wadis* that dotted the land. The girl named Yael turned her head slightly, the only sign that she had heard her friend's call. Then she kept running, sweat dripping off her face and mixing with tears. Her legs burned and her lungs heaved with exertion, until finally, exhausted, she dropped to her knees in the shade of a large rock.

Moments later the other girl appeared, even more fatigued and, if possible, hotter. "Yael, why did you not wait for me? I'm your friend, I want to help you."

"No one can help me, Abigail."

Abigail threw her arms around her friend. "Oh, Yael! Adonai Elohim can help you!"

Yael shook her head soundlessly as she buried her face in her white robe and sobbed. *Abigail doesn't understand. Abigail isn't the one being forced to marry against her will. Abigail will get to stay in the village among her own people and not have to, have to....*

Yael could go no further with her thoughts. Despair overwhelmed her and tears ran faster down her cheeks.

"Please, Yael." Abigail attempted to pull the crying girl to her feet. "It's already late and soon it will be dark. We must get back to the others and not risk being alone in the desert at night."

"I don't care. You go back."

Abigail blanched. Since the girls had been infants, their elders had drilled into them the crucial importance of never, never being stranded alone in the wilderness after nightfall.

"Yael, I'm not leaving without you. Please come with me."

"No," Yael whispered. "I'd rather die than marry Hever the Kenite."

"All right." Abigail dropped down to the ground. "Then I'll stay here and die with you."

Yael stopped crying and eyed her friend dubiously. She couldn't be certain whether Abigail was crazy enough to do that. The two girls sat silently for several minutes, enveloped in the immense stillness of the wilderness surrounding them. A lizard darted out from a hidden crevice in the rock. A wolf howled somewhere in the distance as a hawk circled overhead, seeking its prey. Yael shivered.

Abigail took her friend's hand and held it tightly. "Look, Yael...look at this rock."

"What about it?"

"Can you move it?"

"Of course not! Abba and ten of his friends couldn't move this!" Despite herself, Yael was beginning to be interested in the conversation.

"Well," Abigail said, "I want you to think of the Lord as an unmovable rock in your life."

Yael snorted.

"Stop, Yael!" Abigail cried. "The Lord is very real and He wants to be with you."

Yael's eyes flashed with anger. "No, He doesn't. If He did, then why would He send me off to live among a strange people with"—she spat the name contemptuously—"Hever?"

Now Abigail began to cry. "I don't know! It does not make sense to me; but His ways are above our ways and His thoughts above our thoughts." She turned her big brown eyes on her friend and continued earnestly. "This is hard for me, too. I love you and will miss you terribly! But I know that the Lord has His hand on your life and that there are great things in store for you to do. Now please," she pleaded, "come back with me. Even now the sun is beginning to set."

Both girls looked to the west and saw that, indeed, the sun had sunk low in the sky.

Yael stood up. "All right, Abigail. I'll go back. But only because of you."

Abigail scrambled to her feet and hugged her friend. "Come. Let's hurry."

They walked quickly back toward town. Daughters of the Tribe of Judah, the two girls had lived in Beersheva all their lives and considered themselves closer than sisters. Abigail, who at just fifteen was the elder by three months, was small and sweet-looking. Big doe-like eyes sparkled from a heart-shaped face surrounded by curly black hair that fell in ringlets when it was not forced into a thick braid. Her curvy figure had developed early, and she had lately become conscious of many male eyes upon her. In fact, marriage for Abigail loomed on the horizon as well...only she was to marry Nathan the Levite and so would remain here for the rest of her days.

Yael, though younger, was the taller of the two. Her graceful, dignified style of movement had distinguished her at a young age. She could leap and run effortlessly, reminiscent of the mountain goat for which she was named. Her smooth brown hair fell to below her waist when loose but was now caught up in a bun at the back of her neck. Intense green eyes drew attention to her lovely face, complimented by a long, straight nose and full lips that gave her a regal air. She, too, had unconsciously attracted the attention of many, including Hever the Kenite.

Streaks of purple, orange, and pink covered the sky as the sun sank below the horizon. Normally, Yael would have gasped with pleasure at the magnificent colors, but tonight she had no comment. The two girls held hands, each taking comfort in the other. Every so often, Yael's eyes would brim with tears, then she would shake her head angrily and brush them aside. As they approached the walls of Beersheva, her pace slowed until she stopped walking entirely.

"I cannot do it, Abigail," she whispered. "Look how beautiful our beloved Beersheva is! I cannot bear to leave her."

They stood silently as the colors of the sunset reflected off the white limestone walls of the city, sending shimmering waves of pink across the desert. Carefully cultivated vineyards threw patterns of green mingled with the browns of the sandy ground. Far off to the north, the mountains of Judea stood majestically, while in the foreground, rows of date trees waved their tall, stately palms in the evening breeze.

Abigail said nothing. She, too, loved their wonderful desert home, but she would never have to leave.

A sudden commotion broke the silence. Several men burst out of the gateway of the town and ran toward them. Abigail recognized the one in front as Kasha ben Shelah, Yael's father.

He grabbed Yael by the arm and pulled her toward him. "Yael! Where have you been?"

When Kahsa's three companions caught up to him, Abigail recognized them as Kenites from their brightly colored desert garb. One of the men stepped forward authoritatively and placed his hand on the shoulder of Yael's father. It was Hever.

He never took his eyes off Yael as he spoke to her father. "Careful, Kasha. We've signed the *ketuvah*. She's my bride now."

Kasha ben Shelah dropped his hand from his daughter's arm and took a half-step back.

Abigail watched uneasily. *I've never seen him so easily cowed before.*

Yael stood very still, head bent, eyes on the ground. Hever put his hand under her chin and forced her to look up at him. Hever smiled at her with his lips but not his eyes. "Yael, my beloved, you must never, never run off like this again. I would *hate* for you to be harmed in any way."

Yael averted her gaze.

Now Kasha turned to Abigail. "Come. Your parents are frantic. Let's all get back inside the city walls." The group turned and made their way inside the gates just as the last vestiges of color evaporated into darkness and the night descended on them.

It was the morning of Yael and Hever's wedding. Yael sat very still as the women circled around her. One applied kohl to her eyes, one deftly braided her hair, while yet a third pushed dozens of bracelets up her arms. They chattered incessantly, elated at the prospect of a week of wedding festivities. Yael closed her eyes in a vain attempt to shut them out.

Tavita, the makeup artist, surveyed her work and beamed. "*Yafah, yafah!* You look beautiful, absolutely beautiful! What does the mother of the bride think?"

Yael's mother, who stood anxiously off to the side, peered closely at Yael's eyes without looking into them. Yael stared straight ahead and ignored her mother completely.

"A little more, Tavita," her mother said. "She still looks too young."

"Bah." Tavita spat. "She *is* young! She'll be old like me soon enough!"

One of the younger girls corrected her. "You're not old. You're well-preserved."

Tavita shot her a withering glance and seemed about to reply when Yael's mother interrupted. "Let's go, ladies. The wedding ceremony begins in one hour, and I know the bridegroom is restless to..." She faltered as she saw the flash of pain that passed over Yael's heavily made-up features. "...to begin on time," she finished lamely.

Yael had fought bravely with her parents up until the last moment, doing everything she knew how to do. She had cried, screamed, pouted, threatened, cajoled, whimpered, and now tried the silent treatment, all to no avail. Her parents steadfastly refused to call off the wedding. She sat now in her father's home for the last time as an *almah*, virgin, attended to by those she loved and from whom she would soon be separated. Her tears had dried, replaced by a stoic acceptance of her fate.

Abigail had slipped in to see her whenever possible these last few weeks, and had encouraged her that God would watch over her. She tried to assure Yael that great things were in store for her if she would only keep her eyes on Him. Yael did not want to insult her friend's faith, but the truth was that God was becoming less and less of a reality to her as she sank into a state of despair. Fortunately, her naturally cheerful disposition prevented her from completely succumbing to depression.

As the youngest child of six, Yael had been petted and indulged and given entirely too much freedom. Her father's profession as a potter kept him in his workshop from early morning until dusk; and with six children, money went out as quickly as it came in. Yael's earliest memory happened when she was three years old and her father had yelled at her mother for spending too much money at the *shuk*, marketplace. "You're a foolish woman who doesn't know how to restrain herself," he had raged. Ema had run out of the room, crying. Little Yael had hidden herself under a chair until capable, bossy, ten-year-old Shoshannah had found her later while sweeping and dragged her out of her hiding place.

Yael's mother was perpetually busy with the children, the house, or selling the family pottery in the *shuk* in the center of town. Many times the family's hectic schedule had allowed Yael to slip away unnoticed, to roam the fields and run as she pleased. But all of this had come to an abrupt end last month when Hever had come to Beersheva.

The visitors had caused a stir when they entered the town. It had been noon on the first day of the week, the day after Shabbat, and the *shuk* had been crowded with townspeople. Yael was working at her family's pottery booth with her brother Shimon, and the two had been bantering back and forth when suddenly Shimon nudged his sister and pointed.

"Look! Look at that procession!"

A line of camels sauntered down the narrow street. There must have been at least half a dozen of them, enormous desert camels, like those the Midians rode. Tightly woven blankets in brilliant purples, reds, and blues covered the camels. Enormous saddlebags hung from the sides of the camels, bulging with goods that the men had brought to barter.

"Kenites!" Shimon breathed.

Each of the men sat tall and erect, their stern countenances made even more severe by the curved swords and short daggers strapped to the men's sides. Shimon was enthralled by their warrior-like appearance, but Yael found them merely frightening.

The men dismounted in the center of the square and arranged to stable their animals. They proceeded to walk the length of the market. Yael and Shimon continued to watch them between helping customers. Suddenly the Kenites stood in front of their stall.

Shimon jumped to his feet. "Shalom. How may I help you?"

The man in front stepped forward. "Shalom. We have just come from the east, from Arad, and we wish to buy some of the renowned Beersheva pottery. Please show us your finest bowls."

"Yes, sir!" Shimon reached over to the shelves that displayed several eye-catching bowls. He lined the bowls up on the counter for inspection. Three of the men examined the merchandise closely while the others seemed distracted. Then one of the men poked his companion. "There he is!"

Everyone turned. A well-dressed man strode purposefully toward the group at the pottery booth. Yael and Shimon guessed from the respectful bows of the other men that this man was their leader. One of the men spoke, confirming their suspicion. "Master Hever, we are taking a look at the local pottery."

"Good." The man named Hever stood a bit taller than his companions. Shrewd brown eyes, high cheekbones, and thin lips graced a handsome face marked by a natural air of authority. Although he was no older than thirty, he seemed positively ancient to Yael; yet in a strange way, she found him fascinating.

Without realizing it, she stared at him from her place behind the counter. Perhaps feeling her eyes upon him, he turned and met her bold gaze. His mouth turned up at the ends in an odd smile. Yael flushed a dark red at her own boldness but felt helpless to look away. After several long moments, she tore her eyes away from his and modestly lowered her head. No one else seemed to have noticed what just happened. Hever and his men skillfully bargained with Shimon and eventually left with several of their best pieces. Yael sighed with relief as they left.

*That's the end of them*, she thought.

Unaware of her distress, Shimon was counting shekels. "That was great. I can't wait to tell Abba about these sales." He busied himself about the stall for several minutes, rearranging things and humming to himself. Finally, he stopped and turned to Yael. "So, what did you think of those men?"

"Mmm...I don't know."

Shimon raised his eyebrows in surprise. "You? Since when don't you have an opinion about something? Maybe even two opinions."

She grinned at his teasing, then grew serious. "They made me nervous. Especially the leader. The one they called Hever."

Shimon pulled an imaginary sword from his side and jabbed into the air. "He looked like a warrior. But he came in peace. I wouldn't be concerned." He smiled reassuringly at his sister. "You'll probably never see them again, anyway. They don't strike me as the types to hang around."

Shimon was terribly wrong. That very day, Hever set out on a far more serious buying expedition: to discover who Yael's parents were and acquire their daughter as his bride.

The task proved simple. Hever's men made a few inquiries at the *shuk* and learned that Kasha was the potter and Yael his daughter. First Hever ingratiated himself to Yael's father by paying him a visit at the workshop and flattering his work. Next, he began to ply Yael's parents with expensive gifts. Soon everyone in the family was quite taken with him. Everyone, that is, except Yael. Despite her usual fearlessness, something about Hever terrified her.

It quickly became apparent that Hever wanted to take Yael back to Arad as his wife. At first Yael was confident that her parents would refuse him, but as time went by, and the offerings from Hever piled up in their modest home, she became more and more horrified at the possibility that they would accept him.

Abba and Ema tried to reason with her. "What is it about him you don't like?" they asked.

Yael wished she could make them understand the fear she felt inside. "I don't know exactly. He has a look in his eyes that frightens me."

Her parents glanced at one another. Her father raised one eyebrow... not a good sign.

Her mother sighed. "Well, let's get to know him better. We're sure you'll change your mind."

But she didn't change her mind. A sick feeling in the pit of her stomach began to gnaw at Yael. Her normally healthy appetite diminished, and she lost weight as the gravity of her situation grew more apparent. *They're really serious*, she thought. *They want me to marry him and go to Arad.* And so in the end, Hever had prevailed.

Yael reflected on all these things as the ladies prepared her for her wedding. As Tavita put the finishing touches on her makeup, Yael's oldest sister, Shoshannah, entered the room.

She glanced curiously at Yael. "They're ready. Abba says to come out now."

Yael's mother answered. "Thank you, Shoshannah. Tell him we'll be right there."

Shoshannah nodded and left the room.

After she had gone, Yael's mother took a deep breath and walked over to her daughter. Kneeling by the side of the chair, she placed both hands on Yael's upper arms and tried to look her in the face.

Yael turned her head to the side.

"Yael, Yael," her mother begged. "Please don't shut me out. I love you very much. Your father is convinced that this is the best thing for you and I must obey his decision. Please don't leave angry."

The pitiful sound of her mother's voice unleashed something in Yael. She knew it was out of character for her mother to willingly enter into any type of confrontation and that to say this must have taken a great deal of courage for her. This show of love from her mother broke Yael's stubborn pride. The stony look faded from her expression.

Her mother clasped Yael to her chest. "My little girl, I love you so much!" She sobbed. "I will miss you every day of my life."

At this Yael began to cry as well.

"Stop!" Tavita dashed at them from across the room. "The eye kohl will run! No crying!"

Both mother and daughter looked up. The sight of Tavita was so comical they had to laugh. It was in this state of hugging, laughing, and crying that Shoshannah found them when she returned. Annoyed by their tardiness, she stood in the doorway with one hand on her hip. "Abba says I'm not to leave this room until you come with me."

"All right, all right, I'm ready." Yael disentangled herself from her mother's embrace and stood up. "Let's get this over with."

Shoshannah's frown relaxed into surprised admiration. "Oh, Yael. You look beautiful."

"Do I?" Encouraged by the reconciliation with their mother, Yael, for the first time, exhibited some curiosity about her appearance.

Ever helpful, Tavita appeared at her elbow with a hand mirror. "Look, look! With the Good Lord's help"—she pointed at the ceiling—"we did a great job."

Intrigued, especially by her sister's rarely offered affirmation, Yael studied her reflection in the glass. "Oh!" Deep green eyes framed with thick, dark lashes stared back at her. Her long, heavy, sleek brown hair, expertly braided, rested on top of her head like a crown, with wildflowers from the desert hills woven throughout the braid. Emotions and crying had only succeeded in heightening Yael's naturally rosy color and enhanced her beauty. The richly embroidered gown that Hever had insisted she wear clung tightly to her body, giving emphasis to the shape of her hips and the rounded swell of her young breasts. Thin, delicate, gold sandals made her little feet look like the feet of a princess. Gold and silver bracelets, earrings, necklaces, and a small ruby nose ring flashed and glittered as she turned this way and that.

Her sister Yohanna, who had been standing shyly in the background, now came forward. "Here, Yael," she said, holding a gauzy, gold veil out in front of her. "I hate to cover up part of your hair, but you need this." She reached up and expertly twisted the veil around Yael's hair and face until only her eyes were visible.

"Thanks, Yohie." Yohanna gave Yael a quick kiss on her veil-covered cheek.

All of a sudden, everyone became aware of the beating of drums. Yael's mother drew a shaky breath. "Okay, it's time." She smiled tenderly at her youngest daughter and took one of her hands. Shoshanna held the other, and together they escorted Yael out of the house and into the narrow street. Once outside, the pounding of the drums became louder, more insistent. Slowly they walked toward the town square, where the wedding ceremony was to happen. The whole town, it seemed, had turned out. Hundreds of people sat on the ground or on pillows, talking, shouting, whispering and coughing. In the space of a few weeks, Hever's wealth had become legendary, and all sorts of folks, some whom Yael knew quite well and some whom she had barely met, had come to see the wedding and partake of the countless delicacies that awaited them after the ceremony.

It was not quite mid-morning, but already the sun filled the sky with its intensity. Drops of perspiration formed at the back of Yael's neck. As she approached the square, the beating of drums was joined by the haunting, melodious strumming of a lyre. Gradually the crowd grew quiet and heads turned in Yael's direction. She felt a strange sense of unreality. Head held high, emotions on hold, Yael allowed herself to be led by her mother and sister to the makeshift altar set up in the shade of a tamarisk tree.

There with Yehuda, her childhood priest, stood Kasha, Hever, and Hever's friend, Ishmar. In a glance she noticed the priest looked bored, her father sheepish, Hever triumphant, and Ishmar, kind. *Oh well,* Yael thought. *It's happening. I may as well make the best of it. Maybe I've been wrong and Hever is better than I think.*

"*Baruch atah Adonai, Eloheinu, Melech haolam...*" The chanting of Yehuda's opening prayers cut into her thoughts. Yael closed her eyes as she let the marriage prayers drift over her. A delicate touch on her elbow prompted her to open them. It was Yehuda, signaling her to do the *Shevat Berachot,* the Seven Blessings. Yael was supposed to walk around the bridegroom seven times as the priest recited the blessings.

Yael felt dizzy, uncertain. Then, from the corner of her eye, she spotted Abigail sitting toward the front of the congregation. Yael turned slightly and the two girls locked eyes.

Abigail smiled at her and nodded as if to say, *yes.*

Yael breathed deeply. *Okay, okay, I can do this.* She stepped toward Hever. At first she looked down at her feet, but by the third blessing her confidence rose. She straightened up and held her head high. At the sixth blessing, Yael accidentally brushed against Hever. The touch was like a splash of cold water. She stopped.

"Go on." The words were spoken so quietly that Yael thought she had imagined them. "Now!" The command made her jump. It was Hever. No one but Yael appeared to have heard. Quickly she completed her final circle around him, careful to keep her distance.

Yehuda poured wine out of a clay jar into an exquisite cup that Yael's father had made. It was about five inches high, with a pedestal stem of Egyptian cobalt blue. The rounded cup part was light blue, and dark blue pomegranates encircled the rim. He spoke a few words, then handed the cup to Hever. Hever took a sip himself, then lifted the edge of Yael's veil so she, too, could drink.

Suddenly, it was over. The crowd erupted into shouts, clapping, and foot stomping as cries of "*Mazel tov*" and "*L'chaim*" reached Yael's ears. The musicians took up their instruments and soon the sounds of drums and the lute filtered throughout the assembly.

Kasha strode to the edge of the *bimah* and clapped his hands loudly. After a few tries, he silenced the crowd long enough to be heard. "Thank you! Thank you for gracing us with your presence at my daughter and new son's wedding!"

More cheers and whistles.

"And now," Kasha continued, "Please join us in celebrating." He launched into the blessing over the food. "*Baruch Atah Adonai, Eloheinu Melech Ha Olam, ha motzi lechem min ha aretz.* Blessed are You, O Lord our God, King of the Universe, who brings forth bread from the earth." Kasha pointed to the elaborate tables laden with dish after dish, and then, nodding to the musicians to start back up, he waved to the crowd and stepped back.

The party, which was to go on for close to a week, began in full force. Hundreds of men, women, and children, happy, laughing, talking, surged over to the food. And what a feast it was! Hever had spared no expense to enable Kasha to throw the kind of party that ordinarily Kasha could never have afforded. Bowls filled with purple and white flowers adorned long, wooden tables covered with linen tablecloths. Platters of roasted lamb liberally doused with garlic and cumin and cooked to perfection emitted a fragrant aroma. Trays of grape leaves stuffed with seasoned goat cheese alternated with saucers filled to the brim with humus, a bean paste made with chick peas, crushed sesame seeds, olive oil, and garlic. Bowls of dates, raisins, and almonds and dishes of olives tempted every palate. Baskets overflowed with freshly baked pita, the round, flat bread of the Negev, and stood at the ends of the tables like sentinels guarding an army camp. Pitchers of new wine were continually replenished by a whole army of servers. Juicy pomegranates lay sliced open, their ripe, red seeds symbolizing hopes for a fruitful union for the new couple. And dozens of honeyed desserts left more than a few children with sticky fingers and achy stomachs by the end of the day.

Yael stood uncertainly, surveying the scene before her. *Now what?* she wondered silently. *Where did Ema and Abba go?* She peered at the crowd, searching for them. There was Ema, organizing food, overexcited as usual, but Abba had disappeared. She caught sight of him giving instructions to the wine steward. He pointed at something, waved exaggeratedly, and laughed. *He likes all this extravagance,* she noticed with surprise. *He seems different...almost puffed up.*

"Yael."

"Abigail!" Yael smiled happily at the sight of her friend.

Abigail had dashed over to the *bimah* the second the ceremony had ended. She had waited patiently until she saw that Yael was alone and then had run over to her. Now that she could see Yael up close, looking so different and so much older in her wedding attire, Abigail was suddenly struck by shyness. "Congratulations on being married," she said softly.

Yael smiled wryly. "Thanks."

Both girls looked at each other uncertainly, not sure how to handle this crisis now that it was upon them.

"You look beautiful," Abigail said.

This rallied Yael. "You should have seen Shoshannah's face!" she began, turning to what had always been a favorite topic among them, when Hever walked over. He put his arm possessively around Yael.

"Hello, Abigail," he said.

"Hello, Hever. *Mazel tov.*"

"So what do you think of my beautiful bride?"

"I love her, you know that. She's dearer to me than a sister." Abigail looked straight at Hever and suddenly the power of God came upon her. "Adonai would say to you, 'This one is a precious doe in My sight and you are to treat her with kindness and love all the days of her life. I will be her Rearguard and her Protector and if she abides in Me she will be safe.'" When Abigail finished speaking, she took a step backward, a little stunned by her own boldness.

Yael's eyes grew misty. "Oh, Abigail, how beautiful!"

"Of course I'll love her," Hever said. "She's mine." He put his hand on Yael's elbow. "Please excuse us. I wish to get my wife something to eat before I take her to the bridal chamber." His emphasis on this last phrase caused both girls to blush hotly.

Yael called over her shoulder as Hever steered her ahead of him through the crowd. "Good-bye, Abigail! I'll see you before we leave for Arad."

"Good-bye, Yael. I will be praying for you!" Abigail shouted as Yael and Hever disappeared into the festive throng.

Several hours later, Yael lay on the bed in the makeshift bridal chamber in her childhood home and blinked back tears. Her long, brown hair, arranged so beautifully that morning, now hung in tangles. Her golden veil and bridal dress lay askew on the floor, where an impatient Hever had pulled them from her. Yael had known what to expect. The mating of the sheep and goats alone had been instructive, apart from her mother's teaching. But the reality of the act with a man she barely knew had completely overwhelmed her.

*It was not that he was really unkind,* she reflected. *Just that he was, well, not gentle.*

"You are beautiful, so beautiful," he had murmured into her hair. But when she had cried out, he ignored her pain. "I knew you were meant to be mine the first time I saw you, when you looked at me. I had to have you. And now I have."

"I hope you are happy." She sobbed.

Hever cupped Yael's face in his strong hands and forced her to look at him. "We are meant to be together, my little Yaela. You would be wise to learn to love me." He leaned down and kissed her deeply.

The muted sounds of the wedding festivities penetrated the stone walls of the bridal chamber. Yael thought about all of her family and friends having such a great time while here she was, mere feet away, struggling through the hardest thing she had ever had to do. Tears of self-pity formed in her eyes and slid down her cheeks.

Hever watched her silently at first, tracing the path of a tear with his finger. "Don't cry," he said hoarsely, and in his voice was a concern that surprised her.

His unexpected tenderness made Yael cry harder.

Suddenly he sprang up from the bed and hastily pulled on his clothes. "I'm starving. You should rest. I'll bring you back a plate of food."

And with that, Hever went back to the winks and laughter and goodwill that awaited him at the feast.

Yael pulled herself out of bed and wrapped herself in a robe. She sat down in a chair, lost in thought, as the evening shadows gradually deepened and the room became dark.

*Okay, Lord,* she prayed hopefully, *Maybe I've misjudged Hever. He's not the most sensitive man, but he's my husband now. Help me to give him a chance. Open my heart. Make me love him. Please, Lord. Help me to have the faith that Abigail has.*

Yael leaned back and closed her eyes. The day had taken its toll and, exhausted, she fell asleep....

Much later that night, Hever quietly opened the door and entered the dark room. He put a plate down on the small table near the door and then felt his way over to the bed. Once there, he disrobed and quietly eased himself onto the bed, at which point he discovered that Yael was not there. An exclamation of surprise escaped his lips that immediately caused Yael, in the chair on the other side of the room, to jolt awake. "Who's there?" she demanded, momentarily confused.

"Yael," Hever whispered, "what are you doing over there? Come to bed."

For a moment, Yael stayed frozen in position, unwilling to obey. Then she recalled her very recent prayer, asking God to help her be a good wife. So she slowly stood up and walked over to the bed.

"Come on." Hever put his hands on her upper arms and lifted her over to himself.

The smell of new wine hit her in the face and she turned her head to the side. "How are the festivities?" she asked.

"Winding down. Look, I brought you some food. Sorry it's so late, but it seemed that half the town wanted my company as they drank my wine." He laughed.

"You've taken Beersheva by storm."

"Except for you."

She couldn't tell by his neutral tone whether his last comment had been a question. "I...I don't know what to think yet."

He lay silently for a moment. *Maybe he'll fall asleep,* she thought. But his voice came from the darkness beside her. "Why don't you take your robe off?"

Yael stiffened. "P-please, my lord, I am not ready for..."

Hever cut her off with a wave of his hand. "No, no, don't worry. I just want to hold my new bride while I sleep."

Tentatively, Yael took her robe off and neatly placed it at the foot of the bed. Hever ran his hand up her back and pulled her down against his chest. She allowed herself to be held by him. He wrapped his strong arms around her and instantly fell asleep. As she lay there listening to his breathing, she gradually began to relax.

*Why, he can be quite sweet,* she told herself. *Thank you, Lord, for making this easier.*

Soon Yael was fast asleep as well.

# SIX

The week that followed would remain a cherished memory for the rest of Yael's life. Hever loved Yael passionately, and she found herself won over by his ardor. Fear and distrust melted away as she discovered a world of lovemaking and luxury unlike anything she had experienced before. She lay about on pillows while her new husband fetched her trays of delicacies that she would eat ravenously. She even shared wine with him, which made her giddy and lightheaded at first, then headachy and sick later.

"You can't keep up with me, so don't try," he had said lazily, wrapping her long hair around his hand as he pulled it back from her face while she threw up in a bowl.

"Trust me, I won't," she gasped, deciding she hated wine.

Yael's mother waited until Hever left the room the morning of the second day, then knocked timidly at the door. Yael was sitting up in bed, idly brushing her hair. "Come in," she called. When her mother entered the room, they both looked at each other, and then, embarrassed, turned away.

"How are you, my daughter? Did everything go well?"

"Yes, Ema, I'm fine."

Her mother stood there awkwardly. "I'm here to get the sheets."

"Oh, yes!" Yael had forgotten all about that. It was standard practice for the bridal sheets to be gathered up by the bride's parents to be shown as proof of the bride's virginity. She vaguely recalled the whispering and giggling that went on the day after her sister, Shoshannah, had been married, but she hadn't been terribly interested at the time. Quickly, she slipped out of bed, pulled her robe over her head, and belted it tightly at the waist.

"Here, Ema, let me help you," she said.

Together the two folded the blankets and put them to the side. Then they stripped off the sheet and folded it into a small square. Her mother grunted with satisfaction when she noticed the spot of dried blood.

Sheets under her arm, Yael's mother hovered uncertainly. "Would you like to talk about anything?"

Yael gazed at her mother and loved her. "No, Ema. I'm all right."

Her mother looked relieved. She shifted her weight from her left foot to her right. "Abba and I have something we would like to give you and Hever later, when you're both up and about."

"Okay, Ema. I'll look forward to that." Impulsively, Yael reached over and gave her mother a kiss on the cheek. Pleased, her mother smiled, then quickly left the room.

Later that afternoon, Yael and Hever sat side by side in the enclosed courtyard of her parents' home. Outside, the sun was at its peak, but here in the courtyard, it was cool and shady. Potted lilies in shades of red, scarlet, and white infused the space with color. Fragrant myrtle plants scented the air. *I will miss this spot most of all*, Yael thought.

"Here they are!" Her father's voice broke into her thoughts. Yael's parents swept in to the courtyard, her mother like a fluttering bird, her father more like the proverbial cat that swallowed the canary. Yael and Hever stood to greet them.

"My new son! Daughter! It gives me great pleasure to see you!" Kasha hugged both of them, then bade them to sit back down. "I have a very special wedding present for you."

He gestured to his wife, who ducked back inside the doorway leading to the living quarters and re-emerged with a large object covered with a cloth. Kasha grabbed it from her outstretched hands and put it on the ground in front of Hever and Yael. All four of them stared at it.

"Go on, go on!" Kasha said. "It's yours."

Mystified, Yael watched as Hever lifted the cloth. They both gasped. Underneath was the finest piece of pottery that Kasha had ever created. The smooth, glazed, symmetrical bowl had been baked in the blue, scarlet, and purple colors of the Tabernacle. Expertly engraved around the sides of the bowl was a pictorial account of Moshe leading the Israelites out of Egypt, through the parting of the Red Sea, and into the desert. Mount Sinai, the tablets of stone, the golden calf... they were all there. The final engraving showed the crossing of the Jordan River and the hint of the Promised Land.

Generations of pottery-making skill, learned by his forefathers in Egypt, and continued through the generations, culminated in this one exceptional piece. Its artistry surpassed anything Kasha had previously created. Yael knew what a sacrifice it was for him to part with it. "Oh, Abba! I will treasure it always. It will remind me of all of you." She stopped, not trusting her emotions.

Hever picked up the bowl and silently examined it. He let out a low whistle and shook his head. "This is magnificent." He set it down carefully and pointed to a depiction of the Israelites in the desert. "You see, the Kenites and Israelites lived side by side, like so." He interlocked the fingers of both hands together. "And now our destinies have met again."

They all smiled uncertainly at one another. Yael's mother spoke up. "You will excuse me, please. I need to supervise the preparation for tonight's continuation of the wedding feast."

"Good-bye, my dear mother," Hever said.

"Good-bye, Ema," Yael said, as she gave her mother a peck on the cheek.

"How much wine have we used?" Kasha called after her.

"All the good wine has been drunk, so tonight will be the first of the 'mediocre' wine." She smiled self-consciously and hurried out.

Kasha and Hever looked at each other.

"Beersheva loves a good celebration," Kasha said.

"Indeed." Hever picked up the bowl. "If you'll excuse me, Father. And my Yael." He smiled so intimately at her that she blushed and looked down. "I will give Ishmar this bowl to pack for our journey home." He gave a slight bow and left the room.

He left Kasha and Yael alone in the courtyard. There was an uncomfortable silence. Kasha studied his hands. Yael stared at her lap.

Kasha spoke first. "Yael."

She looked up. "Yes, Abba?"

"I want you to know that I love you very much and will miss you." Sentiment did not come easily to Kasha. He wiped his brow from the effort and went on. "I really do believe that you will have a good life with this man. He is very wealthy."

"I love you, too, Abba." Yael ran over to her father and he hugged her tightly, kissing the top of her head.

The bridal week was coming to an end. Shabbat would be Yael's last full day in Beersheva. Although Hever's men had spent much of the week preparing for their journey to Arad, last-minute details consumed Hever so that he was loath to sit still on this day of rest.

"Don't you do Shabbat, my lord?" Yael asked.

"To some extent."

"What does that mean?"

"It means that Moshe's commands are for the Israelites."

"But I thought the Kenites put themselves under the covering of Israel."

Hever frowned. "Look, Yael, these are not questions for a woman to worry about." He silenced her with a kiss, brushing aside any further debate.

But the issue came back to nag at the corners of Yael's mind. Still immature in her own relationship with God, she did not know how to effectively dialogue with someone else. Yet, as a daughter of Judah, she knew in her bones that every word spoken by God to Moshe on Mount Sinai was true. *If only I were as smart as Abigail! Abigail would be able to convince Hever that he should follow God's commands.*

Saturday evening at dusk, as Shabbat ended, Abigail came to say goodbye to Yael. They had managed to convince the rest of Yael's family to leave so they could spend their last few minutes together alone. Hever was already off with Ishmar and the rest of his men, preparing for the next day's departure.

"I have something for you," Abigail said shyly. She took a little package from the pocket of her dress. It was prettily wrapped in a palm leaf and tied with twisted grasses.

"How clever," Yael said.

Yael carefully untied the makeshift ribbon and unfolded the palm leaf. Nestled in the center of the leaf was a necklace. She picked it up and examined it curiously. The chain was a long strand of dried flax, and attached to it at the center was a small piece of polished wood. Yael peered more closely. On the wood were four Hebrew letters: *yod, hay, vav, hay.* "Adonai's name!" she marveled.

Abigail smiled proudly, her dimples showing. "I want you to always have the Lord's name close to your heart, to remind you that He is right here." She pounded a small fist against her own chest. "You only have to call Him."

"I think life with Hever will be better than I expected," Yael said confidently, the glow of her bridal week still very much apparent.

Abigail took her friend's hand and clasped it tightly. "I don't know what your future holds, dear Yael. It may or may not be as you think. What I do know, however, is that Adonai is with you and you must remember that. So please, wear the necklace!"

Yael smiled and kissed Abigail on the cheek. "Of course. I will treasure it always." She handed the necklace to Abigail as she turned sideways and lifted up the back of her hair. "Would you please tie it on for me?"

Abigail knotted the flax string behind Yael's neck. After a few moments, Yael spoke. "You know, Abi, I've been thinking."

"Mmm," Abigail said, still intent on getting the knot just right.

"There's sure to be travel between Beersheva and Arad. They're not that far apart. We can send messages back and forth and, who knows, maybe visit?"

Abigail hugged Yael. "That would be great. I'm going to miss you terribly."

Yael hugged her back. "Me, too."

Hever shook Yael awake the next morning while it was still dark. At first Yael clung to the warmth of her blankets, turning over on her side and pulling them up to her chin.

"Come on!" Hever said. "It's time to go!"

Yael opened her eyes groggily. Hever had been out until very late last night, and Yael had been asleep for hours when he finally slipped into bed next to her. Now he was filled with nervous energy and ready to go. "Come on," he said again, when she continued to lie in bed.

"All right, all right. Be nice to me." She sat up and felt around in the dark for her robe.

Hever sat next to her and ran his hand through her long, sleep-tousled hair. "Forgive me," he murmured. "I am anxious to return home. With you."

Yael dressed quickly and followed Hever out of the room that had housed them for their week-long wedding celebration. She had said all her good-byes last night, but Ema had promised to be up this morning to see her off. As they moved silently through the dark house on their way to the front door, her mother emerged from her bedroom. "Are you going already?" she whispered, careful not to rouse the rest of the household.

"Yes," Yael whispered back. Mother and daughter hugged. Yael laid her head on her mother's shoulder. "I love you, Ema."

"I love you, too." They clung to each other.

"Mother, we really need to head out now." Hever quietly but firmly broke up their embrace.

Yael's mother put a restraining hand on Hever's arm and looked up at him pleadingly. "Promise me that you'll take good care of my little Yaela."

Hever took her small hand and held it. "Of course I will. We look forward to seeing you in the future."

"As Adonai wills," his new mother-in-law said.

"As Adonai wills."

And then they were gone. They made a hasty exit out the front door, down the narrow street to the town square where Ishmar, Reuel, Zur, and Nadab waited with the heavily laden camels.

"Ah, there you are!" Ishmar said when he saw them. He and Hever turned aside for a few moments of whispered consultation while the other men waited, still and impervious. In one agile movement, Hever swung himself up onto the back of his camel, signaling Reuel, Zur,and Nadab to do likewise. Ishmar approached Yael. "My lady," he said with a dignified bow, "this camel will be yours to ride." He pointed to the smallest camel in the pack. "May I help you up?"

Yael nodded, her heart in her throat as she gazed at the animal commonly referred to as the "ship of the desert."

Ishmar read the look in her eyes. "Don't worry. I will tie her to the back of my camel. Just be sure to hold on." He held out his cupped hands, a makeshift stirrup for her to step up and hoist herself onto the camel. Yael grabbed the edge of the colored blanket that covered the camel's hump and deftly ascended the animal. *Not bad for a first try*, she thought grimly. Ishmar mounted his camel with the same effortless agility the rest of the men had shown, and the caravan surged forward.

Hever was far ahead of them. Already he had left the city gate and was heading east into the first faint blush of pink as the dawn broke on the land. Then they were all outside the walls.

Yael turned her body around as far as she safely could from her perch atop the camel to take a last lingering look at her home.

*Beersheva, Beersheva*, her heart cried, *how I will miss you!* She sighed as she turned forward, gathered her cloak around her chest, and shivered in the cold morning air.

# SEVEN

It was mid-morning when the caravan stopped to take their first break, but to Yael it seemed as though they had traveled for days. Every muscle in her body ached, unaccustomed to the jolting and bumping of the camel ride. As they rode east, the heat of day had sprung upon them like a lion pouncing on a young goat. Yael had long since discarded her cloak and partially covered her head and face with a linen head scarf to protect herself from the blistering sun. But her inability to use two hands while holding onto the camel had made this a sloppy operation at best.

It was with great relief that she observed Ishmar's camel slowing down near a grove of palm trees clustered around a small spring, which stood out as a traveler's oasis in the midst of the barren hills. Shading her eyes from the sun with her hand, Yael peered into the palm trees and could barely discern Hever sitting in the shade. Nadab untied one of the bags from the camels and carried it over to Hever, much as a servant would wait upon his master.

*Hever is like royalty,* Yael thought. *He's like a prince among these people. I guess that would make me... a princess!* Immensely pleased with this logical progression of thoughts, Yael did not notice Ishmar standing patiently next to her camel.

"Excuse me, my lady. May I help you down?"

Yael held her head high as she imagined a princess would. "Certainly."

Ishmar grasped her hand and guided her safely down off the camel, then stood discreetly with his back to her as she recovered her balance, adjusted her clothing, and smoothed her hair. Hours of sitting alone on her camel with only her own thoughts to keep her company had led Yael to reflect compulsively on the previous week. Over and over, she had rerun in her head the scenes of intimacy between herself and Hever and the romantic words he had spoken to her until her cheeks burned. Now she couldn't wait to encounter him.

As they approached the rest of the company, Yael fully expected Hever to detach himself from his companions and welcome her with the same eagerness he had shown during their bridal week. Disappointment stabbed her like a sharp sword when he barely nodded in her direction. She lingered nearby for a moment, then walked alone to the spring, where she knelt down at the bank and thirstily scooped water up to her lips. The coolness of the water was delicious, and she soon became lost in the sensation of restoring her parched body to comfort. Her thirst quenched, she removed her head scarf and splashed her face and hair with water. Then she pulled off her sandals, hiked her white linen dress up to her knees, sat at the edge of the spring with her eyes closed, and dangled her feet in the delightfully cool water.

It was in this state of relaxation that Zur found her when he went to the spring to fill the waterskin. Yael heard him approach and opened her eyes just in time to see his shocked look at seeing his master's wife with her legs bare.

"E-excuse me," he stammered as he backed away and returned to the campsite.

*Oh well*, Yael thought. She felt too tired to move and too discouraged from Hever's inattention to make the effort. Her head swung around quickly, though, when a moment later Hever came up behind her. "What are you doing?" he hissed between clenched teeth.

Yael looked up at him defiantly and splashed her feet in the water. "I'm hot."

"I don't care," he began.

"That's obvious."

He glared at her. "Yael, you are not an undisciplined goat running around the desert anymore. You're my wife, and you will behave properly. Pull your dress down, cover your hair, and come eat while there's an opportunity."

Yael didn't budge. Hever squatted down and gripped her arm. Yael flinched and attempted to jerk free but he held her even tighter.

"What's the matter with you?" he demanded angrily. "Why are you behaving like this?"

"Why am I...?" She stopped herself. Tears of frustration filled her eyes. She longed for Hever to hold her close and tell her that he loved her, but

80

pride would not allow her to say so. "Never mind," she said. "Let's go."

She pulled her arm away and this time he let go. She stood up, slipped into her sandals, and wrapped her head scarf around the back of her wet hair with angry, deliberate motions.

Hever watched her a moment, then turned on his heel and strode over to the group of men. He sat down and, frowning, chewed on the fig that Reuel offered him. Yael slowly approached the group. The men were eating and drinking, deep in conversation. No one looked up when she came. She stood silently until Hever turned to her.

"Here. Sit. Eat," he said and gestured to Ishmar, who immediately presented Yael with a hunk of bread, a small portion of cheese, and three figs. She slid unnoticed onto a shaded patch of ground a short distance from Hever and his men and wordlessly contemplated her piece of bread. She briefly considered staging a hunger strike, but her growling stomach overcame her emotions and, within minutes, she had eaten every morsel.

Snatches of murmured conversation floated her way as she sat there. Gradually she gathered that they would rest here at the oasis during the heat of the day and remount just before sunset. They would reach Arad by early morning the next day if all went well.

*Well?* Yael thought bitterly, *hah!* She reached up to her neck to scratch a bug bite and instead her fingers found the necklace from Abigail. As her hand closed over the shiny wood surface, she remembered what Abigail had told her. She closed her eyes.

*Lord,* she prayed, *Abigail told me that You're with me. I feel so alone right now. You know that I didn't want to marry Hever, but then, well, I guess he won me over this last week. Now I feel,* she groped for the word, *rejected, dismissed, insignificant.* Tears formed in her eyes and she bit her lip. *Help me not to give in to emotion but to be strong, a true daughter of Judah.*

Suddenly a hand clamped down on her shoulder. Yael gasped loudly, startled, and her eyes flew open.

It was Hever. He winced. "Don't scream."

Yael took a long look at him. His face, which had become so familiar this past week, seemed like a stranger's all over again. His curly black hair was pulled into a short ponytail. A sparse beard partially covered his square jaw. Brown skin accentuated his white teeth. In one short week, she had, in turn, hated, loved, and hated this face.

Now his tired brown eyes looked deeply into her red-rimmed green ones. "Yael," he said softly, "you need to pull yourself together. Zur is putting up a tent for us and we will sleep until late afternoon. Then we ride again."

Abruptly he released her shoulder and turned away. She looked past his tall figure and saw the small goat's-hair tent. Yael watched as Zur drove in the final tent peg, took a blanket from one of the saddlebags, fixed the blanket on the ground inside the tent as a pallet, and backed out, gesturing to Hever that the tent was ready. Hever went inside.

The rest of the company had made pallets for themselves under the palms in the shade behind the tent and had already lain down. Everyone, it appeared, was exhausted.

Yael waited until she was sure Hever had fallen asleep, then crept into the tent. Hever lay on his side with his robe off and his eyes closed. Yael sat down cross-legged on the blanket and removed her head scarf. The heat inside the tent was almost unbearable. Reluctantly she took off her long, white linen dress. Clad only in an undergarment, she quietly lay down next to Hever, closed her eyes, and let sleep engulf her.

Yael dreamed while she slept. . . .

*She, Hever, and Hever's men were riding through the desert, parched and dry, eyes strained from looking for water. Far ahead on the borders of the horizon was a faint line of green. They directed their camels toward it, riding furiously, wind in their hair. "If only I can get there, I will survive," she told herself. Frantic, they urged the animals on, but no matter how far they traveled, they never got any closer to the oasis. The heat was suffocating. It closed down around Yael so she could not breathe. . . .*

Struggling, she forced herself up through layers of sleep into consciousness, only to find that Hever's mouth was on hers and he had her in a tight embrace. "What are you doing?" she gasped, when she regained her breath.

"Shhh." He pointed in the direction of Ishmar and the others. "We don't want to be overheard." He looked down at her. "You're quite a deep sleeper, aren't you?"

"I was dreaming."

"Ah." He drew her into another kiss.

Yael pulled away from him. "Leave me alone."

He frowned, perplexed. "What do you mean, leave me alone? You're my wife."

"You've been horrible to me all day."

"What are you talking about? I've barely seen you today."

"Exactly. And when you have, you've treated me badly."

He laughed. "How have I treated you badly?"

"You've ignored me." Yael stuck out her lower lip, a gesture that had been in hibernation for over ten years.

"I'm not ignoring you now." He reached for her again.

Yael slapped his hand. "You should have paid this much attention to me earlier. Now it's too late."

Hever's eyebrows shot up. "Earlier? You mean, in front of my men?" He shook his head. "I thought you Judahites were better behaved than that. We Kenites don't make love to our wives in full view of the world."

"That's not what I mean!" she whispered fiercely. "You've been acting all day as if you don't even like me!"

Hever smiled. "Careful, Yael. You're sounding less and less like the girl who was so desperate not to marry me that she ran off into the desert by herself."

Yael flushed. "I...I feel differently now."

Hever took her hand and raised it to his lips. "I know you do, my beautiful wife. But you must understand that I'm a leader among my people." His voice became more determined. "I will not follow you around like a moonstruck calf. I would be held in contempt were I to do that, and rightly so. Do you understand?"

Wordlessly, Yael nodded. Hever reached for her again, and this time she did not resist him.

Toward sundown, their small party loaded up the camels and prepared for the night of travel. Ishmar handed Yael an extra blanket in addition to the cloak she had loosely draped around her shoulders. "I know it's still warm out, my lady, but bundle up because it's going to get cold fast."

When everyone had mounted, Hever let out a *whoop*, and they left the oasis and headed back into the barren landscape. As the sun slowly sank behind them in the west, orange rays illuminated the desert sand with a golden aura. Yael caught her breath. With her sense of peace with Hever restored, she felt free to enjoy the adventure before her. She reached forward and affectionately patted her camel's neck, using the nickname she had given her at the beginning of the journey. "There's a good girl, Gamala," she murmured, as the two of them swayed along behind Ishmar.

Night descended quickly. Overhead the stars grew brighter and brighter as all about them the air became as black as soot. As Yael gazed in awe at the majesty of the nighttime sky, the word of the Lord to Avram, recited in her hearing many, many times throughout her childhood, came clearly to mind: *"Look up at the heavens and count the stars—if indeed you can count them. So shall your offspring be."* Yael had always held a special fondness in her heart for the stories of the patriarch Avraham.

She recalled with a smile the many times she had played "Avraham and Sarah on their many travels" as a little girl with her brother, Shimon. They would chase each other through the fields and pretend they were journeying to Egypt, or to the trees of Mamre at Hebron. When other children entered into the story, Shimon would introduce Yael to them by saying, "This is Sarah. She's my sister," and they would all howl with laughter. Yael always wanted to recreate the love triangle with Hagar, but Shimon would never agree to that. Instead, he would insist on reenacting yet another battle scene in which Yael would play a conquered king. Often the only girl in a group of several boys, all brandishing homemade swords and spears, Yael would return home with Shimon at dinnertime covered in dirt from head to toe. Ema would scream and scold when she saw them, threatening to lock them in the house the next day so they would stay clean. But by the time Abba returned from his workshop, Yael and Shimon had been scrubbed clean like little angels.

Then, when she turned twelve, her relationship with Shimon had taken a new turn. Her menstrual cycle began, her body changed, and the carefree days of romping through the vineyards with Shimon and his friends ended forever. Now Abigail, who had always been Yael's friend, became almost like a sister. *No, better than a sister.* Yael corrected herself with a smile as an image of bossy Shoshannah flashed in her mind.

Probably the best times with Shimon in recent years had taken place at the *shuk*. In between customers, Yael and Shimon talked continually, enjoying a sense of camaraderie that had years of history behind it. It was only fitting that Shimon had been with her when she first saw Hever. She drew her eyebrows together in concentration as she remembered Shimon's final words to her from last night. "Arad is really very close," he had said. "I plan to see if I can expand Abba's trade and make regular trips east. I'd like to keep my eye on you." Then he had hugged her and whispered in her ear, "You're Avraham now, going to a new land."

"Oh, no, I'm not," she had replied. "I'm more like Sarah, or, or, Hagar!"

His eyes had grown serious, though a smile tugged at the corners of his mouth. "You're not Hagar," he had said. "Always remember: you're the free woman, not the slave woman." And then others had crowded in to kiss her good-bye and Shimon had vanished from the room.

Now his words reverberated in her ears as she pounded along the desert road under the stars, wind in her hair, the cold night beginning to penetrate cloak and blanket. She straightened up in her saddle and grasped the reins proudly. *I'll try to remember, Shimon. I'll try to remember that I'm the free woman.*

It was just after dawn when they arrived at the outskirts of Arad. Bone weary and chilled from the all-night ride, Yael clung to Gamala's neck, eyes shut tight. The last several hours had tested her almost beyond her endurance, effectively separating her from her former life in Beersheva in a way that little else could have done. Even the camels seemed fatigued as they walked slowly and ponderously across rocky, sandy soil and sparse vegetation.

Hever's shout roused Yael. Off in the distance, the walls of Arad stood tall and proud in the dark shadows of sunrise, almost as a mirage, with an enormous village of tents surrounding the outer wall of the city. *At last!* Yael thought. She smoothed her disheveled veil with one hand and covered herself so only her eyes showed.

With the strengthening rays of the sun, signs of life had begun to stir among the village. Women emerged from tents and set about building cooking fires. Smoke rose up in spirals, promising food and warmth after the cold, desolate journey through the wilderness. Faintly at first, Yael could hear the cries of babies awakening. The day had dawned.

A tousle-headed child stumbled out of a tent after his mother when he happened to look to the west. His sharp young eyes picked out of the landscape the caravan of camels as they approached. Excited, he ran and pulled on the hem of his mother's garment until she, too, gazed out at the horizon and noticed the party advancing. She ran and told someone else, pointing and gesturing. Soon several people had gathered to watch the caravan's steady approach.

"It's Hever! Hever has returned!" The cry went up, and soon hundreds of men, women, and children poured out of their tents to greet the caravan. From her perch on top of Gamala, Yael watched, fascinated, as Hever reached the first of the people. He jumped down from his camel and threw himself into the arms of a distinguished-looking man who had led the way. *Is that his father?* Yael wondered. Others bowed slightly from the waist, as Yael had observed Ishmar, Reuel, Zur, and Nadab do. Several of the older women wept and laughed all at once, while a small group of younger women waited to the side and watched eagerly for the rest of Hever's men to arrive. An elderly couple greeted Zur with smiles and hugs, while Reuel and Nadab disappeared into the embraces of two young women, small children bouncing alongside.

Ishmar pulled his camel to a halt, slid down, and came over to help Yael dismount. He grinned up at her, his tanned face weary but happy now that he was home. "Well, are you ready to be inspected, my lady?"

She nodded. "I think so." Ishmar held out his hand and Yael grasped it tightly as she attempted to leave Gamala as gracefully as possible. Once she had steadied herself on the ground, Ishmar walked with her to the crowd that had gathered around Hever and the rest of the men.

Heads turned in their direction and a wave of silence washed over the group. Turning, Hever saw Yael approach. He stopped talking and quickly walked over to her. Placing his hand under her elbow, he released Ishmar with a nod and guided Yael over to the elderly man with whom he had been speaking. Hever bowed and then straightened up and faced the man. "Father, this is my bride, Yael, daughter of Kasha ben Shelah, of the tribe of Judah."

Yael sank to her knees and bowed low with her forehead grazing the dust. She then arose and took her first good look at Yitro, her father-in-law and head of her new family.

"Welcome, Yael, daughter of Kasha ben Shelah," the old man greeted her. Standing straight, he was almost as tall as his son, with a dignified and courtly bearing that made him the natural focal point in a crowd. The only sign of his advanced age was a thickening around the middle of his otherwise muscular frame. Gray hair, curly like Hever's, showed from around the edges of his turban. His face was deeply lined from decades of squinting into the desert sun, but his eyes were intelligent. His smile was like the sun coming out in full strength.

Yael couldn't take her eyes off him. *He looks like a king,* she thought. He smiled at her now, and Yael sensed the tension in Hever dissipate. She herself could have wept with relief.

Yitro took Yael's right hand and Hever's left and held them together with his own. "You have chosen well, my son. May God's richest blessings be on you both. May the blessings of the breast and womb be yours. May your beautiful young wife always satisfy you and may you look only to her for your needs." He kissed them both, wiped his eyes, turned to the side, and called out in a strong voice, "Marta!"

Instantly a short, plump woman emerged from the many people standing behind him and came over to Yael. Smiling broadly, she hugged her close, kissed her on both cheeks, and said tenderly, "Welcome, Daughter!"

Yael responded shyly, conscious of many curious eyes watching her. "Shalom."

Marta turned to Yitro. "My lord," she beseeched him. "Look at this girl! Exhausted from her journey! Let me take her to my tent so she can rest."

Yitro nodded in agreement. "Go."

Before she even had a chance to glance at Hever, Yael found herself bustled off by the energetic Marta. Out of nowhere, several women appeared alongside them. Yael was so tired by now that she let herself be led like a limp doll. After a few minutes' walk, Marta stopped next to one of the larger tents. She lifted the flap and held it open for Yael to enter. Unlike Marta, Yael had to stoop down to get inside. She had been disappointed by the sea of tents, not understanding until now that the Kenites lived outside the city walls and not inside. Tent dwelling had never appealed to her; it seemed dingy and dirty. Now, however, she gasped in amazement.

The interior of Marta's tent was spectacular! Heavy, brocaded carpets with swirled patterns covered the floor. Bronze and ivory jars stood on display in various corners. A large mattress stuffed with straw and covered with luxurious Egyptian bedding lay heaped to one side. A sweet smell perfumed the air. Yael did not have much time to take in all the new sights, though, because as soon as they entered the tent, Marta issued commands to two of the three girls who had followed them in. The two girls escorted Yael to a chamber pot where she could relieve herself. Next, they carefully undressed her as the third girl returned with a basin of warm water, which they used to sponge-bathe Yael. After patting her dry with a soft towel, they gently rubbed perfumed lotion into her skin and pulled a long, clean, white linen nightdress over her head. Finally, they led her to a low stool and served her a bowl of steaming cracked grain cooked in goat's milk with chopped dates. "Eat, eat!" Marta said, happy at all the progress.

Yael tasted her first spoonful and ate hungrily of the delicious cereal. As she ate, the youngest of the girls, a dark beauty with flashing eyes, approached her timidly. "May I brush your hair, my lady?"

Yael smiled gratefully and nodded. The girl, named Simcha, unpinned Yael's long hair, exclaiming as she did so. "Look at this gorgeous head of hair!" The other girls rushed over, laughing in such a way that Yael forgot to be self-conscious and laughed with them. Fatigue, cleanliness, and a full stomach had knocked down all of her defenses. She let them tuck her into Marta's bed and smooth fluffy blankets around her.

"Sleep, sleep, new wife of Hever, sleep."

Yael smiled drowsily. She tried to keep her eyes open long enough to say, "Thank you," but before the words left her mouth, she was asleep.

# EIGHT

It took the better part of a week for Yael to sort out all of the immediate family relationships; it seemed everyone was somehow related to everyone else. She had spent the first three days in Marta's tent while Marta had led an energetic campaign to cleanse Hever's tent and make it suitable for a young bride. "He has lived alone too long," she told Yael, fingers pinching her own nose shut for further emphasis. Yael laughed. She loved Marta's easygoing style and irreverent attitude. In fact, she adored everything about Marta. Under her new mother-in-law's care, Yael blossomed like a new rose.

Marta's three maids kept a shy, respectful distance at first, conscious of Yael's status as the wife of Hever. But Yael's youthful high spirits won them over, and soon Simcha, who was thirteen, and Anna, who was sixteen, prattled away with her as if they had been lifelong companions. "We never thought Hever would marry a woman so approachable," Simcha said boldly one day. But when Yael quizzed her further on why this was, Simcha pursed her lips and turned away. Yael was puzzled but chose not to pursue the topic.

Later that same day, Marta summoned Yael. "You need a hand maiden," she said. "My wedding gift to you will be one of my maids. Pick whomever you want."

Yael was thrilled at the idea of a companion. "I want Simcha," she said immediately. Simcha smiled prettily and bowed her head in acquiescence.

On the third day, Yael moved her belongings into her husband's tent. In ceremonial fashion, she led a procession of several girls, each of whom carried a portion of her possessions, to the tent of Hever. There Hever stood at the entrance. His tall, powerful frame appeared extremely masculine to Yael after several days of living among women. Her heart beat faster as she approached him. He smiled when their eyes met and reached out to take her hands in his. He bent down and brushed her cheek with his lips. "I've missed you," he murmured in her ear. Then he opened the flap of the tent and moved aside to welcome her into their new home.

Yael's eyes slowly adjusted to the dimness of the interior after the glaring sun. Blinking, she gazed around. Her eyes alighted on a tall, gracefully carved pedestal table against an outer wall. A familiar object perched on the table. "Oh!" she said. Residing in solitary splendor sat the wedding present from Kasha, which Yael had aptly named "the Exodus bowl." She ran over and traced the ornamental bowl's curve with her finger. "This reminds me of Abba and Ema. Thank you, Hever."

He came over to where she stood and put his arms around her. "You're welcome. How do you like Mother?"

Yael's eyes brightened with enthusiasm. "I adore her. How lucky you are to have grown up with such a wonderful mother!"

"It pleases me that you like her." He was about to kiss her when they heard a soft scuffling noise just outside the tent.

Yael pulled away from Hever's embrace. "Oh! I forgot about Simcha and the girls outside with all my things." Sighing, Hever walked to the tent flap and lifted it open for the bevy of young girls to flood into his space. Yael noticed how they peeked at him when they thought he wasn't paying attention. *Hever is quite the attraction around here*, she thought. Hever settled himself down to watch the show, but almost immediately Zur's solid frame filled the entrance to the tent. He gave a short bow. "I beg your pardon," he said to Hever. "Your father requests your immediate presence."

Alarmed, Hever sprang right up and followed Zur outside. Yael watched him go, realizing her life was now bound up in his. She would be restless until she could see him again.

A full assembly of Hever's elders had gathered at Yitro's tent. Hever bowed to his father, then to each of his three uncles. Sitting among them was a young man unfamiliar to Hever. He had apparently just arrived at the camp. Not older than twenty-five, he had blazing black eyes, which smoldered in a face women would have described as handsome. Despite his youth, the man had a military bearing and a powerful presence. His style of dress identified him as an Israelite from the North country. His interest seemed to quicken when his eyes met Hever's.

Hever turned to Yitro. "I understand that you wish my presence, Father."

"Yes, my son. Come and join us." The old man's voice was grave.

They were seated on cushions around a low table. Zur had set the table with a pitcher of water, a bowl filled with almonds and dates, and a plate stacked with slices of barley bread. For the first time, Hever noticed Ishmar sitting discreetly in a dark corner of the tent. Ishmar inclined his head toward him and Hever returned the silent greeting.

Yitro turned to the young stranger. "Barak, son of Abinoam, this is my son, Hever."

The two men stared at each other and a heavy sense of destiny filled the air. Barak's eyes bore into Hever's as though he could see into Hever's very soul. Hever felt a roaring in his ears and his head grew light. He looked away.

"Barak has come to us from Kedesh in Naphtali with the news that King Yavin of Canaan has begun to overrun Israel," Yitro said.

Eliav, one of the uncles, spoke. "This is hardly a surprise. We all know that Adonai warned the Children of Israel that if they followed the detestable practices of the enemy nations and worshipped foreign gods, then curses, confusion, and ruin would come upon them. And so they have." He sat back and folded his arms against his chest.

Hever's jaw tensed. *Religious fanatic*, he thought.

Yitro addressed Barak. "What would you ask of the Kenites?"

Barak leaned forward earnestly, his body taut with restrained energy. "I believe we can drive Yavin into the sea," he said. "Right now he's conquered Naphtali, Zebulun, and Issachar, and has made headway into the hill country of Ephraim. If we raise an army, we can drive him out and destroy him!"

Uncle Reuven, the pragmatist, spoke up. "What type of forces does Yavin have?"

"The worst of it is nine hundred iron chariots in Haroset HaGoyim."

There was a collective hissing of breath as each man present contemplated the destruction nine hundred iron chariots could reap. The history of the Kenites was intertwined with that of the Children of Israel; the Kenites were descended from Moshe's father-in-law. Stories of God's miracles during the Israelites' exodus from Egypt—the parting of the Red Sea and the destruction of the Egyptian army, chariots and all—had been drummed into their memories since infancy. It was clear Barak believed God could and would do it again. Silence reigned as each man wrestled with his own faith. Finally, Eliav spoke.

"It seems to me," he said heavily, "that God is punishing us for our prostitution..."

"Eliav! Be careful," Reuven said.

Eliav ignored him. "For selling ourselves to false gods on every high hill and under every spreading tree. Sin and wickedness abound." He addressed Barak. "I admire you, young man, for your courage and determination. I believe there will come a time in your life when God will use you. But"—he shook his head sadly—"I don't think that time is now. I believe that the Lord God Himself sent these nine hundred iron chariots into Israel to punish her for her sin. If we fight, we will be fighting against God!"

Pandemonium erupted as everyone began speaking at once. Yitro stepped in to moderate but his effort was as useless as trying to hold back the tide. The debate raged for hours.

The Kenites decided not to help. Bitterly disappointed, Barak made plans to leave early the next morning. He walked out of Yitro's tent and intended to walk around the outskirts of the tent city and cool off in the early evening air as he awaited the meal being prepared for him in Ishmar's tent.

Hever walked alongside him. "Mind if I join you?"

Barak paused. Right now he was suspicious of all Kenites, sorry that he had wasted his time by coming to this forsaken wilderness camp for nothing. Discouragement rolled over him like a wave and he desperately needed to find his sense of direction from God. Besides, this son of Yitro's alarmed him. But he knew he could not refuse the request.

"Sure," he replied.

For a while the two men walked together in silence. The harshness and heat of the desert during the day were offset by its beauty in early evening. Soft, fresh air perfumed by the local foliage wrapped around Barak like a cool garment. He breathed deeply, releasing the tension in his chest as he exhaled. He relished the peace and stillness after the hours spent arguing with the Kenites. Then he remembered Hever. He turned in mid-stride, examining the man beside him. The setting sun cast its lengthening rays across Hever's face, accentuating his high cheekbones and angular face, giving him a hawkish look.

Barak got that uneasy feeling again. "So, son of Yitro. What do you want of me?"

Hever didn't respond immediately and the two men continued walking. Finally, reticently, he spoke. "Tell me about this God of yours."

"I thought that you Kenites knew the God of Israel. Certainly Eliav spoke of Him."

Hever scowled. "I have not been impressed by the faith of Eliav! He uses God as an excuse not to move." Before Barak had a chance to disagree, Hever continued. "I have not seen a man of my own generation so excited and intimate with God. I have to tell you that I myself doubt that He is any different from Molech, or Asherah, or Baal."

Barak was aghast. "How can you possibly believe that? It wasn't so long ago that He parted the Red Sea and sent the ten plagues against Egypt! Have any of these other 'gods' done anything like that?"

Hever dismissed the miracles with an imperial wave of his hand. "Yes, yes, I know all the stories. But in my own lifetime, I have not seen anything miraculous. And I am not willing to risk my life against Yavin because your God may not be powerful enough to save us. And then where would we be? At the mercy of nine hundred iron chariots with horses swifter than eagles!"

*Arrogant fool,* Barak thought. *How can you question the power of Adonai?* He masked his disgust. "The point is moot, anyway. Without an army, I can't meet Yavin on the battleground. I did not hear Adonai as well as I thought I did. But that only means that the problem lies with me, not with Him."

Hever was about to reply when he spied two familiar figures gliding toward him. He sucked in his breath and squinted. *Yael and that new maid of hers. What are they doing wandering around at this time of night?*

Yael ran toward him as Simcha trailed self-consciously behind. Yael's voice rang out like a silver bell. "Hever!"

The truth was that Yael had spent a fidgety day waiting for Hever to return. She had been disappointed when he was called away so suddenly, before they had a chance to spend any time together in their new home. Eating dinner with Marta and several of the other women had been nice, but when the meeting in Yitro's tent had obviously broken up and Hever still hadn't returned, she grew increasingly restless. Finally, she'd grabbed Simcha. "Come on, I need to take a walk. I'm sooo bored," she'd said.

Simcha giggled. She had never met anyone like this impulsive Israelite girl. The two girls covered themselves with veils, dashed out of Yael's new tent and onto the rocky path that circumvented "tent city," as Yael had dubbed it. They hadn't gone too far when Yael caught sight of Hever and a male companion she didn't recognize. Now she faced Hever and Barak, flushed and excited, more like an eager child than a newly married woman.

Hever was irritated at the interruption, which seemed undignified and entirely too informal. Still, he could not help but be gratified by Yael's sudden devotion to him after all those aggravating weeks when she refused to look at him. And her captivating beauty gave him no small measure of pride in introducing her as his bride. "Barak, this is my wife," he said.

A look of admiration mingled with surprise passed over Barak's face. He bowed slightly. "Most pleased, gracious lady."

Simcha waited off to the side, careful not to draw undue attention to herself, yet curious enough to take it all in. Whenever she thought it safe to do so, she peeked at Barak. She already considered him the handsomest man she had ever seen.

Hever turned to Yael. "Barak comes from Naphtali."

Yael immediately perked up at the mention of Barak's home tribe. She bowed gracefully. "I myself am from Judah."

Barak raised an eyebrow at Hever. "You have married an Israelite?"

When Hever ignored him, Yael jumped in. "What were you two discussing?"

"We were discussing whether or not there is a God in Israel," Barak said. His face was grave, but his eyes twinkled.

"Why, of course there is!" she said. She reached into her robe and drew out the necklace from Abigail that was tied around her neck. "Look! This is His Name!"

Barak bent down to examine the pendant more closely. Yael flushed at the nearness of this strange man. His eyes met hers and he held her gaze as he spoke to Hever. "She's right," he said, smiling. "Here's definite proof."

The conversation became more serious when Barak told Yael about King Yavin's invasion of Israel to the North.

"That's horrible!" she said. "How can we stop him?"

Barak laughed mirthlessly. "If only you were Queen of the Land, my lady."

"We're not going to fight," Hever said.

"Why not?"

"Because all of those iron chariots would mow us down like flowers in a field, only at the end the smell would be rotting corpses and not myrtle."

Yael shuddered. She stared at her feet, deep in thought. Finally she said, "Don't you think Adonai would fight for us the way He did for Ehud against the Moavites?"

Hever rolled his eyes, exasperated. "Don't tell me you believe all those old stories."

"They're not old stories!"

"Your wife is right," Barak said.

"Look," Hever said. "I've had hours of discussing this and I'm finished with it." He shook Barak's hand. "A pleasure to meet you, my friend. You had better find your way to Ishmar's tent before they give up on you." He turned to Yael and ignored her troubled look. "Come, Yael, I am taking you home for the night."

Yael looked back at Barak as Hever led her away, with Simcha trailing behind. Yael waved at Barak. "May Adonai be with you."

Barak watched them walk off into the night, perplexed at the union of this unbelieving Kenite and this beautiful daughter of Israel.

After returning Simcha to Marta's tent for the night, Hever watched silently as Yael brushed out her hair and prepared for bed by lamplight. She did not know what to say to him. Hearing him call the miracles of Adonai "old stories" had alarmed her beyond expression. Who was this man she had married?

She tensed when he got out of his chair and came behind her. He ran his fingers through her hair, then rested his hands lightly on her shoulders. "You were very friendly with Barak of Naphtali, weren't you, my love?"

Yael kept her voice low. "He is a kinsman, a fellow Israelite. Should I have been unkind?"

His hands tightened on her shoulders. "You are my wife now. The Kenites are your kinsmen—not some stranger from Naphtali."

Yael squirmed under his grip, but he didn't let go. "Tell me your true opinion about Adonai," she demanded hotly.

"My opinion," he said, as he jerked her up and twisted her necklace from Abigail, "is that you should stop wearing this necklace that tells everyone you belong to Him."

"Let go!" she cried as he tore the necklace off her and pocketed it. "Give that back to me! It's from Abigail!"

He pulled her against himself. "You can have it later. After I remind you that you belong to *me*."

Yael was furious. Her pent-up desire for Hever mixed with anger at his possessiveness aroused her passionate nature to a combustible level. She made love to him with a ferocity that both shocked and excited him. Without knowing it, Yael had set a dangerous precedent in their marriage.

# PART III

# DEVORAH

### 1222 BC—1217 BC

# NINE

The ostracism of Amos and Leah caused a terrible rift in the community of Ramah. As Avraham and the others had hoped, some families turned away from their worship of foreign gods and quietly disposed of their household idols when they saw what happened to Amos's family. Unfortunately, others grew more defiant than ever. Pagan worship spread like an insidious cancer, and unity in Ramah was fast becoming a distant memory.

During this time of turmoil, Kenaz, now one hundred and five years old, took ill. He had outlived his wife and children; only a granddaughter remained to tend to him. Dinah was in her fifties, widowed, and although she sometimes complained about the irascible old man, in truth she was completely devoted to him. Now Kenaz lay in bed, growing weaker each day.

Devorah went to see him immediately when she heard of his failing health. She had gathered a bouquet of Kenaz's favorite flowers, which she clutched in her hands as she stood at the threshold of his house and knocked. Dinah met her at the door.

"How is he?" Devorah asked.

Dinah smiled sadly. "Not so good, I'm afraid."

"May I go and sit by his bed?"

"Of course. He'll be so glad to see you. You've always been one of his favorites."

Devorah handed Dinah the flowers and followed her to the small room where Kenaz lay. Dinah opened the door and motioned her in. "He sleeps almost all the time now," Dinah whispered.

Devorah gazed with fondness on the ancient face, now relaxed in peaceful slumber. *How small and vulnerable he looks.* She watched him for a while and prayed as he slept. After a few minutes he stirred and opened his eyes. When he saw Devorah, a smile touched the edges of his mouth. "You've come to see me!" His voice trailed off into a spate of coughing.

Dinah came into the room. "Is everything all right, Saba?" She put her hand on his forehead.

Kenaz attempted to swat her hand away but only got his arm a few inches off the bed before it fell weakly back. "See how she fusses over me. She acts like I'm sick!"

Devorah and Dinah exchanged amused glances. "I'll be in the next room, Devorah. Call if you need me."

Devorah took one of Kenaz's cold, papery hands and clasped it in her young, warm ones. "You need to be nicer to Dinah. No one else would have put up with you the way she has."

The old man's eyes watered. He squeezed Devorah's hand lightly, like the fragile fluttering of a butterfly. His lips moved soundlessly.

"You know," she said tenderly, "ever since I was a little girl, you and I have always had a very special connection."

Kenaz responded so softly that Devorah had to bend over with her ear to his mouth to hear him.

"...our trip to Shiloh when Ehud prayed for you?"

"Yes, yes, I remember. I have treasured his words and recalled them many times over the years."

"They're not just his words." Kenaz attempted to sit up. "They're God's words." His breathing grew more rapid and he fell back on the bed.

Devorah stroked his hand soothingly and put her face close to his so that he could see her easily, without effort. "Kenaz, please take it easy. If anything happens to you, Dinah will be really upset with me."

"Pah!" He spat weakly. "I must tell you..." Another coughing fit erupted. Devorah heard Dinah's footsteps come quickly toward the door and then retreat back down the hallway when the coughing ceased. "Devorah, the Lord has great things in store for you."

Devorah nodded as he spoke, holding tenderly onto his hand. "Thank you, Kenaz," she whispered. "Your affirmation means a great deal to me."

Kenaz shook his head, frustrated. "You don't understand. It's more than affirmation." He rallied all of his strength, desperate to communicate clearly to Devorah while there was still time. Suddenly his gaze sharpened and he looked directly into her eyes. An odd chill ran down Devorah's spine. "I see the same spirit in you that I saw in Ehud when he rallied the troops to fight against Moav. God wants to do something extraordinary in you, Devorah. Don't miss out on any part of His plan for you just because you are a girl." Exhausted, he ceased speaking, and collapsed against his pillows.

Devorah squeezed his hand and kissed his wrinkled brow. "Thank you, Uncle," she said. "I will hold your words close to my heart."

Satisfied that he had accomplished his goal, Kenaz soon fell into a deep sleep. Devorah sat there for another hour, watched him sleep, and mulled over what she had heard.

Two days later, at mid-morning, Devorah's brother Yitzhak appeared at her door. He gave a cursory knock before bursting into the front room, chest heaving from running.

Devorah hurried out to meet him. "What is it? Is it Kenaz?"

Yitzie nodded. "Early this morning. He will be buried tomorrow."

Devorah hugged her brother, and together they wept at the loss of this man who had been like a member of the family for so many years. Though Kenaz had seemed ancient from their earliest memories, they could not imagine life without him.

Devorah brushed away tears with the back of her hand. "How is Dinah?"

"I don't know. Abba and Ema could probably tell you. Are you going to come over to the house?"

"Later. After Lappi is home from the fields, I'll tell him the news and we'll come by."

"Okay. I better get back." He looked down and shuffled his feet. "I know how special he was to you. I love you."

She hugged him and kissed his cheek. "I love you, too."

He broke free of her embrace, grinned at her, and sprinted out the door.

A month after Kenaz's funeral, Devorah sought her mother out on a morning when Miryam was alone doing housework.

Miryam spotted her daughter from the front window. "Hello, hello! To what do I owe the pleasure of this visit?"

Devorah hugged her mother. "Do I need a reason to visit my mother?"

"Of course not. How are you, *beeti*?"

"Fine." She grabbed a rag and silently began to help with the dusting.

"How are you doing with Kenaz being gone?"

"Oh, I'm fine." She grew silent again and this time Miryam didn't press her.

Presently Devorah said, "Ema?"

"Yes, *beeti*?"

"How does a woman know if she's going to have a baby?"

Miryam's heart skipped. She came over to Devorah and put her hand on her daughter's shoulder. She forced herself to sound calm. "Well, first she misses her monthly cycle."

"Check." Devorah said, reddening a little.

"Second, her breasts may feel tender."

Devorah touched herself lightly. "Check."

"Third, she may find that foods she normally ate without a problem now make her throw up."

"Definitely a check on that."

"And finally," Miryam said, "she tells her beloved mother, who then makes a huge fuss over her and takes care of her."

Devorah grinned. "Here I am."

The next seven months brought great joy and expectation to Devorah and Lappidot. Together they worked at building an addition onto their home— Lappidot did most of the actual labor, while Devorah brought him tools and kept him company. Lappidot's love for his wife grew even as the baby grew within her. Devorah, in turn, grew in her respect and admiration of him as he took charge of his household and took care of her.

Devorah had wondered whether she would know when the baby was coming; but when the pains finally came, she had no doubts.

"Lappi, it's time," she said when she felt the first strong contraction. "Please go get Ema and Avdah."

He bolted out the door without another word.

Time dragged on endlessly as she counted the pains and waited. When Lappi, Miryam, and Avdah finally appeared in the distance, Devorah stood in the open doorway of her home, one hand on the doorpost and the other cupping her belly. She tried to wave at them, but a pain gripped her so keenly she doubled over, breathing hard until it subsided. When she could straighten up, she saw that Lappidot had broken away from the women and was running toward her. She laughed softly though gritted teeth. "Thank you, Lord, for my Lappi."

He reached her and held her closely. "Are you okay?"

"I think so." She squeezed his hand, relieved to see him.

"Come on. I'm putting you to bed. Your mom and Avdah will be here any minute."

He steered her toward their bedroom, but she protested shakily. "I'm okay walking around..."

Another sharp contraction took her by surprise. Doubling over, she eased herself onto the bed with Lappidot's help. When the pain lifted, she stayed curled in a fetal position.

"I'm going to see where your mom is," Lappidot said.

"No, don't go! Please stay here with me."

He sat down next to her and massaged her shoulder.

Another contraction hit. "Aahh," she exhaled, then held her breath while she waited for the pain to subside.

"Don't hold your breath; let it out and breathe quickly," he said.

As she struggled to follow his advice, Miryam and Avdah rushed in. The two women quickly rearranged the room and gathered the items they would need to deliver the baby. Miryam kissed her daughter on the cheek, then kissed Lappidot. "Go outside and wait. We'll call you when we need you."

"Are you sure there's nothing I can do?"

"Nothing! Go!"

He kissed Devorah on the lips. "I'll be praying for God to ease your pains and bring forth a healthy son."

She smiled at him. "Or daughter. I love you."

"I love you, too." They stared into each other's eyes. He lingered.

"Go!" Miryam demanded.

"I love you," Devorah whispered again.

"Me, too." He backed out of the bedroom door.

Twelve hours later, Devorah gave birth to a healthy son.

"He's the most beautiful child I've ever seen," she murmured as she held the tiny, squirming bundle. "Look at his perfect, round little head." She looked up at Avdah. "Where is Lappidot?"

Avdah found Lappidot pacing around and around the house as he prayed loudly, beseeching God's mercy. He exhaled with relief when he saw Avdah's smile. She ushered him into the bedroom and tiptoed out.

"So *that's* what you look like!" Lappidot exclaimed when he saw his son.

As if on cue, the baby turned his head and seemed to look in the direction of Lappidot's voice.

Devorah gasped in amazement. "Lappi! He knows who you are!"

"Of course he does." Lappidot smiled broadly as he bent over and examined the baby for the first time. "I'm his father." His tone grew serious. "Are you okay, Devi?"

Devorah smiled and the furrow in his brow relaxed. "Just exhausted. And sore. I'll be fine." She rested her head on Lappidot's shoulder as they gazed down at their son. "I expected him to be cute, but I never thought that he would be this *extraordinary*," she said. They stared at him some more, transfixed by his intelligent, knowing eyes, rosebud mouth, little pink tongue, and soft brown hair. "What should we name him?"

Lappidot didn't respond right away. As they looked at the baby, he gave a big yawn, revealing two rows of toothless pink gums. Devorah and Lappidot looked at each other. "Kenaz!" they said simultaneously, laughing.

Devorah had been prepared for the joy of motherhood, but she hadn't been prepared for the challenges. Of course she had expected the baby to wake up during the night, and in fact remembered her younger brothers crying a lot when they were little. But having primary responsibility for the care and feeding of such a tiny, helpless life overwhelmed her at times.

Lappidot did what he could to help, but he had the animals, the fields, and the farm work to do. He couldn't function if he didn't sleep. It naturally fell to Devorah to get up and feed and change little Kenaz when he woke up at night. And wake up he did. Not until he was six months old did he finally begin to sleep for eight-hour stretches. By then Devorah and Lappidot perceived themselves as experienced parents.

By day, Devorah carried little Kenaz in a scarf-like sling that she tied across one shoulder as she went about her daily errands. When she stopped to chat with people, which happened frequently, Kenaz often popped his fuzzy little baby head out of the sling and stared with his wide, knowing eyes. Exceptionally bright and adorable for his age, he became immensely popular.

When Kenaz was one and a half years old, Devorah became pregnant again. This time Kenaz required so much of her attention that she didn't have time to focus on every little aspect of her pregnancy. Almost before she knew it, she was in labor again.

God blessed the labor, and it went smoothly. Devorah and Lappidot found themselves parents again, this time blessed with a girl. They named their new daughter Tirzah. Pretty and delicate-featured though she was, Tirzah proved far more difficult than her brother. Devorah was woefully unprepared for the crying and screaming that permeated their household almost from the first day. Not even nursing would appease Tirzah during her crying fits. The only remedy, they discovered, was for Lappidot to dance with little Tirzah and sing one of his worship songs. Unfortunately for Devorah, Lappidot worked all day. When Miryam could take a break from her housework, she came by and sang and rocked Tirzah. That helped a bit, too. But the lack of sleep, the constant crying, and the additional burden of Kenaz, who transformed from a happy toddler to a jealous, clingy sibling, all conspired to quench Devorah's naturally buoyant spirits.

For the first time in her life, Devorah felt far from God. More often than not, she slept through her pre-dawn prayer times. *I'll have plenty of time to sit and pray during the day when the baby is napping,* she would rationalize to herself. Then she would reach the end of the evening, fall into bed exhausted, and realize that although she had kept up an interior dialogue with God all day, she had missed sitting quietly before Him.

"Don't worry," Lappidot whispered as they snuggled in bed one night. "The Lord gives special grace to nursing mothers."

"How do you know?"

"Believe me. I'm the husband God gave you so I must be right."

Devorah shook her head at his silly logic, but she did feel a little less guilty.

Unbeknownst to Devorah, God was testing her heart. She had been in many ways the ideal child: precocious, thoughtful, kind, obedient to her parents, and an earnest seeker of God; yet *because* of all these wonderful attributes, a root of pride had taken hold in her. Now her circumstances were beating that pride out of her on a daily basis. No longer self-satisfied about her clean house, her well-fed husband, or her close relationship with God, Devorah lost her sense of superiority over the neighbors, friends, and relatives that surrounded her. In fact, now that she herself fell short of her own high standards, she began to feel *compassion* toward the very people she once held in contempt.

When Devorah searched her heart and saw the sin and wickedness that existed there, she shuddered with revulsion. *How can you ever use me, God? I've been so arrogant all these years, reveling in being everyone's special pet.*

Buried under the weight of self-condemnation, she slunk through the rest of that day in a fit of depression, just hanging on until Lappidot came home. He had barely walked in the door when Devorah, with Tirzah struggling on her hip, blurted out a litany of her own sins and character flaws.

"...And so," she said, shoulders bowed, "I realize now that God can't possibly use me. I'm completely unfit to serve him." Tears came forth in a torrent and spilled down her cheeks.

"Shhh, Devi." Lappidot stroked her hair. "It's not as bad as you think. This is actually good news. Here, give me the baby." He took Tirzah and settled her on his lap. Kenaz raced in from the next room and jumped on his lap as well.

"What do you mean, 'good news'?" she said.

"Can you feed me first? I'm starving."

"Fine. But it's not very good. I can't cook either." She dropped a sorry looking bowl of lentil stew in front of him.

Lappidot groaned. He said a hasty blessing over the food and began to eat. Devorah sat across from him and dabbed at her eyes, while the children, thrilled to see their Abba, behaved better than they had all day. The baby, who had spent half the day screaming, now gurgled happily in her father's arms while the two-year-old who had had a death grip on his mother's leg all afternoon slid off of his father's lap and played contentedly on the floor with one of his little wooden animals.

"Okay," Lappidot said between mouthfuls. "Tell me how you feel."

"I feel like God is upset with me." Tears came again.

"And why is that?"

"Because," she said, "I'm proud. I'm arrogant. I don't get up in the morning to pray the way I should..."

"Devi." Lappidot pulled out his chair and placed the baby on the floor. He put a spoon in her chubby fist and she chewed contentedly. He held his arms out. "Come here."

She came over and sat on his lap and he put his arms around her.

"You know, don't you, that the Lord disciplines those He loves? What child isn't disciplined by his father? Avraham disciplined you and you respected him for it, right?"

She nodded silently.

"Okay, then. God is treating you as His child. Your Abba disciplined you for a little while as he thought best; but God disciplines us for our good, that we may share in His holiness."

"But this is so hard," she cried.

"Of course it is. No discipline seems pleasant at the time. Only later it produces a harvest of righteousness and peace if you have been trained by it. You're being trained, Devi."

She blew her nose. "I thought so, too." She sniffled. "I've always thought that God had a very special plan for me. But lately it all seems to have fallen apart."

"No, no, that's not true," Lappidot said. "Just because you're in a difficult place doesn't mean anything's changed from God's point of view. You're doing great. You really are." He ignored the skepticism on her face. "Strengthen your feeble arms and weak knees and be the warrior God called you to be, okay?"

"How? How do I do that?"

"You know how. We call on God to give us the strength. Can we pray together right now?"

She cleared her throat and blew her nose again. Closing her eyes, she nodded. Lappidot held her tighter on his lap. "Adonai," he prayed, "thank you for my wife. Thank You that You deem her worthy as a child of Yours and that You are disciplining her through this time of difficulty. Please open her eyes so she can see how much You love her, and let her know this is only a temporary season. Let her experience joy and blessing. Strengthen her so that tomorrow holds no fear. Bring back her zeal for life."

"Lord, thank you for Lappidot," Devorah said. "Thank you also for the two beautiful children You've given us. I'm sorry that I'm so ungrateful and all I can think about is I'm tired and it's too noisy. Forgive me. Help me to keep my eyes on You and not on my circumstances. I really love You, Lord." Her voice broke. "And I want more than anything to be useful to You." She stopped.

They sat silently. The only sounds were those of Tirzah sucking on her spoon, punctuated every so often by Kenaz mimicking different animals as he played with his toys. Peace settled in the room. Devorah, her eyes still closed, felt almost lulled to sleep when Lappidot gently said, "Amen?"

"Amen," she said.

Lappidot cleared his throat. "On to another topic. I heard something today that I need to tell you."

She frowned. "Is everything okay?"

"With us, yes, *motek*." He kissed her hand, then shook his head sadly. "It's about Amos and Leah."

"What happened?"

"Apparently he and another man got in a fight at the Canaanite temple over one of the prostitutes there. The guy pulled out a knife and slit his throat. Amos is dead."

Devorah's face blanched. "Oh no. How awful! When was this?"

"Last night."

"How is Leah taking it?"

"I don't know. That was all I heard. If you want to call on her tomorrow and see what you can do to help, that's fine. But you're not allowed to bring the children, and I insist that you take Yitzhak with you. Understood?" He looked at her severely.

Devorah bowed her head meekly. "Understood."

The next day, Devorah brought her children to her mother's house, and she and Miryam packed up a big meal for Leah. Yitzhak came and the two of them walked to Leah's house to offer their condolences. There they encountered a large crowd of Canaanites and even some Ephraimites who, like Leah and Amos, had turned away from Adonai and taken to idol worship. All around them, people wailed loudly, gnashed their teeth, and gashed themselves with knives. In the center of it all sat Leah. She moaned and cried hysterically, with tangled hair in her face, clothes torn, and ashes on her head.

Yitzhak and Devorah worked their way through the crowd in an attempt to pay their respects. Several people pushed at them in an overtly hostile manner.

"Maybe we should just go," Devorah whispered to Yitzhak.

Just as they turned to leave, Leah looked up and spotted them. Her eyes narrowed dangerously and uncontrolled rage erupted. "Why are *you* here?" she screamed. The wailing stopped as everyone stared at them.

Devorah took a deep breath. "We heard about your loss, Leah." She stepped closer to Leah and laid the baskets of food carefully on the ground. "We only want to bring you some food and offer comfort."

"My life is over." Leah sobbed angrily. "There's no comfort anymore."

"Oh Leah." Devorah knelt beside her and grasped her hands. "The Lord God of Israel is your comfort. Don't turn away from Him." She hugged Leah.

Briefly, Leah let herself be held, then recoiled and pushed Devorah away. "No! It's too late for that. Please leave."

"It's never too late to turn back to Adonai." Devorah reached to touch Leah's arm, but a hand seized her wrist. Horrified, she stared down at the long, crimson nails that dug into her flesh, then looked up into the hate-filled eyes of a Canaanite woman.

"You heard her. Get out of here," the woman hissed. "You and your god are not welcome here. Now go!"

Yitzhak stepped forward to defend his sister, but Devorah quickly shook herself free of the woman's grasp. She put a hand on Yitzhak's arm. "No," she whispered as she stood and steadied herself. "Let's just leave."

She glanced down once more at the pitiful figure on the ground. "Call me if you need me, Leah."

In the wake of these events, Devorah's life steadily improved. The baby's screaming fits grew less and less frequent; and Devorah generally found ways to cope with the ones that remained. As time went on, Kenaz regained the sense of security he had temporarily lost when his little sister was born, and he became more independent. Instead of struggling against the hardships, Devorah surrendered herself to motherhood. As a result, her attitude improved immeasurably; and as her attitude improved, so did her circumstances.

Just about the time Tirzah reached two years of age, and Devorah gained a foothold on her time, the Lord prompted her to pick the harp back up.

Through Lappidot's instruction, she had become passably competent at playing the harp. She strummed it nicely, and had learned to play a half dozen or so of her husband's songs by memory. After Kenaz was born, she still picked it up occasionally, but when Tirzah had arrived, Devorah had abandoned her music completely. Every so often Lappidot would encourage her to play, but she always had a reason why she couldn't. One Shabbat afternoon their little family was relaxing in the courtyard, shaded from the sun by the big date palm that stood sentry over the house. Kenaz and Tirzah chased each other around the enclosed area in some sort of game. Devorah sat on the stone bench beneath the palm and luxuriated in the peace of Shabbat, content to be between meals and thrilled that she was forbidden from doing housework until sundown. Lappidot sat down beside her, harp in hand.

"Are you going to play, *dodi?*" she said drowsily.

By way of response, Lappidot set the harp in position and started strumming. He closed his eyes and sang softly, "Alone anointed is the Father, coming back to rule forever...."

Normally Devorah would have enjoyed listening to her husband sing, but today the music agitated her. Her pleasant, relaxed mood fell from her and a gnawing restlessness took its place. *What is wrong with me?* she thought. Then all at once she realized what was going on. *I'm jealous! I want to do what Lappi's doing. I don't want to just sit here as an audience.*

"Hey, Lappi," she said softly.

He opened his eyes. "Hmmm?"

"You know what?"

"What?"

"I'm thinking that maybe I should pick up the harp again. What do you think?"

He broke into a laugh. "I think *Baruch ha Shem.* It's about time."

She took a playful jab at his ribs. "Very funny. Will you help me?"

He puckered his lips. "Only if you kiss me."

She batted her eyelashes at him. "I'll do more than kiss you."

"Devorah, I'm shocked! You, a mother in Israel, to say such things." He seemed anything but shocked, however, as he set the harp aside, pulled her onto his lap, and kissed her passionately.

This scene drew the two children over like magnets. Kenaz began to chant, "Abba's kissing Ema, Abba's kissing Ema."

Lappidot sighed and drew back from Devorah. "You know there's only one thing to do in a situation like this."

"What?"

"Tickle the four-year-old!" He jumped up and grabbed Kenaz, who screamed happily. Lappidot pounced on him, pushed him down onto the grass, straddled him with his legs, and playfully tickled him.

Devorah covered her eyes. "Lappi, stop!"

"Oh, he loves it," Lappidot said. "Look at this." He stood up, gripped Kenaz by the ankles, and swung him around.

"Don't hurt him!"

"Aaahhh," Kenaz yelled, wide-eyed and delirious with joy.

Tirzah reached for her daddy with chubby baby arms. "Me too, me too!"

Breathing hard, Lappidot set Kenaz on the ground. "Now it's your sister's turn," Lappidot said as he picked up the toddler and gently spun her around. "How about you, Devorah? Do you want a turn?"

She crossed her arms against her chest and shook her head. "I think you're all *meshugga*," she said, but she batted her eyelashes at him over the tops of the children's heads.

# TEN

Nine months later, almost to the day, Devorah and Lappidot were blessed by the birth of a second boy. They wanted to name him Avraham; but tradition would not allow them to choose the name of a living relative. As a compromise, they chose Avi, which means "my father."

Devorah gained competence as a mother every day. At the ripe old age of twenty-two, she could not remember a time when she *didn't* have a baby on her hip as she cooked, cleaned, and washed. Devorah used the time leading up to Avi's birth to practice the harp and become proficient at it. She struggled at first but eventually won the battle of self-discipline. On days when she desperately wanted to close her eyes for ten minutes or sit under a tree and gaze off into the hills, she forced herself to seize hold of that valuable time and doggedly practiced her instrument. After several months, when she could play a song almost as well as Lappidot, something interesting happened.

One day she began to strum one of Lappidot's songs when she changed the tune slightly and soon found herself singing prayers that were circulating in her head. The next time she sat down with the harp, she first asked Adonai to bring forth what He would have for her. As she picked at the strings, she let her fingers play without too much thought, and again sang words of honor and praise to God. *Am I writing songs like Lappi?* she wondered. But it wasn't the same thing. His were songs of praise and worship, while the words that came to Devorah from Adonai felt like words of *prophecy*.

*Oh my*, she thought, startled by the realization. She asked the Lord to guide her, and tried strumming a simple arpeggio pattern on her stringed instrument. The word *Messiah* came into her mind. *What is it, Lord*, she prayed. *What about the Messiah?* Words tumbled from her lips, dropping into the air like ripe olives:

*"The Messiah will come,*

*From Yehudah*

*From the lion*

*The lion will crouch, it will spring, it will crouch, it will spring.*

*The Messiah will come,*

*With eyes dark as wine,*

*With teeth whiter than milk,*

*Wielding the staff, the staff, and holding fast to the scepter.*

*Come quickly, O God, and deliver us from our sins!"*

Devorah sang the words God had given her, and as she did, she marveled at His kindness in speaking to her. She had never connected the patriarch's blessing over his son, Yehudah, with the coming Messiah. It amazed her that the Lord had just dropped the whole thing into her lap. Awed and humbled, she stood and placed the harp on the chair she had just vacated. Then she lay facedown on the ground in total submission and clasped her hands over her head.

"O Lord," she prayed, "thank You for using me. Thank You for this gift You've given me. Show me how to glorify You with everything I do. Help me not to disappoint You but to live for You always. In Your blessed Name, amen." She lay there until Kenaz and Tirzah ran in from outside, hungry, disheveled, and in need of Ema's attention.

"What's Ema doing?" Tirzah asked, eyes wide.

"She's talking to Adonai."

Pulling herself off the floor, Devorah hugged both children hard. "You are so smart," she said to Kenaz. "That's exactly what I was doing. Who wants a snack?"

"I do! I do!" both children shouted at once, just as baby Avi woke up from his nap and started to cry.

Lappidot was just as excited as Devorah about the song when she played it for him later that evening. "This is really excellent," he said. "Why don't we work together and see what God gives us as a team?"

She hugged him. "Oh, I'm so happy I could burst!"

But the collaboration would have to wait. Pesach was upon them, and this year the whole family, including Devorah and baby Avi, would travel to Shiloh for the Feast of Unleavened Bread. Together with Devorah's parents, brothers, Amram, Aharon, Micah, wives, and little ones, they made quite a large party.

Kenaz at five was almost the age Devorah had been so many years before when she met Lappidot for the first time at Sukkot in Shiloh. "Remember?" she asked Lappidot.

"Remember?" He laughed. "I still have the bruise from where I bumped into you."

"Oh, stop it. That was such an amazing time. I still remember Ehud's prayer over me."

Devorah noticed the frown that passed over Lappidot's face at the mention of Ehud's name. "What is it, Lappi?"

Lappidot sighed. "It's been ten years since Ehud died."

Devorah nodded.

"In that time, we Ephraimites have turned from Adonai to idols in droves. Do you remember how packed Shiloh was that year we met?"

"Of course. It seemed like the whole world was there. But I was seeing it from the perspective of a child…."

"Well, I was older and I remember it very well. Wait and see what it's like at Pesach this year. Keep in mind what it looked like when you were seven, and tell me what you think of things now."

"Fewer people, I'd imagine."

"Far fewer, I'm afraid."

Lappidot's prediction proved sadly true. When their group arrived at Shiloh, Devorah thought at first that they had arrived a day early. "Oh my goodness," she said as she stood atop the hill from which she and her father had first viewed Sukkot so many years ago. "Lappidot, you were right. There's hardly anyone here." Small groups like theirs were scattered sparsely across the grounds, in stark contrast to the bustling crowds of years past.

Devorah saw that Avraham, too, was distressed. Her mother spoke into her father's ear and the two of them turned away, arms intertwined. She thanked God silently for Kenaz and Tirzah, who jumped up and down gleefully. Compared to their small town of Ramah, the valley dotted with men, women, children, and yet-to-be sacrificed Passover lambs seemed enormously exciting.

Kenaz pulled at Lappidot's sleeve. "Abba, can I run down ahead of you and look around?"

"Mmm..." Lappidot scanned the crowd with one hand shielding his eyes. "Okay, son, sure. Just wait for us over there." He pointed to a spot that seemed to have a lot of children running around. "Are you taking your sister?"

Tirzah clapped her hands together excitedly. "Me, me, me!"

"Sure."

"Okay." His father waved them ahead. "We'll catch up with you in a bit."

Lappidot sought out Devorah. "So, what do you think?" He gestured toward the panorama below them, including the sight of Kenaz as he scampered down the hillside, then waited for Tirzah to catch up.

Devorah sighed. "It's a huge difference from fifteen years ago. My parents look pretty upset." She pointed discreetly behind them.

Lappidot glanced over his shoulder. Avraham and Miryam walked slowly, deep in conversation.

"You know, Lappi," Devorah said, "the state of our nation is troublesome, and I agree with you that it's a big deal, but this is baby Avi's first Pesach, and Kenaz and Tirzah are old enough to understand more about it. Can't we enter into the spirit of the holiday even if not that many other people are here? I know that I, for one, am really looking forward to roasted lamb and bitter herbs."

"Of course." Lappidot put his arm around her. "We'll have a great family Pesach."

Devorah settled the baby into a more comfortable position in the baby sling. "Good."

A few minutes later they reached the edge of the valley and made their way to the spot where most of the people from Ramah had congregated. Kenaz and Tirzah trailed along at the end of the group, greeting other children wherever they happened to find them. Everyone worked together to set up camp amidst the tumult of children and lambs running loose. When the work was done, family by family, they prepared the evening meal.

Since coming down the hill into Shiloh, Avraham had been unusually pensive. After dinner, Devorah noticed that instead of playing with the grandchildren or sitting and relaxing as he normally would, her father purposefully set off through the camp, greeting people everywhere from all tribes.

Devorah joined her mother, who *was* sitting and relaxing. "Ema, what's Abba doing?"

"He's just talking to folks." Miryam reached down to massage one of her feet.

"Here, Ema, let me do that." She sat on the ground in front of Miryam and took her mother's foot onto her lap.

"Oh, *beeti*, you must be tired too," Miryam said weakly.

Devorah winked. "Don't steal my blessing."

"I wouldn't dream of it." Miryam sighed contentedly as her daughter rubbed the travel weariness from her feet.

"So," Devorah said. "What's Abba really doing?"

"He's looking for like-minded people."

"Ah."

Devorah mulled this over. Her mother appeared to not want to say too much so she didn't push. Instead, she worked on Miryam's feet for a few more minutes before she stood up. "I'd better round up the kids and get them to bed. Avi already has a head start on the rest of us, and I don't want him to wake up before I even have a chance to sleep some myself."

"All right, honey. Give your old mother a kiss before you go."

Devorah leaned down and kissed her mother affectionately. "I love you, Ema."

"I love you, too. *Lilah tov.*"

"*Lilah tov.* Say good night to Abba for me."

"I will."

Even with a smaller crowd, Pesach in Shiloh proved to be a tumultuous, heady, exciting time. The bleating of lambs mingled with the cries of children when they realized these adorable, cuddly pets would soon be slaughtered to become their Pesach dinner. Mothers shushed little ones as rows of Levitical priests sharpened their knives. An on-site butchering factory was necessary to handle the flood of lambs.

Since Lappidot and Devorah's household was too small to eat an entire lamb, they would share one with Avraham, Miryam, Yitzhak, Yaakov, and Yosef. Four days prior, back home in Ramah, Avraham and Yitzhak, now a strapping lad of sixteen, had waded through the flocks of sheep, looking for the lamb that would suffice. After several sweaty hours going back and forth, trying to make a decision, Yitzhak spotted four spotlessly white legs huddled under a protective mother sheep. He called his father over, and the two of them examined the lamb together. "Yes," Avraham grunted. "This one will do nicely."

In accordance with the word of the Lord as given through Moshe, the lamb was a year old male without spot or blemish, taken from the sheep or the goats. However, this particular lamb, with its snow-white woolly face and big, soft eyes, had a very protective mother. She made menacing noises and bristled aggressively when Avraham and Yitzhak started leading her baby away. They had to push at her with their shepherd's crooks. Hardened though he was to the plight of sheep, Avraham always felt a twinge when he finally succeeded in capturing the lamb.

That had been the tenth day of Nisan. Today was the fourteenth day and the lambs were being slaughtered with the recognition that the blood of the innocent lamb would atone for the sins of the people. Just about every family, to some degree or another, had become attached to their particular lamb.

"It was Adonai's intention," Avraham explained to his sobbing grandson, "that we grieve at the killing of the lamb so we can begin to understand the sacrifice that is being made in order to cover our sin."

Kenaz failed to find comfort in these words; only the strong, brown, leathery arms of his *saba* helped him regain his equilibrium.

Soon the air was filled with the scent of warm blood as hundreds of animals gave their lives. "It's a good thing God said to slaughter them at twilight when it's cooler. If it were the hottest part of the day I think we would be passing out from the stench," Lappidot said to Devorah only half-jokingly. She wrinkled her nose and covered Avi's head with a light blanket.

"It makes me think of the Canaanites—those nasty ceremonies where they drink blood," she said. "I don't know how they do it."

"The worst part isn't so much that they do it, but that they entice Israelites to do it as well."

"What do you think some of the people who aren't here this week are doing back home?"

Lappidot shrugged. "Probably best not to think about it."

They turned as Yosef ran over to them. "Hey, come on, you two! Our lamb is up next!"

Lappidot and Devorah followed Yosef up to one of the many altars. A weary, blood-spattered priest held up his knife. "Who's next?"

Avraham held a solemn Kenaz by the hand and stepped forward. "We are," he said.

The priest peered nearsightedly at Avraham. "Is it...?"

"Phineas? Is that you?"

Phineas nodded and the two men hugged as Devorah and Lappidot exchanged glances.

"So good to see you, my friend. It's been awhile." Avraham pointed to the clan behind him. "You remember my wife, Miryam, and this is the rest of my family."

"A wonderful family," Phineas said. "Okay, is everyone ready?"

They all tentatively nodded as Snowy (named by Tirzah) the lamb bleated softly and nuzzled his nose into the back of Kenaz's legs. "I want everyone to take turns putting their hand on the lamb's head so that you all agree you're taking part in its death."

Solemnly, they all obeyed, even down to a sniffling Tirzah.

"Good," Phineas said. "Everyone understands that if you don't share in the sacrifice, then you don't share in the atonement from sin, right?"

"Right," they all said in unison.

"Good." He reached out to pat Tirzah on the head, hesitated when he noticed how bloodstained his hands were, and decided against it. Instead, Phineas scooped up Snowy in his arms, placed him on the altar, motioned to Avraham and Lappidot to hold him down. He then stood behind the lamb and, with one quick motion, severed the jugular and windpipe of the animal, using a sharp blade with no nicks in it.

Tirzah's face registered surprise that Snowy appeared to feel no pain. Spurts of blood gushed out from the sliced throat in rhythm with the faltering heartbeat of the lamb. They all stood transfixed, staring at the dying animal. Within three minutes, Snowy began to kick convulsively as his nervous system shut down. Next he lost consciousness, and then he was dead.

Holding the carcass by its back legs, Phineas poured the blood into a shallow basin off to the side of the altar. In a few minutes, the animal was completely drained of blood, and he and Avraham tied it by its feet to a pole.

Phineas smiled at them. "Nice to have met all of you." He turned to Avraham. "Always good to see you, my brother."

"Same here." Avraham clasped him heartily on the shoulder, before turning away.

As the family proceeded to the cooking pits, they heard Phineas shout hoarsely, "Next!"

Later in life, when Devorah reflected on the events that had transpired in her life and the lives of her family, she would always remember the beauty and fellowship of this first night of Pesach, the spring she was twenty-three. Alongside Israelites from every tribe and clan, they roasted their lamb over the fire—head, legs and inner parts, just as God had commanded Moshe. They spread liberal amounts of bitter herbs on the cooked meat and scooped the whole thing up with brittle pieces of unleavened bread, or *matzah*, which Miryam and Devorah hastily kneaded and baked while the lamb was roasting. Skins of new wine came out of tents and off the backs of long-suffering donkeys, and soon the Passover was underway.

Lappidot, Devorah, their children, and the rest of the ben Yosef family joined several other families and together they all recounted the story of the Exodus from Egypt. Lappidot particularly added to the narrative when he passed on some firsthand remembrances of his great-grandmother.

One young boy had been absently tossing tiny bits of wood at the smoldering fire while the familiar story of the Children of Israel leaving Egypt was recounted. When he heard about Lappidot's great-grandmother, he drew his head up sharply and a flicker of interest sparked in his dark brown eyes. "She was really there?"

Lappidot smiled at the boy, a wiry, strong lad from the area around Yerushalayim. A Benjamite. "Yes," Lappidot said. "She was probably about the same age you are now when they escaped Pharaoh. How old are you?"

"Twelve."

Lappidot considered. "Yes. She may have even been a little younger. But then of course she wandered in the desert until she was over fifty years old."

The boy's mother spoke up."That's incredible."

Lappidot nodded. "You know, even though she lived an extremely long time once she was in the Promised Land, it was the Exodus and the time in the wilderness that defined her life and everything she did. She always had trouble reconciling herself to the rest of us. She thought we were spoiled." He grinned unapologetically. "By the way, I don't believe we've met. I'm Lappidot, this is my wife, Devorah, and our three children."

"My name is Rivkah, and this is my son, Yishai." She gestured broadly to five other kids younger than Yishai, some of whom were asleep. These are some of my other children, and my husband, Kish."

A short, stocky, dark-haired man sat next to her and gnawed an entire leg of lamb. His friendly brown eyes crinkled at the corners when he smiled. "Shalom. It's good to be together with people who love the Lord." He looked meaningfully at them.

"How are things in Benjamin?" Lappidot asked.

"Probably not much better than Ephraim."

"Kish!" Rivkah pulled at his forearm. "Let's at least get to know them before...."

She stopped speaking as Avraham suddenly clapped his hands sharply. "I'm glad we're all making new friends. But we still have to go through the ten plagues before we can put the little ones to bed." This last remark came with cries of protest from the little ones in question.

They listened to the stories until well past midnight. The following day, now that the Pesach meal was eaten, the Israelite community began to celebrate the seven-day Feast of Unleavened Bread. They remained at Shiloh, making bread without yeast, and cleansing their tents of all leaven. Kenaz and Tirzah sat on Avraham's lap, one on each knee, as he explained the custom to them.

"The leaven," he said, "represents sin. Have you watched your Ema make bread?"

Both children nodded.

"Have you noticed that she uses just a little yeast, but it works through the whole batch to make it rise?"

Again they nodded.

"Well, it's the same way with sin. At Pesach we cleanse our lives of all sin because even just a tiny amount can destroy us." Avraham leaned back, satisfied that he had presented a very lucid explanation for his small grandchildren.

"Saba?"

"Yes, Kenaz?"

"What's sin?"

"Oy!" Avraham smacked his hand against his forehead while both children giggled.

Not until the journey back to Ramah did Devorah have a chance to speak with her father. Lappidot had taken baby Avi, and Devorah, relieved of her sweet burden, felt energized and free. She saw her father walking alone and hurried to him before someone else noticed and got there first.

"Abba." She panted, out of breath from the sprint to catch up to him.

"Shalom, my daughter." His face broke into a wide smile. "You're a blessing to the eyes."

Devorah laughed gaily and took her father's arm. Although Lappidot had long ago taken his rightful place as the "man" in her life, she still treasured the special bond that existed between herself and her father. They were very much alike.

"I've been wanting to talk with you," she said. "You're not easy to get alone."

He half-turned, eyebrows raised toward her as they walked. "Is something the matter?"

"No, no. Nothing's wrong. I just wanted to know what's been happening this week. It seemed that whenever I looked for you, you were in yet another huddled conversation with a person I had never before seen from either Judah, or Dan, or Asher, or Zebulun or...."

"Don't forget Ephraim."

"Or Ephraim," she said. "But tell me: what are you up to?"

"I'm not 'up' to anything." Avraham wiped the sweat from his forehead with the edge of his sleeve. Already the day grew hot. "Those of us who still take the Lord's commands seriously enough to travel during the Feasts quite naturally find each other. And we talk."

For a few minutes Avraham didn't say anything. Father and daughter walked in companionable silence. "I will tell you, though," he said in a lower tone that made Devorah's ears perk up. "I will tell you that for some reason even men I had never met before last week treated me with respect and deference. Like a leader."

Devorah's heart swelled. Of course these men treated her father as a leader. He was! Besides Lappidot, whom Avraham had mentored, Devorah had never met anyone who could compare with him. "So what does this mean, exactly?"

Avraham looked straight ahead. "I'm not sure. Let's wait and see if anyone turns up in Ramah. I've let men know that my door is always open."

Devorah wanted to ask her father for more details, but at that moment a very familiar *waaa* reached her ears. She and Avraham looked back and saw Lappidot walking quickly toward them, holding baby Avi under the armpits at arm's length in front of him. "Devi," he yelled as soon as she was within earshot, "somebody's hungry!"

"Okay, I'm coming," she shouted. She gave her father a quick kiss on the cheek. "I enjoyed our talk, Abba. Perhaps we can finish it later?"

"Perhaps." He smiled at her. "Go tend that precious son of yours." Devorah ran off to meet up with Lappidot, who gratefully handed her the baby.

"Here I am, you little smoosher," she said to Avi, whose tiny mouth opened the moment he saw her. Devorah took the baby and nursed him as she walked, having mastered this skill years before with Kenaz.

The days following Pesach teemed with activity. First, there was the settling back into the everyday routines and recovering from time spent on the road. Then, soon after they returned home, Kenaz and Tirzah got sick—nothing serious, but enough to consume any spare time Devorah might have squeezed from her daily schedule to practice the harp. Eager as she was to get back to her prophetic music, she had to remind herself that her family was her main priority. Then, shortly after the kids recovered, something unexpected happened.

One morning, as Devorah raced around her little home, cleaning, cooking, and tending to the children, there came a knock on the door. "Coming," she yelled. She flung the door open and found herself face-to-face with Leah.

"Leah!" The last time she had seen Leah was the day after Amos was killed. If Leah had looked bad then, now she looked awful. Her clothes hung from her emaciated frame; big, dark circles ringed her eyes; and several of her teeth were missing. Devorah stood aside so Leah could walk in. "Please come in."

Leah reluctantly moved forward a few steps, eyes to the floor.

Devorah's heart ached with pity. "It's okay. You're welcome in my home."

Leah began to weep.

Devorah hugged her gently. "It's all right."

Kenaz and Tirzah crept into the room and stared, wide-eyed. Over Leah's shoulder Devorah mouthed the words "Go away!" to them and pointed to the door. Reluctantly, they wandered off to play.

"You must be hungry," Devorah said. She brought Leah some food, which Leah ate greedily. "Where are the kids?"

"Shmulie ran away six months ago." Leah's voice broke. "I don't know where Naomi and Ben are right now…probably searching for anything edible." She tried to smile.

"Bring them here," Devorah said. "We'll take care of you while we figure out what to do."

"Devorah, I am so ashamed." Between sobs, she shared how Amos had become enticed into the fertility goddess worship. Soon he began sleeping with multiple temple prostitutes, and then he encouraged Leah to join in.

"I never even considered the sinfulness of our behavior. All I could think about was holding onto Amos. I knew that if I defied him, I would lose him to those people and that lifestyle. So I went along with it." She paused.

"And then?"

"Then Amos was killed. Our money ran out, and I had no place to turn. The Israelite community had cut us off, and our so-called 'friends' at the temple didn't want to help us. They told me if I needed money, I could sell my body at the temple. So I did."

Shaking with remorse and shame, Leah described some of the bizarre and unnatural acts the temple priests had required of her. "I can't tell you the worst of it," said Leah, staring down at her clenched fists. "It's too horrible."

"You can tell Adonai. He knows."

Leah lifted her head. "I already have. That's why I'm here. One day I felt so low I wanted to die. And from the depths of my misery, I came to my senses and cried out to God. I remembered what you said to me—'It's never too late to turn back'—and I begged Him to forgive my sins and restore me to Him. Since then I have not been able to shake your image from my mind. Devorah, I am so sorry for the way I sinned against you. Will you forgive me?"

Devorah flung her arms around her friend. "Of course I forgive you. And Adonai has forgiven you as well—you know that, don't you?"

"I guess so… I don't know."

"Oh, but He has," Devorah said. "A humble and contrite spirit God will not despise. If you truly repent of your sin before Him, He is faithful and just to forgive. He will restore you, Leah."

Leah's face crumbled into tears. "I've been so lost."

Devorah held her close. "I know, I know. It'll be okay."

Later that day, Leah and her two children moved in with Devorah and Lappidot. Miryam came by with Avdah, and together the three women helped bathe, feed, and tend to the needs of Leah, Naomi, and Ben. While they slept that night, secure for the first time in years, Lappidot and Devorah sat with Avraham and Miryam to discuss the situation.

"Obviously she can't stay here long-term," Miryam said.

"I have an idea," Avraham said. All eyes turned to him. "We have a woman in our community who is all alone and could use some help. Why don't we suggest that she take Leah and her children on as servants in exchange for food and lodging?"

"That's a great idea," Lappidot said. "Who is the woman?"

Devorah's eyes sparkled. "I know. It's Dinah, isn't it, Abba?"

"That's right. I think this is an arrangement the Lord will bless in a powerful fashion."

So it was that Leah was restored to the believing community of Ramah; and Dinah, bereft since the death of her grandfather, Kenaz, had a new purpose in life.

Already the feast of Shavuot loomed close. Devorah felt an urge to return to her music before things got busy. *Okay, Lord,* she prayed one morning. *Help me have time to write music today.* It had already been several weeks since they had returned from Shiloh. The house was clean, dinner preparations made, clothes washed, Kenaz and Tirzah had eaten and were outside playing, and baby Avi fell asleep nursing and had stayed asleep when she placed him in his little bed.

*I can't believe it,* Devorah thought. *I can finally play the harp again.* She went and retrieved the harp, dusted it off, tuned it, and gently plucked the strings. *Ahhh.* It felt good to be playing again. For a little while, she worked at running through some of her repertoire and softly, so as not to wake Avi, she sang to the Lord. When she reached a natural pause in her worship, she asked the Lord to release His song anointing on her. Expectantly, she poised her fingers over the strings and waited. And waited. And waited. Nothing came.

*What is it, Lord?* Devorah prayed. She could feel a sense of His presence, yet the gifting she had so anticipated failed to materialize. Disappointed, with a heavy heart, she put away her harp just as baby Avi awoke from his nap with a cry.

When Lappidot came in from the fields that day, Devorah intended to discuss with him what had happened. But he was late, and hot, and sweaty, and hungry. She put aside her own needs and tended to him and the children. By the time she was free to talk to him, he had already fallen asleep, exhausted from the physical toil of his day. As she lay in bed next to him and listened to the sounds of his breathing, she brought before the Lord her frustration about her music.

*Do you love Me? Is that You, Lord? Do you love Me? O Lord,* Devorah prayed, *You know I love You. Then why did you despise My Presence today? How did I despise Your Presence?*

Then she remembered. She had not been interested in being close to God. All she had wanted was to write powerful songs. The *reason* for the songs had become secondary to the songs themselves.

Stricken to the heart, she slid out of bed and fell to her knees. *Forgive me, Lord,* she cried. *Forgive me for making an idol of a gift You gave me.* Bitterly repentant for her cavalier treatment of the Lord of the Universe, she relinquished ownership of song writing and gave it all back to God. When at last she got up off her knees and climbed back into bed, she felt drained but at peace.

# ELEVEN

Devorah wearily ran her hand through her hair and sighed. Her daughter lay on the floor kicking and screaming yet again over virtually nothing. The house, generally neat and charming, was in a state of disorder. Unwashed dishes from breakfast sat in the wash bucket, the floor was unswept, beds were still unmade, and dirty laundry sat in a pile in the corner. Dinnertime was approaching far too quickly.

*How many times can we eat lentil stew?* Devorah thought grimly. Exhausted, overwhelmed, and slightly nauseous, she nudged her screaming child with her toe.

"Come on, come on, that's enough. Stop it, Tirzah!"

Tirzah kicked her leg at Devorah and screamed louder.

Baby Avi, disturbed from his nap by the noise, started to cry. Frustrated, Devorah debated spanking Tirzah as hard as she could but decided she had better cool off first. She scooped up the baby, ran outside the house, and sat down on a stone bench in the shade of the large date palm that grew in the middle of their courtyard. "It's okay, Avi, it's okay," she said to the baby as she began to nurse him. She stroked his soft little head as she sought to pull herself together.

It was a beautiful, hot day. The heady smells of fruit trees mingled with the sounds of honeybees and birds as they went about their daily business. The courtyard reflected intense white sunlight, causing Devorah to squint as she peered in the direction of her home. Without an audience, Tirzah's cries had begun to wane. Soon there was only the intermittent muffled sob.

*Maybe she'll just pass out on the floor.* Devorah closed her eyes and leaned against the tree. *Help me, Lord*, she prayed. *I thought that I was called to do great things for Your Kingdom, and I can't even handle a three-year-old!* Tears spilled out from under her closed eyelids as she wrestled with self-pity. *O Lord, I'm so overwhelmed. Help me!*

As Devorah prayed, both the baby and Tirzah fell asleep. Lulled by the sudden quiet and the warmth of the sun, Devorah drifted off as well. About a half hour later, she was startled awake by a shadow passing in front of her. Slowly she opened her eyes and discovered her husband, who stood there and gazed at her with a tender smile.

"Oh, Lappidot!" As soon as Devorah saw his beloved face, her tears, forgotten while she slept, welled back up. "I'm so glad you're home." She squinted into the sun. "Where's Kenaz?"

Lappidot sank onto the seat beside her. "He's with your father. Tell me what's wrong."

"I...I have nothing to feed you...the house is a mess...I'm so over-whelmed..." Tears turned into wrenching sobs as she recited her litany. "I just can't handle Tirzah. She's too much for me." She put her head on his shoulder and gave herself over to her misery.

Lappidot laughed softly as he smoothed his wife's hair away from her face. "You are the most competent person I've ever met. I refuse to believe," and he gestured toward the house, "that the little *boobah* in there can win."

"I'm not competent."

"Stop it. Of course you are. You're tired, is all."

"And I don't feel well, either. I'm kind of nauseous."

The same idea occurred to both of them simultaneously. They stared at each other.

"Do you think...?!" Lappidot said excitedly.

Devorah groaned."Oh, no."

"Sweetheart, no wonder you don't feel well. Soon you'll feel much better, I promise," Lappidot said as he kissed his wife.

Startled, baby Avi opened his eyes. When he saw his Abba, his little baby face lit up in a big grin. Lappidot grabbed the baby from Devorah's lap and began dancing wildly around the courtyard with him. "You're go-ing to be a big brother," he sang to the delighted baby.

Tirzah emerged, stumbling, from the darkened doorway of their home, rubbing sleep-weary eyes. "Ema, Abba," she wailed. Lappidot caught sight of her and swooped her up in his other arm. Tirzah relaxed and started giggling.

Devorah felt all of her earlier emotion dissolve, only to be replaced by the real affection that she felt for her husband and children. *Okay, Lord, okay, I understand. You're making me a mother in Israel. This is a good and worthy calling. But please, please, Lord. Please help me accomplish this life with grace. I need You every minute.* She stood up and started walking toward the house.

"Hey!" Lappidot yelled after her. "Where are you going?"

"Inside, to make us lunch. How about some"—she hesitated—"lentil stew?"

"Lentil stew?" Lappidot repeated. "I *love* lentil stew!" He twirled the children around and around the courtyard until they shrieked with laughter.

It was a spectacular fall day. Wildflowers dotted the green hills, the sun shone brightly, and fleecy white clouds made patterns against the soft blue sky. The temperature was just mild enough to be comfortable, but not too hot. A faint smell of ripening apples hung on the breeze. It was also Shabbat, the day God gave to the Israelites as a day of rest.

Avraham paced impatiently around Devorah and Lappidot's little courtyard. He had been waiting for some time now for the two of them and their children so they could all walk together to the weekly Shabbat gathering in the village square. Every so often, he would squint up at the sun, judge its position in the sky, and shake his head.

"We're coming, Abba," Devorah called from inside the house. Avraham looked up hopefully.

"Saba!" Kenaz came running out of the door first.

Avraham's tanned face crinkled into a big smile. "Kenaz!" he responded.

The boy jumped into his arms. Next came Lappidot. Avraham noted he looked a little hollow-eyed this morning.

"Sorry we're so late today, Abba." He grinned apologetically. "It's been rough getting the kids together."

Finally, Devorah emerged. She carried baby Avi and had Tirzah by the hand. Tirzah's face was red and Devorah had that stressed look. She prodded the little girl toward her grandfather. "Go, go to Saba."

Tirzah took a few tentative steps but stopped when she saw Kenaz in Avraham's arm. She shook her head. "No. *He's* there!" She pointed an accusatory finger at her older brother.

Avraham, the master peacemaker, worked it out. "Come to me, Tirzah," he coaxed. "Look! I have an arm just for you." He waved his empty arm at her.

Tirzah stared at him suspiciously. Then she glared at her brother, who stuck his tongue out at her.

"Kenaz!" Devorah scolded.

Avraham got down on one knee and lowered Kenaz to the ground. He held out both arms and looked at Tirzah with his warm, brown eyes. Love for Grandpa won. She ran over to him and hid her little face against his shoulder. He hugged her and stroked her long, black ponytail.

"What's the matter this morning, little dove?"

Tirzah mumbled something into his shoulder.

"What?" He held her away from himself so he could hear her voice.

"I said, it's not easy being three!"

Everyone started laughing. At first, Tirzah didn't know what to make of the levity, but then she too joined in. Devorah laughed so hard that she was doubled over with tears in her eyes.

Avraham felt joy flood his being as he watched the stress drain from Devorah's face. "This is good," he lectured the children. "Shabbat is a day of joy, not a day of gloom and anger. Let's hurry now, so we don't miss any more of the service. The boys will wonder what became of us."

The three adults and three children exited the courtyard and walked briskly down the dusty street to the center of town. Kenaz held tightly to his grandfather's hand, Lappidot hoisted Tirzah to his shoulders, and Devorah carried the baby tied in a shawl around her neck. Devorah breathed in the fresh air with delight, her mood lightening with every step. *God is good*, she thought. *He has given me the ability to shed unhappy moods the way a snake sheds its skin. I will be joyful in all circumstances.*

Her train of thought was cut off as their little party reached the center of town. *Where is everybody?*

Amram the Levite, elderly and stooped, stood next to the well and read from Beresheet the account of Yosef and his brothers. Since Yosef was the father of Ephraim and Manasseh, this was always a popular choice in Ramah. Sitting on the grass in front of him, listening intently, were Devorah's three brothers, and a handful of families in addition to them. Miryam had stayed home today with a fever. No more than thirty people filled the courtyard.

Devorah turned questioning eyes to her father. He shook his head at her, put a finger to his lips, and proceeded to sit down on the ground next to his sons. Kenaz sat in his lap.

Tirzah, humming a song just a little too loudly for Devorah's comfort, had spotted her best friend, Noa, and had run over to sit with Noa and her parents. Devorah and Lappidot settled themselves on the perimeter of the group so if Devorah needed to nurse baby Avi, she could be somewhat discreet.

Throughout Devorah's lifetime, Shabbat morning had been a time for the entire town to gather together to praise God and bring Him worship with voice and instrument. Since her earliest memory, Amram the Levite had read a portion from the writings of Moshe and several of the men would then discuss what it meant. If visitors were in town or strangers passed through, more often than not, they joined in. Since Ehud's death, however, fewer and fewer people were interested in keeping Shabbat. What had once been a service packed with people had dwindled to a remnant. It was the smalltest turnout on a Shabbat that Devorah could ever remember. *What was becoming of Israel?*

She turned to look at her husband. "What do you think?" she whispered.

He shook his head and then pointed his finger up to the heavens. "Don't worry, God is here," he whispered back. He took her hand and squeezed it.

Devorah smiled, but her spirit was deeply troubled, her earlier joy gone. She listened to Amram's nasal tones as he recounted the jealousy of Yosef's brothers over the richly ornamented robe with which their father, Yaakov, had favored him over the rest of his sons.

"And when they saw him in the distance, before he reached them, they plotted to kill him," Amram recounted.

Devorah closed her eyes as he spoke. *It's amazing we ever survived as a viable people*, she silently told the Lord. *You have pulled us out of our stiff-necked, evil ways again and again. It's been ten years since Ehud died, and most of the Israelites are indistinguishable from the nations around us. Look at this! It's Shabbat, and almost no one is here. This is disgraceful.*

Tears formed in her eyes and rolled down her cheeks. *Where are Your people, Lord? Why isn't anyone hungry for You? Why are the worthless gods of the Canaanites more attractive than the one true God of heaven and earth, the Creator of all that is? Is there no one left who will serve You with all his heart?*

*There's you.*

The words startled Devorah. She opened her eyes and looked around. Lappidot, the baby asleep on his lap, was intently listening to Amram. No one else was near them.

Devorah closed her eyes again. *Is that You, Lord?* she asked, hopefully.

*I will draw My people back to Myself, and you will point the way.*

*But Lord,* she protested, *I'm only a woman. How can this be?*

Again the Voice came to her. *I will draw My people back to Myself, and you will point the way.*

Devorah began to sob. She felt Lappidot's hand on her head, stroking her hair.

"What is it?" he whispered in her ear.

She couldn't respond. The sobs grew more and more intense, and her whole body began shaking. Lappidot set the still sleeping Avi on the ground and gathered Devorah in his arms. By now they were attracting attention. Amram paused in his explanation of Yosef to peer nearsightedly in their direction.

The sobs came up from Devorah's belly and ripped through her small frame. Gradually, they decreased, but by this time most of the people were gathered around her. Kenaz and Tirzah huddled under Avraham's arms, like baby birds under their mother's wings.

"What's happening?" someone said.

"Shhh," another said. "She's speaking!"

Devorah pulled herself out of Lappidot's hold and stood up. She raised her arms high above her head and tilted her face toward heaven. All eyes turned in her direction as the power of the Lord came upon her and she began prophesying in a loud voice.

*"Adonai says: 'When I led you out of Egypt, out of that smelting furnace,*

*with a mighty hand and an outstretched arm,*

*and brought you here, into this good and spacious land,*

*a land flowing with milk and honey,*

*a land with houses you did not build,*

*with vineyards you did not plant,*

*with fields you did not sow,*

*I warned you not to follow other gods.'"*

Devorah closed her eyes as she listened for God. She resumed:

*"'But you have disobeyed me,' says the Lord.*

*'You have prostituted yourself on every high hill*

*and under every spreading tree.*

*You have bowed down to stone and wood,*

*saying 'My father! My mother!'*

*Because of your detestable idols,*

*God's wrath will burn like fire*

*with no one to quench it.*

*'I am sending a destroyer against you,'*

*declares the Lord.*

*'He will lay waste to your houses and fields,*

*your flocks and herds.*

*He will take your sons and daughters for himself*

*and you will be desolate.*

*I have decided this thing,'*

*says the Lord.*

*'In its time I will do it swiftly.'"*

She stopped and waited. That was it. The Lord had finished speaking through her. Trembling, but emboldened by the Spirit, she remained standing, keenly aware of everything that was happening around her.

Instantaneous conviction rippled through the small crowd. Everywhere Devorah looked, people knelt or lay prostrate before the Lord in repentance for their sins and the sins of their fellow countrymen. Kenaz copied his grandfather, and knelt on the ground next to Avraham, who prayed silently. Little Tirzah watched everyone in quiet astonishment; baby Avi slept peacefully through it all. Amram continued to stand where he had been teaching and held his hands up in the air. "Have mercy on us, Lord. Have mercy on us!" he wailed.

*Lord,* Devorah prayed. *Thank You for using me! I don't know what's coming, or how, but I want to be with You every step of the way. Thank You, Lord, for Your protection and Your love.* She watched in awe as people responded to God's voice with repentance. She felt a pricking within her spirit. *I do understand, Lord…these people are Your remnant here in Ramah. I pray that those outside the camp will also respond with a repentant heart. Show us how to speak forth Your word so boldly that all who hear will turn from their useless idols and fornications and come and kneel before You, our King.*

And so Shabbat Shuvah, the Sabbath of Repentance, came to a close.

# PART IV

# YAEL

## SUMMER, 1215 BC—1213 BC

# TWELVE

Weeks and months went by, and life for Yael became a simple routine. Yael came to understand that Hever would seek her out mostly at night, while her days would be spent in the company of other women. Marta put her to work grinding grain, cooking, making cheese, milking goats, and carrying water. She also instructed Yael in the traditional rug weaving from sheep's wool and dyeing using various desert plants—a trademark of the clan. To Yael, this seemed an excessive amount of work for the wife of an important man, but she realized gratefully that her days were much shorter and less intense than, for instance, Simcha's. She also took joy in the motherly affections showered on her by Hever's mother; she hadn't counted on missing her own mother quite so much.

To Yael's great disappointment, her emotional bond with Hever was far less stable. Hever didn't seem capable of a steady, nurturing love; rather, their relationship tended toward the sensual and obsessive. The companionship Yael so strongly desired from her husband remained almost totally elusive. Yael felt something missing, but was too confused to know what was wrong and too proud to ask for help.

She also missed the city life Beersheva had to offer with its *shuk* and permanent homes. Already, Yitro had called for the Kenite clan to pull up stakes and move several miles north as summer intensified and pasture lands for the animals grew scarcer. Yael learned it was women's work to set up tents. Although the men pulled them down and packed them away on camels, the women drove the tent pegs into the ground with hammers.

It was at the height of summer, when the clan had just set up a new camp, that Yael realized a great deal of time had passed since her last menstrual cycle. Her first impulse was to coyly hint at pregnancy to Hever, but when he spoke sharply to her that night over some inconsequential aspect of housekeeping, she held her tongue and decided she would keep her secret to herself as long as possible.

The next day, however, as Yael worked on rugs with Marta, the heat overcame her and she fainted. The next thing she knew, she lay on Marta's bed with a wet cloth on her forehead as Simcha fanned her relentlessly with a fan made from bird feathers. Marta stood over her. Her hair was covered, and her bright black eyes crinkled with laughter like twin beacons of light. She pointed a strong, brown finger at Yael as her voice shook with gaity. "So," she said, "you have something to tell me, do you not, little daughter?"

"I think I am to have a baby, Mama," Yael admitted.

Marta hugged Yael close to her, smothering her face in her broad bosom. The comforting smells of garlic and mint filled Yael's nostrils. "I am so happy. So happy," she repeated. "What does Hever say?"

"Uh, nothing yet. I haven't told him."

Marta gazed down at Yael with knowing eyes. "You need to tell him today, Daughter. It will not be good if he finds out about this baby after half the clan knows!" And with this last statement, she subtly gestured with her head in the direction of Simcha, who carefully and nonchalantly feigned ignorance.

That evening, after Hever came back from supervising work with the flocks, he washed his hands and sat down while Yael served him a meal she had prepared herself. It was roasted wheat with chick peas, garlic, olive oil, olives, goat's cheese, and round crusty bread on the side. After a few bites, he looked up at her. "You know," he said, "you're really getting much better at this."

"Thank you, Hever," said Yael, pleased. Back home, Ema and Shoshannah had done most of the cooking, and consequently that skill had been sadly lacking in Yael's brief domestic repertoire. Now, with Marta guiding her, she found she enjoyed the creative challenge of putting a meal together.

Yael studied Hever as he ate. He seemed mellow tonight. This was probably as good a time as any to tell him the news. She drew a deep breath and quietly spoke his name.

"Huh?" Already he had finished what was in his bowl and was in the process of wiping up the oil with a piece of bread. "What is it?"

"I have something to tell you," she said, and she blushed.

"What is it?" he asked again, alert and attentive now.

She began in a very small voice. "It looks like we're going to..." She cleared her throat. Lifting her head, she looked in his eyes. "We're having a baby."

Yael hadn't given much thought to Hever's reaction; she was too preoccupied with her own. But now she was surprised to see a variety of emotions pass fleetingly across his features. Shock, fear, resignation, hope. "Are you sure?"

"Quite."

"Well, then," he said, as he pushed back his chair and came over to her, "congratulations are in order." And he held her closely. The sweetness of the gesture pierced Yael's heart and she started to cry. Hever awkwardly patted her on the back. They stayed like this for a few minutes until Hever said, "I'm going to take a walk and do some thinking. I'll be in later, okay?"

She nodded *okay* and watched him with big, bright eyes as he pulled on his cloak and slipped out of the tent. Believing he would return soon, she cleaned up from dinner and puttered around, killing time. When it grew apparent that Hever would not return anytime soon, Yael undressed and got into bed. She didn't understand Hever's reaction. She only knew that she had told him something that affected both of them tremendously and that consequently he had not wanted to be with her this evening. Suddenly she felt very lonely. Her initial instinct was to pray, but she stopped herself. Ever since the argument after Barak's visit, Yael had avoided reaching out to Adonai so as not to antagonize her husband.

She lay on her back in bed and rested her hands on her belly. She wanted desperately to call out to God but was ashamed to after months of silence on her part. Tears rolled down her cheeks until, emotionally drained, she fell asleep.

Yael never knew what time Hever came to bed that night; but when she awoke the next morning, he had already left for the day. Dejected, she dragged herself out of bed only to be hit by a wave of nausea. She grabbed a bowl just in time to retch into it. Rinsing her mouth with some water, she crawled back into bed and lay there, dizzy.

A little later, Simcha came to attend to her as she did every morning. She knocked tentatively but entered the tent when there was no response.

Seeing her mistress lying in bed so still caused Simcha to give a gasp as she rushed over to Yael's side. "My lady, what's the matter?"

Wearily, Yael opened her eyes. "I'm fine, Simcha. Really. I'm just feeling sick this morning."

"Is it because of the...?" Simcha stopped and clasped a hand over her mouth.

"Oh, you know, do you?"

Simcha nodded guiltily.

"Don't worry," Yael said more gently. "The secret's out, and I certainly can't hide it forever."

"Of course you can't," Simcha agreed. She took a cloth, wet it, and tenderly sponged Yael's face. "Let me take care of you, my lady," she urged. She brushed Yael's hair as best she could and smoothed out the bedclothes. Next she heated some water and brought it to Yael along with a small piece of bread. "Here, try to eat this. You'll feel better."

"I should get up and not lie around all day uselessly." Yael tried to sit up, then paled and lay back among her pillows.

"Oh, no, my lady! Having a baby is not useless. You need to store up your strength so the baby will grow healthy." Simcha bustled about, happily taking charge.

Yael opened one eye. "How do you know so much about this? You're younger than I am."

"Yes, but I am the oldest of ten children and I helped my mother at the last five births," Simcha said proudly. "You do what I say and you'll be fine."

Yael closed her eyes and was quiet. The sounds of Simcha cleaning and ordering the tent combined with the early morning stirrings outside proved comforting to her. She felt better. She roused herself on one elbow. "Simcha," she called.

"Yes, my lady?"

"Have you seen Hever?"

"He went to the fields very early this morning with the other men, my lady."

"Did he seem preoccupied?"

"Of course," Simcha said. "After all, it's only natural that he should be concerned, given what happened to him in the past."

*Past? What past?* Yael's eyes narrowed. "What do you mean?"

Simcha clasped a hand over her mouth, realizing that she had made a serious error. "Uh," she stammered. "Perhaps you should talk to Marta about this."

Yael, miraculously healed, jumped out of bed and lightly ran across the room to where Simcha stood. She grasped both of the girl's thin wrists with her hands and held on tightly. "Tell me, Simcha. Tell me what you know."

Simcha started to cry. "I'm going to get in so much trouble."

"Too late. Tell!"

Simcha pulled her hands away and tucked a long strand of dark hair behind her ear. Next she blew her nose loudly. Yael waited impatiently. Finally Simcha spoke. "Okay, I'll tell you what I know." She looked at Yael anxiously. "You know about Hever's first wife, right?"

"WHAT?" Something inside Yael exploded. "WHAT FIRST WIFE?"

Simcha drew a shaky breath. "Okay, here's what happened. When Hever was very young, not even twenty, he married one of the local girls here..."

"What was her name?"

"Nedra. Anyway..."

"What did she look like?"

Simcha smiled at Yael. "She was beautiful, my lady, but not as beautiful as you."

"Humph. So, what happened?"

Simcha began to enjoy telling the tale now that it was out in the open. "Well, they were very much in love. Hever was very different then, or so I am told, since I was only a baby when these things took place. It came about in the course of time that they discovered they were going to have a baby. Naturally, they were thrilled, and there was much celebration in the camp over the pending arrival of Yitro and Marta's first grandchild."

"Naturally," Yael said wryly.

"When it came time for Nedra to give birth, we all prayed to Adonai for her safety and protection. She was in high spirits, eager to bring a son to Hever, whom she adored. But"—Simcha raised her eyes to heaven and spoke dramatically—"it was not meant to be. My mother was the midwife. She said the poor girl labored courageously for two days before she succumbed to loss of blood and breathed her last."

"And the baby?"

"The baby was born dead, my lady. It was a very sad time. I understand that Master Hever was out of his mind with grief. No one expected him to remarry. We were all delighted when he returned with you as his bride last spring. Especially me," she added.

But Yael by now was too lost in her own thoughts to notice Simcha. This revelation, shocking though it was, also helped to explain much about Hever that had confused and alarmed her. She was mortified at being deceived by an entire village about her own husband; yet, at the same time, a wave of tender love for Hever swept through her. *How tragic his life has been. No wonder he is afraid to love again.* Suddenly, a plan, full-blown, presented itself to her. *Of course….*

"Simcha!"

"Yes, my lady?"

"Help me dress in one of my nicer garments and do my hair. I have an errand to run."

"Yes, my lady." Mystified, Simcha quickly obeyed.

Hever, Ishmar, and most of the able-bodied men in the camp were out in the hot, summer fields harvesting this year's bumper crop of millet. Normally a man of Hever's status would not need to work as a common laborer, but this year's harvest was such that every hand became necessary. Hever welcomed an excuse to be away from home all day, anyway. His response to the news of Yael's pregnancy startled even himself. His anguish over Nedra and their infant son lay buried under years of anger and repressed grief. Yael had a way of kicking at and exposing parts of him that were still too raw for him to handle.

Stripped to the waist and sweaty, the men were taking a mid-morning break in the shade of a hastily constructed hut set up next to the fields for just this purpose. They passed around a skin of water, each one drinking thirstily. Hunks of bread dipped in olive oil served as fuel for their bodies until they stopped later that day for a full meal.

The women remained at the camp, where they cooked, cared for the children, swept out tents, beat the rugs, washed clothes, and generally maintained things at home. The one thing from which they were exempt was field work. Naturally, the men were astonished when one of them spotted Yael and Simcha approaching the hut.

Hever's jaw clenched. *Those two are entirely too independent,* he thought as he watched the two girls cautiously picking their way through the rocks and clumps of hard earth that surrounded the field. "I will see what they want," he said loudly. He ignored the questioning glances of his co-workers as he headed over to his wife.

A sense of purpose had motivated Yael to pull herself together and journey in the hot sun to find Hever. Now that she had found him, however, she began to lose her nerve. She and Simcha stood uncertainly at the edge of the partially harvested millet field. Yael shielded her eyes with her hand and watched as Hever emerged from the little hut and made his way toward them.

"What are you doing here?" he said hotly when he reached her.

Yael was about to respond angrily when she stopped herself. *No!* She thought. *I've come here to reach out to him.* Instead, she bowed down before Hever with her face to the ground. She fell at his feet and said, "Don't be upset with me, my lord. I have sought you out this day because I love you." She reached out and took his hand and kissed it.

He was startled by this new, submissive Yael. Normally, she would have sulked for days after being deserted as she had been last night.

Hever pulled her to a standing position. They looked into each other's faces. Yael was very beautiful. Her green eyes glittered and her full, shapely lips were slightly parted. Loose strands of long, brown hair blew across her heat-flushed face in the mild breeze.

Simcha looked away.

Hever stared at his wife, mesmerized. "I love you, too," he admitted hoarsely. He wrapped his arms around her, for once heedless of the public display of his emotions.

"I needed you last night," Yael whispered in his ear, as he crushed her in his embrace.

"I'm sorry," he whispered back. "I promise that we will talk tonight for as long as you like. This isn't the best place or time. Let me walk you part of the way back, okay?"

"Okay," she agreed, amazed at the new softness in him.

Husband and wife turned and headed in the direction of the camp, as Simcha trailed along behind them. Back at the shelter hut, a group of men stood with their mouths hanging open.

"Was that really Hever?" one young man asked.

"My guess," his companion said, "is that if you say anything in front of him you'll find out soon enough he's one and the same!"

Laughing, they all ventured back into the cloudless sun and resumed gathering the millet for next year's food.

The next several months brought a change in Hever that astounded all who knew him. For the first time in more than a decade, he allowed himself to hope. He opened up to Yael and truly began to love her. His eyes lit up when he saw her, and as she visibly grew, so did his love for her. They spoke together of their plans for this child and for their life together. The future seemed bright with promise.

After the initial bout of nausea, Yael felt wonderful. She enjoyed being pregnant, and her beauty glowed with an intensity that caused many to cast admiring looks her way. Her increased comfort with her husband led her to delve more deeply into Kenite society, and she became open and friendly with everyone she encountered.

Yitro and Marta could not have been more pleased. Hever was their only surviving child, and he had never been as open and effusive as either of his parents tended to be. When his first wife and infant son perished on the same day, all semblance of peace had vanished from his soul. Yitro and Marta often wept privately as they helplessly watched him grow more and more brittle. At first, people forgave him for real and imagined slights, but as the memories of Nedra and the child faded, Yitro and Marta found themselves covering time and time again for Hever's dark and abrupt moods. When he'd returned from his buying expedition at Beersheva with a very young bride, they had been shocked. But it didn't take long to realize that Yael had the potential to be a wonderful blessing for Hever, should he allow it.

Marta and Yitro had painfully debated whether to tell Yael about Nedra. *No*, Yitro had decided. *If Hever finds out that we took matters into our own hands, it will cause much trouble.* Simcha's revelation of the story had come as a relief to them, as they were no longer bound to secrecy. And in the end, it proved to be a blessing to Yael and Hever's relationship as well. Still, Marta and Yitro feared Yael's trust in them would suffer irreparable damage. Marta prayed for courage and then addressed her daughter-in-law in total humility.

"My daughter," she said one day soon after the news had been revealed. "We love you and never meant to hurt you by keeping Hever's past a secret. We just did not feel free to speak of it. Can you ever forgive us?"

Yael looked at her mother-in-law and could not help but love her. "Of course I forgive you, Mama. Let's put it behind us."

From then on, Marta felt free to rejoice in the pregnancy and in her son's newfound happiness. She and Yael spent many happy hours planning for the new baby, and sometimes even Hever joined them, a new light in his eyes.

As in every passionate relationship, the times of affection were coun-terbalanced by outbursts of temper on both sides. But the dark, brooding quality of their lives had lifted, and for the first time, Yael felt optimistic that she could build a happy life with Hever. Both of them eagerly looked forward to this coming child.

A month earlier than expected, on a cold and rainy winter's morning, Yael went into labor. Simcha had enthusiastically filled her in on all the gory details which Marta, in her prudence, had either glossed over or cho-sen not to discuss, so Yael immediately knew the baby was on its way. "Sim-cha," she shouted, "come quickly!"

"What is it, my lady?" asked Simcha, wiping her hands on a dish cloth. "Oh!" she said when she saw Yael bent over, pain contorting her features. "Is it the baby?"

"I, I think so." Yael gripped one of the tent poles with one hand while she massaged her belly with the other. "Call Marta, and let your mother know."

Simcha stood frozen.

"Now!" Yael barked. Simcha jumped into action and raced out of the tent to find help.

Fifteen hours later, Yael lay back on the bed, panting. The baby wouldn't come and she could feel her strength ebbing. The worried looks that passed between the older women told her something was wrong.

"What is it?" she said. "Why isn't the baby coming?"

"Shhh." Aida, the midwife, tenderly wiped her brow with a wet cloth. "Everything is fine. Save your energy for the baby." She turned and whis-pered something to Marta, who shook her head.

"AHHH!" Yael screamed as another contraction tore through her. The pain stabbed like a sword and lasted a full minute. When it was over, Aida inspected her. "You're not ready to push yet," she said grimly. "Take a deep breath and hold my hand."

Yael started to cry as another contraction began. "I can't do this any-more." She sobbed. "When is it going to stop?"

Marta stroked her hair. "Soon, soon," she said soothingly. "The first is always the longest."

"I want my mother," Yael cried pitifully, no longer a proud married woman, but a scared young girl. She screamed again and again as the pain continued to rip through her, and still the baby refused to be born. Several harrowing hours later, Aida was able to make an incision and pull the baby out. He was dead—strangled by his own umbilical cord. Aida breathed into his mouth and massaged his tiny chest to cause his heart to beat, but it was of no use. He remained blue and lifeless.

Meanwhile, Yael was badly torn and nearly unconscious. Marta and another woman worked frantically until at last they stopped her bleeding. Yael had lapsed into a deep sleep, mercifully unaware that her baby was dead.

"It's just as well," Marta said. Her shoulders sagged, and tears of grief and exhaustion filled her eyes. "She will have plenty of time to mourn when she wakes."

Aida roused her daughter, Simcha, who had crawled under a pile of rugs on the other side of the tent and fallen asleep. "Go sit by your mistress and call us if she awakens."

Simcha stared at her mother through sleepy eyes. "The baby?"

Aida shook her head. "Dead."

Eyes suddenly bright with tears, Simcha stumbled over to the bed where Yael lay. She knelt by the side of the bed and cradled her mistress' limp hand in her own.

Leaving her there, Marta, Aida, and Aida's helper left the tent and emerged into the cold, morning air. A gray, dreary dawn silently came upon the earth as the sky lightened by degrees. Marta turned to her two companions. "Go to your beds," she said. "I will break the news to my son."

Marta's legs felt old and tired. She trembled with anxiety over the devastation this news would bring to Hever. *Oh Lord,* she begged, *please bring my son joy in his life. He has known so much heartache. Help him, Lord.* Marta shook her head. Her prayer bounced back at her. The heavens were like bronze today. She cautiously opened the flap to the tent where Hever was staying. He sat cross-legged on the makeshift bed, eyes dark as he stared at the wall across from him. Marta sat down quietly next to him. She tried to embrace him, but his body was stiff, unyielding.

"Son," she began.

"Don't, Mother. I already know."

"How?"

"It was too much to expect happiness." His voice rose. "The gods hate me."

"Oh no, my son! Adonai loves you; he gave you Yael."

"Loves me? If He loves me so much, then why does every baby born to me die before it sees the light of day? How is it," he gulped, "that Nedra is no more?" His features twisted in anguish. "Yael will probably die, too."

"No, no, son, don't say that! Yael is alive! She will live!" Marta put her hand on his arm. "She needs you, Hever. She's a frightened young girl, far away from her mother and father. I beg of you, don't turn away from her now that she really needs you. Right now she's in a deep sleep, but very soon she will awake and discover that her son is no more. You must be with her and comfort her."

He stared at his mother with hollow eyes. "How can I comfort her? I have nothing to give."

Marta got down on her knees before her son and took his cold hands in her own. "Please, my son, pray with me. God will give you the strength you need to get through this. And the hope."

Hever wavered. Then he pulled his hands away. "I will not pray to a god who killed my child." He jumped to his feet, grabbed his cloak, and stormed out of the tent.

"Hever!" Marta called. He didn't answer. She sank to the floor and gave herself up to a good, hard cry.

When they told her about the baby, Yael could not find the strength to cry. Quiet and unresponsive, she sat and stared at the wall for hours, as grief carved a hollow pit inside her. Simcha sat at her feet all day, feeling her mistress' pain as though it were her own. Marta and two of her maids stayed in the tent as well. They all tended to Yael while Aida the midwife appeared every few hours to check on her.

The dead baby lay in a tiny box on a pedestal across the room. Tradition would have him buried at sundown. Yael had not asked to see him; neither had she mentioned Hever, though her heart quaked at the thought of his reaction to this terrible news. Toward late afternoon, Hever came. The already quiet tent became deathly still and everyone, even Simcha, bowed in his direction and left the couple in privacy.

He came and approached the bed where Yael lay. He sat down heavily next to her, and both remained silent for a few moments. Finally he took her hand. "I'm sorry," he whispered hoarsely.

Yael turned her head and loved him. "No, my lord. It's I who am sorry. I"—her voice broke—"very much wanted to give you a son."

Hever bent down and kissed her gently on the lips. "I understand you're quite hurt, physically."

She nodded. "I think it will be a while before, before..."

"I know." He caressed her cheek.

Then he stood up and walked over to the small box that held his dead son. He gazed down at the tiny, lifeless form and clenched his fists. "Have you seen him?"

"No."

"Do you want to?"

She shook her head. "I'm afraid."

He picked up the box and carried it over to the bed. "I think you need to see what he looks like before he's in the ground."

Yael shut her eyes tightly. "I'm afraid."

"Look!"

Apprehensively, she opened her eyes and glanced into the box. The baby lay there so peacefully: a beautiful baby, the child of her dreams. She reached out a hand to touch him, but Hever caught her wrist. "No," he said. "Just look, don't touch."

Yael nodded numbly, and at last the tears came. After a few moments, Hever took the box and replaced it on its pedestal. He returned to Yael and sat down beside the bed. "Try to sleep some more. I'll stay with you until it's time for the burial." He leaned back and closed his eyes.

"Hever?"

"Yes?"

"Do you think I'm a failure?"

Wearily, he shook his head. "It's not you, Yael. It's me. Me. I'm the one God wants to destroy."

Yael was horrified. "Oh no, my lord. He doesn't want to destroy you! He's..."

"Shhh." Hever put a finger over her lips. "No more talking. Just sleep now." He closed his eyes as well and soon both of them had slipped into a deep, numbing sleep.

"My lord," Marta said as she nestled in her husband's embrace one dark night several weeks later, "How do you think Hever is handling his loss?"

Yitro made a *hmmm* sound somewhere between his throat and his chest... a signal to Marta that he needed time to think before answering.

She waited patiently. She loved this man the Lord had given her and fervently hoped that her son would find such peace in the arms of his wife.

Yitro interrupted her thoughts. "I'm pleased that he is making an effort to carry on after his disappointment. This shows character. However, I am not convinced that his recovery is genuine."

Marta nodded. "I know what you mean. He says and does all the proper things, but still, he seems off."

Both husband and wife sighed in unison. Worrying about Hever had become a regular part of life's routines.

*Maybe it's my fault*, Marta thought. *I was so happy to have a child who lived that I spoiled him rotten. And Yitro, bless his heart, wasn't much better. Hever has always been demanding and unyielding.* Aloud she said, "I do hope he's being kind to Yael. I understand all too well the pain she's experiencing."

Yitro closed his hand over his wife's as he pulled her closer to him. "I know you do. But I don't think you need to worry. This little girl our son has chosen is as tough and resilient as the mountain goat for which she's named."

"Do you think so?"

"I'm sure of it," he said confidently, and he turned over on his side and went to sleep.

# THIRTEEN

Once Yael had recovered physically from childbirth, she began to feel better emotionally as well. Spring arrived, and the desert was beautiful: warm during the day and cold at night. Red poppies dotted the fields and the fragrance of myrtle scented the air. The rich, fertile smell of newly planted earth filled Yael with hope for the future. Hever, though moodier than he had been during the pregnancy, still seemed to love her, which gave her much-needed reassurance. And Marta was especially warm and motherly toward her, for which Yael was extremely grateful. Her new family had become quite precious to her.

News from outside filtered through occasionally. King Yavin of Hazor had begun to make bolder and bolder forays into Israel. At first he had kept to the north, but now his vicious raids reached as far south as Hebron. Horrified whispers circulated, hinting at entire villages murdered, with the exception of virgin girls who were raped and then taken as slaves and concubines.

At first Yael had been too preoccupied with her own grief to pay much attention to the stories of the raids. Besides, villages like Kedesh, Gilead, and Tirzah seemed so remote to her. But Hebron was practically in their backyard, and was also dangerously close to Beersheva. Suddenly she became keenly aware of the threat this king posed to her own people.

Hever, Yitro and the uncles and elders now met frequently in Yitro's tent. One day the meeting lasted for several hours—far longer than the others. Yael decided to see if they were finished meeting and if Hever wanted dinner; but before she had a chance to announce herself, she heard shouts from within the tent.

Yitro's voice came through the goatskin wall loud and clear: "I'm ashamed. Ashamed! I can't believe that a son of mine, flesh of my flesh, would suggest such a wicked thing! Leave this tent!"

Utterly shocked, Yael barely had time to collect herself and hide on the other side of the tent before Hever stormed out, walking with a cold and silent fury that sent a chill up her spine.

Dreading Hever's wrath should he discover her, Yael made haste to return to their tent by a shortcut. Her fears were unnecessary; he didn't come home for nearly two hours. Yael hoped that a long walk in the desert would help him cool down, but when he entered the tent, she could see by his tensed jaw that he was still very angry.

"Welcome home, my lord," she said carefully. She arose from the lounge on which she had been lying and bowed before him. "Would my lord like something to eat?"

"Yes."

Yael had already decided to feign ignorance. "What is it, my lord? Why are you so upset this evening?"

Hever glowered at her with furrowed brow, his face dark. "My. Father." He spat the words out one by one like poison darts. "I am done with him. Done!" He slammed his fist so hard into his other hand that Yael jumped.

Yael hurriedly tried to soothe him. "No, no, my lord. Your father loves you dearly. Whatever has happened?"

"It's a military issue. Nothing you would understand."

*Oh really?* Aloud she said, "Your servant is interested in whatever concerns my lord. Please tell me what has happened."

He looked up, annoyed. But when she smiled, she saw his defenses go down slightly.

"All right," he said. "Basically I believe we would be wise to join forces with Yavin in order to protect ourselves. I proposed sending an envoy to him with terms for an alliance, and my father—"

"You can't be serious!" she said, all efforts at appeasing Hever forgotten in her horror. "You would take sides against *Israel? Against me?*"

"Not against you. I don't see it as taking sides against anyone. I see it as making a wise alliance with a force more powerful than ourselves."

Yael was aghast at his cold logic. "But *I* am an Israelite! Have you forgotten?"

"You were born an Israelite, true. But now you're the wife of a Kenite. Your identity has changed."

Yael's green eyes flashed dangerously. "I am a daughter of Israel, of the tribe of Judah. *That* is something you will *never* change." She turned to leave, but he grabbed her by the wrist and swung her around to face him. His eyes held that same cold fury she had seen when he left his father's tent, but she could no longer control her disdain.

"You've forgotten yourself, my lady." He pushed her down onto the bed. "Let me remind you exactly who you are."

Disgusted with his intentions, Yael fought him off, but her resistance only aroused him more. Frustrated and helpless against his strength, she had no recourse but to submit to an act which had until now been done mutually in love. When it was over, tears of anger and loathing streamed down her cheeks as she stared silently at the wall.

"Look at me," he said.

She refused.

He took her by the chin and held his face two inches from hers. "Never forget," he said coldly, "that I bought you from your greedy father and that I own you. Do not cross me!" He rose up, dressed, and went out into the night.

Impenetrable walls went up between Hever and his entire family that awful night. Never again would he and Yael enjoy the lighthearted intimacy they had shared during her pregnancy; the very fragile bond of happiness between them had broken down irreparably.

Of more immediate consequence was the breakdown in relationship between Hever and Yitro. Yitro's rebuke had stung Hever sharply. However, instead of repenting for his disloyalty toward Israel (and, by association, the God of Israel), Hever nursed his wounded pride until the sting of his father's words grew into a festering ulcer. He steadfastly refused his father's pleas for reconciliation; in fact, so convinced was he of his own righteousness and of his father's sin that even Yael began to second-guess what she knew to be true. *If only Abigail were with me. She would help me make sense of all this.*

One night Marta showed up at their tent. Yael's heart sank at the sight of her beloved mother-in-law's tired, haggard countenance. The feud between her husband and only son had taken its toll on her normally happy disposition.

Undaunted by Hever's stony-faced silence, Marta entered the tent and walked over to him. "Hever, please. I've come to talk sense to you."

Hever glared at her. "He wants nothing to do with me, Mother. I'm simply obeying his wishes."

"How can you say that? You know he is terribly upset by your anger..."

"My anger? My anger?" The veins on Hever's neck stood out. "He's always made it quite clear that I don't measure up. He's so smug and superior..."

"No, he is not!" Marta said sharply. "Your father is a king among men and it's time you acknowledged that instead of always trying to exalt yourself. He's done nothing but love and care for you. No one was more upset for you when Nedra and the baby—both babies—died!"

The mention of his dead wife coupled with the reminder that he had failed to father living children sent Hever's temper spiraling out of control. "Get out!" he shouted at his mother. "Get out of my tent now!"

Yael and Marta both gasped in shock at the dishonor Hever had heaped on his mother's head. Heedless of the danger, Yael rushed over to him and grabbed his arm. "Hever, please! Stop it! Do not treat your mother this way!"

Snarling, Hever shoved her to the floor. "Keep out of this!" he screamed at her. Breathing hard, he swung around to face his mother. But she had fled.

News of the ugly scene spread like wildfire, and soon the Kenite community was in an uproar. Meetings with Yitro, Marta, the uncles and several elders within the clan ensued. Once he gained control of his temper, Hever realized he had backed himself into a corner. He formally apologized to his father and his mother the following day, then announced his intentions to separate himself from the Kenite community. Ishmar, Reuel, Zur, Nadab, and their families, through either choice or obligation, aligned themselves with Hever, as did three disgruntled families who were looking for a change in leadership. Yael gave Simcha the option to stay, but her young handmaiden would not hear of it. "I will be with you, my lady," she said, head bowed.

Hever gave the orders, and preparations for moving commenced immediately. Yael's heart broke within her as she watched her possessions packed up and loaded onto camels. "Be careful!" she pleaded, when the wedding bowl from her father toppled from its pedestal into the waiting hands of a servant. The engraved pictures on the sides of the bowl of the Exodus from Egypt mocked her. *That's me,* she thought bitterly. *Reverse exodus. From the Promised Land to the desert and now, who knows where?* Hever had not made known his destination. Yael knew only that they would initially head north toward Hebron.

A year ago, Yael would have fought valiantly with Hever over this move. Now, however, she feared engaging him too strongly. She risked his wrath only once, when she beseeched him to reconsider. "My family won't even know where I am," she said, eyes bright with unshed tears. "I had hoped my brother Shimon would come soon to visit us, but now, now…" Her voice broke.

"Don't hold your breath waiting for your brother to show up. You said good-bye to your family a long time ago. You belong to me, and you will go wherever I tell you."

Yael bowed her head and bit her lip. She was trapped and they both knew it.

The day before they were scheduled to leave, Yitro and Marta came to their tent. Yael rushed over to welcome them. "Mother, Father. Please come in. Sit down."

Hever stood tall and unyielding, but the pulse at the base of his neck jumped like mad. "What can I do for you?" he said coldly.

Yitro rose and faced his son eye-to-eye. "Your mother and I respect your decision to leave," he said gravely. "We have not come to dissuade you. Sometimes," and here he turned and smiled tenderly at his wife whose red-rimmed eyes testified to days of weeping, "it's best to go separate ways. We had hoped that you would understand and seek after the ways of Adonai, but we see that this is not to be. We will, however, continue to pray for you as long as we live. Shalom, my son. Go in peace and may God be with you."

Hever unstiffened slightly. "Thank you, Father. May God be with you and Mother, as well." He kissed them both good-bye.

"I will see you outside," Yael said. When they were out of sight from Hever, Yael threw herself on her mother-in-law's neck and wept bitterly. "I don't want to leave you."

Marta cried with her and for several minutes the two women clung to one another. Finally, Yitro put his hand on Yael's back as she slipped out of Marta's embrace and wiped her eyes on the sleeve of her robe. Yael looked up at him expectantly.

Yitro spoke slowly and with great deliberation. "Yael, my daughter. I want you to know that Marta and I could not love you more dearly if you were our own flesh and blood. We do not hold you in any way responsible for this difficulty." He waved his arm in the direction of the tent. "We promise to pray for you faithfully and we look forward to seeing you again in either this life or the next." He bent down and kissed her on the forehead.

"I love you too, Father," Yael whispered through her tears.

Late the following afternoon, Hever the Kenite separated himself from the rest of his clan. Clouds of dust swirled through the air as lines of heavily laden camels shuffled impatiently on the desert sands. Great flocks of sheep and goats *baaaed* and *maaaed* loudly, while young boys yelled and pushed at them, strenuously attempting to keep the animals together. Relatives and friends clung to each other and wept. And at the head of this cacophony, Hever barked commands in all directions.

Yael felt strangely detached from this wild scene. She had recently discovered she was pregnant again, and intermittent bouts of nausea provided an oddly welcome distraction from her grief. Besides, any minute now she expected her husband to come to his senses and make up with his father. She could not believe their disagreement over this king in Hazor had led to a complete break in community. It was as if something evil had overtaken Hever. She shuddered. *If only I could stay with Yitro and Marta!*

Ishmar interrupted her thoughts, ever polite and deferential. "Come my lady," he bowed. "Your camel awaits." He leaned forward and spoke softly. "I managed to get Gamala for you." Yael's head jerked up and she stared at him. The ghost of a smile touched her lips; the first in days. "Thank you, Ishmar."

And then, in a flurry of good-byes, they rode away. This time Yael did not look behind her as she had when she left Beersheva. Tears blurred her eyes and she stared straight ahead. Instinctively, she reached up and fingered the YHVH necklace from Abigail which she had recovered from Hever and always wore. This time, though, it failed to bring the comfort that it had in the past. Yael felt very far from God. *He must not like me*, she thought sullenly, *to have allowed my life to go so badly*. Tears of self-pity slid down her cheeks until the jolting of Gamala and the fatigue of the journey drove all emotion from her.

They made slow progress with all the little ones and animals. It was well into the evening when they stopped and made camp partway to Hebron. All involved were so bone tired that it was a quick meal and sleep. By daybreak, the journey began again. Simcha had walked the day before, but now she shared Gamala with Yael. The younger girl's wide-eyed curiosity over new vistas grew contagious. Soon Yael found herself perking up and taking an interest in her new surroundings as well.

Toward the end of the day, they rode slowly uphill as they approached the city wall of Hebron. Bits and pieces of tales concerning the city's history jumbled together in Yael's mind. She knew that this was Caleb's inheritance in the Land. She also knew that this was where Avraham, Sarah, Yitzhak, Rivkah, Yaakov, and Leah were buried. She had always imagined a sort of kinship between Beersheva and Hebron, as both places were so closely associated with the Patriarch Avraham. In anticipation of her first sight of Hebron, she was able to shake off some of her sadness and regain her spirit of adventure. *Maybe this will be better than I expect*, she thought hopefully.

Hever and Ishmar rode far ahead of the rest of the travelers. Mindful of the rumors that Yavin had attacked Hebron, they advanced with caution toward the city. To their great relief, everything seemed peaceful and unmolested. They beckoned for the caravan to follow them.

At the city gate, Hever spoke to someone who gave him permission to set up camp outside the walls for the night. Hever also paid for the privilege of using the town well. He sent several of the women with their jars on their shoulders to draw water for the people and the animals.

Yael went to work and helped the other women set up several makeshift tents for the night. She found that she was particularly skilled at banging the tent pegs into the ground. "It must be all of my pent-up frustrations," she said half-jokingly to Simcha after her maid admired the skill and power with which Yael directed her hammer.

Hever came to check on their progress. He was likewise impressed with Yael's prowess. "Not bad," he said. Yael stopped hammering and looked at him. These were the first words he had spoken to her since they left Arad.

"Why, hello," she said.

"How have you been holding up this trip?"

"All right." She treaded cautiously, unsure of his motives for being friendly.

"Just all right?"

"Well, actually, before we leave Hebron, I'd hoped to visit Avraham's burial place." The words tumbled out before she had time to consider them.

Hever raised his eyebrows. "That's an odd request."

"Is it?"

"I'll see what I can do. No promises." And then he kissed her cheek and moved on to supervise others.

Yael stared after him as she reached her hand to touch the spot he had kissed. "I won't understand him if I live to be one hundred," she murmured.

Simcha edged closer to her. "What did you say, my lady?"

"Oh, nothing." She smiled at Simcha, who smiled back, happy to see her mistress and master kinder to one another for the moment.

That night Hever showed up in Yael's tent after she and Simcha had fallen asleep. He lay close to her and held her all night long.

Early the next morning, before the sun rose, Zur blew a shofar to awaken the company. Its thin, mournful tone swirled and reverberated throughout the hills, effectively rousing young and old alike. Deeply asleep only a moment ago, Yael now moaned as she struggled to open her eyes. A wave of morning sickness gripped her stomach, and before her brain fully engaged, her body slammed into full gear as she flung herself out of the tent and, just in time, threw up in the dirt.

Sleep-tousled, Simcha came outside with a blanket, which she wrapped around her mistress. "Come back inside, my lady," Simcha said as she led Yael into the tent. "Here. Sit down while I fetch you a cup of water."

Hever sat up in bed and tied his outer garment around his waist. He looked extremely alert considering the time. Now he placed his hand on Yael's forehead. "Tell me why you threw up."

Yael's green eyes flew open. "I should think it's rather obvious, my lord."

"Why haven't you told me before now?"

"I was afraid to." She looked away. "The last time didn't go so well."

Hever's face softened. He crushed Yael in his embrace. "This one will," he said fiercely. "This one will."

Later that morning, when they had been on the road heading north for less than two hours, Hever led the company off to the left onto a large field. The entire company came to a halt as Hever announced they would take a

154

short detour to visit Avraham's tomb. "I believe it's over there." He pointed toward the end of a long field dotted with terebinth trees. The small, exceedingly shady trees made a very inviting picture in the hot mid-morning sun. Soon every child old enough to walk ran excitedly to those deliciously cool trees. "Look for the cave!" Hever shouted after them.

Yael slid off Gamala, astonished at Hever's sudden generosity. "Oh, my lord!" She bowed low before Hever. "Thank you for honoring your maidservant in this way!"

Hever took her by the elbow and pulled her to her feet. "Come," he said, not unkindly. "Let's take a walk and go see this tomb of yours."

"Not *my* tomb!" She giggled, unexpected joy bubbling up in her like the rushing waters of a cold brook in the spring.

They picked their way through the tall grasses at the edge of the field beneath the shade of the terebinth trees. Yael sighed happily. Soon, they reached the spot where all of the children were clustered. One small girl wandered in circles and howled for her mother.

Yael went to comfort the child, but Hever stopped her. "Look! Her mother is coming even now." Indeed, Zur's young wife swooped down on the child with an apologetic look, and they could hear her soothing noises as she carried the girl off.

*That could be me soon,* Yael thought, and the idea frightened and attracted her all at once.

Hever walked through the group of children, who immediately darted to either side to let him pass. Ahead lay a low cave, with a sign scratched into the stone wall. In Hebrew, it read *Avraham* and *Sarah.* He whistled and carefully rubbed his hand over the ancient letters.

Yael came up from behind him and peered at the sign as well. "Amazing! Just think. This tomb is over 700 years old!" Even the pushing, shoving, noisy children behind them suddenly became reverent as they gazed up at the ancient tomb.

Yael sat on the ground in front of the cave, cross-legged, chin in her hand. *I can't believe that this is the final resting place of Avraham avinu,* she mused. *Maybe Shimon is right; maybe I really am like Avraham, going off to a distant land. It must be a sign from heaven that I have been allowed to see this site.*

She was so preoccupied with her own thoughts that she failed to hear Hever and Ishmar herding everyone back to the camels. Soon she was the only one left. She turned when Hever called her name. He stood in the middle of the field beckoning to her. She waved at him, then slowly and regretfully rose to her feet, blew a kiss in the direction of Avraham and

Sarah, and joined Hever for a final walk beneath the terebinth trees.

# FOURTEEN

Several hot, tiring, dusty days later, the company approached the hill country of Ephraim between Ramah and Beit El. They set up camp at the outskirts of a little village. Hever negotiated with the village elders for water usage, and returned to announce that they would spend several days to rest and regain strength.

These words were sweet music in Yael's ears. The pregnancy, traveling, summer heat, and emotional anguish over leaving Arad had worn her out. *"Baruch ha Shem,"* she muttered to Simcha under her breath as they got out their hammers and—yet again—pounded tent pegs into the ground.

Later, after the tents were erected and the food cooked, eaten and cleaned up, Yael sat outside with Hever and watched the sun set. Flames of deep orange, rosy pink, and scarlet red filled the sky. New and exotic smells from the local foliage scented the soft air. Yael's eyes, accustomed from birth to looking out at the barren desert landscape, feasted in astonishment on the lush forests and distant hills before her. "How beautiful," she said to Hever. "I have never seen so much *green*."

"It does not have the power of our desert," he said, a faraway look in his eyes.

Yael put her hand over his. "We can always go back," she said tenderly.

He snatched his hand away as though it burned. "There is no going back. Not ever!"

"Okay, okay." *Hever is impossible,* she thought crossly. *He's touchy about every-thing.* "Where are we going, anyway?"

"You'll know when we arrive," he said in a voice that made it clear that the discussion was over.

Yael sighed. Pouting, she crossed her arms and continued to stare at the sunset, only now through furrowed brows. Just then Ishmar and his wife, Ria, walked past them, obviously enjoying the warm summer evening and each other's company. They stopped to talk when they saw Hever and Yael.

"Shalom," Ishmar said.

"Shalom," Hever replied, glad for the diversion.

Yael forced a smile to her lips but still felt grumpy. "Shalom," she said tersely.

"Shalom." Ria giggled nervously. Still relatively unacquainted with the master's wife, she regarded Yael's beauty and spirit with a measure of awe. Yael, although younger than Ria, had not paid much attention to her. Ria seemed boring compared to the vivacious Simcha.

Now, however, Ria stood there with an expectant look in her wide, dark eyes; and Yael found herself responsible for drawing Ria into a conversation when the two men plunged into a discussion regarding travel plans. *There's no way that Ria will say anything first,* she thought. *It's up to me to make an effort.* Sighing inwardly, she patted the grass next to her. "Sit down, Ria. Come and visit with me."

Eagerly, the older girl gracefully lowered herself to the ground, carefully holding her upper body straight. "Thank you," she said, her words punctuated with another nervous laugh.

"So what do you think of this new country we're in?"

Ria's face lit up. "Oh, I think it's just beautiful! I never knew anything could be so green!"

"Do you miss the desert?"

"I do not yet know. Right now I'm on an adventure I never expected. There will be plenty of time for homesickness later."

*Wisely said,* thought Yael. Maybe she had been too hasty in her judgment of Ria.

"I find it very beautiful here as well," Yael said. "My father used to say that the tribes of Ephraim and Manasseh received the best part of the land since Joseph was the favored son. I used to think that he was exaggerating, that nothing could be as magnificent as Beersheva. I see now that he was correct."

"Perhaps..." Ria began in a soft, hesitant voice. "Perhaps during the time we are resting here, we can venture out and see more of this area?"

Yael studied her dubiously. "Do you really think we can wander around on our own?"

"No, no, not on our own!" Again, the tinkly laugh. "I think perhaps Ishmar would be willing to escort us."

At the sound of his name, Ishmar paused in his discussion with Hever long enough to smile at his wife. He extended his arm in her direction and she reached up so their fingertips touched together briefly. A pang smote Yael's heart. Aloud she said, "That would be lovely."

Now it was Hever's turn to notice the women. "What would be lovely?"

Ria was too flustered to speak to the master, but Yael felt bold. "What a beautiful country you've led us to, my lord," she said smoothly. "We were hoping that we could see even more of it during the next few days. Would you be able to take us around?"

Hever immediately shook his head. "I'm much too busy, you know that. Possibly I could spare Ishmar for a few hours...."

"Oh, thank you, my lord!" Yael clasped Hever's hand and kissed it, an action which effectively ended the discussion. The plans for the next day made, Ishmar and Ria said good night and vanished into the evening shadows.

Hever stood up as well. "It's late," he said. He reached out his hand and pulled Yael to her feet. "Come. Let's go in for the night." Yael took a final deep breath of the cool, evening air before being swallowed up by the walls of the tent for the night.

Early afternoon the following day, Yael and Ria succeeded in cajoling Ishmar to take them to the nearest town. He arranged for each of them to ride a donkey on the tour. "We'll go to Ramah," he said. "It's closer."

"What is special about Ramah?" Ria asked.

Ishmar scratched his head. "I think this is where Rachel's Tomb is, but I'm not totally sure."

"Oh, yes, it is!" Yael said. "I had forgotten, but you're right. She is buried in Ramah."

"What was she doing there?" Ria said.

"As I recall, Yaakov, his wives, concubines, and children were on their way from Beit El to Hebron...."

"The opposite of us!" Ria exclaimed.

Ishmar smiled at his young wife. "Not exactly the opposite. We're not staying here forever; just for a few days."

Yael ignored the interruption. "Anyway, Rachel was pregnant with Benjamin, her second son, and began to give birth. She had great difficulty, and when the baby finally came, the midwife said to her, 'Do not be afraid, for you have another son.' As Rachel breathed her last—for she lay dying—she named her son Ben-Oni, son of my trouble. But his father named him Benjamin."

"That is so sad." Ria dabbed at her eyes with the sleeve of her robe.

Ishmar listened with interest. "How will we recognize this tomb?"

"Moshe tells us that over Rachel's Tomb, Yaakov set up a pillar and that it's there to this day."

"A pillar!" Ishmar said with a grin. He pointed to the fields that bordered the outskirts of Ramah, now visible in the distance. "Maybe we'd better ask those people in that field. Otherwise this could be a longer ride than we expect."

Ria made a face at her husband and all three laughed. Yael had never known a couple could be so lighthearted toward each other. She felt like a carefree young girl with Ishmar and Ria, and not the burdened, pregnant, serious wife she had become. *It's because of Hever*, she said to herself. *I'm always worried about what he's doing, or saying, or may do or may say.* She sighed.

Ria looked with concern at Yael, who jogged along on her donkey a few feet away. *She is so sweet*, she thought. *Ishmar is right; I should become friends with Yael. She has no one in her life to trust or depend on.*

As they neared the harvesters in the field, Ishmar called out in a loud voice, "Greetings, friends!"

Surprised faces swung toward them. Three men stared silently, suspicion coloring their features but a fourth answered quickly. "Shalom! Who comes here?"

Ishmar dismounted from his donkey and held his hands out, palms facing heavenward, to show that he was friendly and meant no harm. "I am Ishmar, a Kenite from Arad. These two women are my wife and the wife of my master, Hever."

"What are you doing in Ramah, Kenite?"

"A fair question!" Ishmar smiled broadly, and his teeth gleamed white against his bronzed skin. "We have separated from our clan and are traveling north, seeking new land."

"Where are the rest of you?" On closer inspection, the man proved to be young, ruddy, and handsome.

"They are back at the camp, in the direction of Beit El. We have come to explore your beautiful land and perhaps find the tomb of our mother Rachel."

The man's face brightened. "You're close to Rachel's Tomb right now." He pointed to a small hill at the edge of the horizon to the right of the border of the cultivated field. "Do you see that hill?"

"Yes."

"Back in there is the tomb."

"How will I recognize it?"

"You'll find a pillar and there you are."

"A pillar. Thank you," Ishmar said dryly as, behind him, Ria and Yael dissolved into giggles. The man looked curiously at them.

"What is so funny?"

"Private joke." Ishmar extended his hand. "Thank you for your help, uh—" He realized he had given his name but had not heard the other's name.

"Lappidot. It's Lappidot." They shook hands. "God be with you."

"And with you, Lappidot." Ishmar and the girls waved at their new friend, who waved back before returning to the work of the fields.

After their inspection of Rachel's Tomb, the two girls asked to go into the village and look around, but Ishmar gently refused. "I promised Hever I would only be gone a few hours. We must head back toward camp now."

Yael would have argued, but she didn't want to get Ishmar in trouble. Reluctantly, they mounted their donkeys and pointed them back toward camp.

As they approached Lappidot's fields, they could just see him, seated on the ground eating. His companions had left, but now a woman and several children clustered about him. When Lappidot saw them, he rose and waved. "Come, friends!" he shouted, cupping his hands to his mouth so they could better hear him. "Come and join us!"

"Oh, let's!" Yael said. "Please, Ishmar! We won't stay long!" Ria added her pleas to Yael's, and poor Ishmar would have been a hard-hearted man indeed to refuse.

"How did you like Rachel's Tomb?" Lappidot said when they had pulled close to him.

"Wonderful, wonderful!" Ishmar said. "Such a bond with the past, is it not?"

The two men bowed slightly to each other, then Lappidot beckoned to the woman who stood at his elbow. "I would like you to meet my wife, Devorah." He presented her to them as if introducing them to a queen. "And these," he gestured to the five children, from ten-year-old boy to sleeping infant, "are my children."

"A beautiful family," Ishmar said.

Yael and Ria nodded their agreement. Yael studied the wife of Lappidot. A relatively young looking woman, probably no more than ten years older than Yael herself, Devorah was slender, of average height, with curly, red-blonde hair carelessly pulled back from her face in a loose bun. Freckles dotted her long nose, and green eyes (*like mine*, thought Yael) sparkled with a lively intelligence. Her lips were parted in a welcoming smile, and an aura of peace and contentment spilled forth from her like cream overflowing from a dish. When she spoke, her voice was pleasing to the ear.

"Welcome to Ramah, friends! Please come and share the meal with which the Lord has blessed us!" A little boy with bright eyes peered out at them from behind her robe.

In no time Yael found herself seated next to Devorah, with a hunk of barley bread and a piece of cheese in her hands. The children had already flocked to Ria like flies to honey. The baby continued to sleep peacefully, unaware of all the activity around him.

Devorah turned to Yael. "It's interesting that we should meet up with you today. The children and I rarely visit Lappidot when he's working, but the Lord kept impressing upon me that it was *imperative* I take plenty of food and come here. In fact"—she laughed delightedly—"I wanted to leave the house about now and not when I did, but the Lord told me, 'GO!'" She reached out and touched Yael's hand. "I'm so glad, Yael, wife of Hever, to meet you."

A lump formed in the back of Yael's throat. Never, *never* had she encountered a woman like Devorah. Something about her made Yael want to cling to her and beg to stay. She swallowed and could barely control the tremor in her voice. "I, too, am very glad to meet you, Devorah, wife of Lappidot."

The two women talked freely about their lives. Yael briefly explained to Devorah the story of her life in Beersheva, how Hever had taken her to Arad, and that Hever now led a contingent headed somewhere north.

Devorah grew thoughtful when Yael touched on the subject of Hever's reaction to Barak, son of Abinoam. "I have heard of this young Barak. He is a warrior in the hand of the Lord; someone not to be trifled with, I think."

At this point the baby awoke and began to fuss loudly. Devorah scooped the infant up in her arms. She turned her back on the two men and put the baby to her breast.

Yael watched shyly. "I hope to have a healthy baby soon."

Devorah did not appear surprised. She nodded as if Yael had confirmed something for her. She was silent for several moments and looked to be weighing words carefully in her mind. When she did speak, her question startled Yael. "Tell me, Yael, wife of Hever, what you know about Adonai."

"What I know about Adonai? But why do you ask?" Out of the corner of her eye, Yael noticed that Ishmar glanced their way, suddenly wary.

"The Lord has spoken to me about you," Devorah said gently. "Your answer to my question will determine what He will have me say."

Yael stared at Devorah, speechless. Even Abigail, who loved the Lord more than anyone Yael had ever known had never behaved as strongly and confidently this woman. It was as if the Lord Himself were seated beside Devorah, and the two of them conversed. "I will do as you ask," Yael said.

She glanced tentatively at Ishmar, who suddenly turned back to Lappidot as if guided by an invisible hand. Ria followed the four oldest children on a tour of their favorite places in the field. Yael and Devorah sat in complete privacy.

"I have always known about Adonai," Yael said. "There is a great deal of history surrounding the patriarchs in Beersheva, you know. My parents followed the Law of Moshe, but they didn't seem to really *know* God apart from that, if you know what I mean."

Devorah nodded.

"If it hadn't been for my dear friend Abigail, I don't think that I ever would have understood nearly as much about God as I do." She stopped and stared out at the horizon as longing, unbidden, rose up in her voice.

"Go on," Devorah said kindly.

"Abigail didn't just follow the Law, then complain about how annoying and time-consuming it was, like my family did. She loved the Lord and spoke about Him as if, as if...." She paused to search for the right word.

"As if He were her Beloved?"

"Exactly! I've never thought about it in quite those terms before, but that's exactly what she did! That's what you do, too, isn't it?"

Devorah's eyes shone with joy. She placed her hand over Yael's. "I'll tell you a secret. Walking intimately with Adonai is available to everyone. The eyes of the Lord are forever upon the earth, looking to see who will love

Him and obey His commands."

Yael's eyes brimmed. "But you don't understand. My husband is hostile to Adonai. We've left Arad"—here her voice broke—"because he wants nothing to do with the things of Adonai."

"Yael, Hever will have to answer to God for the choices he makes, but he holds no power over *your* walk with God. That is in your hands alone."

Yael stared down at her hands. "I don't know what I want. I'm afraid of antagonizing Hever."

Devorah raised her eyebrows. "Is this Hever so fear-inspiring?"

"Sometimes he is quite sweet. But I never know how he will respond to something."

"I believe that Adonai protects His own. If you hold fast to Him, He will hold fast to you. No one—I repeat, *no one*—can snatch you out of His hand."

Yael's eyes flashed angrily. She tried to keep her voice calm. "Perhaps it is easy for you to say that. Your husband adores you and obviously loves Adonai." She tried to pull her hand away from Devorah, but the older woman held it firmly. "For me, it is very different."

"Yael, how do you imagine God?"

"I don't know. I guess I don't really imagine Him at all. I just see His name written in letters in my mind. Why?"

"Let me tell you how I see Him." Devorah released Yael's hand so she could draw pictures in the air with her finger. "He's like a son of man, dressed in a robe reaching down to His feet with a golden sash around His chest. His hair and head are white like wool, and His eyes blaze like fire. His feet glow like bronze in a furnace and His voice is as the sound of rushing waters. His face is like the sun shining in all its brilliance."

Yael listened, transfixed.

Devorah continued. "He's the King of kings and the Lord of lords. On His head are many crowns. The armies of heaven follow Him, riding on white horses and dressed in fine linen, white and clean. Out of His mouth comes a sharp sword with which to strike down the nations. He's the ruler of all that is."

"Unbelievable." Yael shook her head. "You see all that?"

"That, and more. He's available to you, too. Not just to me." While Yael pondered this, Devorah added, "He spoke to my heart regarding you."

Yael's heart pounded in her chest. "When? Now?"

"No. Before. When you were still far off in the fields, while you rode on your donkey. He told me about you."

"But that's incredible. You hadn't even seen my face!"

"*I* hadn't, that's true enough. But Adonai is Lord of all, Yael. He knew you when you were still in your mother's womb. I am merely His maidservant whom He has graced to use occasionally as a messenger."

"What did He say?"

Devorah closed her eyes. Her lips moved but no sound came out. Yael watched her expectantly, wide-eyed. Suddenly she spoke. "The Lord would say: 'Most blessed of women be Yael, the wife of Hever the Kenite, most blessed of tent-dwelling women. Do not be afraid to stand strong for Me, for I will protect you. I will be a husband to you, says the Lord your God. Though your mother and father forsake you, I will be with you. I will wipe every tear from your eye and will lead you in the way everlasting. Do not be alarmed by what comes. Draw close to me and know that through you a mighty victory will be won for Israel.'" She opened her eyes and looked intently at Yael. "That was the message. You are to memorize this and hide it in your heart. The Lord has spoken and He will not go back on His word. Is He a man that He should lie?"

Yael was completely undone. She sobbed, softly at first, but then deep, cleansing sobs of wonder and release. Devorah held her and stroked her hair tenderly.

A shadow fell across the two women. They looked up to discover Ishmar standing there, concern etched in his brow. "What's wrong?" he said.

Yael smiled weakly. "Nothing, Ishmar. I'm fine. My new friend was praying for me and I got a bit overcome."

Ishmar's expression seemed to say *a bit?* But he merely politely inclined his head and bowed graciously to Devorah. "A thousand thank yous for your kind hospitality, my lady, but I must bring Yael and Ria back to our camp now. We have been away longer than we should have been." He glanced nervously at the late afternoon sky.

Lappidot came and stood behind his wife. "Our prayers are with you. Go in peace."

After several more good-byes and hugs, Ishmar, Ria and Yael mounted their donkeys and rode back to camp.

Two weeks later, Hever and Ishmael led their people to the territory of Naphtali, up by the town of Kedesh. There they pitched their tents by the great tree in Zaanannim. At the time, Yael had no idea why Hever had chosen that specific location.

The land was even hillier and greener than the territory of Ephraim through which they had passed. Several kilometers to the east was a small lake, the closest Yael had ever lived to a real body of water. To the northeast stood the majestic Mount Hermon, whose snow-capped peaks seemed like the foothills of heaven itself to these desert nomads. Yael's eyes thirstily drank of the land's refreshing beauty.

Hever set up a camp structure very similar to his father's back home. Fields close to the dwellings would carry a rotation of basic crops: wheat, barley, and millet. Home gardens provided herbs, beans, garlic, cucumbers, lentils, peas, and onions. Lush grazing fields for the animals lay all around them. In a few short weeks, the community flourished under the enormous, spreading tree.

Fall turned to winter, and winter melted into spring. At the first spring thaw, Yael went into labor, and with the help of the Lord, plus the ministrations of Ria and Simcha, she gave birth to a son. This time, the baby was born alive, and Yael and Hever both were overcome with joy. They named him Hadash, because Hever exclaimed that life was beginning anew for him.

Although she had yearned for a healthy baby, Yael soon discovered that motherhood was an exhausting and difficult job. She arose several times during the night with little Hadash, and a good two weeks passed before she could nurse him without pain. Nothing, however, had ever given her as much joy as nuzzling his sweet little face with its big, solemn dark eyes and black hair that stood straight up. She found herself staring at him constantly, transfixed by his beauty. She didn't quite trust anyone else to handle Hadash. When Hever swung the baby around in his exuberance, she wanted to scream and snatch him away.

Only after Hadash was born did Yael realize the extent to which their entire community had held its breath during her pregnancy. Now tension dissipated in all quarters. Simcha, in particular, bounced about with such an excess of good spirits that Yael good-naturedly threatened to sell her to the Arab merchants.

"Like Joseph?" Simcha asked, dark eyes flashing mischievously.

"Trust me," Yael said dryly. "You will not wind up as prime minister of Egypt."

Every so often Yael would think about Devorah, wife of Lappidot, and when she did, she yearned to see her again. *If only Devorah lived nearby,* she thought. *I would sit at her feet and turn my ear to the wisdom that falls from her lips like jewels.* The only other person in her life who seemed the least interested in Adonai was Ria. And she really didn't know Him yet. Yael shook her head sadly. *I guess it is not to be. But at least I have my little Hadash.*

The relationship between Yael and Hever continued pleasantly enough. The birth of a son did much to encourage Hever; and for a short time he seemed willing to concede there was something to this Adonai worship after all. After several months, though, the novelty of parenthood diminished, and Hever ceased to be mindful of the gift God had given him.

Hever and Ishmar began to routinely take a couple of camels and ride off for several days at a time. The first time this happened, Yael asked Hever where he had been. When Hever seemed reluctant to give her an answer, she pressed him further.

"You are the last person here that I would tell!" he snapped, and after that enigmatic statement, he left the tent, leaving her startled and confused.

Two months later, as Yael watched Hever and Ishmar pack up provisions and load the camels with gifts, the truth dawned on her. She stood in the early morning breeze, wrapped in a cloak, and watched as they headed southeast, in the direction of Hazor. *Oh, I see,* she whispered aloud. *You are going to do traffic with Israel's enemies.* Shaken, she turned and went back into her tent, to nurse Hever's son.

# PART V

# DEVORAH

## 1212 BC—1195 BC

# FIFTEEN

*For the Lord gives wisdom,*

*and from His mouth come knowledge and understanding.*

*He holds victory in store for the upright,*

*He is a shield to those whose walk is blameless,*

*for He guards the course of the just*

*and protects the way of His faithful ones.*

—PROVERBS 2:6-8

Years passed. The Lord added two more children to Lappidot and Devorah's young family before He closed Devorah's womb. Fourteen months after Avi was born, Devorah gave birth to another son. They named him Shuvah, as their prayer was that Israel would return to the Lord. When Shuvah reached the age of four, Devorah gave birth to her fourth and final son. They named him Yehoshua, *God saves.*

Lappidot and Devorah's life was full, but happy. The difficulty of the early child-bearing years had given way to a household dominated by older children who no longer woke during the night and cried uncontrollably. Baby Yehoshua was a peaceful child who slept well—truly every mother's dream.

The Lord restored Devorah's song-writing anointing, and both she and Lappidot continued to write songs as they were able. In addition to the harp, Lappidot had made a set of drums using goatskins as heads and carved the body from the wood of an oak tree he had cut down one year. Kenaz took to the drums, and it became a special bond between father and son to play music together.

Devorah and Lappidot gained a certain renown for themselves with their music. These past five years had brought streams of visitors to Ramah—mostly to see Avraham. The songs sung in their presence made their way to every corner of Israel, from Dan to Beersheva.

Avraham's life changed considerably as well. Known and respected throughout Israel as a man who understood the heart of the Lord, Avraham received visits daily from those who still truly wanted to follow the commands of Adonai. Men unhappy with the deterioration of Israelite society clustered about him. At first, he had been rather overwhelmed by it all.

"Miryam," he said one night to his wife when the last visitor had finally left. "I have to say that I feel unworthy of all this attention. What do you think of all this?"

"I think that God is doing something stunning in our lives, and it would be disobedient to reject it for any reason."

"You are a wonderful wife," he murmured, kissing her hand.

"However…"

"Uh-oh." He paused in mid-kiss.

"You're spending so much time meeting with all these different people that our house is falling apart! I've been telling you there's a leak in our roof for some time, plus the fence in the sheep pen needs mending, plus…."

Avraham raised his hand. "I agree. But it's difficult to tell someone who just traveled from a long distance that you're too busy to talk."

"I know, Avraham, I understand. But tell me. Have any of these people offered you any money?"

Avraham frowned. "Nearly all of them."

"And?"

He looked at her. "And I always reject it. You know I'm not in this to get rich, Miryam. I don't want to be accused of anything unrighteous."

She waved her hand dismissively. "Yes, yes, we all know that about you. But perhaps you're supposed to accept the money so that you can hire men to do the work you no longer have time to do." It seemed so logical to her.

"I'll pray about it."

"Avraham! Why won't you accept the money? Isn't it obvious that this is God's provision for us?"

He glared at her. "I will not put an open chest in front of my home and turn this into a sideshow," he said loudly. "You would see then that the fastest way to lose God's hand of favor on our lives would be for us to seek riches for ourselves in His Name."

Miryam started to cry. Avraham almost never raised his voice with her. "You know that's not what I meant," she said shakily. "But while you're giving advice and spending time with all these interesting people seeking God on this and that, I'm the one who's trying to hold both the household and the farm together."

Avraham put his arms around her. "I'm sorry. Give me a little time to hear God's heart on this matter, okay?"

Eyes closed, she nodded.

The next morning, Avraham took Miryam aside. "I want you to know that I sought the Lord like I told you I would."

"Yes?" Miryam set down her basket of laundry. "What did He say?"

"I believe that you're right. What we'll do is accept enough money to maintain our lifestyle as if I were still working full-time in the fields and with the sheep, and the rest we'll distribute to the poor."

"Oh, Avraham!" Relieved, Miryam threw her arms around him. "I love you!" Humming one of Lappidot's songs, she picked the laundry back up and proceeded with her chores, leaving behind a bemused husband.

Men kept streaming into Ramah from all over. They brought enough gifts to keep Avraham, Miryam, and their family solvent as well as provide alms for the poor. Avraham dispensed advice justly and liberally. He encouraged men everywhere to put away their foul and unclean idols and return wholeheartedly to the Lord their God. He was never as prominent a judge in Israel as Ehud and Othniel had been before him. But he was widely accepted and respected throughout the land by the faithful remnant.

Now it came to pass that the Philistines grew bolder and bolder and made forays into the territories close to the Great Sea. They struck at Dan, the western half of Ephraim, Judah, and Manasseh. A great hero arose in Israel named Shamgar, son of Anat. He gained renown for himself when he struck down six hundred Philistines with an oxgoad. After that, the Philistines retreated to their fortified towns and country villages and did not attempt to subjugate Israel again for many years.

Lappidot wrote a song about how Shamgar saved Israel, and this song was sung more often than all of his other songs put together. Singers at all the watering holes and wells throughout Israel repeated it until even the little children knew the words.

At about the same time, Lappidot and his family began to hear about the rise of the king of Canaan, named Yavin, who reigned in Hazor, and his army commander Sisra, who lived in Haroshet HaGoyim. Because the Israelites continued to do evil in the eyes of the Lord, God made them subject to Yavin, who cruelly oppressed them. Yavin had nine hundred iron chariots at his disposal, and was virtually invincible.

King Yavin started his campaign by attacking the unfortified Israelite villages at the borders of territories such as Asher, Naphtali, Zebulun, and Manasseh. His raiders would swoop in, kill all the men, rape the women, and take them and the children as plunder along with all goods and animals. They kept the people they wanted and sold the rest into slavery. Then they would put the villages to the torch. Helpless and terrified, the Israelites lived in fear of Sisra and Yavin. But they still did not repent of their idols.

Eventually, instead of murdering all the men, Yavin sent Sisra to round up a few key men in each place he sought to conquer, and put them to the sword in front of the petrified populace. He then placed the rest of the town under his "protection" and imposed heavy fines and taxes on them. The Israelites groaned under their burden. But they still did not repent of their idols.

Some towns defended themselves more successfully than others. The mountainous regions in Ephraim afforded a natural advantage, as they were difficult to access with the iron chariots. The southern regions, especially in the desert, were also more difficult to conquer, for Yavin's headquarters remained in the north.

So it was that Ramah did not suffer like the rest of Israel. In her heart, Miryam felt convinced of God's protection over her family. She knew this would sound proud and arrogant to the uninitiated, so she did not voice this sentiment aloud. But she could tell that Devorah felt similarly.

Nevertheless, despite the safety of Ramah, the surrounding areas where the Canaanites resided were still subject to attack. It became harder for men to find their way to the house of Avraham as the power of the Canaanites increased and the open roads grew more and more dangerous for men traveling alone. Those who absolutely had to travel relied heavily on hidden, winding paths in a territory rife with wild animals. Often, a man would hide from a Canaanite soldier only to find himself face-to-face with a bear. These were awful times for the Israelites.

A growing segment of the population, mostly young men, itched with eagerness to meet Sisra in battle.

Avraham advised against it. "The hearts of Israel are turned away from the Lord God, and He is allowing this trouble. You cannot win because you will be fighting against Him." He shook his head sadly. "It will only be when men throw away their idols and come before the Lord with repentant hearts that the tide will turn and God will give us victory."

One bright-eyed youth who had made the journey from Beit Horon spoke up. "When will that be?"

"When will that be?" Avraham stretched his hands out wide and looked upward at the sky. "I cannot answer that question. I am not a seer. I only know that the Lord will not give victory now. Even in their distress, the hearts of the people wax cold."

Some of the young men glanced at each other. They all respected Avraham and venerated his wisdom but they were impatient to war against the despised Canaanites and push them out of their land. "Moshe said to drive them out," they said.

Avraham shook his finger at them. "Moshe also said that if you do not obey the Lord your God and do not carefully follow all His commands and decrees, then He will cause you to be defeated before your enemies. He said that you will come at them from one direction but flee from them in seven, and you will become a thing of horror to all the kingdoms on earth. Your carcasses will be food for all the birds of the air and the beasts of the earth, and there will be no one to frighten them away."

Despite themselves, these passionate young men knew Avraham's warnings were true. They had heard the story of one belligerent youth who failed to heed Avraham's words of caution.

"I will not accept predictions of defeat!" the young man had said to a like-minded friend. "We must destroy the Canaanites!" He had gone back to his home in Manasseh and succeeded in attracting a large band of followers—headstrong youths who were unwilling to wait for the Lord Himself to lead them into battle. They plotted an ambush against Sisra and several of his battalions but were no match for the experienced commander. Sisra mowed them down with his iron chariots like daisies in a field of new spring grass. The blood spilled that day brought grief to many a mother's heart in Israel. When news of the slaughter reached Avraham, he was inconsolable for days.

"Oh!" he cried, ripping his clothes and throwing dust on his head. "Oh, that I had better communicated to them the hopelessness of fighting Sisra without God to defend them!"

Lappidot went and reasoned with him. "Abba, you did everything you could. Your words were choice morsels spoken in wisdom. That boy chose against them. His blood and the blood of his followers are on his own head."

Avraham nodded sadly. "I understand, my son," he said heavily. "But it is an awful thing to see men cut down in their prime. They never had the chance to take a bride or father a child." He raised his hand and then let it fall back limply at his side. "The Almighty has laid a heavy burden on me. I grieve for our people in their misery and distress."

Lappidot sat down next to his father-in-law. He didn't offer any more advice or encouragement. He merely kept Avraham company as Avraham prayed and sought God. Later that day, after his father-in-law arose, washed his face, and asked Miryam to bring him something to eat, he thanked Lappidot. "Having you with me, keeping quiet, blessed me more than I can say."

Lappidot went home and told his wife what had happened that day. She shuddered at the mental image of all those young men lying slain in a battlefield, covered in their own blood. She thought of Kenaz, her beloved firstborn, who sat under a tree and whistled cheerfully as he whittled a small animal from a piece of oak. The ten years since his birth had passed so quickly! In only ten more he would be old enough to fight in the army. "Look at him," she said in a choked voice. "What those poor mothers must be going through!"

Lappidot came up behind her and wrapped his arms around her. "Pray that the Lord would bring comfort to those mothers," he told her. "That's right and proper. But don't become fearful about our children. Those men died out of rebellion. They rushed into battle without the Lord's protection. He loved them enough to warn them, but they mocked His warning. God willing, none of our children will ever be that arrogant."

"You're right." Slipping around in his grasp, Devorah turned so she faced Lappidot. She put her arms around his neck and pulled his head toward her. "Kiss me. I love you," she whispered fiercely.

"Gladly," Lappidot murmured as he kissed her again...and again.

That summer brought forth a good harvest for Lappidot and his family. Long, hot days and cool nights combined to make a long threshing season for the wheat crop. Most days Kenaz worked alongside his father, and Devorah watched with satisfaction as her son grew sturdy and brown in the summer sun.

Every so often, Devorah would pack a lunch and take all the kids out to the fields, where they would sit in the shade, eat, and visit with Lappidot and Kenaz.

One morning, on one of the days when Kenaz had stayed back at the house to help Devorah with various chores, she had a strong impression from the Lord to go with the children to the fields.

"But Lord," she said, "I purposely kept Kenaz home because of all the things I need to do here today." She proceeded to list for Him all of her projects. But she felt disobedient even as she went through her list. She sighed.

"Kids," she yelled. "Pull yourselves together. We're going to pack up some food and go see Abba today." She braced herself for complaints: it was a long hot walk to the wheat fields. Tirzah especially did not like to go out in the blazing heat of midday. But to Devorah's surprise, Tirzah, of all the kids, waxed enthusiastic.

"Oh, Ema! That sounds like such fun. Can I help with the food?"

Devorah stared at her. *Can this be my daughter? Now I know this is from You, Lord,* she thought.

"That would be wonderful, honey. Why don't you go borrow the big basket from Savta." Happily, Tirzah ran off, her long dark ponytail swaying behind her.

An hour later, they were almost ready to go when the baby fell asleep. *Hmmm,* Devorah thought. *Maybe I'll wait until he's had a decent enough nap. I don't want him to be too cranky.* She was all set to get Kenaz started on a specific job when she had the most urgent sense from the Lord that she was to GO NOW! "Okay, Lord," she said. "I see that you have other plans for me today." Immediately she gathered the kids and the food, tucked the sleeping Yehoshua into her baby sling, and left the house.

The early afternoon was hot and still. Very few people were outside, but those who were waved and smiled when they saw Devorah and her children. *A mother and a prophetess in Israel,* people described her these days.

More and more, she was seen and respected as one who heard from the Lord. Now she walked along the dusty summer path that dipped down to the wheat fields, and wondered aloud why the Lord had been so insistent this afternoon. None of the kids asked her any questions. They were used to her speaking to God and to herself.

When they arrived at their usual shady spot, the children gratefully threw down their burdens and clamored for a drink of water. Devorah untied the skin that held the water and they took turns drinking.

"Is there enough for me?"

They all turned around. "Hey, *dodi*," Devorah greeted her husband.

Lappidot, dirty and sweaty, smiled broadly at the sight of his family. Devorah kissed him gingerly and handed him the waterskin. He drank thirstily, the lines of his throat taut.

After they sat down to eat, Lappidot asked Devorah, "What brings you here today? I thought you had entirely too much going on at home."

"Well, it's the oddest thing," she said. "I had no intention of coming, but the Lord absolutely *insisted* that I pack up a huge amount of food and meet you here."

Lappidot raised his eyebrows. He smiled knowingly. "That's very interesting," he said, biting off a large chunk of bread.

Devorah watched him intently. "Tell me. What's going on?"

Lappidot finished chewing before he answered. Devorah's eyes never left his face. "I had some visitors this morning. One man and two women on donkeys. They were from a group of Kenites who are traveling north from Arad. They were out looking for Rachel's Tomb." He took another big bite and waved what was left of his piece of bread at her. "This is good."

"That's it? Three Kenites were out wandering around our fields on a sightseeing tour? That sounds very odd. I'm surprised they've made it all the way from the Negev without running into trouble with Sisra and his men."

Lappidot shrugged. "We don't know what alliances have been formed."

"So what did you think of them?"

"They seemed nice enough. One of the women may have been an Israelite. I don't know. It was a pretty short encounter. I gave them directions and off they went."

"Do you think they'll be back this way?"

"Probably. It's the only path that makes any sense to get back to where they're going. In fact"—he peered into the distance in the direction of

Rachel's Tomb—"I do believe that our friends are on their way."

Shading her eyes with her hand, Devorah could just barely make out three figures on the horizon. "You're good at this. Should we invite them to sit and eat with us?"

"Definitely. It seems pretty obvious that the Lord wants you to meet them." By now all of the children, with the exception of the baby, could see the strangers approaching. Kenaz, Tirzah and Avi jumped up and prepared to race over when Lappidot stopped them. "Kids," he said sternly, "Sit down. We think the Lord wants us to get to know these folks, and we don't want to scare them off by pouncing on them. Understood?"

"Yes," they all mumbled, and they sat down reluctantly.

When the trio on donkeys rode closer, and it was clear they had seen Lappidot, Devorah and the children, Lappidot stood up. "Come, friends! Come and join us."

It looked like a hurried exchange of some sort took place, then the man and two women rode up to the family.

Devorah quickly rose from where she had been sitting and stood quietly behind her husband. She studied the strangers as they dismounted from their donkeys, noticing that they were all attractive young people. The man seemed an affable sort, with a quick, intelligent way about him. He was tall and dark skinned, in the manner of the Kenites. One of the two women smiled sweetly and shyly. *His wife*, Devorah thought. But her attention rested on the second woman. *She's the one*, breathed the Spirit of God.

The second woman stood tall and dignified. Her hair was swept back from her face and partially covered by an embroidered scarf. *They must be wealthy*, Devorah observed, recognizing the costliness and intricate needlework of the head covering. The woman was fairer than her two companions, and did seem more of an Israelite than a Kenite. Exquisite green eyes glowed with an intensity that took one's breath away. Her shapely figure held an extra curve, and Devorah's practiced eye immediately understood she was carrying a child. Although she appeared to be several years younger than Devorah, her face held a maturity and depth of experience that belied her years.

While Devorah studied the woman, Lappidot had engaged the man in some introductory small talk. Now he pulled her into the conversation by introducing her and the children.

"A beautiful family," the man said.

"Welcome to Ramah, friends! Please come and share the meal with which the Lord has blessed us!" Devorah greeted them kindly, trying not to stare at the woman but aware that the Lord wanted her to make contact.

The man then told them that his name was Ishmar, and introduced them to his wife, Ria. The second woman, he proudly informed them, was Yael, the wife of his master, Hever.

Devorah seated herself next to Yael. She found herself fascinated by this unusual young woman. Devorah kept in constant internal prayer while talking with Yael, trying to determine precisely how the Lord would have her handle this encounter.

She believed Yael knew God, but not in the intimate fashion she should. So she encouraged Yael to describe her relationship with Adonai. Eventually, she described her relationship with her husband, Hever the Kenite, letting Devorah know that he was an obstacle to her walk with the Lord.

At this, Devorah protested. "Hever will have to answer to God for the choices he makes, but he holds no power over *your* walk with God. That is in your hands alone." Even as Devorah said the words, she knew how difficult it would be for Yael to follow after Adonai. Still, she pressed on. She believed Adonai had His hand on Yael in an extremely significant way. She felt the Spirit of God coming alive inside her with power. Speaking prophetically, Devorah described for Yael a physical manifestation of God. She spoke of one like a son of man, with a golden sash wrapped round his chest, and eyes blazing like fire. She spoke of his feet, glowing like bronze in a furnace; and of his voice like the sound of rushing waters. Yael listened, enthralled.

The Spirit of God made Devorah bold. She told Yael how God loved her; how he wanted her for His own. She heard His voice in her head, much as she had years ago at Shabbat Shuvah, the Sabbath of Repentance. She told Yael that the Lord had a word for her, and Yael seemed eager to hear it.

Devorah gave forth the word as the Lord gave it to her. Closing her eyes, focusing on what Adonai would have her say, she allowed the words to tumble forth. Words of love, encouragement, and tenderness. Words specific to Yael about her future. Words that spoke of a great victory for Israel and Yael's part in it. Words of commitment and power.

Words that pierced Yael to the core of her being and reduced her to tears. Ishmar had come over to be sure no harm had befallen his master's wife.

Yael assured him she was fine. The tears dried. He didn't press the matter. The time had come for Yael, Ishmar, and Ria to take their leave. Devorah and Yael embraced tenderly. In a very short time, their hearts had been joined. Devorah knew she would never forget this day.

"I will keep you in my prayers, Yael, wife of Hever." Devorah held her new friend's eyes with a steady, clear gaze.

"A thousand thank yous," Yael said. She mounted her donkey, waved, and they rode back to the road that led to their temporary camp on the way north.

"Well." Lappidot put his arm around Devorah now that they were alone. "What was that all about?"

Devorah shook her head, eyes bright as she stared into the distance after the retreating trio on their animals. "I can't talk about it yet," she said in a low voice. "It's too soon. Can I tell you later?"

"Of course," he assured her, studying her profile, thinking how today had brought a new strength to her.

Devorah remained unusually pensive the rest of that day. After she and the children returned home, they finished their chores for the day and had supper. Lappidot came in after all the children had gone to sleep. He found Devorah sitting outside on the ground, arms hugging her knees, head thrown back so that she could see the stars.

"Hey," he called softly, as he came up the path to the house.

"Hey," she called back, smiling in the dark, happy to see him.

He came over and threw himself on the ground beside her. "What is it?"

"I'm just looking at the stars and remembering God's promise to Avraham."

"How his descendants would be more numerous than the stars in the sky?"

She nodded. "They are, you know. The woman Yael that we met today…she's from Beersheva of the tribe of Judah. That's pretty far-flung from Ramah or Beit El in Ephraim."

Lappidot put his hand on Devorah's back. She put her head on his shoulder. "You were quite taken with her, weren't you?"

"I can't stop thinking about her. It was such an intense time talking with her today. You know, the Lord gave me a word for her and used me in her life, which is always satisfying. But I also believe He connected us spiritually; and one day that will manifest itself somehow in the physical here on earth."

"Something is bothering you. What is it?"

"The Lord had me tell her that she would be used to bring victory to Israel. I had a brief flash of metal on metal and then blood. Lots of blood."

"Did you tell her?"

"About the victory, yes. I gave her the words that the Lord gave me. But I didn't describe my impressions. I fear for her, Lappi."

"Then pray. Use what God gave you and cover her in prayer as often as she comes to mind."

She traced the outline of his face with her finger. "I love you. I want you to know that I appreciate you so much."

He chuckled. "Did I do something wonderful today that I can't remember?"

"You do something wonderful every day. Finding out about Yael's life today made me realize that there is no better husband in the world. Do I seem ungrateful to you?"

"Never." He kissed her on the lips.

"We're so blessed, Lappi." She clung to him.

"I know," he whispered into her hair.

# SIXTEEN

Thirteen years passed. Life changed in so many ways. The oppression of life under Yavin had become unbearable. Most people could barely subsist under the heavy taxation. Rebellion against Adonai and a slavish adherence to idols had reached its peak. Slowly but surely, people realized the harsh consequences of idol worship and sought to return to Adonai. Still, they were a growing minority in the land.

For the past five years, Avraham had held court under the huge date palm on the road from Ramah to Beit El. He had divided the Ramah property among each of his three sons and their families. Yitzhak, as the eldest son, inherited the actual house, while Yaakov and Yosef built their own homes on adjacent sections. Meanwhile, a group of Avraham's followers joined together with Avraham's sons and constructed a small but beautiful home for Avraham and Miryam right near the landmark date palm, where Avraham would be more accessible to travelers. All day long he sat under the tree and the people came to him.

As Devorah's children grew, she became more and more involved with her father's judgeship. Avraham requested that she serve at his side when possible. Her gifting and knowledge proved invaluable time and time again, and many of the men and women who came to Avraham for wisdom looked gladly to Devorah for answers as well.

When Devorah reached her fortieth year, Miryam took sick and died. Everyone was in shock. The illness, abrupt and unexpected, lasted less than forty-eight hours. Two days prior, bustling about the house, energetic as always, Miryam had put down her kneading basket to good-naturedly chide her husband for working too hard.

"Look who's talking," he said. "You think you're a woman of thirty."

Suddenly Miryam put her hand to her head and grimaced.

"What's wrong?" Concerned, Avraham took a step toward her.

"I...I don't know," she said, face ashen. "My head hurts."

"Come lie down." He gently took her hand and led her to the bed. Avraham settled her in, and then soaked a cloth in cold water. He placed it tenderly on Miryam's forehead. Her eyes were closed.

"How are you feeling?" He stroked her hand.

She didn't respond. She had fallen asleep.

Avraham placed his hand on his wife's forehead and prayed to the Lord for her to be healed. It was highly unusual for Miryam to behave this way. Anxiety pricked at him. After he had prayed, the anxiety backed off, but he had no real sense of what was going on.

Just then his youngest son, Yosef, knocked at the door. Gratefully Avraham let him in and told him what had happened.

"I'll go get help, Abba," Yosef said.

By evening, the tiny house was crowded with people. All of Miryam's children and grandchildren gathered about her, praying. Friends and neighbors brought food and offered advice. Everyone had a medical opinion. Miryam still slept, but her breathing became more and more shallow.

Avraham sat closest to her, his long, gray beard wet with tears. As he held her thin, limp hand, he rocked back and forth and prayed silently. On the second day, Miryam drew her feet up, breathed her last, and was gathered to her fathers.

Avraham tore his clothes, put on sackcloth, and mourned for his wife many days. His sons and daughter, son-in-law, daughters-in-law, and grandchildren all tried to comfort him. But he was deeply bereaved.

During this time, Devorah pushed her own grief aside to minister to the needs of those around her. Not only was there the sorrow of the family to deal with, but also the long lines of men and women whose lives Miryam had touched over the years and who came, heads bowed, to offer condolences. More often than not, Devorah discovered that many of these conversations started with the person offering comfort, and ended with Devorah comforting them. And so it was that she won the hearts of the people of Israel.

Not until weeks later, when the hectic pace slackened and life crawled back to something approaching normalcy, did Devorah discover the huge well of sorrow within herself.

"I miss the honey cakes Savta used to make," Shuvah said one day.

For Devorah, that innocent comment released a torrent of tears that lasted for days. She put on sackcloth and refused to eat. Tirzah, now a married woman of twenty-one with children of her own, sat with Devorah for hours, stroking her hand and speaking soothing words. Devorah's sons offered comfort awkwardly, uncertain how to act now that their strong mother was in need. Lappidot held her close and quietly prayed for her, having learned over the years that the less said, the better. However, the family grew more and more concerned when she continued to refuse food. It was on the third day that Devorah suddenly ceased crying. She arose, washed her face, put on lotions, and changed her clothes. Entering the kitchen area, she helped herself to some food and ate.

Her family watched in pleased bewilderment. "What has changed, Ema?" Shuvah asked.

Devorah replied, "Inside me was a deep well of tears for my mother. I will miss her until the day I go to be with Adonai. But many of the tears have been shed and the Lord has cleansed me of my immediate sorrow." She took Tirzah's new baby on her lap and held him close.

When the season of Avraham's grief had seemingly abated, he threw himself into his work tirelessly. Every day except Shabbat, from dawn until dusk, he met with people. Always available, he continued to be a blessing throughout the land. Devorah came and stayed with him often, and helped him with his ministry obligations as she was able. Others contributed to keeping house and preparing food for him.

One day, Devorah packed some food and set out walking along the road from Ramah to Beit El. It was early morning, and the first rays of sun shimmered through the few faint clouds hovering over the eastern horizon. The bleating and mooing of sheep and cattle filtered to the road from the fields and pastures. Birds awoke and sang to one another from the lofty branches of tall trees. Devorah walked the familiar two miles to the great date palm quickly, hoping to arrive before anyone else. It was rare these days to spend time alone with Avraham, and lately she grew more concerned about him. Since Miryam's death nine months before, he had grown thin and frail.

When she drew near the gate of the little house, she saw with relief that the grounds were deserted. Stepping up to the front door, she knocked briefly and opened it.

"Abba," she called. "It's me, Devorah. Are you up?"

"In here," Avraham said weakly. She walked into the bedroom and found him slowly, shakily, rising from his knees beside his bed. He smiled when he saw her.

"Oh, Abba. Am I interrupting your prayer time?"

"I'm always happy to see you," he said. "Why are you here so early?"

"I miss you," she said simply. "I'm selfish. I want to have you to myself for a bit." She waved her basket back and forth. "I brought breakfast for us."

"Ah. Good. Then let's go eat." He held out his arm and she took it, noticing how emaciated it was. As they walked to the dining table, Devorah felt extremely conscious of the fact that her father was no longer the strong hero of her childhood. Now she was the stronger of the two. Her throat tightened.

"What is it?"

Wordlessly she shook her head. A few tears escaped and seeped down the sides of her face. Finally, she was able to hoarsely say, "I love you, Abba."

He held her close then, against his chest, like he used to do when she was a little girl. "Oh, my Devi, don't be sad. I've had a full, rich life. Adonai has been very good to me. I miss your mother..."

"But..."

Avraham shook his head. He continued to speak. "I've done what the Lord had for me to do. I've run the race and fought the fight. And now I'm finished."

"How can you say that?" she cried. "What about all the people who come here every day, seeking your wisdom like, like..." She groped for the right words. "Like the way the lilies of the field seek the sun?" She looked at him triumphantly.

Avraham sat down and patted the chair next to him. "Come. Sit here." When she had sat down, he took both of her hands in his and peered intently into her face.

She gazed back at him unflinchingly. "Tell me, Abba."

"There's something we need to talk about. I want you to know that I've prayed long and hard about this. Just this morning, in fact, right before you came here, I again spoke to the Lord concerning you, and finally I have peace."

Her face grew warm and her heart leaped within her. "Of what did you speak?"

"Do you not know?"

"Is it...?" She faltered. "Does it have anything to do with judging Israel?" Even as she said the words, she felt a sense of unreality.

Her father's warm brown eyes, filmy with age, crinkled at the corners. His love for Deborah shone in them. "Surely you know, my daughter, the calling the Lord has placed on you since you were a tiny child."

Devorah bowed her head. Then she looked back up at her father. "Never has there been a woman judge in Israel," she said, in a thick, choked voice. "Not even Miryam, sister of Moshe, held such a high position. Often I have thought, as you say, that the Lord was calling me to such a role, but always I assumed that it would be in subservience to Lappidot. I did not believe that it would be me."

"Oh, Lappidot will stand with you. He is your husband; he is your authority. But it is *you* who have won the hearts of this people. It is *you* whom the Lord our God has chosen." His once-strong hands, now claw-like and shaking with age, gripped hers. "Do you remember," he said urgently, "when you were a child and we went to Sukkot and Ehud prayed over you?"

"How could I ever forget?"

"I knew then. The Lord showed me. I have done everything I could, as the Lord allowed, to train you for this day." He held her hands tighter. "A battle is in your future, Devorah. God is calling you to mighty deeds. Our people are in bondage. They are starting to groan and cry out to the Lord. Yavin and Sisra will not dominate us forever. Those who oppress Israel will vanish like smoke!" He released her hands and leaned back, exhausted.

She knelt on her knees before him and laid her head on his knee. He stroked her hair gently. "Abba, to go forward without you..." She faltered.

"Adonai is with you, my daughter. I am looking forward to my reward in the hands of Adonai." His hand rested heavily on her head. "I am looking forward to going where Miryam has gone." His eyes closed and his speech slurred. Devorah struggled to understand him.

"What is it, Abba?" she whispered.

"I am looking forward to..." His eyes opened then, as if he saw something in the corner of the room, at the ceiling. A beatific smile lit up his grizzled face. "Look! The Angel of the Lord has come to make me a pillar in the temple of my God!"

Devorah swung around and stared. The air around where Avraham looked seemed to swirl faintly. A great sense of peace descended upon the room. She felt as if a heavy weight pushed down upon her, forcing her to the ground. She lay facedown in a position of worship for what seemed like days, or hours, or minutes. She couldn't tell. Slowly, the heavy quality of air in the room returned to normal. Devorah sat up slowly, like one who had been drugged and only now regained consciousness.

Rising to her feet, she approached her father, who remained sitting in his chair, eyes open, a smile on his lips, immobile.

"Abba?" Tentatively, she reached out her hand to touch him but stopped just short of contact. The beloved face before her was no longer her father. She knew that his spirit lived on in a place inaccessible to her during this lifetime.

During the days of mourning, when Devorah's grief waxed darkest, the Lord gave her a song.

*"He who overcomes will be*

*a pillar in the Temple of our God.*

*Temple, temple, temple of God.*

*Never will he leave*

*Never will he leave*

*Never will he leave.*

*I'm in the Temple of God."*

"Oh, Abba, Abba," Devorah breathed as she ceased singing but continued to lightly play the harp. "I can see you now. You *are* a pillar in God's temple. Never again will you hunger, or thirst, or feel the scorching heat of the sun beat down on your head. What a beautiful place it must be."

Her fingers slowed and gradually stopped. "But, oh," she whispered, her voice choked with emotion, "I miss you *so* very much."

# SEVENTEEN

It took nearly a year before Devorah fully occupied the position of judge. It seemed natural in the eyes of many for Lappidot to succeed Avraham; and for Devorah to assist her husband.

Lappidot, however, felt uneasy about this and never received a clear calling from God. "I know that people expect a man to lead them," he said to Devorah one night when they lay in bed together. "But I believe God wants you for this."

The fact that Lappidot had come to this conclusion without any prodding from Devorah struck her as quite significant. She had decided early on that she wouldn't try to control the situation but would allow the Lord to place her where He wanted her.

"Well," she said hesitantly. "I agree that God is calling me to this. But how does this function with our life?"

"I'm not sure. I do know that standing in the way of what God wants to do is a bad idea. We'll just have to work it out as we go along."

So they did. Devorah walked to the great date palm four days a week and sat under it all day long, holding court. Word spread that the anointing of the Lord rested upon her and that she was an acknowledged prophetess. From Dan to Beersheva, the Israelites who braved the treacherous journey came to her to have their disputes settled.

Everywhere, at all times, in and out of season, Devorah sought to lead people back to the Lord their God. She admonished, prayed, argued, counseled, prophesied, sang. She poured herself out for the Lord like a drink offering on an altar.

Her fame grew. And so did the demands on her time. Soon she was traveling to the great palm, now known everywhere as the *Tomer Devorah*, every day except Shabbat. Lappidot was reluctant to complain, as he knew without a doubt that Devorah was endeavoring to perform the Lord's work to the very best of her ability. But their hectic lifestyle wore at him.

He missed his wife. So many others pulled at her for time and attention that she came home even more physically and emotionally drained than when they'd had small children. The special things she had done for him all the years of their marriage dwindled and died down as her energy diminished. Cooking for him, rubbing his tired shoulders at night after long days in the fields, sitting and talking to him when the house grew quiet after it was dark—these things became only memories for Lappidot.

Probably the most upsetting change in their lives, though, was Devorah's lack of interest in him physically.

"I love you," she would murmur tiredly late at night, her face already half-buried in a pillow. "But I just can't right now. I'm too exhausted."

He sulked at first, then grew angry. They fought—their first full-blown fight in years. He complained about their suffering sex life. She defended herself. "I am doing what we agreed was from God," she said quietly, hands on her hips, eyes glaring.

"You are not acting like my wife anymore," he shouted, his voice shaking. The tension of the last few sacrificial weeks crushed him, and something inside him snapped. Suddenly all the anger drained from him and he sat down, put his head in his hands, and wept.

Devorah watched, horrified. Never, *never*, in all their lives had she seen Lappidot give in to such despair. *O Lord*, she prayed silently. *What shall I do? Where have I failed?*

*He's right.*

*How is he right, Lord? How? Everything I do, all day long, I do for You. How have I failed?*

*Do not deprive each other*, she heard God's voice utter in her ear. *Do not deprive each other, except by mutual consent, and then only for a limited time so that you may devote yourselves to prayer.*

Devorah bowed her head. Self-defensiveness crumbled and repentance came in its place. *Forgive me, Lord. I have withheld myself from my husband. I have sinned before You and before him.* She kept her head bowed until she felt the forgiveness and mercy of the Lord wash over her. Then she walked over to Lappidot, knelt down, and put her arms around him.

"Forgive me. I love you. I'm sorry that I put you last. I'm sorry that I took advantage of your love for me."

Lappidot raised his head from his hands and looked into her eyes. His eyes were wet. "I forgive you."

They stared at each other for several moments. Then they kissed. A long, sweet kiss—the first one in a long time.

Devorah stood up and held out her hand.

"Come," she beckoned, eyes steady on his face. "Let's renew our marriage."

He took her hand and she led him into their bedroom, where they made love with a passion and intensity that brought them to new levels in their love.

Later, when they had dressed and shared a meal, they discussed their options. "Why don't we move to the house your parents lived in," suggested Lappidot. "It will save you all of that walking."

Devorah stared at him. It had never occurred to her to ask Lappidot to live so far from their land. "But what about you? How can you work as hard as you do and then add the walk on top of it?"

"Well," he said slowly. "I've been thinking about all of this on those nights when I've been too wound up to fall asleep." He looked at her meaningfully. She blushed. "And I think it's time to give the land and the flocks to our boys and for me to come and help you."

"But what about Yehoshua?" she said. "He's too young to be alone at home!"

Lappidot shook his head. "He won't be alone," he said. "His brothers are with him." He paused. "Besides," he admitted, "I've already made inquiries into having Avdah come and keep house for them."

"Avdah!" Devorah repeated. Avdah had faithfully served Avraham and Miryam for many decades and had retired to a tiny house by herself upon their death. She had seemed to Devorah to be extremely content to putter around and tend her garden. "Is she really willing to cook and clean and wash again?"

"She would do anything for you. Besides, she came to me first and hinted broadly about how boring it is to take care of only one person."

"How broadly?"

Very." He ran a hand through his red hair, now tinged with gray. "I've been praying a lot about the judgeship and it's time for me to step in and be an on-site support for you. We should do what your father did, and accept enough money to support ourselves so that we're both free to fully move forward." He leaned forward and lowered his voice, even though they were alone. "You do realize, don't you, that Adonai has set you up to do more than decide questions about whose ox has strayed and where the boundary lines are. He has called you to galvanize a nation so that we can destroy Yavin and his forces."

Her defenses went up. "I thought that was what I was doing. All I do is encourage and exhort people to leave their idols behind and return to Adonai."

"Yes, you do. God has used you mightily."

Devorah sat back, mollified.

Lappidot sighed and pushed forward. "Maybe I'm not being clear enough. I'm not suggesting that you haven't been effective. What I am saying is that the time has come to *mobilize an army* so that God can use us to take Yavin down."

Devorah shook her head. "Israel isn't ready yet. I don't believe we're in a place yet where we can assume that the Lord will rescue us from our oppressors."

"Well," said Lappidot. "Do you believe that we're close?"

Devorah stared at him. "Yes," she said, her voice trembling ever so slightly. "Yes. I believe that we're close."

"Okay, then. Don't you think that it would be a good idea to begin to establish contacts so that when the Lord says 'Move!' we can act quickly?"

"I need to pray."

"Can we do it together?" He held his hand out toward her.

"You are my lord and master." She took his hand and pressed it to her cheek. "I would be honored to pray with you, my husband."

Lappidot and Devorah moved to the little house across the road from Tomer Devorah on the road from Ramah to Beit El. They went to their Ramah home once a week in the afternoon leading into Shabbat. After Shabbat, they returned. Their three youngest sons freely traveled back and forth between both homes. Within the year, both Avi and Shuvah had found wives. Avdah retired—permanently this time. Avi built a home on the family property for his new bride, while Shuvah remained in the family home with his wife. They graciously consented to have Yehoshua live with them temporarily. At fifteen, it would not be long before he also found a wife. Kenaz, Tirzah, and their families stayed back in Ramah except for occasional visits.

It quickly became apparent that Lappidot was an excellent facilitator. He made contacts all over Israel with men of like mind who sought to build up enough military strength that they might defeat the despised Canaanites.

King Yavin of Hazor grew older. And as he aged, he became overconfident. Were it not for Sisra, his commander, even now the Israelites would have been tempted to rip off the yoke from around their necks. But Sisra's strength and vitality went on undiminished. Middle age had taken down neither his stamina nor his cunning; he remained a dangerous opponent.

Devorah and Lappidot discussed Sisra repeatedly. "It's as if he's protected by something," Devorah said one morning as they sat at their kitchen table. "It doesn't make sense that at fifty he should be as strong as when he was thirty."

"He's against Israel," responded Lappidot. "Which means he's fighting the God of Israel as well. So whatever is helping him hates the God of Israel."

Devorah looked appalled. "Do you think that he has the personal protection of *hasatan*, the adversary?"

"Don't you?"

"Well, yes, I suppose he does, but I never thought about it in those terms before. I knew he had chosen evil but I hadn't considered that *hasatan* himself would be protecting Sisera's rear flank. What do you think we should do?"

"I think we should gather as many people as we can who will truly pray with all their hearts, and pray for holes in the armor of Sisra's protection."

"That's a great idea, Lappi. Can you get that going?"

"Right away, *motek*. I already know the first person I'm going to enlist for this prayer group."

"Who?"

"You." He grinned as he stopped to kiss her surprised face. Then he headed out the door and across the way to Tomer Devorah.

Devorah, her daughter Tirzah, her childhood friend Marta, and her brother Yitzhak's wife, Azra, formed a weekly prayer group. Each had been praying all along for the deliverance of Israel, but now they banded together and focused on the evil forces in the heavenlies that would seek to destroy Israel. They cried out to Adonai with one voice, on their faces before Him. After several weeks, each woman, apart from the others, felt a desire in her own heart to fast one day a week. Undetected areas of sin in their lives came to light, and amazing things began to happen in their personal lives as the Lord brought them to repentance.

About six months in, discernible changes in the hearts of their country-men became more and more evident. Reports filtered in that from every tribe, in every town and village, more and more people were crying out to Adonai for help from the oppression of Canaan.

"You would think that we would have cried out to Adonai twenty years ago," Azra said one day when the prayer group met.

"Ah, but we weren't ready then. It's taken twenty years of being beaten down for us to finally start to repent as a nation." Marta replied.

Devorah looked at each of the women in the prayer group by turn, her eyes bright. "I'm excited. It feels like we're...almost there."

Tirzah raised her hand timidly. "Ema, how shall we pray tonight?"

Devorah was quiet for a moment. "Pray that all Israel would cry to the Lord for help. Pray that the coming battle would be won in the heavens before it's ever fought on earth. Pray that the Lord Himself would fight for us. Pray that we would never fall away from Him but would be with Him forever. And pray for me, that I might lead Israel in such a way as to bring Him honor." She stretched out her hands to the Lord God, lifted her face toward heaven, and began to worship Him in song. Tirzah, Marta, and Azra joined her, praising and thanking God for His great goodness and merciful hand. Azra pulled out her tambourine and led the women in dancing while Devorah sang the prophetess Miryam's victory song:

> *"Sing to the Lord, for He is highly exalted.*
>
> *The horse and its rider He has hurled into the sea..."*

The women danced and sang to the Lord until, exhausted, they fell to the ground on their faces and pleaded with Him for the salvation of Israel.

Their men, likewise, prayed and sought the Lord fervently. It became more and more apparent to those with ears to hear that God was on the move. Lappidot formed alliances with many men. This constituted dangerous work, for at any moment any one of them could be cut down by the Canaanites as they traveled and gathered together. The safety of all involved was nothing short of a miracle.

During one of Lappidot's excursions north, he and Devorah's brother Yaakov headed toward the town of Kedesh in Naphtali. The route would take them eight miles northwest of Hazor. It took all of Yaakov's skills as a guide to skirt them safely around Hazor and into Kedesh. It was here that Lappidot met with Barak, son of Abinoam.

As a young man, Barak had tried to raise an army to fight against Yavin almost twenty years before, when Yavin first attacked Israel. The timing had been wrong, though, and the Lord did not give him the coalition he desired. Bitterly disappointed, Barak had no choice but to return to his hometown and continue on with his life as best he could. Always, in his heart, he counted the days until he could route the despised Canaanites. Again and again he went before the Lord to ask, *Is it now?* Time and time again, he received a *no* in his spirit.

Now he received as honored guests the husband and brother of the prophetess and judge, Devorah. The three men talked long into the night, realizing they were of one heart and mind.

At the end of the visit, Barak bowed to Lappidot and Yaakov. "My brothers," he said gravely. "May the Lord, the God of Israel bless you and keep you safe. I do not doubt that the Lord will use you to deliver Israel from the hand of her oppressors. Do not forget your servant." The muscles in his neck visibly tightened as he swallowed. "I long to be one of the first to wield a sword when we destroy the enemy."

"God will use you mightily," Yaakov said.

Then Barak prayed over Lappidot and Yaakov for protection on their return journey. He cautioned them to avoid Zaanannim. "It is the home of Hever the Kenite," he said. "He is loyal to Yavin."

*Hever the Kenite?* Lappidot narrowed his eyes as he searched back in his memory.

Barak noticed Lappidot's consternation. "What is it?"

"Does he have a wife named..." Lappidot struggled to pull the name up out of the recesses of his memory. "Is it, Yael?"

Barak's eyes lit up. "You know of her?"

"I met her many years ago when they were traveling north from Arad."

"I, too, had the honor of meeting her many years ago." Barak leaned forward. A flicker of longing crossed his face. "Tell me more. Was her husband with her?"

"I never met her husband."

"You missed nothing then."

"An unpleasant sort, I take it?"

"Very unpleasant." Barak sighed. "Stay away from him. He will tear you to pieces like a she-bear."

"And his wife?"

Barak's face softened. "She is like the spring flowers after the winter rains. One of ours. A daughter of Judah. Far too lovely a wife for that Kenite."

"Oh, yes, I remember now. She and my wife were quite taken with each other. Devorah even had a word for her from Adonai. It had something to do with a battle."

At the mention of the word *battle*, Barak's black eyes glittered. "It's soon, my friend. The Lord has roused Himself. He will come like a pent-up flood and sweep away our enemies."

"Then let us be ready when that moment comes." Lappidot and Yaakov turned to leave.

"Amen. Shalom, my friends. God's peace be upon you."

"And upon you," they said. Waving good-bye, they slipped off into the underbrush, and then headed south toward Ramah. They hurried home, eager to share with Devorah and the others about the open door the Lord had given them in Naphtali.

# PART VI

# YAEL

### 1210 BC—1197 BC

# EIGHTEEN

Three years passed. Rumors of King Yavin's cruel and barbaric raids against Israelite towns penetrated even Hever's closed settlement. Although Hever never included Yael in the discussions, she overheard snatches of conversations that made her bones melt in fear. King Yavin possessed nine hundred iron chariots, and with these chariots, his army ruthlessly mowed down anything that stood in their way.

One day Yael discovered Simcha crying piteously as she ground wheat berries into flour. Yael ran to her. "Whatever is wrong, Simcha?"

"Oh, my lady!" Simcha gasped. Tears rolled down her cheeks and her hands shook. "I'm so frightened!"

Yael put her arms around the shaking girl. "What's happened?"

Simcha sniffled loudly as she wiped her eyes with her sleeve. "It's that awful king Yavin of Hazor!" She lowered her voice. "I've heard they burn villages, kill the men, and take the women captive. I can barely sleep at night for worry!" She continued to weep loudly.

"Oh, Simcha! How long have you been afraid like this?"

"Since yesterday when I overheard Ria and Ishmar talking."

Yael's eyes narrowed. "Where were you that you overhead their conversation?"

Simcha's cheeks reddened. "Uh," she delayed, head down, "I guess I was on the other side of the great tree when they were speaking to each other."

"How could they not have noticed you?"

"I was very quiet."

Yael folded her arms and looked thoughtfully at Simcha, who contin-

ued to avert her face from her mistress. For some time, Yael had suspected Simcha of eavesdropping, but had scolded herself for being too suspicious. Lately, Yael had been so engrossed in motherhood that she had failed to really notice Simcha. She did so now and realized her young, vivacious friend had matured into a curvy, beautiful young woman of seventeen. "Simcha," she said, "it's high time we married you off."

"As you will, my lady," she said obediently, but there was a flash of desperation in her eyes before she picked up her discarded millstone.

That evening, Yael approached Hever about Simcha. She briefly told him what had occurred that day and mentioned her plan to marry Simcha off as soon as a suitable match could be found. She was entirely unprepared for his violent reaction.

"Absolutely not!"

"What do you mean, 'absolutely not'? I had already been married for three years by the time I was seventeen. Simcha is far too old to be single! If we don't move soon, she's going to get herself into trouble."

Hever stood there, arms folded against his chest, and stared at Yael. His eyes had a faraway look.

A growing apprehension gnawed at her heart. Something was up. "Tell me what's going on, Hever."

He sighed. He cleared his throat. "I have decided to take Simcha as a second wife."

"WHAT!" Yael's stomach lurched.

He averted his gaze from Yael's stricken face. "You heard me. "

Yael began to cry softly. "She's my *maid*! Why would you want to marry my maid?"

Hever's face hardened. "I want more children, and Simcha is a logical choice. Naturally, as the first wife, you will still have some authority over her. I will buy you a new maidservant."

"Why do you want to do this, Hever?" Yael pleaded. "Please keep me as your only wife. It's hard enough being married as it is...."

"I've determined to do it." His expression remained impassive, but his voice softened a bit. "Look, there's something else you should know."

"What else could there be?"

"Simcha is pregnant."

White-faced, eyes wide, she looked up at him. "Is it...?"

To his credit, he blushed. "Yes. I'm sorry about this, Yael." He stood there hesitantly. "Can I do something?"

She shook her head. "Go." She sobbed. "Just go." As he continued to stand there, her voice rose in pitch. "Go!" she screamed. "*GO!*"

He turned to leave and she crumpled to the floor, weeping for all that was and all that would never be.

Within the week, Hever officially made Simcha his wife. She glowed with happiness and held her head high as she established herself in her own tent.

Yael addressed her only once. "I'm disgusted with you," she hissed. "You are a nasty little sneak. May Adonai deal with you." And she turned her back.

Simcha was outraged. At first she had felt guilty over her secret trysts with Hever. Yael had always treated her with kindness and she genuinely loved her young mistress, but the excitement of having the master pursue her was positively intoxicating. When Simcha realized she was pregnant, though, fear had stabbed her in the belly like a sharp sword. Her initial reaction had been to confess everything to Yael and throw herself at her feet. Hever's continued attention, however, kept her from this noble plan. When Hever learned of the pregnancy and offered to marry her, any semblance of humility in Simcha dissolved. She felt as if she owned him and the world was hers for the asking. She began to convince herself that Yael would get over it quickly.

When Yael finally confronted her, instead of reacting with sorrowful repentance, she grew angry and belligerent. "Hmmmph. It's too bad you couldn't keep your husband happy," she said and flounced out of the tent.

For days, Yael could barely force herself to leave her tent. Shame covered her head like a mantle and she couldn't bear to face the people of the community. Although she knew intellectually that she was not at fault, the fact that her husband had preferred another woman to her—and not just another woman but *her very own servant*—humiliated her almost beyond endurance.

Little Hadash further distressed her. Not only did he keep asking why she cried all the time, but he also wanted to know why Simcha was no longer with them. Years of watching Simcha clean, grind grain, and take care of the tent had naturally made the little boy think of her as family.

Finally Yael gathered enough courage to choke the words out. "Simcha has her own tent now and is also married to Abba."

Hadash's reaction was almost worse than Hever's infidelity. "Hooray!"

he exclaimed, clapping his chubby hands together. "Does that mean that she's my Ema too?"

A fresh outburst of grief from his mother frightened him so badly that he hid in a corner of the tent until the storm subsided.

Now that his relationship with Simcha was out in the open, Hever also became more boldly open about his association with Yavin, King of Hazor. No longer feeling the need for secrecy, Hever openly flaunted his influence with the king. Most of the Kenite community stood in awe of Yavin, and took pride in their master's good standing with this most powerful of kings. Yael, on the other hand, felt like a traitor to her own people, but she knew better than to rebuke her husband. As the news of raids and ambushes against Israelite villages proliferated, the small band of Kenites felt safe and secure under Yavin's protection. Before Yael's eyes, Kenites who had once felt kindly disposed or even neutral toward Israel now took on the Canaanites' hostile attitude. And although the Kenites had loosely participated in the worship of Adonai by observing the Passover each year, now they dropped all pretense of loyalty to Adonai and began to adopt the pagan religion of the Canaanites.

When Simcha reached her seventh month of pregnancy, Hever erected his first altar to the Canaanite goddess deity Asherah. He supervised the work of three men, but he himself laid the cornerstone. Hadash was desperate to help, so Yael came and stood silently while the work progressed.

Relations between Hever and Yael had all but ceased since Hever had married Simcha. Only lately had some of the tension eased. So it was with a sinking heart that she observed this latest infraction.

"What are you doing?"

"Building an altar."

"What kind of an altar?"

"For Asherah."

"Oh, Hever, *why?*"

"Quiet!" he said, dark eyes flashing. He extricated himself from his project and came over to where she stood. "Come with me!"

He took her by the wrist and pulled her to the outskirts of the tents where no one would overhear them. Little Hadash stayed behind, fascinated by the building of the altar.

"Look," he said, "people are excited about worshipping Asherah, and I don't need you causing confusion by coming against it."

"Oh, Hever." Yael closed her eyes in frustration. She opened them and their startling green color reflected back the afternoon sun. "You will bring curses down on our heads by mocking Adonai."

Hever folded his arms against his chest and pursed his lips in a straight, tight line. "How can I say this, Yael? Have you or have you not noticed that we've thrown in our lot with King Yavin?"

She nodded miserably.

"All right, then. Tell me: who does the king worship, Adonai or Asherah?"

"Asherah."

"Precisely. And that's who we're going to worship. Not Adonai." He gave a short laugh. "The god of the Israelites appears to have lost interest in His people. At least we're on the side of the winners." He put his thumb and forefinger under her chin and looked deep into her eyes. "You are to forget this nonsense about Adonai and worship Asherah with the rest of us."

Numbly, Yael shook her head *no*. "I'm sorry, my lord, but that is impossible," she whispered, tears filling her eyes.

"We'll see about that. I will talk to you more about this later." He hurried back to his work.

Yael instinctively reached her hand to her throat and felt the YHVH necklace from Abigail. Lately she had fished it out of its secret hiding place and wore it hidden under her dress.

*Oh Lord*, she prayed. *What should I do?* Then the thought came to her unbidden, *What would Devorah do?*

*She would stand against the paganism*, Yael thought. *But Lord, I am alone here. How can I stand against not only Hever, but everyone in the community?*

The words came to her then: *You are not alone. I have others, even here.*

Yael lifted her head. "Who, Lord?" she said aloud.

But the Voice was silent.

Two months later, Simcha went into labor and gave birth to a lusty, black-haired baby girl. The labor went easily for a first child, and it was not many hours before Simcha happily held her newborn in her arms and nursed her. Yael dutifully attended to Simcha along with the midwife and Ria. She worked just about every day on forgiving Simcha and not letting a root of bitterness grow up in her heart to choke her. Still, she could not help but compare the difference between the easy time Simcha had and the awful time she had with the first baby.

*Lord, is this the reward for sin? How can adultery end like this? I know that You are a merciful God, but You are also a God of judgment. Where's the judgment here?* Yael sighed, straightened her shoulders, and left the birthing tent to search for Hadash.

The day after Simcha gave birth, the head Canaanite priest from Hazor came to meet with Hever. Recently he had returned from an extended visit from Rabbah of the Ammonites, east of the Jordan River. There he had been quite fascinated with the Ammonite deity, Molech. Ishra was a short, slim, swarthy man, with narrow, hawk-like features and rubbery lips. He continually looked about him, disdain dripping off him like rainwater off a roof. Hever seemed unusually eager to please Ishra; his normally abrupt disposition magically transformed into that of an obsequious underling when he was in the high priest's company.

"We are honored and most grateful to have you visit our village, Ishra," Hever said. He barked orders at various servants, who scurried to bring refreshments to their honored guest. When Hever and Ishra sat down to enjoy the hastily prepared feast, Hever brought his new baby daughter out and showed her off to the priest. "As you can see, the gods have shown us great favor."

The priest's interest quickened when he saw the baby. Deftly and thoroughly, he reached for the infant and examined her. A cold smile touched his lips. He handed the child back to Hever, who proudly returned her to her mother. When Hever rejoined the priest, the Canaanite leaned forward and said something inaudible to everyone except Hever. Hever jumped backward as if stabbed, shock reigning over his features. The priest laid his hand on Hever's arm and spoke urgently, soothingly. Hever held himself stiff at first; then slowly his shoulders slumped and in a strange, detached fashion he nodded in agreement. Not long after, the priest took his leave. Hever refused any more food and drink. He spent the rest of the day and night alone.

The following morning, Hever grimly entered Simcha's tent and ejected everyone so he could talk to Simcha alone. Several minutes passed when suddenly the most chilling screams emanated from the tent and reverberated throughout the camp. Everyone spilled out of their tents to see what had happened.

Ashen-faced, Hever exited the tent as Simcha followed him, wild-eyed and disheveled. "NOOOOOO!" she shrieked, as she clutched at him like a madwoman.

Hever brushed her off and strode past dozens of curious eyes to his own tent.

Simcha, meanwhile, collapsed to the ground and sobbed hysterically.

Yael reached her first. "Simcha, what is it? What's wrong?"

For several seconds, Simcha frantically gulped for air, unable to speak. Finally, she raised her finger and pointed it in the direction of Hever's tent. "He wants to kill my baby!" she gasped. And she screamed and screamed.

Yael held her by the shoulders and shook her. "Stop it, Simcha!" she demanded fiercely. "What do you mean, he wants to kill your baby?"

Simcha tore at her long, black hair. "For the goddess Asherah," she moaned. "As an offering for the goddess Asherah!" And she slumped to the ground, inconsolable.

Yael stared at Simcha's distorted features in shock. Her mind raced wildly. *Surely Hever would never...* She wavered. *Or would he? Well, why not? He's thrown his lot in with those uncircumcised barbarians. They commit all sorts of atrocities for their bloodthirsty gods.* Forgetting past history, Yael put her arms around the grief-stricken mother and rocked her back and forth. "We'll fight this," she murmured into Simcha's hair. "We will fight this."

But try as she might, Yael could not prevail against her husband. He grew more and more determined to sacrifice the baby, and many others in the camp agreed with him. *Think how Asherah will bless us,* they said. No one seemed to put it together that a god who killed could not be trusted to bring life. Hever dismissed anyone who tried to reason with him. Depending upon their level of importance in his eyes, he either plied them with convincing words or merely told them to go away.

Ishra came to the camp once more to confer with Hever the day before the sacrifice. The sight of the barbarian priest consumed Yael with dread and loathing. She avoided meeting him and kept Hadash away as well—a difficult task, since the boy wanted to be in the middle of everything his father did.

"Why can't I go with Abba?" he wailed as he sought to elude her grasp. Impatiently, she smacked his little behind hard, closing her ears to his outraged yelps.

She pointed to Ishra. "You are to stay away from that man," she said sharply. The little boy's face hardened, but he obediently followed his mother back to their tent.

The morning of the sacrifice dawned hot and hazy. Not even a whisper of a breeze ruffled the leaves on the trees. The altar of Asherah seemed to pulsate in the shimmering heat, as if anticipating its blood offering. Hever circled the camp and barked orders, his eyes hard and empty.

In the distance, muffled drumbeats reverberated. *Boom, boom, boom.* Ishra and his fellow priests slowly marched into the camp from Hazor. Yael expected to see two or three men and was stunned to see at least thirty. One in particular wore an embroidered purple robe and a heavy gold medallion against his chest. The others treated him deferentially, and when Hever saw him, he fell to the ground and bowed with his face to the dust.

"Arise, Hever the Kenite," the man said in a bored tone.

"Thank you, O king!" Hever rose to his feet. "Your servant exists merely to do your bidding. Thank you for gracing my humble camp with your presence."

"That's King Yavin!" Yael exclaimed, as she peered out from her hiding place behind one of the tents.

Hadash jumped up and down. "Let me see! Let me see!"

"Shhhh!" Yael clamped her hand over his mouth, but it was too late. The king's sharp ears heard the boy and he looked in their direction.

He leaned over and said something to Hever, and then the next thing Yael knew, Hever was walking toward them.

"Abba!" yelled Hadash gleefully as he ran toward his father. Yael tried to grab him by the back of his hair but she missed. Her heart thumped as Hever came right over to where she had been crouching.

"Come," he intoned, his voice expressionless. "The king desires to meet you."

Sweaty and nervous, Yael got up and followed Hever to the spot where the king and his entourage waited. She stood before him, and found it hard to believe this average-looking man was the evil oppressor of Israel.

Hever pushed his fist into her back. "Bow!"

Stubbornly, Yael inclined her head but did not fall to the ground as her husband had.

The king appeared not to notice. He studied her face intently, no longer bored. "Who is this woman?"

"She is one of my wives, your Majesty."

"Is she the mother...?" The king let the rest of the question hover in the air.

"No." Hever shook his head. "She is the mother of my son." He motioned to Hadash, who clung to his father's leg as he stared at the king with big, round eyes.

The king turned back to Yael. "What is your name?"

"Yael. Of Beersheva," she added defiantly.

For some reason, this response amused the king. He laughed, which prompted all the men around him to laugh as well. When he stopped, so did they. "Come here," he commanded Yael. She slowly stepped closer to the king. When she was within an arm's length, he reached over and pulled off her head covering so that her long, brown hair tumbled about her shoulders. Behind her, Yael heard Hever's sharp intake of breath, but he said nothing. Next the king traced the outline of Yael's face with his forefinger. "I am impressed, Hever the Kenite, that you have such a beautiful wife. She would make a spectacular gift for the commander of my army, Sisra. Do you not think so?"

Hever gulped and turned pale. "Your Majesty, she is my wife."

The king laughed again. It was not a pleasant sound. "I am playing with you, Kenite. Obviously the gods have blessed you by presenting you with such a magnificent woman. And after your act of obedience to Asherah today, you will be highly blessed among men." So saying, the king waved his hand and dismissed Yael, who backed away, grabbed Hadash, and ran back to her tent.

Ishra stepped forward from his position behind and to the right of the king. Ceremonial paint covered his face and chest, and he wore only a loincloth. "It is time to begin. Bring the baby now."

Resolute, Hever went to Simcha's tent and returned with the baby. Simcha remained behind, sequestered and sedated; her moaning filtering faintly through the still air.

Ishmar took the baby from Hever. He held her up for all to see how perfect and healthy a child was being presented to the goddess Asherah.

The newborn waved her tiny fists in the air. Distressed by the strong hands clamped like iron around her torso, her face turned red and she began to cry.

In her tent, Yael covered her ears with her hands in an attempt to drown out the pitiful crying. "Don't you dare leave this tent!" she commanded Hadash sternly.

Strange chants accompanied by the beating of drums penetrated the goatskin walls of the tent. Fervently Yael prayed, silently at first and then out loud. Hadash stared at her with big eyes, until curiosity overcame him and he ran to the front of the tent to watch Abba, the king, and the strange, painted man.

"Get away from that entrance and sit on your bed!" screamed his mother.

Startled by her anger, Hadash fell to the floor, crying. Stricken, Yael ran over to him and held him close. "I'm sorry, sweetie," she said hoarsely. "Ema isn't mad at you. I just don't want you to see the awful thing that's happening outside."

"How can it be awful if Abba is there?"

Yael didn't answer but hugged him even closer. Hadash put up with it for only a moment before he squirmed restlessly. "Let go, Ema. It's too hot."

Just as Yael released him, they heard the tortured screams of the baby. Both Yael and Hadash jumped at the sound. Dead silence followed, during which Yael burst into tears and called on the name of Adonai. Again, and again, and again. Shaking and trembling, she pleaded with the Lord to have mercy on the tender soul of the baby and to comfort Simcha.

After a short period of silence, a cacophony of noise erupted. From inside the protected walls of their private tent, it seemed to Yael and Hadash as if everyone in the camp screamed and shouted at the same time, as Ishra led the crowd in praises to the goddess Asherah.

The pounding of the drums resumed. Softly at first, then louder, and louder, the sound grew until it seemed as if the whole earth groaned and shook with each beat. Yael thought she would go mad from it. "Help us, Lord. Help us," she moaned, pulling at her hair, as sweat and tears mingled on her face. "We are despicable in Your sight." She covered her face and wept.

That night Yael hid in her tent and trembled at the raucous revelry undulating around her. It shocked her to realize that the men and women among whom she lived and worked could celebrate such cruelty. Burning an innocent baby to death on a stone altar! And then rejoicing until dawn! Throughout the camp, men and women drank wine until they stumbled around drunk and then engaged in lewd sexual acts in front of one another. Yael felt sickened by the loud, bawdy comments and drunken laughter that filtered through her walls almost until dawn. What had overtaken Hever and his people?

*O God,* she whispered into her pillow, *surely the human heart is desperately wicked. Who can know it?*

When the sun rose the following morning, Yael got up, dressed, and splashed her sleep-weary face with cold water. She observed gratefully that Hadash remained sound asleep; his soft breathing rose and fell rhythmically. Taking only her YHVH necklace, which she tied around her neck and hid, as usual, she quietly lifted the flap of her tent and walked outside for the first time since yesterday afternoon.

The sight that greeted her made her gasp in horror. The normally well-ordered camp lay in shambles. Empty wineskins abounded, broken pottery littered the paths, men and women slept where they had passed out the night before, and odors of vomit, urine, and feces assaulted her nostrils. She forced herself to look toward the altar and found, to her profound relief, that it, at least, had been swept clean.

She lifted her robe so that it would not touch the ground, and hurried through the camp to Simcha's tent. Not sure whether Hever would be inside, she paused, her heart pounding. *Don't be such a frightened little fool*, she told herself firmly. *Just go in.* Tentatively, she pushed open the goatskin flap and peered in. The inside of the tent was dark and it took a few moments for her eyes to adjust. Presently, she discerned that Simcha was alone, tossing and turning on her bed in a drug-induced stupor.

Yael sat on the edge of the bed and laid her hand on Simcha's curly black hair. As she stared down at the semiconscious girl, all remaining traces of bitterness and anger drained from her. The only emotion Simcha evoked in her now was pity.

Simcha's eyes fluttered open. "My baby, my baby," she whimpered, new tears forming, dripping out of the sides of her red, swollen eyes. Slowly she focused on Yael, confused. "What are you doing here?"

"Shhh." Yael stroked Simcha's hair tenderly. "Adonai my God told me to come and offer you comfort."

"The God of the Hebrews? I thought His law said adulterers should be stoned to death." She turned her face to the wall. "You were only ever kind to me. I sinned against you, my lady."

"Yes, you did. But you sinned against Adonai first. If I can forgive you, can not the King of the Universe forgive you, whose mercy and compassion knows no bounds?"

Simcha was silent, her face turned to the wall. Finally, she spoke, fists clenched. "I've been punished, haven't I?"

"Adonai didn't kill your baby! It was that wicked, bloodthirsty demon, Asherah, who stole your child from you." Her voice grew softer. "If you repent of your sins, and turn to Adonai, He will forgive you and restore

208

you to Himself."

Simcha's mouth hardened. She closed her eyes. "Please leave me now. I want to be alone."

Yael opened her mouth to say something but closed it again. *Too much too soon* came unbidden into her mind. She tucked a stray curl behind Simcha's ear. "Okay," she said, standing up. "I'll come and check on you later." She stood silently for a moment, watching Simcha, who appeared to have drifted off into unconsciousness. "Shalom," she whispered and quietly left the tent.

After she was gone, Simcha briefly opened her eyes, shut them again, buried her face in her pillow, and sobbed uncontrollably.

# NINETEEN

The weeks following the death of Hever and Simcha's baby marked a loss of innocence for the camp of Hever the Kenite. A clear line had been drawn between righteousness and wickedness; and to Yael's great disappointment, most of the camp rushed to the side of evil.

Ria proved to be the exception. One night, a few days after the Asherah celebration, Ria appeared unexpectedly at Yael's tent. When Yael bade her enter, Ria stumbled in and burst into tears. Yael hurried over to comfort the shaking woman. "What is it, Ria?"

"It's Asherah! I hate having her presence here. She's so *nasty!*"

"It has been pretty horrible, hasn't it?"

Ria nodded. "I don't want to worship a bloodthirsty god who kills babies. I want," she hesitated, "I want to know more about the god of the Hebrews."

Yael's heart leaped within her, but she masked her excitement and spoke calmly. "What would you like to know?"

"How do I get to know Him?"

It was a good question. Yael herself had grown up with a knowledge of Adonai, but it was the testimony and example of Abigail and then Devorah that had caused her to reach out and seek Him for herself. She smiled at Ria. "I'm not an expert, but I do know that Adonai is a jealous God who will not share you with others. If you truly come to Him, you have to put away all other gods."

Ria considered her thoughtfully. "I'm ready to do that. What do I do next?"

*What do you do next?* Yael wondered. *Lord,* she prayed silently, *I'm no Abi-*

*gail! What do I tell Ria now?* Suddenly it came to her: prayer.

She held out her hands to Ria. "Let's pray."

The other woman wordlessly reached out and locked Yael's hands with hers.

Yael closed her eyes and began, "Adonai Elohim, Ria and I come to You filled with grief over what has happened here. It is not only sorrow over the murder of an innocent baby, though that in itself is terrible enough. It is also despair over the wickedness that we see around us. Adonai, Ria has told me that she wishes to follow You and You alone. Please, Adonai, forgive her all of the sins she has committed against You and against others. Cleanse her, Adonai, and make her pure in Your sight. Lift up her countenance so that she may glory in Your Presence. Open her eyes so that she may see You. Open her mind so that she may understand Who You are."

The words rolled effortlessly off Yael's tongue. She felt as though Adonai Himself said the prayer and she merely served as a conduit. She opened her eyes and looked at Ria, whose head was bowed and whose body was shaking.

Closing her eyes again, Yael continued to pray. "Protect both of us, Lord, and lead others to us. Make us a light among the Kenites to draw those called to belong to You. We pray Your victory over Asherah and over any other idols who would seek a foothold here. Bring Hever and Ishmar to an understanding of who You are and a desire to know You. Be with us now and bless Ria. In Your holy name, Amen."

"Amen," Ria said softly. She lifted her head and gazed at Yael. Her eyes were bright with tears but her face was no longer downcast. "Thank you."

"Thank *you*," Yael said, eyes warm and glowing. "You don't know what an encouragement it is to me that you have come here tonight."

"I had better be going. Ishmar will be looking for me soon."

"How *is* Ishmar with all of this?"

Ria's face momentarily lost some of its newly acquired glow. "Not so good. He's very loyal to my lord Hever, you know."

"Yes, I know." The two women looked at each other with understanding. Reluctantly, Ria donned her cloak and prepared to return to her own tent.

"*Lilah tov,*" she said.

"*Lilah tov.*" Yael watched as Ria went out into the night.

By the end of the following year, Hever's camp boldly and unequivocally aligned themselves with King Yavin and his gods. Yael sought to live as peacefully as she could with her husband under the circumstances; the greatest challenge for her was raising their son. Young Hadash adored his father and ran to be with him every chance he could. Now that the boy was six years old, Hever took him along occasionally when he grazed sheep or supervised field work. To Yael's horror, Hever even took Hadash on a visit to the royal city of Hazor. Hadash came back from the trip in a defiant and rebellious mood, and it took weeks before he would again obey Yael in even the simplest matters.

Yael tried on several occasions to reach out to Simcha. After that initial visit, however, on the day following her baby's death, Simcha hardened her heart to Yael's advances. At least publicly, she seemed to be devoted to Asherah. "I expect to give birth to many children as a reward for my obedience and devotion to the goddess," many heard her say. Hever spent more and more time in Simcha's tent; and the formerly vivacious and fun-loving girl became coarse, loud, and haughty.

Yael and Ria arranged to meet every week to pray together, and Yael would recount to Ria everything she could remember from the Torah of Moshe and the stories of Yehoshua, son of Nun. She could kick herself for not paying more attention when she had had the opportunity during her girlhood in Beersheva. "Oh, why didn't I memorize more!" she often said aloud. She discovered, though, that if she sat quietly and asked the Lord to re-establish His word in her, that many times whole sections of stories flooded back into her mind.

Ria particularly liked hearing about Rivkah and Yitzhak. "It's so romantic!" she said when she learned about their first meeting, and how he took her to be his wife and so was comforted after his mother's death.

Yael laughed. "There's more to God's word than romance!"

Many times, they prayed for their husbands. Ria prayed passionately for Ishmar, beseeching God for his eyes to be opened to the darkness and perversity of the Canaanite ways. Once she stared at the ground, eyes lowered, and made a confession. "I believe the Lord wants me to abstain from food until sundown on the first day of every week until Ishmar comes to faith in Adonai."

"Are you going to obey?"

"I've been doing it for the past four weeks."

*The past four weeks!* Ria's faith had already grown by leaps and bounds. Yael stood convicted by Ria's selfless devotion in pursuing God for Ishmar's salvation. *O Lord,* she prayed, *soften my heart towards Hever. I am not nearly as diligent as Ria in praying for him. Help me to love him and not despise him.* She smiled at her friend. "That is wonderful, Ria. I am so proud of you."

Ria glowed from Yael's words. Although she and Yael had grown close in this hostile environment, she remained in awe of the beautiful woman from Judah. Besides her position as the master's first wife, Yael had a commanding presence in her own right. Even the most ardent worshippers of Asherah whispered among themselves but dared not speak out against her. Hever himself seemed divided in his own heart about Yael. He refused to let her openly worship and speak of Adonai; yet at the same time he did not force her to participate in the adulation of Asherah. As a result, she occupied a unique position within the community.

Despite continued relations with Hever, Yael had failed to conceive another child since the birth of Hadash. For several years, she had been so busy with the demands of her son that she hadn't given the lack of additional babies much thought. Lately, though, she grew increasingly restless. She sought the Lord and came away feeling that He had sovereignly closed her womb. *Please Lord,* she prayed, *fill my life.*

In the spring of Yael's twenty-fifth year she met a man whose destiny would be irrevocably intertwined with hers. It was a clear, glorious day. Mount Hermon stood still and resolute, shrouded in dazzling white, drawing the eye ever northward. Birds sang sweet songs, unconcerned with the troubles of men, while soft breezes swept over the camp. Yael sat outside the entrance to her tent and worked on grinding grain with her new maidservant, Fatma. This was a woman who lacked Simcha's beauty and vibrancy, but Yael felt confident that Fatma would not wind up as wife number three.

She felt physically good. The sun, not too hot, poured down upon her, caressing her with its warmth. She wiggled her bare toes in the lush grass, and stretched her legs out in front of her. Fatma worked quietly, and Yael was free to pursue her own thoughts. She hummed an old worship song, remembered from her childhood, when Hever popped up in front of her, looking urgent.

"What is it?" she asked lazily, her hand shading her eyes so she could look up at him.

"I need you to prepare a feast for this evening. A very important visitor will be with us." Hever stood importantly; self-satisfaction spread across his face.

*Uh-oh. What's going on?* "Who is it?" Yael asked sweetly.

Hever placed his hands on his hips. "It's Sisra," he said with a smile.

Yael stared at him aghast. *Not Sisra! Not the cruel beast who had led his men to raid, plunder, burn, and rape her people over the past ten years?* Aloud she said, "But why, Hever? Why must such a one as that come here?"

"Silence!" he roared at her. "After King Yavin, he is the most powerful man in the world. It is a great honor that he comes to pay us a visit." He shook his finger at her. "Prepare a meal worthy of such a great man. I want him to see that the clan of Hever the Kenite is not a bunch of poor shepherds!" He turned to leave but swung back around. His eyes glinted. "Oh yes. See to it that you look especially lovely."

She swallowed nervously. "Why, my lord?"

"Because you will be serving us tonight. I want Commander Sisra to see that my wife is equal to any woman he has ever seen." With those final words he spun on his heel and worked his way through the camp, shouting orders in anticipation of Sisra's visit.

Yael sat, shocked, her happy mood shattered. *Well, I'm not going to do it,* she thought defiantly. She crossed her arms against her chest and set her mouth in a firm line. *I'm not going to paint my eyes and wait on the butcher of Israel!*

Just then Ria hurried over to her. "Have you heard the news?" she said, big eyes wide.

"Yes." Yael glanced furtively over her shoulder at Fatma, who ground away at the mill as if she were alone in the world. "I will have nothing to do with that *meshugga.*"

"But Yael, how can you not? Master Hever will be very, very angry with you."

"I don't care."

Ria stared down at the grass. Then she said timidly, "Let's pray about this."

"What?"

Ria lifted her head and spoke more boldly. "Let's ask God what He wants you to do." She held out her hands to Yael. "Let's pray."

Yael stared at her, annoyed. *Who did this girl think she was, anyway? Who was she to question the decisions of the master's wife? Hmmmph.* But as she glowered at Ria's sweet face, flushed a pretty pink color, she grew ashamed. "All right. Let's pray."

"Good." Ria sat next to Yael and held her hands. Quietly, she began to pray, "O Adonai, we come before You and praise Your holy name. We bless You and praise You for Your goodness and mercy that endures forever. Adonai, You know that we are unsettled by the news that Sisra is coming to our camp today. You know that this is a man who has done everything in his power to destroy Your people. You know that Yael, out of a sense of righteous anger, does not want anything to do with this man. So we come before You now, your humble maidservants, and ask that You would guide us as to the proper decisions. We want to do Your will, Adonai. Not ours. Not even the master's. But Your will. Amen."

"Amen." The two friends sat, eyes closed, waiting for direction from the Lord. After several minutes, Ria pulled her hands loose and opened her eyes. Yael did likewise.

Ria's eyes glistened. "So, what did you hear?"

"I'm not sure," Yael said. "What did you hear?"

Ria caught Yael's eye. "I think that you are supposed to listen to your husband."

Yael sighed and looked away. "All right, all right."

"What did you hear?"

"I heard the words *obey your husband,* but I'm not happy about this at all." Yael stuck out her lower lip, like a vexed child.

Ria burst out laughing.

Yael glared at her. "Why are you laughing?"

Ria hugged her and kissed her on both cheeks. "I can't help it. I love you so much. Send Fatma to fetch me when you need me to help prepare for tonight." She waved gaily and raced off.

The rest of the day was frenzied with preparations. It turned out that Sisra was coming with a delegation of fifteen men, a few top bodyguards, and this was considered a light visit. They were fortunate, because he had been known to show up for a meeting with a hundred men, terrifying his host.

It would keep all of the women in the camp hustling all day long to prepare a feast for sixteen warrior-type men that would impress Sisra. Several hours later, with the lambs roasting, the bread dough rising, the skins of new wine cooling in the brook, the tables set, and Fatma taking care of Hadash's needs, Yael had enough time to retire to her tent to dress.

*Look especially lovely,* Hever had commanded her. *Hmmm.* She smiled grimly to herself. *Okay, then. I'll look fabulous.* She took off her robe and dipped a cloth in a bowl of water. Quickly, she rinsed herself down and then rubbed scented ointment on her body. She chose to wear the white, embroidered dress that Hever had bought her for their wedding so many years ago. She sat down at the dressing table next to her bed and peered into the little mirror perched there. The face that stared back at her *was* lovely—no longer the fresh face of a young girl but rather that of a mature woman. She gazed into her own eyes, sighed, then took the lid off of a tiny ivory container that housed her eye kohl. Hever had bought her several intricately designed cosmetic jars from traveling Egyptian merchants during one of his erratic bursts of generosity. They were really quite beautiful. Yael rubbed her forefinger over the lotus blossom design. Memories crowded into her mind, but she shook them away. Resolutely, she applied the kohl to her eyes, slanting it up at the outside corners for a slightly exotic look.

Fatma re-entered the tent. "Ah," Yael said. "Just in time to do my hair. No one can braid like you!"

Fatma beamed with pride as she hurried over to her mistress. She had always been creative with hair, and the thick, silken tresses of the master's wife were a special delight. While running a comb through Yael's hair, she chattered about the bustle of activity in the camp in anticipation of Sisra's visit. "The food"—she groaned with pleasure and patted her stomach for emphasis—"smells wonderful!" She pulled Yael's hair back, holding it first this way and then that as she wrinkled her brow in concentration, determining precisely what she was going to do for a hairstyle. "Do you have anything particular in mind?"

"Master Hever requested that I look especially lovely," she said innocently. "Make sure that Commander Sisra appreciates me."

Fatma guffawed. "Ha ha, my lady! Were you to cover yourself in veils from head to toe, the Commander would still be able to see you are the most beautiful woman in the world."

Yael smiled at this obviously excessive compliment. She bowed her head slightly. "Thank you, Fatma," she said demurely.

No more was said for the next ten minutes as Fatma set about braiding Yael's hair. She laced together several thinner braids and wrapped them around Yael's head, securing them with two small ivory combs. The final effect was not unlike a royal crown. Finally, she stood back and surveyed her work. "What do you think, my lady?" She handed the mirror to Yael.

Yael studied herself. *I look magnificent*, she thought, but then she had a qualm of conscience. *Am I going overboard trying to show up Hever?* She couldn't decide, and the minutes were slipping by at an alarming rate. Outside, a shofar blew, and she could hear Reuel shouting that the commander had been spotted with his men just over the crest of the hill to the south.

Fatma ran to the tent entrance to look. "Hurry, my lady!"

Yael shoved several bracelets on her slender arms and dabbed her wrists

216

and the hollow of her neck with perfume. Wrapping a gauzy veil partially over her hair, she thrust her feet into delicate leather sandals and hurried from her tent, with Fatma close on her heels.

As she emerged into the late afternoon sun, the air permeated with the pungency of cooking lamb, she was amazed to see that Hever had mobilized everyone, even the children, into action. The camp had been spruced up, people wore their finest clothes, and an atmosphere of celebration had taken hold.

*O Lord*, she prayed, *I'm obeying my husband like You told me to, but I don't understand why You want me to give honor to a man who has sought to destroy Your people. Help me to do what You want.* She waited, listening for the Lord's voice, but heard nothing. Straightening her shoulders and taking a deep breath, she walked over to the tables to give final instructions to the girls who were setting up.

When everything seemed in order and the serving girls had embarked on their various tasks, Yael turned and saw with surprise that several horses had approached and the riders were dismounting. Too far away to see the features of the men clearly, she tried to guess which one was Sisra. *He must be the one in white with the embroidered belt*, she thought. Her suspicions were confirmed when Hever approached the man, kissed his hand, and knelt before him. Sisra put a hand on Hever's back and seemingly bade him to arise. Hever waved his arm and servants led the sixteen men to chairs where they could rest after their journey. Servant girls hastened forward with buckets of water to wash the dusty, travel-weary feet of Sisra and his men.

A hand tapped Yael on the back. She turned and found herself staring down into the big, brown eyes of her son. "Abba wants you," he said. His eyes widened as he saw her. "Ema, you look beautiful!"

"Thank you, Hadash." She kissed the top of his head, which was a lot higher up than it used to be.

Under the spreading leaves of the great oak, Hever and Ishmael conferred with Sisra and several of his lieutenants. Hever caught sight of Yael as she approached and motioned her over. Sisra's back was to Yael. Hever's mouth dropped as he took in the full extent of her dramatic appearance. She smiled modestly. "Here I am, my lord," she said, coming to a stop before him.

Hever cleared his throat. "Commander, I would like to introduce you to my wife, Yael." Sisra turned and looked full into Yael's face at the same moment that she beheld him. A bolt of lightning could not have generated more electricity. Yael drew in her breath sharply. Sisra blinked. Time stopped. Yael felt flushed all over and her head buzzed. A slow smile curved upwards on Sisra's lips.

"Delighted," he murmured. He held her fingertips lightly in his hand, and his eyes never left her face. "My compliments, Hever, on your choice in women."

"Thank you, Commander," Hever said smugly as two of Sisra's men exchanged knowing looks.

"Please," Yael said when she recovered her breath, "come and sit down so that my lord may be refreshed after his journey."

Sisra released her fingers and proceeded to the place of honor that had been set up for him. After he sat, the rest of his men were shown to their places, followed by Hever, Ishmar, and the rest of the Kenite men, with the exception of the musicians who would play during the meal.

Yael had to force herself to function. She gave orders to several of the servant girls and they circled the tables, pouring wine. She was intensely self-conscious, feeling Sisra's eyes on her as she moved about.

Yael had imagined Sisra as a malevolent, dark monster—something subhuman. The reports of destruction and cruelty he had waged against Israel had created a seething hatred in her. She expected him to be revolting, horrid, loathsome—quite the opposite of the attractive man who had suavely and charmingly greeted her moments ago. For a man nearing forty, he cut a figure of someone much younger. His upright, trim, muscular figure bespoke his military lifestyle. Shrewd, sensual eyes radiated intelligence. Handsome features combined with the force of a powerful personality that radiated outward from him like spokes on a wheel. Yael suddenly had difficulty remembering that she despised this man. In fact, she longed to return to the table and encounter him again.

"Let me help." Yael grabbed a platter of figs from a startled serving girl. Balancing it deftly on her shoulder, she gracefully walked over to where Sisra was sitting, to the right of his host, Hever. Silently she placed the platter on the table in front of them.

Sisra paused in his conversation with Hever and met her eyes. "Thank you, beautiful Yael."

She smiled at Sisra and noted with satisfaction the frown line between Hever's eyebrows as he watched her. "Let me know if you need anything," she said, then walked slowly and deliberately back to the serving area.

When she got there, Ria reached out and stopped her. "What are you doing? Why are you dressed like that?"

"Ria," Yael said, one hand on her hip and the other pointing a finger at Ria, "you're the one who told me to obey my husband! That's what I'm doing!"

Ria's mouth twisted into a wry smile. "I've never seen you look like this before, Yael, and I've known you for years. What is Sisra going to think?"

"I don't know." She averted her eyes from Ria's gaze. "What do you think of him?"

"What do *I* think of him? I think that he's one of the most evil men on the face of the earth! Why? What do *you* think of him?"

"Oh," Yael said evasively, "I don't know yet. He's attractive, isn't he?"

"Attractive?" Ria exploded, then lowered her voice so no one would overhear them. "How can you possibly think of him as attractive? Don't you know how much Hebrew blood is on his hands?"

Ria's words pierced Yael to the heart. Ashamed, she looked down at her hands. "You're right, Ria," she said softly. "I don't know what's come over me. I just want to obey my husband like we heard in prayer. That's all."

Yael's contriteness mollified Ria. She hugged Yael.

As Yael continued to direct the functional aspects of the feast, she had cause from time to time to be within several feet of Sisra. She couldn't help but notice that the commander's eyes were drawn to her, no matter what he was doing. With Ria's words ringing in her head, Yael attempted to be coolly detached but could not help looking back at him. His seductive power drew her.

*What in the world is wrong with me?* she cried silently to the Lord. *Why am I suddenly obsessed with this man? He is Israel's worst enemy since Pharaoh! If I had been one of the slaves in Egypt, would I have flirted with Pharaoh in between plagues?*

By the end of the evening, when the slanting rays of the sun set over the valley, Yael slowed down and began to observe the scene. Simcha now stood behind Hever, her hand on his arm as he laughed and spoke enthusiastically with Sisra. She, too, had worn her most alluring dress and had made herself as beautiful as possible. She entered into the conversation with the two men and flirted with Sisra in the most outrageous fashion. Hever didn't seem to mind.

*Look at them,* Yael thought. *They're both such whores with him.* Then she glanced down at her own beautiful dress and skimpy sandals, and realization hit her full force. Shame filled her. *O Lord,* she cried, *I'm not any better than Simcha, am I?* Suddenly, all the illicit desire for Sisra turned to ashes and fell as dust to the ground. As unobtrusively as possible, she turned and tried to slip away to her tent for the night.

Sisra saw her go. He dropped all pretense of interest in whatever story Simcha was telling. "Wait!" he ordered. Yael froze, but she didn't look back.

"Yael!" Hever called out in a voice thick with wine. "The Commander is asking for you. Come here!"

Reluctantly, she walked back over to them. Hever grinned drunkenly, Simcha pouted jealously, and Sisra stood and extended his hand toward her. Cautiously, she gave him her hand and purposely stared at his chin instead of meeting his eyes.

"Such a pleasure to meet you, Yael."

She continued to look at his chin.

"Look at me," he said.

She raised her eyes to meet his intense, confident, seductive gaze. He lowered his voice until it was barely audible. "You are so beautiful," he began.

"No." She took a step backward. He tightened his grasp on her hand.

"Let me finish."

*I shouldn't listen to him. Help me not to listen to him.* But his words created such intense longing in her that she allowed herself to be drawn closer to him. Hever and Simcha watched them quizzically from a short distance but did not attempt to interfere.

"I find you very beautiful," he continued, "and I want you to know that I will find a way to make you mine." He boldly stared into her eyes before bending over to kiss her hand. In a louder voice he said, "Thank you for your wonderful hospitality. I will report to King Yavin that the generosity of the tent of Hever the Kenite far exceeds all expectations." He released her hand and she hurried away.

The next morning, when Yael awoke, she put on her usual working dress and covered her hair with a scarf. As she slipped unobtrusively out of her tent, she noticed with both relief and disappointment that Sisra and his contingent had gone. "Good," she said aloud. She kicked at a small rock on the path in front of her. "That's the end of that."

But it wasn't. As the days and weeks went by, Yael found that she could not stop thinking about Sisra. A hundred times a day, his image passed through her mind. She felt as though she lived in two realities: her daily life with Hever, and her fantasy life with Sisra. Usually her fantasies would begin with Hever's untimely death, followed by the immediate arrival of Sisra. After he made her his wife, she would bring him to an understanding of the sovereign nature of Adonai. He would then renounce all wickedness and spend the rest of his life (with her by his side) repairing the damage he had done to Israelite towns. Somewhere toward the end, they would travel south to Beersheva, whereupon Yael's parents would toss palm branches at them and beg them to bless their household with their presence.

Yael's relationship with the Lord was strong enough that she understood the destructive power of her thoughts and fantasies. Several times a day, she would ask God to cleanse her of impure thoughts; but, in direct opposition to these prayers, her mind would irresistibly stray in the direction of Sisra. At the mere mention of his name, her cheeks would redden and she would feel as if she had been caught in the midst of something illicit.

Oddly enough, no one else seemed to notice. Hever, thrilled with how well Sisra's visit had gone, believed his star was rising high with King Yavin. He foresaw only fabulous opportunities for himself in the coming days. Sisra's obvious attraction to Yael pleased Hever; it had been his idea all along that Sisra should be impressed by his beautiful wives and so think highly of him.

In fact, Sisra's appreciation for Yael's beauty had renewed Hever's interest in her. Since the sacrifice of Simcha's baby the preceding year, Hever and Yael had kept their contact with each other to a bare minimum. Hever's deep sense of shame and loss and his arrogant loyalty to Asherah had clashed with Yael's pure lifestyle and deep faith in Adonai. Occasionally, Hever visited her at night, but she remained only coldly submissive. They had less and less to talk about, until only Hadash remained a topic of mutual interest. And even the subject of the boy was problematic, as they disagreed more and more on how to raise him.

By the time Sisra came to visit, the marriage had dwindled to nothing more than a legal arrangement. Hever seemed barely conscious of Yael at times. But after witnessing the way Sisra responded to her, Hever suddenly became interested again. He visited her tent often in the weeks after Sisra left and grew angry when she merely went through the motions with him without any excitement.

"Let's see you flutter your eyes at me the way you did for the Commander," he said angrily one night.

She looked at him innocently. "What are you talking about?" After so many years of marriage to Hever, Yael had become skilled at diverting him when he became belligerent.

"I could see how fascinated you were by Sisra. It doesn't take a sage to figure that out."

"I was only obeying your instructions, my lord," she said coolly.

Determined to force a reaction from her, Hever handled her more aggressively than usual that night. Yael fought him off, with the unfortunate consequence that he came to her tent even more often. She had always felt able to tolerate him before; but now, in contrast to Sisra, he seemed positively vile. She cried out to God about her accursed situation, but the heavens were as brass.

# TWENTY

Weeks later, a messenger from King Yavin rode into the camp. Dusty and disheveled, he immediately sought out Hever. When he had been led into Hever's presence, he bowed with his face low to the ground.

"Arise," Hever said. "What can I do for you?"

"King Yavin requests that you accompany me back to Hazor, my lord. He wishes to confer with you on matters of the utmost importance."

Hever composed his face into one of thoughtful contemplation, but inside he was jubilant. At last, the king recognized his need for him!

"Of course," he said smoothly. He clapped his hands. "Servants! Wash the feet of our honored guest and bring him food and drink to refresh him after his journey." Turning to the messenger, he asked when they should leave.

"As soon as possible, my lord. Tomorrow at daybreak, and we need to make haste."

"As you say," Hever agreed.

Hever put Ishmar in charge of the camp, and the next morning he and the messenger mounted horses and headed southeast toward Hazor.

Yael watched Hever leave with gladness in her heart. With him gone, she had freedom to breathe. "Don't hurry back," she muttered quietly.

As she stood there, Hadash stumbled sleepily out of the tent, rubbing his eyes. Yael reached to put her arm around the boy, but he eluded her grasp. "Where's Abba?"

Yael pointed into the sunrise at the two figures on horses disappearing into the horizon. "He's gone, but he'll be back soon."

"He's *gone?*" The boy's voice rose in a plaintive wail. "Why didn't he say good-bye to me?"

"Shhh, Hadash. It all happened very suddenly. Why don't you go back to bed? It's still very early."

"I don't want to go to bed!" The boy's young face was pinched with anger. He stamped his foot. "I want Abba!"

"Stop it, Hadash! You're much too old to be throwing tantrums like this. What would Adonai say?"

Hadash scowled. "Who cares what He would say! He's the god of the losers! I'm going to worship Asherah, like Abba and the king!"

Yael's voice shook with anger. "Get in the tent now!"

"Fine." He backed away from her. As he headed toward the tent, he yelled over his shoulder, "You're not my master. Abba is!" And with that he fled from his mother's presence.

Yael sank down onto the ground. *Lord, help me,* she prayed. *My life is out of control.* A tear trickled down her cheek until it fell off her face into the dust.

By mid-afternoon, Yael was able to talk to Hadash and pray with him. Although the boy genuinely loved his mother and regretted hurting her feelings, Yael could sense that she was losing him to a culture that hated Adonai. She clasped him close to her and kissed his hair, but after a moment he squirmed, anxious to be free.

"Can I go play, Ema?"

"Yes, go. Go." When she released him, he sprang from her like a hare set free from a trap. Without a backward glance, he flew out of the tent, off to find other boys like him. Yael watched him go and turned to find Fatma.

Before she had gone very far, however, a shout went up in the camp. Several horses were spotted winding along the crest of a hill to the south-west. Ishmar summoned all of the men and, silent and grim-faced, they fetched weapons lest these prove to be unfriendly visitors.

"Who do you think is coming?" Yael questioned Ishmar, as he stood on the highest piece of ground in the camp and squinted into the distance.

"I have my suspicions, my lady." His answer was friendly. Yael's friend-ship with Ria had not gone unnoticed by Ishmar, who benefited greatly from Yael's positive influence on his wife.

"And those are...?"

Ishmar pointed at the steadily advancing figures, outlined by the sun as it sank toward the western sea. "The markings on those animals resemble those of Commander Sisra."

"Oh." Yael spoke in a monotone but her insides went icy. *Sisra! What was he doing, coming here just when Hever had been called away! Unless...* a startling idea formed in her head. *Would he have arranged.....? Oh, no!* She went hot and cold with dreaded anticipation. "Well," she said, her voice determinedly light, "if it is my lord Sisra, then we will have to welcome him as Master Hever himself would have."

"I should know in about ten more minutes." Ishmar turned his attention fully on their unexpected visitors.

Yael waited quietly for Ishmar's determination. Inside, though, she felt as if her whole being had just changed from slow and unhappy to breathless and excited in a moment. She held her hand to her eyes and peered toward the men on horses but was unable to tell who they were. *Ishmar is much better at this than I am*, she thought. Then a revelation struck her: *I can't wait to see him*, followed by an insincere *Lord, help me*, instantly succeeded by *Do I have time to run to my tent and change?* That last impulse was happily only a fleeting one when she realized if she were to do that, she might as well hang a sign around her neck announcing her interest in Sisra.

"Yes," Ishmar said.

"Yes, what?"

He looked at her. "Yes, it is Commander Sisra, my lady." He paused. "I don't know why he would come here, though. I hope everything is all right." He scratched his head. "I'm going to alert the camp. Will you give orders as to hospitality when they arrive?"

Yael bowed her head. "But of course."

Ishmar looked at her thoughtfully. "Talk to Ria first. Have her help you."

"All right." She responded obediently, but a voice inside her screamed, *"Ria will know something's up."*

As Ishmar hurried off in the opposite direction, he muttered under his breath. "Okay, let's see what we're in for."

Ria, guileless as ever, failed to see the blackness in Yael's heart. "Why would he possibly be coming here?"

"I don't know, but I guess we'll find out soon enough," Yael said, while the voice inside her head screamed, *Liar, liar! He's coming because of you!*

A young boy stuck his head in the tent. "He's here, he's here! The Commander is here!"

"Thank you, Etnan," Yael and Ria said simultaneously.

Etnan jumped up and down once more before dashing off to spread the word some more. "I'm surprised Hadash isn't with him," Ria said as she prepared to leave the tent.

Yael tried to keep her voice from trembling. "Oh, he's probably already over by Commander Sisra."

"Before we go, do you want to pray with me that the Lord's will in all this would be accomplished?" Ria held out her hand to her friend.

Yael hesitated. She really did not feel that she was in a place to speak to God right now. "Um, it's a good idea, but we're already late. Why don't we try to grab some time in a little bit and pray then?"

Ria looked at her oddly but merely bowed her head. "As you wish," she said and followed Yael out of the tent.

When the two women reached the center of the camp where Sisra and eight of his lieutenants stood, they saw that the majority of their people already stood there expectantly, waiting for information.

Ishmar stood next to Sisra, conferring with him in low tones. Out of the corner of his eye, he could tell that his wife and Yael had joined the crowd. He bowed respectfully to Sisra and stepped backwards, gesturing in her direction. "Ah," he exclaimed, loud enough for her to hear. "I see that the master's wife has arrived. She may be able to give my lord the Commander more information." He beckoned to Yael to come over to them.

Heart pounding, Yael walked slowly over to where Sisra waited. The crowd melted before her on both sides as people made room for her to pass. When she was directly in front of Sisra, she bowed down before him with her face to the ground. As she arose, he reached out and, taking her hand, helped her to her feet. When Yael looked into Sisra's eyes, she saw reflected back the same intense desire that had gripped her daily since they had met.

Sisra spoke first. "How are you, my lady?" His voice sounded gentle, almost soothing.

"Your maidservant is well, my lord," she said, unable to take her eyes from him. "It is I who must ask my lord the Commander what we, his humble servants, can do for him. To what do we owe the honor of this visit?"

"I have actually come to see the master Hever on some important business."

"Ah!" Yael lowered her eyes. "Does not my lord know that King Yavin has summoned him to Hazor on important business just yesterday?"

"This surprises me." Sisra appeared anything but surprised. He rested his hand lightly on the hilt of his sword, which was strapped around his waist. Drumming his fingers, he appeared to be deep in thought. Suddenly he snapped his fingers.

The lieutenant standing to his right, a particularly lethal looking man, jumped to attention. "Yes, Commander?"

"It appears that we have just missed Hever. Let's stay here for the night and then head to Hazor in the morning and try to catch him there."

"As you say, sir." The lieutenant immediately turned to confer with Ishmar, who nodded agreeably.

The women hurried to prepare food for their unexpected guests. They took a fattened calf and butchered it at once. Next, they took yeasted dough and formed it into loaves, which they baked over an open stone pit. Fatma, who was particularly skilled in the area of sweets, whipped up a concoction with dates, almonds, and honey for after the meal.

Yael herself helped somewhat, but for the most part she enjoyed the status of master's wife. She thrilled to the pleasures of Sisra's obvious desire for her and made every effort to be in his presence. She ignored Ria's worried face and several suspicious glances from Simcha and gave herself over to the desires that had been battling for control within her. At one point during the dessert, Sisra grasped her hand and kissed it, heaping lavish praise on her for the delicacy of the honeyed treats he had just consumed. Yael boldly looked into his eyes and smiled at him.

As she bade her good nights and went to retire to her tent that evening, Ria intercepted her. "My lady," Ria called quietly, lest anyone should overhear.

*Oh no.* Yael stopped and met her. "Yes, Ria," she said mildly.

"My lady." Ria appeared frightened, flustered. "I don't want to overstep my bounds, but..."

"Then don't."

Ria's face blanched white.

Immediately, Yael was stricken to the heart. She touched the other woman's arm. "I'm sorry, Ria. Forgive me. That was rude."

Ria nodded, head down. When she lifted her head, there was a new resolve, a new boldness on her face. "I forgive you. But please don't go any further with the Commander. The Lord is against it. You will bring disaster down on your own head if you, if you..." She couldn't bring herself to say the explicit words.

"Thank you, Ria," Yael said stiffly. "I will consider your words."

"As you will, my lady." Light and purity reflected off her face and she looked so much like Abigail in that moment that Yael, staring at her, became temporarily confused.

"A-Abigail?" she stammered.

"What is it, my lady?"

Yael blinked. There was Ria, standing before her, big eyes tender with love. She averted her face. "Oh, nothing, Ria. Just a foolish fancy. I think that I've been with the Kenites too long." She gave a short, mirthless laugh. "I'll see you in the morning."

"Sleep well, my lady."

"And you." Ria hurried off to the tent she shared with Ishmar as Yael proceeded to her own tent. Her whole mood of exhilaration fell shattered to the ground. Instead of sighing with delight over the powerful good looks of Sisra, she found herself remembering Adonai's words through his prophet, Moshe: *If a man commits adultery with another man's wife—with the wife of his neighbor—both the adulterer and the adulteress must be put to death.* She shook her head, annoyed at this forgotten verse of the Law.

*I'm not planning on committing adultery,* she thought. *It's just that it's so nice to have a man like Sisra pay attention to me. This will lead to nothing.*

A voice pricked at her conscience. *He's a pagan who hates Israel. You're married. What are you doing?*

*I'm not doing anything,* she said. *I'm being hospitable to a man whose feet my husband licks the dust off of.*

*Sharing your bed is not the type of hospitality that pleases God.* She began to argue back when she reached her tent, pushed through the flap, and gasped! "My lord Sisra! What are you doing here?"

"Isn't it obvious?" He studied her with a boldness that frightened her. "I came because I want you, my lady Yael. I have had your face always before me since the day we met. And I think you want me too, is that not correct?" He folded his arms and waited, confident of her desire.

Now that the object of her fantasies and desires stood before her in the flesh, Yael wavered. She was still very drawn to Sisra, but the haunting word *adulteress* pounded in her head. His arrogance threw her as well. This man was not the idealized Sisra of her dreams.

"I think you should go before anyone sees you," she said nervously, eyes bright. "I'm sorry that I gave you the wrong impression." And she moved to the left so that he could walk past her and out of the tent.

Sisra laughed, a little menacingly. He strode over to Yael and cupped her face in his hand as he ran his other hand down the firm lines of her body. She shivered.

"I know that you want me, my lady," he said, his voice husky. "Why do you think I came here?"

"I...I thought you came to see Hever," she stammered.

"We don't have to talk about Hever." He pulled her face toward him and kissed her.

It was the kiss that shocked Yael back to her senses. She had imagined a kiss like those from her happiest times with Hever—a kiss that spoke of passion, love, and oneness. Instead, Sisra's kiss was bold, arrogant, and dominating. A picture flashed in her mind of the thousands of Israelite maidens whose virtue Sisra had destroyed, even as their fathers, brothers, and betrothed lay dying, run through by his cruel and indifferent sword.

"No!" She pulled away from him, but he came after her, completely unaccustomed to being denied.

He pushed her down on the bed, and she struggled against him, desperate to avoid the very thing she had thought would satisfy her longings. "Stop it!" she cried. She twisted her head from side to side to escape his kisses.

Bewildered, he paused in his pursuit. "What is it? What has changed your mind?"

His hesitation enabled Yael to elude his grasp and sit up. Breathless and shaky, she confessed to him that she was utterly and entirely wrong to have led him to believe that she was willing to lie with him. "I cannot commit adultery," she said, cheeks burning with shame.

"I don't understand," he said, his passion ebbing. "I could tell from the first moment I saw you that you do not care for Hever."

"This isn't about Hever," she said. "This is about..." She knew that she was taking her life in her hands, but she plunged on anyway. "This is about the Lord God of Israel."

Sisra's mouth tightened. "He is a weak god," he said disdainfully. "I have crushed His people and He has done nothing. He is not like Asherah, or Molek, or Ba'al."

Yael's stomach lurched. "He will move in power when He is ready. I cannot lie with you because I would be sinning against my God."

Sisra looked away from her. He appeared to be thinking. Yael held her breath.

Abruptly he stood up. "I will not take you against your will," he decided. "I will not dishonor Hever the Kenite in that way."

Yael let out a sigh of relief.

"But I am confident that soon you will see the folly of following this God who does nothing and you will call for me. And then I will come to you, my lady." Bowing slightly to her, he exited the tent.

Yael fell to her knees and prayed aloud to Adonai. *Oh, thank you, Lord, thank you*, she wept. *Forgive me for dishonoring Your Name. Forgive me for leading Sisra to believe that I would be willing to deny You for my own satisfaction. I know that it was You who saved me just now.*

She cried out to the Lord for a long time that night, until at last she felt clean again. Only then did she crawl into bed and drift off to sleep.

The next morning Yael reluctantly left her tent, afraid to encounter Sisra. By telling him that she believed in the God of Israel, she basically had announced that she was hostile to him and all that he stood for. Motherhood proved stronger than fear, however. Hadash had spent the night at the tent of his friend, Etnan, and Yael felt uneasy about his safety with the Canaanites in the camp.

As Yael exited her tent, Fatma was already up and hard at work preparing the morning meal over the stone cooking pit. The smell of last night's feast, heated up and roasted, assaulted Yael's nostrils.

"*Boker tov*, my lady." Fatma eyed her mistress with more interest than usual.

"Good morning to you as well, Fatma." Yael averted her eyes as shame over last night's events welled up in her.

"I prepared food for our visitors. They took it with them for later as they were in a hurry to be on their way."

"They have already left?" Relief washed over Yael like a flood.

"Yes, my lady. Master Ishmar saw them off."

"Thank you, Fatma. I am going to find Hadash and then both of us will be back for some food." Yael's spirits lifted considerably once she realized that she would not have to face Sisra this morning.

"As you will, my lady." Fatma turned back to her task. When Yael had walked off a few paces, Fatma lifted her head and watched the retreating back of her mistress. "There will be trouble over that one," she muttered to herself, shaking her head in concern.

Hadash and Etnan had spent the morning snooping around Sisra and his contingent, desperate for any contact. After the men departed, the boys followed the procession of horses with their eyes until even the tiniest speck became invisible. Disappointed that the exciting group of warriors was gone, they headed back into the camp. Yael retrieved her son as he scampered down from the top of the highest hill of the camp.

"Hey, boys," she called when she saw them. "What are you doing?"

"Morning, Ema." Hadash ran to her. "We watched the Commander leave."

"And how did that go?" She attempted to hug her son, who shook off her embrace. *Too old.* She sighed.

"Okay, I guess," Hadash said. "He wasn't friendly like last night. He seemed kind of—" He groped for the word.

"Angry," Etnan said, suddenly talkative.

"Really." Yael wanted to find out everything the boys knew, but not in such a way as to arouse suspicion. "Tell me what else happened."

"Oh, nothing much," Hadash said. "Only—" He looked at his mother's face and stopped.

"Only what?"

"It's stuff you don't like."

"Tell me," Yael said firmly.

"It's just that the Commander told me to stay away from the God of the Hebrews. He said that the gods of the Canaanites are the gods that will bring me success and make me more like him." Hadash stopped, knowing these words would infuriate his mother.

She didn't yell, though. In a quiet, controlled voice she said to him, "You know that's not true, don't you, Hadash?"

"But he is successful, Ema. And he doesn't believe in Adonai. So isn't he right? Besides," he said craftily, "you like him, too. I can tell."

Yael flinched. *How obvious have I been?* "Commander Sisra is a charming and likable man, Hadash. I admit to you that I have been caught up in the pleasantness of his company and have not stopped to remember who he really is. He has been responsible for much evil, you know. Many people have been harmed because of the Commander. The wicked freely strut about when what is vile is honored among men."

Hadash fidgeted uncomfortably. "Well, I still like him."

Etnan nodded vigorously in agreement. The boys ran ahead of her as she walked them back to camp.

"Go to your tent for breakfast, Etnan," Yael said. "Hadash, you come home with me. You boys can see each other later." The two friends waved and Hadash followed his mother back to their tent to begin the day.

Several hours later, Hever returned home. Hot, weary, dusty, and disheveled, he rode into the camp, obviously in a foul mood. Ishmar rushed to greet him, and the two men closeted themselves off for a conference. Simcha was summoned, and she went with a basin to wash the feet of the master and bring him refreshment after his tiring journey.

Much later Hever sought out Yael. "How are you, my husband?" she greeted him, bowing down. "How was your time with King Yavin?"

"You should know," he said coldly.

Fear gripped Yael's heart. She faltered. "I do not know what you mean, my lord."

"Don't you?" He glared. "My trip was a waste of time. Yavin had nothing to say to me. It was only when I returned here and heard that Sisra had paid you a visit that I realized what was going on."

"Oh, no, my lord," Yael said, trembling. "He came to see you!"

Hever gripped her hair and pulled her head back, dragging her down. "You're a lying whore!" he yelled in her face. "You slept with him, didn't you?"

"No, no, I didn't!" Yael cried, afraid to move. In her heart she knew that even though she had put off Sisra at the last minute, her behavior was not without reproach. "He, he wanted to, but I wouldn't! I would never dishonor you, my lord!"

"You're a liar!" he screamed at her, striking her with the back of his hand across the face.

"No, I'm not! I swear!" Yael cried, attempting to shield her face with her arms.

"I don't believe you!" He hit her again. And again.

"Stop, Hever, stop! I didn't do it!" Another blow. She reeled, sick from the pain, and fell to the floor. He jumped on her. Desperate. she cried out to Adonai, "Lord, help me!"

Fury twisted Hever's features. "Call out to your worthless god! Go on! This one's for Him!" And he pounded her head hard into the floor of the tent. Yael blacked out in a cloud of agony. Satisfied, Hever got to his feet, spit in her bruised, still face and strode from the tent.

Yael never knew afterward how long she lay there, but when she awoke it was to find herself cradled in Ria's arms. "What happened?" she slurred through bruised and swollen lips.

"Shhh. Don't talk. Everything's okay." Ria tenderly stroked her hair and adjusted a light cover over Yael, her eyes dark with anguish.

Yael grimaced. The pain in her head was unbearable, and her face felt wrong to her. She had trouble talking. "Help me Ria. My head… "

Ria soaked a cloth in a bowl of scented water, wrung it out ,and placed it over Yael's face, lightly, so she could breathe. Next she took a bottle of olive oil, and, with trembling hands, applied a small amount to the top of Yael's head near her hairline. Placing her hands on either side of Yael's head, she began to pray. "O Adonai, God of our Fathers, we come before You to plead for mercy for my lady, Yael. Forgive her for her sin, dear Adonai, and cleanse her of all iniquity. You know that she loves You and desires to follow You all the days of her life. We enter Your holy Presence now to ask for healing for Yael. Healing for her head, dear Adonai, and her face. Healing for any part of her body that has been broken or harmed in any way. We ask that You heal her spirit, as well. In Your holy Name. Amen." Ria continued to hold her hands on Yael's head. Yael felt a warm buzzing and noticed with great relief that the pain lessened.

"Ria." She labored to speak. "You need to know that I didn't sleep with Sisra. I couldn't sin against God like that." The tears seeped out from the corners of her eyes and slid down the sides of her face.

Ria clasped Yael's hands in her own. "Oh, my lady. I love you so much. You are closer to me than a sister. It hurts me to see you like this." Her voice broke as she saw her treasured friend lying bruised and beaten, her beauty hidden under a mass of welts and cuts.

"Don't leave me, Ria. I'm afraid of Hever. He wants to kill me."

"No, no, my lady. He won't kill you." Ria stroked her hand. "Ishmar has calmed him down and convinced him of your innocence."

Yael closed her swollen eyes. Moments later they flew open. "Hadash! What about Hadash?"

When Ria didn't immediately respond, she grew frantic. "Tell me, tell me! What's happened to Hadash?"

"Oh my lady," Ria said, "we can talk about that later. Now you should rest."

"No," Yael cried hysterically. "You must tell me about my son!"

"He's the one who found you," she said quietly. "He ran and got Ishmar, who got me. It was traumatic for him."

"Where is he now?"

"With his father. I'm sorry, but no one else would do."

Unspeakable anguish tore through Yael. "Does he know that Hever did this to me?"

Ria shook her head. "I don't know. Pray for him, my lady." She leaned over Yael's shattered form. "No more talking now," she said firmly. "You need your strength to recover."

Exhausted, Yael acquiesced. She soon drifted off to sleep, temporarily numbing the agony of her existence.

It took weeks for Yael to recover. The brutal beating had resulted in three broken ribs, a broken nose, a bruised cheekbone, and a concussion, along with countless cuts and bruises. Miraculously, her teeth and internal organs remained intact.

Ria stayed with Yael day and night, only leaving her side temporarily to snatch a few minutes here and there with Ishmar. On those rare occasions, Fatma filled in. After a week, when some of the swelling had subsided, Hadash came for a short visit. He could barely look at his mother and said almost nothing to her. When he left, Yael wept for hours.

By the second week, she could get out of bed and sit in a chair for brief periods. "Can I see what I look like?" she asked Ria.

"Absolutely not."

"Is it that bad?"

"No, but you still have a way to go before you're healed. It will only upset you to look at yourself now. Wait until the bruises fade and the swelling goes down some more."

"What about my nose?" Yael gently ran her forefinger over the new bump in her broken nose.

Ria studied her lovingly. "It changes your look slightly, but not in a bad way."

Yael sat pensively. "I guess what I look like doesn't really matter anymore. Actually, my looks have been a curse. If I had been ugly, I still would be in Beersheva. I never would have met or married Hever. And I'd never have known Sisra."

"Oh no, my lady! Then where would I be? Were it not for you, I would never have known the one true God! I would be tossing my babies in the ash heap around Asherah like everyone else!"

Yael felt a pang of sadness for her friend. Ria and Ishmar had been married for several years and had still failed to conceive a child.

"And," Ria added shyly, "I wouldn't have known you."

Yael gave a short laugh. "Knowing me seems to be a liability."

"I refuse to allow you to say things like that." Ria's normally soft voice took on a steely edge. "I agree that you haven't acted perfectly at all times, but you have carried the light of Adonai in the midst of this darkness we live in. If it weren't for you, the rest of us would think that idol worship was normal. But because of you, whether or not we choose to do something about it, we are convicted of the wickedness of our ways."

Regret pierced Yael's soul like a sharp sword. "Oh, Ria. I sinned by my behavior with Sisra. Even though I didn't actually sleep with him, I committed adultery in my heart. I encouraged him."

"Well, have you repented of your sin?"

"You know that I have."

"Have you asked forgiveness of your husband?"

Yael blanched. "You know that I have not yet seen him," she said in a low voice.

"Look, Yael," she said gently. "I know that he is not the husband your heart yearns for. I know"—her voice broke slightly—"that he harmed you horribly. And I know that for the last eleven years you've been forced to live with a people who are not your own. But the fact remains that this is where Adonai has planted you. He allowed you to marry Hever and, for some reason, He brought you up from Arad to Zaanannim."

"Wait a minute. Do you think we came north because of *me*?"

"Yes. I do. I think that God used Master Hever's breach with his parents to bring us to this place. I do not believe that it is an accident. I am certain that we are in the will of the Lord."

"Then why is it so hard, Ria?" Tears formed in Yael's eyes. "Why is my life such a battle?"

Ria put her arms around Yael. "I can't answer that, my lady. I am certain, though, that despite the way the master has abused you, that you still need to ask his forgiveness for your involvement with the Commander. Then you will be clean before Adonai. Let Him deal with Hever. It will be much more effective than anything you can do. I promise you that."

Yael dabbed at her nose with a cut square of linen. To blow it in its current state would be agony. "So," she said, half-crying, half-laughing, "when did you acquire so much wisdom?"

"I had a marvelous teacher."

"I think you overestimate your teacher."

"Begging your pardon, my lady." Ria smiled. "You are wrong."

The very next day Hever came in to see Yael for the first time since the beating. He was not contrite, but neither did he appear to still be angry. He seemed to believe she had spoken the truth about Sisra. Yael knew that this was because of the tireless efforts of Ishmar. Hever inclined his head gravely when she haltingly asked for his forgiveness for her inappropriate behavior with the Commander.

After Yael humbled herself and asked Hever to forgive her, an odd thing happened. He no longer seemed like a monster to her. Her fear of him dissipated. As he sat in his chair, unable to show sorrow for what he had done to her, it caused her to pity him, and not hate him. She felt free to study him boldly and felt saddened by what she saw. He was not a monster, she realized, but a diminished human being sinking into a pit of his own making by his rejection of Adonai.

*Oh Lord,* she prayed silently. *Help me to love this man. Help me to pray for him daily so that he will turn from evil and toward You. He is nothing but a puppet in the hands of* hasatan.

Yael spoke her deepest concern aloud. "What shall we do about Hadash?"

Hever's tone was flat. "He's ten now. It's time he left his mother's tent and learned to be a man. I have already moved him into my tent and will keep him there."

Yael nodded. Two weeks ago, she would have argued furiously with him but now she accepted the decision with tired resignation. All her influence had not kept Hadash from desiring the things the pagans ran after. "As Adonai wills."

Hever's features darkened. "That's another thing. We don't worship the God of the Hebrews here. Keep your remarks about your God to yourself. I will not have King Yavin call me a traitor." He looked directly at her for the first time since he had entered the tent. "You have caused enough trouble as it is."

Yael's mouth trembled, but she kept silent. She closed her eyes and leaned her head back. Hever stared at her for a few moments and then, exhaling loudly, stood up and left the tent.

Eventually Yael recovered, and she forced herself to resume life as she had known it. Although Hadash had moved into his father's tent, he still spent considerable time with his mother. Members of the camp gawked at Yael at first, but soon enough she ceased to be a curiosity. Yael and Ria met together at least three times a week, more if they could, to pray and encourage each other. No more news of Yavin and Sisra penetrated the boundaries of their camp,

Yael entered into a new phase in her relationship with the Lord. He became increasingly precious to her, and she began to turn to Him as her husband. He lifted her above the cares and anxieties of her life, and gave her the strength not only to survive, but to prosper.

One day Ria excitedly sought Yael out and the two women walked toward the hills to talk privately.

Yael pounced on Ria as soon as they were out of earshot of the camp. "Tell me! Are you having a baby?"

"Even better." Happiness flooded Ria's face like the sun in its full strength. "Adonai has blessed me abundantly. Ishmar now believes in the Lord God of Israel!"

"Oh, Ria!" Yael kissed her friend on both cheeks. "That's wonderful! Tell me what happened."

"Nothing dramatic. Ishmar has been watching us both for quite a while. He was devastated by Hever's treatment of you. He loves you, my lady."

"And I him."

"Anyway, Ishmar has always been appalled by Ishra and his child sacrifices. He never believed there was anything to this whole Asherah business. But he also never thought Adonai really existed. It was your forgiveness of Hever and your courage to proceed with life in this camp that truly spoke to Ishmar. This morning, he asked me how the love of God could transform him the way it has transformed you and me."

"Oh, Ria, I'm so glad!" Yael clapped her hands together in delight. Suddenly a cloud passed over her features. "But what is he going to do about Hever? You know they spend an enormous amount of time together."

Ria's brow wrinkled. "We haven't figured that out yet. We will have to say and do whatever Adonai prompts us to do. Perhaps Hever will turn to the Lord as well."

"Perhaps." Yael knew in her heart that she lacked faith where Hever was concerned. It seemed more and more impossible for him to desire to follow Adonai. Indeed, since the incident over Sisra, Hever had stepped up his contact with that awful Canaanite priest, Ishra. Yael shuddered inwardly at the thought of him. If *hasatan* were to take on human form, he would be the spitting image of Ishra.

Ria seemed to read Yael's thoughts. "I am worried about Ishra. Ishmar says he has more and more influence over Master Hever. Ishra is encouraging the master to build a temple right in the camp."

"Oh, no!" Yael protested. "We have far too many Canaanite practices happening here already. If Hever builds a temple, then Ishra will stock it with his male and female prostitutes, and there will be no way to shield our children from the corruption."

"I know. But now that Ishmar can join us in prayer, we can fight this evil more effectively. Also remember that Hever will listen to Ishmar in a way that he would never listen to us, my lady."

Yael murmured her agreement. She rejoiced with Ria over the change in Ishmar. But in her heart of hearts, she doubted Hever would ever find his way out of the evil into which he had willingly entered.

# TWENTY-ONE

Quite some time after these things had transpired, an outsider approached the camp. He traveled alone, which showed courage or foolishness in a time where a man alone made easy prey. Seated high on a donkey, he rode past tall, lofty pine trees and wound around the dry, dusty trail that cut through the hills like a white ribbon. When he reached the outskirts of the camp, he dismounted. He shaded his eyes from the hot, summer glare and scanned the camp for signs of life.

Ishmar soon received word that a stranger had arrived. Taking a few men with him, he cautiously greeted the man.

"Shalom, my friend. Do you come in peace?"

"Yes." The traveler took a deep draught of water from the skin tied to his animal.

Ishmar frowned as he studied the man's features. He looked to be about forty years old. His dark eyes smoldered with an indiscernible passion, but the thin lines running from his nose to his mouth denoted a certain weariness. He looked vaguely familiar, but Ishmar could not place him.

"Do I know you?" Ishmar said.

The stranger didn't answer but looked Ishmar full in the face.

"Wait a minute," Ishmar said. "Aren't you the fellow who visited us in Arad many years ago? From Zebulun?"

"Naphtali," the man corrected him, and a slight smile crossed his features. "I am Barak. From Kedesh. We're neighbors." He bowed in respect.

"You're from Kedesh?" Ishmar could not hide his astonishment. "Why, we've been at this camp for fifteen years now. Have you been in Kedesh all that time?"

"Yes, I have." He smiled enigmatically.

The memory of Barak's visit to Arad flooded back to Ishmar. This was the young Israelite who had tried to raise an army against Yavin so many years before. He looked at Barak carefully. "Come. Have the dust washed from your feet and be refreshed. Then you can share with Master Hever why you're here. You do remember Hever, do you not?"

"I most certainly do." Barak led his donkey on a tether and followed Ishmar into the camp. The *plod, plod, plod* of hooves thudded in the dirt, the only sound around them as they walked.

Later, after Barak had accepted some refreshment, Ishmar walked him toward Hever's tent. "I have not told him who you are. I will leave that to you."

Barak stopped walking and considered Ishmar curiously. There was a faint glimmer of hope in his eyes. "You are not what I expected, friend."

Ishmar met his gaze unflinchingly. "It's the influence of the master's wife."

"I remember her very well. An Israelite."

"My lady Yael is from Beersheva, of the Tribe of Judah."

Ishmar motioned toward Hever's tent. Hever sat at the entrance, a look of discontent pulling down the sides of his mouth.

"Master Hever," Ishmar called respectfully. "Here is our visitor." He inclined his head as he withdrew to the side.

Hever looked at Barak with interest. "I know you, don't I?"

"We have met once before. My name is Barak. From Kedesh."

Hever's forehead creased for a moment, then his eyes lit with recognition. "That's right. You came to Arad many years ago, looking to raise an army."

Barak extended his hand. "How do you like it up here in the north?"

Hever scowled. "I'm used to it. Where do you live?"

"Kedesh," repeated Barak patiently. "Close to Hazor."

"Are you involved with King Yavin?"

"Not if I can help it."

Hever dropped all pretense of politeness. "What do you want with me?"

"I know you have been allied with Yavin for many years," Barak said earnestly. "Surely you can see that his kingdom is crumbling. I've come to offer you an opportunity to ally yourself with me. With the winning side, that is."

Hever masked his outrage. He casually picked at his teeth with the edge

240

of his knife. "What makes you think his kingdom is falling apart?"

"It's in the air."

"Maybe in the air you breathe, friend. But not in my air."

"I remember your father and uncles. Would they have allied themselves with Yavin?"

Hatred filled Hever's eyes. "Your visit here is ill-advised," he said coldly.

Barak tried one more time. "Please, Hever. There is still time to save yourself and your followers. The balance of power in this land is about to shift. Soon, very soon, things will change. Now is your chance."

Hever stared at Barak. Unflinchingly, Barak stared back. For several moments, neither man spoke.

Then, Hever stood up, signifying the interview was at an end. "Ishmar," he called, still keeping his eyes on Barak.

"Yes, my lord?"

"Show our friend some Kenite hospitality and send him on his way to-morrow. First thing."

Ishmar inclined his head. "Very well," he said, his voice expressionless.

Without another word, Hever went into his tent.

Ishmar walked over to Barak, who stood silently, clenching and un-clenching his fists, a small nerve under his right eye pulsing.

"Don't let his answer discourage you," Ishmar whispered. "Look! Here comes the master's wife. She is a true daughter of Israel."

Barak turned. Yael was walking gracefully toward them.

Barak drew in his breath sharply. "She is like an angel." He stared, transfixed, as she stopped before him and gave a slight bow.

"Shalom." She extended her hand. "I have heard of your presence among us, Barak of Kedesh. I am honored to have a son of Naphtali here."

Barak bowed in return. "Thank you, my lady. You are very gracious. It seems that you are not in agreement with your husband, however."

"Oh!" She laughed, and the sound was like tinkling bells. "We always disagree where the things of Adonai are concerned."

Yael and Ishmar escorted Barak to the meal Ishmar had ordered pre-pared. Yael began with polite small talk, but Barak plunged into the topic that intrigued him most.

"Are you, then, a follower of Adonai?"

"Yes. But I am not permitted to speak openly of Him in this camp."

"Then why so open with me, my lady?"

She smiled, and warmth radiated from her. "I know you belong to the

Lord God of Israel. You will not betray me, I think." She turned trusting green eyes on Barak.

Though his pulse quickened, he spoke softly. "You are quite right, my lady Yael. I would value your trust as a gift worth keeping."

As Ishmar observed their conversation, he sensed something between them—that Barak was a kindred spirit. Ishmar understood full well the balancing act between faith in Adonai and loyalty to Hever. He and Ria had grown strong in their relationship with God these past several years, and Ishmar had decided early on to tell Hever about his new faith.

Hever had been dumbstruck. "Surely you jest!"

"No, I do not." And Ishmar began in earnest to defend his faith.

"You're out of your mind!" Hever shouted. "This Hebrew god is driving you insane."

"I am not insane, Master Hever," Ishmar said patiently. "What I am saying is true and reasonable. You are familiar with these things and I can speak freely to you." He ignored Hever's grumpy look and continued. "Now is the time to get rid of our worship of Asherah so we can escape Adonai's wrath."

"No! Absolutely not. We have an alliance with Yavin. Pledging allegiance to the God of his enemy would be suicide."

"Please, Hever. The sun will set on Yavin. He will not hold power forever. It is Adonai Elohim who holds the power of life and death over you. Only He can save you."

Hever wavered. Ishmar silently prayed. The heavens stood still as angels waited expectantly.

Somewhere in the distance, a coyote howled. Hever started. He shook his head, slowly at first, then faster and faster. "No," he said. "No. I will not follow the God of the Hebrews." And he turned away.

Oddly enough, he had kept Ishmar in his service. And Ishmar, on his part, had not felt it was time to move on. Now, however, the sight of Barak caused a burning in Ishmar's spirit. Realization hit him with the force of a thunderbolt as he struggled to accept what he believed he was hearing from Adonai. *Is this really what you would have me do, Lord?* He groaned inwardly, knowing the cost.

He took Barak aside after dinner. "Please see me before you leave," he whispered. "I must speak with you." Barak nodded, his dark eyes hooded.

Much later that night, Barak sought out Ishmar. "Tell me what's on your mind."

Ishmar studied Barak. The man's intensity appealed to him. Obviously,

Barak was zealous for God. He was a man who took chances in life.

So would Ishmar. "I, too, am a believer in the Lord God of Israel," he said.

Barak's eyes brightened, but he didn't speak.

Ishmar continued. "Hever knows, but strongly prefers that I keep silent so as not to upset the Canaanites."

"And?"

"And that has been okay for several years. I've grown in my knowledge of God, as has my wife. God has blessed us with twins, whereas previously we were childless. We've also had the privilege of showing several others the truth. But now I believe that Adonai is leading me from this place." Ishmar took a deep breath. "I believe He is telling me to join you in Kedesh."

Barak blinked. "With me? Will Hever let you go?"

Ishmar shrugged and held up the palms of his hands. "He has no choice. I am no one's slave, save God's. But," he said, and his voice grew serious, "I do not doubt that he will make things difficult."

Barak's face was covered in the night shadow, but his voice was hopeful. "What of the Lady Yael?"

"She is a most virtuous woman. I do not think she will desert her husband."

Slowly, Barak nodded. "Of course. How many of you will there be?"

"Four from my family. As to the others, I do not yet know. Perhaps another five."

"All right, my brother." He clasped Ishmar on the shoulder. "But give me a month's head start. To minimize the danger."

"Agreed." Ishmar smiled a bit nervously. The two men parted, but their hearts were as one.

Hever boiled with rage when he learned of Ishmar's plan to leave the camp. One other family announced their intention to leave as well, and, as they also were free, Hever could not force them to stay.

True to Ishmar's predictions, Yael opted to stay with her husband and child. She yearned to leave with her friends, but she knew that Adonai wanted her to stay where she was planted. Besides, her mother's heart refused to be parted from her son while she maintained any influence at all over his life. With each passing year, Hadash became more and more like his father. Only a faint glimmer of light remained in his eyes, but it was enough to give her hope.

All too soon for Yael, the day dawned when Ishmar, Ria, their twins, Perez and Zerah, Yavez, his wife, and three children loaded up their donkeys and prepared to leave the camp. Ishmar had not told Hever they would go to Kedesh. Instead, he used the worship of Asherah and the association with Ishra as reasons to leave. "My family and I can no longer live under such circumstances," he said gravely. "I will head north, toward Haran."

Now he attempted to say a final farewell to Hever, to no avail. Sullen and angry, Hever turned away from any display of kindness or affection.

Meanwhile, Ria and Yael fell on each other's necks and sobbed. "I will miss you so very much," Yael cried.

"And I you," Ria said. "But, my lady, I have faith that we will meet again—either in this world or the one to come."

Yael kissed the twins good-bye. She adored the curly haired, bright-eyed little boys. They had brought much happiness to her life.

In a flurry of dust and excitement, they were gone. Yael stood for a very long time, gazing after them even when the specks in the distance vanished. Not since leaving Beersheva had she felt such grief; yet this time, she felt confident in the knowledge that all was not lost. She knew Adonai had a plan to give her a hope and a future. *Bless them, Adonai,* she prayed. *And bless me, as well.*

Soon after Ishmar's party had left, Hever sent for Zur and Omar. The two men now stood at attention while Hever gave his commands.

"As you know, two families have chosen to turn away from the ways of our camp and have aligned themselves with those who worship the God of the Hebrews. Such disloyalty deserves death." He pointed north. "Tonight, you will go after them. See that no one in their party lives to see the light of day. And say nothing to anyone about your mission."

Two of the camp's most fervent Asherah worshippers, Zur and Omar were only too glad at the chance to gain favor with their bloodthirsty god. They left the camp quietly that evening and rode swiftly north.

As the slow procession of donkeys neared Kedesh, Hever's men overtook them, swords drawn. The wife of Yavez saw them first and screamed. Ishmar swerved around. He could barely make out their faces in the dim evening light.

"Zur! Omar!" he roared. "Would you act in such a foul manner to your own people?"

"You are not our people anymore!" Zur brandished his sword. "You deserve to die."

Ria clutched her boys close to her chest. *Adonai, protect us all,* she prayed desperately. Ishmar and Yavez moved to meet Zur and Omar.

Suddenly, out of nowhere, a group of five men appeared, each armed with swords. Stealthily, quickly, they leaped over to Zur and Omar, and cut them down before Ishmar and Yavez had time to draw their swords.

Zur and Omar gasped for air as the blood drained from their bodies. As they breathed their last, Ishmar peered at the leader of their rescuers. Barak!

Barak had anticipated Hever's treachery. He and several of his men had lain in wait along the rocky crags that lined the road from Zaanannim to Kedesh. He signaled to two of his men. "Take their swords and their donkeys. We need every one we can get." The men obeyed, while two others dragged the bodies off into the underbrush.

Barak called to the astonished travelers. "Hurry! Let's get to Kedesh quickly and safely. We don't want Hever to know where you went." Subdued and shaken, they followed Barak to their new home, thanking God all the while for His protection on their lives.

Torment and doubt gnawed at Hever when Zur and Omar failed to return to the camp. Yael noticed his moods seemed even blacker than usual. "What is it, Hever? How can I help you?"

Hever waved her off. "Go away. There's nothing you can do for me."

Yael's heart filled with pity for him. "You don't have to be so miserable, you know." She reached out to touch him, but he jerked away from her hand as if burned. She looked at him sadly. "I'm here if you need me." Then she turned and walked away.

Hever watched her go. How would she react if she knew what he'd done to Ishmar and Ria? Sadness and regret welled up inside him, and he felt a powerful longing to accept her comfort. He stood up to follow her, when an image of Ishra flashed in his mind. *Do you dare seek comfort from a worshipper of Adonai?*

Hever's spirit shrank within him at the thought of Ishra's wrath. And what had become of Zur and Omar? Icy fear gripped his heart. Sure they had succeeded? He debated sending more men after them. Confusion fogged his mind like mist hovering over a valley.

After a full week had passed, Hever sent out a search party. Three days later, they discovered the decaying bodies. The news of Zur and Omar's deaths, coupled with the departure of Ishmar and Yavez's families, stunned the camp.

Yael took advantage of the crisis. Quietly but effectively, she spoke to the many grieving Kenites about the Lord God of Israel. She explained that no matter how far they strayed, He waited patiently for them with an open hand and an outstretched arm. Some responded well; most did not. Still, Yael felt as though she were soaring on wings like eagles. She knew it was Adonai's strength that carried her, and she only had to obey His direction.

Ever since Ria had left, Yael thought often of Devorah. She had heard from the occasional visitors to their camp that Devorah had become a judge in Israel. Yael knew Devorah held court under the great palm on the road between Ramah and Beit El in the hill country of Ephraim. In her mind's eye, she could imagine the spot, having traveled through on her way from Arad so many years ago. She saw the dry road, pocketed with the imprints of human and animal feet, flanked at either side by masses of wildflowers, bushes, and sparse trees.

She yearned to see Devorah again. Never had she forgotten the awe and delight of that divinely appointed encounter when Devorah had spoken the words of prophecy so many years ago. On her darkest days, she would cry out to the Lord, *O that I had the wings of a dove! I would fly far away and seek out Devorah and Lappidot. I would conceal myself from the storm and tempest!*

It was then that the Lord would speak most tenderly to her and comfort her with His presence. When she recalled the words Devorah had prophesied, her heart would leap for joy within her, certain that God planned to use her in mighty and amazing ways.

Yael would draw lavishly on those times with the Lord and rest in the certainty of His love for her, even as the world she knew experienced a shaking that would forever change her life.

# PART VII

# THE

# BATTLE

## 1194 BC

*On that day God subdued Yavin,*

*the Canaanite king,*

*before the Israelites.*

*And the hand of the Israelites grew*

*stronger and stronger*

*against Yavin, the Canaanite king,*

*until they destroyed him.*

—JUDGES 4:23-24

# TWENTY-TWO

D evorah had led Israel for five years. Her days had become a peaceful, productive routine, balancing ministry with her home life. Then one night she had a dream.

In this dream, she saw the heavens part and the Lord Himself descend with clouds under His feet. She couldn't see His face—the glory was so bright that it burned and she had to look away—but she knew it was Him. The mountains trembled and melted like wax at the presence of the Lord.

God was angry. Smoke rose from his nostrils and consuming fire came from His mouth. Out of the brightness of His presence, clouds advanced and moved swiftly toward His enemies. Massive hailstones, arrows, and great bolts of lightning rained down, and His enemies scattered.

Then she looked down, and far, far below, in the valleys inhabited by men, a great battle raged. A multitude without number surged against each other. She looked closer and saw chariots, swords, and spears. Israel was fighting for its life. The enemy swarmed at Israel from all sides, as hundreds of chariots closed in on her people. Fear and jubilation rose up within her. Gasping, she awoke, and sat straight up in bed.

She seized her sleeping husband by the shoulder. "Lappidot, Lappidot! Wake up!"

One eye opened. "What is it? What's wrong?"

"I just had the most amazing dream. Are you listening?"

"Yes." He propped himself up on one elbow and struggled to wake up. "What happened?"

"It was a dream about Adonai. He was coming down from heaven and He was *furious*. The whole earth shook from His fury. It was unbelievable.

I saw huge mountains shrink in fear." She shook her head in wonderment. "He shot arrows and attacked enemies, *our* enemies."

"Then what?"

"Well," she said slowly. Her voice sounded distant and unreal even to her own ears. "I saw a battle, and I knew without a doubt that the Lord had come down from heaven to fight for us. Oh, Lappidot." Excitement radiated off her like heat off a fire. "It's time! Adonai has given our enemies into our hands! Now is the time to defeat Yavin and Sisra!"

Lappidot lay back on his pillow, brain working furiously as he took this latest information in. After a few minutes he spoke.

"We need to formulate a battle plan. We have to seek the Lord and find out exactly how He wants us to provoke Sisra. We have to sound the battle cry."

They lay silently side by side for the rest of the night, praying, thinking, sleepless. At dawn, as they tiredly ate a quick breakfast, Lappidot said, "You know who our general is."

"Who?"

"Barak, son of Abinoam, from Kedesh. Since you told me about your dream, he is all I can think about."

*Hmmm*, Devorah thought. *Barak. Makes sense.* "What makes you sure?"

"He's been looking to destroy the Canaanites since they started attacking our borders twenty years ago. In many ways, he's a lot like Moshe. Remember when Moshe killed that Egyptian, believing he was freeing the Hebrews from bondage to Pharaoh?"

"Yes," said Devorah. "But he acted in his own strength and not in God's timing."

"Right. So he spent forty years tending sheep in the desert before the Lord said, 'Okay, now.'"

"And Barak has spent twenty years sitting in Kedesh, waiting?"

"Waiting, but not idle. When Yaakov and I met with him a while back, he showed us how he has been secretly training and raising up an army from the towns and villages of Naphtali and Zebulun. I've heard there are raiders attacking Yavin, and they never seem to get caught. I'm almost certain Barak is their leader."

"What kind of man is he?"

"Not much of a personal life, I gather. When I was with him he made some allusion to a wife who died in childbirth many years ago. Doesn't appear to have any children. I'd guess that he's chosen not to take another wife because his lifestyle is so dangerous."

"Lappi, let's take this to our prayer groups for the next three days. We'll fast and seek the Lord about what exactly we should do, and then we'll take action. Okay?"

He leaned over her and brushed his lips against her soft cheek. "Okay, *motek.*" He started to go out the door, then turned around and looked at Devorah. "You know," he said, "I admit that sometimes I've despaired of ever ridding our land of Yavin. It's been so many years." His eyes grew moist. "But the Lord is faithful. He hasn't forgotten us. He is a wonderful God. Today, my heart is on fire."

"Amen, my love. Mine, too."

Lappidot and Devorah, along with the small band of men and women who formed their inner circle, faithfully sought the Lord as to their next step. On the third day of fasting, Devorah heard the Lord speak. She arose from the pallet on which she had lain praying, and summoned everyone to her. "Listen!" she said, her voice still strong despite the lack of food. "Adonai is speaking to me. He wants me to send for Barak and tell him that the Lord, the God of Israel, commands him to take ten thousand men of Naphtali and Zebulun and lead the way to Mount Tabor. He will lure Sisra, the commander of Yavin's army, with his chariots and his troops to the Kishon River and give him into Barak's hands."

Lappidot and Yaakov trembled with excitement. "We will go and bring him to you so you can give him the word yourself," Lappidot said.

"Go, and God be with you," Devorah said.

So the two men went up to Kedesh in Naphtali and met with Barak. They told him all that had transpired. He immediately made preparations to leave with them. Before he left, he instructed his faithful right hand, a Kenite named Ishmar, on what to do in his absence.

Lappidot shook hands heartily with Ishmar when they saw one another.

Barak looked perplexed. "You two know each other?"

"We go way back. To a field near Rachel's Tomb." Lappidot winked at Ishmar. "It seems Adonai has had a plan for us all along."

Ishmar smiled. "God works in mysterious ways. And if He is willing, we will meet again soon. Shalom, my friend."

Along the dangerous route back to Ephraim, the men had ample opportunity for conversation. "How would you rate the effectiveness of our troops?" Yaakov asked as he led the way through the dense underbrush.

"We have the courage of a lion and the fierceness of a bear, but our numbers are small compared to the countless multitudes of Canaanites." Barak ducked his head to avoid a branch as he followed Yaakov single file along the well-hidden path. Lappidot brought up the rear.

"What about the infamous iron chariots?" Lappidot asked.

"Big problem. Those chariots can crush our foot soldiers in the blink of an eye."

"So what can be done?"

Barak laughed grimly. "Pray that Adonai would do to those iron chariots the same thing he did to Pharaoh's chariots at the Red Sea."

"Uh, not to sound like I lack faith, but is there anything else we can do?"

There was a gleam in Barak's eye. "We can engage the enemy on terrain where the chariots are ineffective. Mountains, bodies of water...."

The three men trudged along silently for a long time, each deep in his own thoughts. After a while, Lappidot spoke. "How familiar are you with Yavin's war tactics?"

"Very. I've been watching him closely for twenty years. I'd say I'm an expert."

"How have you observed him?"

"Oh," he said blithely, "there have been all sorts of raids on Yavin's people, and because I live in Kedesh, I've been close enough to the action to watch what's happening."

"Really?" Lappidot suppressed a smile. "How close to the action have you been?"

"Well, brother, it's like this. I've been so close that it's like I'm there myself."

Lappidot shook his head. "I'm amazed you've survived this long."

Barak stopped and turned around so suddenly that Lappidot bumped into him. "I am too," he said earnestly. "I expected to die years ago. It's like I'm veiled to the eyes of the enemy. I even exposed myself to one of Yavin's allies several years ago. A snake by the name of Hever the Kenite. But you know? I never had any lasting trouble from that. I even came out ahead. I got Ishmar from that visit."

"Ishmar?" Yaakov's ears perked up. "Your lieutenant?"

Barak nodded as the men continued walking. "The staunchest support a man could wish for."

Just prior to reaching Tomer Devorah, Barak confided something that had been gnawing at him. "You know, I don't doubt that what Devorah heard is from the Lord. But I wish to place a fleece before the Lord for my own peace of mind, before I endanger the lives of my men."

"What is the fleece?"

"If Devorah agrees to come to the place of battle with me, then I will know that the Lord Himself will fight for us, and that our victory is assured."

Every husbandly instinct rose up in Lappidot. "Do you realize what you're asking?"

"Yes," Barak said quietly. "I do."

Lappidot was about to object when, out of the dim recesses of his memory, he heard Avraham's voice. *Slow to speak, quick to listen.* He took a deep breath. "Let me think about this," he said flatly.

Barak nodded, his eyes fixed straight ahead as he continued to work his way through the forest. "Take as long as you need, friend. We have plenty of time before we reach Tomer Devorah."

After the men reached the great palm, they promptly closeted themselves in with Devorah. She had held court all day under the tree, but her attention shifted often to the northern road, as she checked to see if her husband and brother had returned yet. When they appeared in the distance, she rose quickly to meet them, leaving behind a startled farmer who was in the middle of a story about a gored sheep. "I'll be back with you shortly," she called over her shoulder. Within a few minutes she and Lappidot had met up with each other.

"I'm so pleased to see you," she murmured, as he held both of her hands. She turned and warmly welcomed her brother and then looked at Barak. Lappidot waved an arm toward Barak.

"Devorah, this is Barak, son of Abinoam from Kedesh."

She extended her hand. He took it. "I am delighted to meet the man upon whom the favor of the Lord rests," she said graciously.

"And I am most honored to meet the woman whom the Lord God has deemed worthy to wear the mantle of judge in Israel."

"Thank you. He is a God most worthy of praise." She clapped her hands. "Girls!" she called to several of the maidservants waiting nearby. "Wash the feet of the men and bring them refreshment." Two of the girls ran to get basins of water while two more went to fetch food and drink. "We will talk when you have rested," she said to Barak.

Later that evening, after all had washed and eaten, the three men and Devorah met to discuss war plans. Barak spoke to her of the things he had discussed with Lappidot and Yaakov concerning the number of men he would be able to muster, the effectiveness of the iron chariots, strategy, and geography. When he finished, he saw respect in her eyes.

"You are a man called of God, Barak, son of Abinoam. The Lord God spoke to me about you already. I wish to share those words with you."

"I would be honored."

Devorah paused, and then took a deep breath. Closing her eyes, she reached inside herself and drew back out what the Lord had impressed on her originally. "The Lord, the God of Israel, commands you: 'Go, take with you ten thousand men of Naphtali and Zebulun and lead the way to Mount Tabor. I will lure Sisra, the commander of Yavin's army, with his chariots and his troops to the Kishon River and give him into your hands.'"

Barak heard these words, and after so many years of waiting and watching, they seemed almost unreal to him. *Can this finally be, Lord?* Opening his mouth, he felt compelled to say to her, "If you go with me, I will go; but if you don't go with me, I won't go."

Devorah stared at him, completely taken aback by his request. She looked past Barak at Lappidot, who nodded at her. "I need to pray about your request before I respond," she said. She closed her eyes and asked the Lord, *What should I do?* And instantly she remembered the words she had whispered to the ancient warrior Ehud when she was just a little girl: *"I know I'm just a girl, sir. But I love the Lord God with all of my heart, like Moshe said to do, and I want to lead Israel to victory one day just like you did."*

Yes, she would go with Barak.

She opened her eyes. "Very well. I will go with you. But because of the way you are going about this, the honor will not be yours, for the Lord will hand Sisra over to a woman."

"May it be as He wills." Barak smiled, and all the cares and worries faded from his face. "I don't want the glory. I just want to see Yavin and Sisra destroyed and removed from our land forever."

"So be it." Devorah stood up a bit shakily. "We need to say good night. I'd like to leave in three days. There's a lot to do before then."

Yaakov gladly took his leave, anxious to reunite with his wife for the little time they had before he left again. One of the maidservants showed Barak to a sleeping alcove in the home of Devorah and Lappidot, where he settled in for the night.

Once Devorah and Lappidot were alone in their own room, in their own bed, they felt free to truly greet each other. "I prayed for you continually. God is gracious to us that you are safely back," Devorah said.

He held her close. "And I am so glad to be able to look upon your face."

They spoke in hushed tones of all that had transpired during the time spent apart.

"This is an exciting time," Lappidot said. "Tomorrow we'll send messengers throughout all the territories of Israel, calling men to arms."

"What about our sons? Will they come with us to Mount Tabor?"

Lappidot shook his head. "I think Yehoshua is still too young. He's only eighteen, and twenty is really the age to go to war. Kenaz, Avi, and Shuvah will want to march, though. And I know that all of your brothers will come."

Devorah, ignored his last comment, still focused on her youngest son. "What if Yehoshua insists on coming with us?"

"If he prays about it and believes that Adonai is telling him to go, then he can come with us as a helper, but he's not to take up a weapon and go into battle. Agreed?"

"Yes," Devorah nodded. "Sounds good."

They spoke softly for a while longer before eventually drifting off to sleep.

The next three days were a flurry of activity. In response to Lappidot's fleet-footed messengers, young men and old volunteered to join under the command of Barak from all over Ephraim. A large contingent of well-muscled fighting men marched up from the territory of Benjamin as well.

A messenger returned from the territory of Dan with the welcome news that a contingent of soldiers was on the way and would meet up with them in Kedesh. Dan, a small tribe, was wedged between Judah, Benjamin, Ephraim, and Manasseh with the Great Sea on its western border. Reuben, which was located to the southeast of Ephraim and east of both the Jordan River and the Salt Sea, likewise sent word that their troops planned to march straight to Naphtali.

"I'm relieved," Devorah confided to Lappidot. "I wasn't sure what those two tribes would do."

Lappidot looked pensive. "I am, too. Though I would have preferred they march with us from here, in case we run into any skirmishes along the way." He smiled, irrepressible good humor bubbling to the surface. "Well, it's not for us to worry about. Adonai has all things under control."

"Definitely," Devorah said, as she inspected an ever-growing mound of provisions. "Bered," she exclaimed loudly to an energetic young man on the other side of the mound, "we need more raisin cakes. There's not nearly enough for the number of people going."

"Right away." The young man named Bered bowed respectfully and grinned at them before dashing off to fulfill Devorah's command.

Lappidot studied the young man as he vanished into another building on his way to get more raisins. "He's a good kid."

"He's an excellent aide. No sooner do I ask for something than I find it delivered into my hands." Devorah watched as Bered and another young man carefully added a huge case of raisin cakes to the pile.

Lappidot took his wife by the elbow and led her off to the side.

"What is it?" she said. "What's wrong?"

"Nothing, nothing. I just wanted to tell you what happened with Yehoshua without the whole world listening in."

She studied him expectantly.

"It was as we thought. He desperately wants to fight."

"Did you tell him he can come but he can't fight in the battle?"

"Of course. That's what we decided."

"So how did he take it?"

"He's not terribly happy, but he's willing to be obedient." He leaned closer to her and whispered in her ear. "Just between us, I think when our troops rush down Mount Tabor, we'd better have our youngest son chained to the supply wagon."

"Knowing Yehoshua, he'll start catapulting blocks of raisins with his slingshot," Devorah said wryly. Lappidot let loose a laugh, and Devorah joined in. Weeks of tension erupted out of them as they doubled over in laughter. Before long, they drew a curious crowd.

"So what's the big joke?" someone asked.

Devorah wiped tears from her eyes with the edge of her sleeve. "It was really nothing," she snorted, calming down.

"Brother, we're filled with the joy of the Lord," Lappidot boomed. "This is the end of the oppression of Israel. From now on it only gets better. *Baruch ha Shem!*"

"*Baruch ha Shem!*" someone said, followed by another person. Soon the whole assembly took up the cry. Men and women spontaneously danced and leaped about, putting aside the serious work of preparing for war. All the fears and anxieties that had secretly accumulated in the hearts of men found release in this joyous outpouring of worship before the Lord of the Universe. Just for a moment, the war at hand could be forgotten.

The next morning at the crack of dawn, every troop and helper left the makeshift camp between Ramah and Beit El and followed Barak up to Kedesh. The company numbered around several hundred, including the four sons of Lappidot and Devorah, Tirzah's husband, Ladan, and Devorah's three brothers, Yitzhak, Yaakov, and Yosef. A few women besides Devorah came to help and support her. Tirzah stood by and wept as they loaded up the donkeys in the cold morning air. Countless teary good-byes, jumbled voices, and the rustling of provisions echoed throughout the camp.

As much as possible, they would stay off the main road to avoid drawing attention. Devorah was to ride in front with Barak. She dressed plainly, her hair pulled tightly back from her face, cascading down her back in a long braid. She sat erect on her donkey and assumed military command almost effortlessly, as God-given authority flowed from her. Inwardly, though, she trembled. *Help me, Lord,* she prayed. *Make me the mighty warrior for You that I've always desired to be.* She breathed deeply and felt the peace of God fill her. It was time. She touched Barak lightly on the shoulder. "I think we're ready to go."

Barak lifted the small *shofar* that hung from his saddlebag. Putting it to his lips, he blew three long blasts. The mournful tones of the horn reverberated throughout the valley. Everyone recognized it as the signal to head out.

"May Adonai bless you all and keep you safe," Devorah called out to the crowd staying behind. "We'll be back to proclaim the Lord's victory!"

She exchanged a loving look with her daughter, dug her heels into the sides of her donkey, and rode off.

They rode in a line two across. The cold orange dawn soon brightened into pink streaks across the sky before giving way to the early morning blue that promised a hot day. Barak had deemed it safe to travel on the open road as long as they were in the territory of Ephraim. They would re-evaluate their course when they reached the borders of Manasseh.

Lappidot, meanwhile, rode herd and imposed discipline on the boisterous young men in the company. Trying to turn farm boys into soldiers in a few short days was no easy task. His son Kenaz, a solid, compassionate man of almost thirty, proved invaluable in this regard. Lappidot enlisted his help, as well as the aid of two of his brothers-in-law, and together they brought a semblance of unity to the ranks.

The first day on the road seemed endless. Emotions were raw as the flurry of the last three days of preparation subsided, and each person now rode alone with his or her thoughts. By the time they broke for camp that first night on the outskirts of Manasseh, everyone was exhausted. Nevertheless, Devorah insisted the entire company have a time of worship before they went to sleep.

Shuvah had started out strong this morning, but now he looked at his mother with eyes bleary from fatigue. "Ema," he said, "everyone's dropping. Shouldn't we wait until the morning for this?"

Devorah looked at her third son and loved him. He had her father's coloring, but stood much taller. At twenty years old, his shoulders were broad, his grip firm, and his gaze steady. Surely the Lord had blessed her with her sons! "No, Shuvah," she said firmly. "The only chance we have against Sisra is for the Lord God to fight our battle Himself. We must continually seek Him. He inhabits the praises of His people."

So the company of Israelites spent time every evening and morning in prayer and worship before their King. They purposely did not use any instruments, lest they attract the attention of the Canaanites, but they lifted their voices in song and bowed down in silent prayer.

On the second day, as the company forged through the territory of Manasseh, they were intercepted by a youth of about sixteen years. His clothing torn and face dirty, he emerged from the woods and ran alongside the lead donkeys.

"I have a message for Barak," he yelled.

Barak guided his donkey over to the side of the road. "I am he. What is your message?"

The boy's face lit up. "Oh, sir, I've been waiting for three days, watching for any sign of you. I have a message from the leaders of Manasseh."

"Tell me, son."

Suddenly the boy grew shy as he noticed the great company that stretched far back on the road. He cleared his throat. "Uh, they have received word that you are marching to Kedesh and wish to offer their services as commanders in the field."

Barak and Devorah exchanged glances. Lappidot rode up to meet them. "What's happening?" he asked.

Devorah pointed to the youth. "This brave young man...What's your name, son?"

"Peresh, ma'am," he said, startled to see a lady sitting atop a donkey next to Barak.

"Thank you." She smiled at him, and he, overcome, stared at the ground, pushing his bare toes pushing into the dust. She turned to Lappidot. "Peresh brings us word that the leaders of Manasseh have volunteered to fight alongside us."

"Excellent," he said, the worry on his face replaced by a smile. Barak beckoned to Peresh.

"Yes, sir?"

"How soon until your masters are ready to march?"

"They're ready at a moment's notice. We can catch up with you in three hours' time."

"We?" Barak said coolly, one eyebrow raised.

At first Peresh gulped, then he looked Barak in the eye. "We, sir," he said firmly. "I will fight for Israel."

Barak started to respond when Devorah cut in. "Leave him, Barak." She laid a hand on the boy's shoulder. His face grew crimson at the touch. "He's a fine lad. We'll put him with my son Yehoshua who is running supplies to the troops."

Peresh regarded Devorah with something akin to awe. *Wait until I tell my brothers,* he thought. *A wise and beautiful lady commander. Whoever heard of such a thing!*

"Now go!" she commanded Peresh. "Tell the princes of Manasseh we eagerly await their help. We will be hugging the hill country, heading north toward the border of Issachar, staying to the west of the Jordan River. Join us as quickly as you can!"

"Yes, my lady!" Peresh bowed awkwardly to the three leaders and then turned and scrambled up the hill in furious haste to complete the mission assigned him. Devorah and the others watched him go.

"Send word through the ranks that our brother Manasseh, son of our father Joseph, has volunteered to stand against the enemy with us. It will greatly encourage the men." Devorah spoke these words to Lappidot, who nodded at her and immediately began passing on this new information. Meanwhile, Barak spurred on his donkey, pushing forward with the long journey to Kedesh.

"Barak," Devorah said, "I hope that I did not offend you by stepping in and offering to include Peresh in our company."

Barak spoke slowly and deliberately, with more than a trace of good humor. "I now realize that when I asked you to come, it meant I would be relinquishing some of my authority. However, your wisdom in all matters greatly precedes you, so I rest confident that I will not regret any of your decisions."

"Thank you, Barak," she said. "You are very gracious."

Several hours later, the sentry at the back of the line spotted an advancing company of men. A Levite in the front ranks blew a shofar to identify themselves as Israelites. These were the leaders of Manasseh with a select group of fighting men. The company numbered about two hundred in all.

Their captain bowed down at Devorah's feet. "We are those who love the Lord God of Israel and will give our lives for him."

"Arise," she said. "We are servants of the Most High, like you." The man stood tall and strong, with the erect bearing of a prince. "What is your name?" she asked.

"Ulam, son of Makir."

"Ulam, son of Makir, we are most honored to have you and your men join us in the battle against Yavin and Sisra."

Ulam's mouth tightened. "I will do anything to rid the land of those vermin. They have robbed, destroyed, and oppressed us far too long. Put us where you need us most."

"Barak will instruct you," Devorah said. "Thank you."

The integration of the men of Manasseh into the company proved swift. The men bonded quickly over stories of shared bloodshed, humiliation, and devastation at the hands of Yavin and Sisra. Now that the company moved farther north, the disaster wrought by the Canaanites grew glaringly obvious.

Remnants of burned villages and pillaged fields lay scattered across the country. Men, women, and children emerged from hiding places to bless them as they passed, and Devorah was appalled at how emaciated they were. Over the years, Yavin had plundered more and more of the produce of the fields and vineyards for himself and his people. Those who resisted were murdered as a warning to others.

She wept silently as she sat atop her donkey and gazed again and again at the evidence of the atrocities committed against the Israelites. Every so often, as they passed along the ridge of hills that would eventually take them alongside Mount Tabor, she would notice many altars built on the high places. Altars not to the God of Israel, but rather to other gods.

*How far we have fallen from You,* she cried out to God. *How blessed we are as a people that even though we have been as an unfaithful wife, yet You are calling us back to Yourself by Your infinite love and compassion. As far as the heavens are above the earth and as far as east is from the west, so is Your love for those who fear You. Have compassion on us, O my God! We are but dust, our days are like grass. As the flower flourishes in the field only to be blown over by the wind and be no more, so are we, O Lord our God.*

On the fourth day of the journey, the company entered into the territory of Issachar. This was the last tribe through which they would pass before reaching Naphtali. On the edge of Issachar, just before the border into Naphtali, stood Mount Tabor. All had heard of the prophecy Devorah had spoken forth to Barak, which signified that the battle would commence from Mount Tabor.

"We have yet to receive word from Issachar," Barak said to Devorah as he glanced up and down the mountains.

"What is your opinion?"

"I know many good men here. I'm surprised we have not yet seen a show of support." Before she could answer, they spotted a sudden movement in the bushes halfway up the hillside to the right of them. Barak reined in his donkey. "Whoa. What's that?"

Devorah sat stunned as hundreds of men came pouring down the hillside. As they ran, they shouted and cheered. *Issachar!* Tears filled her eyes as the throngs of new soldiers pledged their allegiance to Barak. *Thank you and praise you, Adonai,* she prayed.

The ranks of the company had swelled to close to two thousand over the course of the journey to Kedesh. As soon as they arrived, Ishmar and a team of aides welcomed the troops and quickly began to assign sleeping quarters and food. Barak immediately sent messengers out to Zebulun and Naphtali and called for more men to come and fight. Valiant warriors streamed into Kedesh singly, in pairs and in groups, until the numbers added up to the ten thousand predicted by Devorah. As far as the eye could see, men prepared themselves for war: they exercised, practiced combat maneuvers, rehearsed battles, and memorized strategies. Overnight, Kedesh had turned from a moderate-sized town to a sprawling military camp.

Barak had told Devorah that Yavin had routinely confiscated all the shields and spears he could find from the men of Israel. Devorah dreaded the disadvantage this would create on the battlefield. However, she soon discovered that what they lacked in shields and spears, they had more than replaced with bows, arrows, daggers, and not a few homemade swords. She smiled to herself as she recalled Lappidot's words earlier in the week: *Adonai has all things under control.*

Meanwhile, no further word came from the tribes of Asher, Dan, Reuben, or Manasseh east of the Jordan. Ulam requested leave from Barak to go directly to the tribes and gather more troops. "I will take only two men with me, and we will go with the swiftness of eagles."

Barak studied him for a few moments before answering. He gazed off to the east, toward Manasseh. "All right. You can go." As Ulam started to leave, Barak put a hand out to stop him. "Wait. We want men whose hearts and souls are dedicated to Adonai. Keep that in mind. And be careful."

Ulam smiled; the stories of generations of strength were written across his face. "I will. When you march from this place to Mount Tabor, I will be with you."

"Good. Go then, and may Adonai be with you."

"And with you."

"Things are going well, don't you think?" Devorah said to Lappidot as they watched a group of young soldiers going through maneuvers.

Lappidot frowned. "Yes and no. The men we have are adapting well, but I'm concerned that so many tribes still haven't sent anyone. Ulam has been gone for three days."

"The word that the Lord gave only spoke about ten thousand men. They're here, plus about two thousand more."

Lappidot gave a hollow laugh. "Our twelve thousand men are going up against nine hundred iron chariots and more trained soldiers than there are grains of sand on the seashore. I have to admit, I'm a little intimidated."

"Lappidot, we can't look at what's physically in front of us. We've got to believe that God is fighting for us—"

A loud shout caught Devorah off guard. She and Lappidot turned as a crowd began to gather around the village gate.

Ulam and his men stumbled into the camp, their clothing torn as if in mourning. They lamented bitterly, at the top of their voices.

"My brothers are dead to me," Ulam shouted in anguish. He sat in the dust and bowed his head in grief.

When Barak reached them, he clasped Ulam to his chest. "What happened?"

"It's my brothers," Ulam said hoarsely. "They will not fight for Israel. They are content to stay among their sheep pens and gaze at the stars. They do not believe the Lord God will fight for us. They believe the Canaanites will slaughter us, and they do not wish to risk their lives." He wailed bitterly.

A wave of unrest permeated the camp. *Where are the rest of our fellow Israelites? Why are they afraid to fight with us?* Men who had previously trusted that the Lord God would deliver them now began to doubt and lose heart.

Lappidot and Devorah watched in despair as morale collapsed all around them. Lappidot sank to his knees. "Forgive me, Adonai. I should never have worried about the number of men we have. I didn't trust You. I have sinned before You."

Devorah knelt down with him, and together they cried aloud to the Lord for forgiveness. As they prayed, the enemy of their souls lost strength. Fear receded and peace settled upon them.

"This is the battle," Devorah said. "Right here. On our knees. What happens later is merely cleaning up in the physical what has already happened in the spiritual." She slipped her arm through her husband's and looked at him tenderly. "Send word through the camp that we will be gathering together to seek the Lord immediately. Tell the Levites among us to prepare burnt offerings for the Lord."

So it was that the whole multitude fell on their knees before the Lord and repented of their unfaithfulness and fear. Sacrifices of bulls and rams went up on altars, and the pleasing aroma wafted up to heaven. Those who had instruments retrieved them, and thousands of voices sang praises to the Lord with harp, lyre, cymbals, stringed instruments, flutes, trumpets, tambourines, and voices. Barak spoke words of encouragement to the men, and a great hush fell over the army. Devorah stepped forward with her head bowed before the men. After a time, she looked up and spoke, and all listened intently to her words.

"We are here," she said in a loud, clear tone, "because we lost faith in the Lord our God and did evil in His eyes. For decades, we bowed down to the countless gods of the pagans, and for that reason we were sold into the cruel and merciless hands of Yavin, king of the Canaanites. The Lord our God is a jealous God, who punishes the sins of the fathers to the third and fourth generation, but shows mercy and love to those who follow Him for a thousand generations.

"It has been twenty years since Yavin first started attacking the towns and villages of Israel. Twenty long years." She took in the sea of faces turned toward her and loved them. "And in that time a remnant has always held fast to Adonai.

"You are that remnant. You are those whom the Lord delights in calling His own. You are those whom the Lord has polished like arrows and hidden in His quiver. You are those whom He has sharpened like swords and hidden in the shadow of His hand. You are a weapon forged for His glory. He will not stand by and watch you go to your destruction.

"What is our faith? It is being sure of what we hope for and certain of what we do not see. We are small and weak in comparison to the enemy, but we are commanded by the Lord of Hosts, and before us is our mighty God.

"What can faith do? Noach, when warned about things not yet seen, in holy fear built an ark to save his family. Our father Avraham went to this land on which we now stand by faith. By faith he believed God's promise that he would have a son, though he was past age and Sarah herself was barren. By faith, when God tested him, he offered Yitzhak as a sacrifice. He who had received the promises was about to sacrifice his one and only son, even though God had said to him, 'It is through Yitzhak that your offspring will be reckoned.' Avraham reasoned that God could raise the dead, and, in a fashion, he did receive Yitzhak back from death.

"And what more can be said? You know about Moshe, the plagues against Egypt, the parting of the Red Sea, the destruction of Pharaoh's army, the falling of the walls of Jericho, the taking of the Land, and so much more.

"Go then. Follow Barak, son of Abinoam. He is the leader whom the Lord your God has chosen to take you into battle. Go with him to Mount Tabor. Be strong and courageous. You have been chosen by the Lord of Hosts to see with your own eyes how He will rescue us. Strengthen your weak arms and feeble knees, because the Lord your God will fight for you if you stand firm and do not shrink back. Now go. Go to your tents and sleep well because tomorrow at dawn we leave for Mount Tabor." She stepped down then, drained from the power of God that had surged through her in such intensity. As she heard twelve thousand voices raised in spontaneous praise and worship she knew deep in her spirit that the battle was won, and that Israel would be victorious.

Lappidot reached her side and stood with her. "Well said, my wife.

Adonai used you mightily."

"It's all of us, Lappi," she said solemnly. "He's using all of us." Together they joined the worship until, spent, they returned to their tents and fell into deep, dreamless sleeps.

# TWENTY-THREE

Sisra's spies reported that the Israelites had mobilized troops to fight him. Immediately, he gathered together his nine hundred iron chariots and all the men he had, from Haroshet HaGoyim to the Kishon River. Next he sent messengers to the scattered outposts of his allies to entreat them to come and help him destroy the Israelites. One of these outposts was the camp of Hever the Kenite.

"Come," the messenger yelled as soon as he galloped into the camp. "Israel has chosen to march against us. Commander Sisra sends word that there will be wealth for each man after we strip the dead and burn the villages to the ground."

Hever's camp had grown considerably larger over the last several years. His alliance with King Yavin had advanced his status from that of a wealthy nomadic herdsman with a small community to that of a powerful local prince. At the chief priest Ishra's insistence, Hever had erected an actual temple to the goddess Asherah, and Ishra made quarterly visits to Hever's camp to maintain the temple. The temple succeeded in attracting several hundred people from around Hazor who subsequently moved to Zaanannim.

In addition, Hever had begun an export trade of wool cloth woven from the sheared wool of his thousands of sheep. King Yavin's protection allowed Hever to trade freely with traveling merchants without fear of attack.

Despite the increase in people and wealth, however, the quality of life in the camp had steadily degenerated. The temple worship gave rise to levels of promiscuity, drunkenness, and violence beyond anything the Kenites had known before. Normal sexual relations between husband and wife became outdated as men and women gave themselves over to the perverse acts of lust and depravity promoted by Asherah. Babies of questionable parentage were routinely born, and just as routinely sacrificed to the flames on Asherah's altar. The Kenites did what ought not to be done and as a result became filled with every kind of wickedness, evil, and greed imaginable.

Cleanliness and order fell to the wayside. The once peaceful community became a writhing cesspool of envy, strife, and deceit. Malicious gossips, slanderers, and murderers, this new generation completely disregarded the authority of their parents and the one true God. Hever had taken to running the camp with an iron fist; in these terrible days, fear was the only voice of authority anyone would hear.

Yael tried to make a difference, but she held little real power. Now a mature woman in her early thirties and mother to an eighteen-year-old son, she possessed a dignity and wisdom borne of much suffering. Still beautiful, the only overt signs of age were tiny lines at the corners of her eyes and an occasional strand of gray in her lustrous brown hair. She continued to grow in the fear and knowledge of Adonai and sought after Him fervently. Hever, on the other hand, became more and more hardened as time went by. He spent little time with Yael and chose instead to lay with whoever his latest and youngest wife happened to be.

After Ishmar had left the camp, Hever took a sixteen-year-old girl as his third wife. After a year, he grew bored with her and took another wife. And then another.

Simcha and the succession of women who followed after her became a cause for sorrow with Yael. None of them showed any interest in the Lord God. Rather, they matched their husband in pagan wantonness. The multitudes of children born to these women were a disagreeable lot. Coarse, whiny, unwashed, sullen and, Yael secretly thought, entirely too much like their father.

The position Yael held within the camp as Hever's first wife forded a delicate balance with her faith in the Lord God. Terribly saddened by the world she lived in, and all but ignored by her husband, she nevertheless carved out a small niche for herself with a few others who shared her morals and her faith. With these few, she held influence and favor. The rest, mindful of her status, thankfully left her alone. She spent her days working at the tasks all women did, grinding grain, cooking, fetching water, cleaning, weaving cloth from the wool of sheep and goats, experimenting with dyes for Hever's export business. Mostly, though, she devoted more and more time to prayer, sequestered from prying eyes in her own tent. *I'm like a prisoner,* she told the Lord. *But I know that when the time is right You'll release me.*

Yael's deepest regret in life was that her son, Hadash, showed no inclination to follow after Adonai. Helpless, she watched as he leaped headfirst into the pit of debauchery that characterized the camp. He already had made three girls pregnant, yet scoffed at the idea of marriage. He treated his mother with contempt and only remained obedient to his father because he respected Hever's power.

Although he worked hard in the fields, tended his father's flocks, and pursued every young female who caught his eye, this used up only part of his excessive energy. He twitched for adventure and action.

When Sisra's messenger reached the camp, Hadash was like a ripe fig about to drop off the tree. And when the messenger added that the Commander specifically requested that if Master Hadash were to come fight, Sisra would use him on his own chariot, Hadash nearly burst from excitement. He idolized Sisra. He immediately rushed to his tent in order to pull together a few belongings.

Most of the other men in the camp heeded the call to war as well. Among them were Reuel and Nadab, both quite powerful in their own right after many years spent serving directly under Hever. Another was Etnan, Hadash's childhood friend. And, despite his age of almost fifty, Hever also prepared to go.

When Yael heard of Sisra's call, she boldly pushed her way into Hever's tent and grabbed hold of his hand. "No. Please don't go. Don't fight against Adonai. You'll only lose! Hever, I know that we haven't agreed about a lot of things and that we have had our differences, but please understand that to go with Sisra now is to court death!"

Hever laughed. It was a harsh, grating sound. "Death? The Israelites have been cringing in fear for years. They are no match for the Canaanites." He laughed again. "They barely have any hand weapons, let alone chariots. We outnumber them twenty to one." He waved his hand at her arrogantly. "It's sheer stupidity for them to challenge King Yavin. I don't know what they're thinking. It's outright suicide."

"No, Hever." Yael gripped his arm but he shook her off. "It's not stupidity. What about all the raids on Canaanite towns that can't be traced? Don't you see? Can't you tell? They have heard from the Lord God of Israel. He's going to deliver them from the hand of their oppressors. Now is the time! I can sense it. If you go, you'll be killed."

He stared hard at her then. "Would you mind that so very much?"

"Oh, Hever." Yael sighed. "You have not made it easy for me to be your wife. But I loved you once. And I wish you no harm. I greatly desire to see you know Adonai before you die."

He had listened intently to her, but at the last statement he sneered. "Oh, you're back to that again, are you?" He turned his back on her.

Yael's heart sank as she realized she had lost him. "All right. I know I can't convince you. But please, Hever, I don't want Hadash to go. He's my son also, and I don't want him exposed to needless danger."

Hever turned to face her again. "He's coming with me."

"No. I won't let him go."

"He's a man, not a boy holding onto his mama's dress. He's ready to fight the enemy and build his own house with the wealth and plunder."

"They're not the enemy!" Yael cried. "They're his own people."

"His people are Kenites."

Yael's eyes sparked with intensity. "The Kenites are kin to Moshe. They would never come against the sons of Avraham. You have forgotten what it means to be a Kenite."

Hever's mouth tightened. He raised his hand instinctively to strike her but slowly pulled it back down again. Since his attack on her over Sisra he had not hit her again. "This topic is closed. Hadash is coming with me." Then, unexpectedly, his voice softened. "Don't worry about us. We'll be back before you know it." He returned to his packing.

Yael left without another word and hurried over to Hadash's tent. She found him polishing his spear, whistling tunelessly. She ran to him and clasped him around his broad shoulders."Hadash," she exclaimed, "put that spear away. You're not going anywhere."

"What?" He pulled away and stared at her belligerently. "Yes, I am. I'm going with Abba."

"Hadash," she said more gently, "listen to me. The Israelites are your brothers. Why do you want to kill them?"

He snorted, annoyed by her persistence. "They are not my brothers. They're our enemies. Abba said so, and so did the Commander."

"Because they said so, does that make it true?"

"You know what? I really don't care. I have the chance of a lifetime to be on the Commander's chariot in a major battle that we're going to win. And I am not going to miss out."

"This is a terrible mistake, my son. You're only eighteen. There will be plenty of battles ahead for you. But I firmly believe that Israel will win this one, and I do not want to see you harmed."

"Oh, Ema." He gave her a tiny kiss on the cheek, hoping to mollify her and get her off his back. "I'll be fine. Before you know it, I'll be home."

Until the moment they rode away, Yael tried desperately to persuade Hever, Hadash, and the other men not to go. But despite her pleas, they gleefully ran off to partake in what they expected to be a rollicking slaughter. Deep in her spirit, Yael knew she would never see any of them again.

Bleakly, she recalled the story of Noach, and how he spent one hundred years building an ark, calling on men and women everywhere to repent before the fury of the Lord overtook them. Out of all the people on the face of the earth, only Noach and his family were deemed righteous by the Lord; only they were permitted to enter the ark and escape the flood that soon drowned everyone else who breathed.

Yael held tightly to her last glimpse of her son; his head leaned forward as he eagerly pressed his donkey faster. His brightly polished spear gleamed in the sun. *Oh Lord*, she prayed. *Be gentle with the young man Hadash for my sake, if not his own.* And she wept bitterly.

# TWENTY-FOUR

arak, Devorah, Lappidot, and their twelve thousand troops arrived at Mount Tabor. The journey spanned two days, during which scouts went before and behind, searching for any signs of an ambush. The company reached its destination without incident, climbed to the top of the mountain, and set up camp. Mount Tabor rose steeply into the air for about seventeen hundred feet. The view from the top was dazzling; one could see for miles, which meant no one could get anywhere near the mountain without being spotted.

Five miles away, Sisra doggedly gathered his troops together in the plain east of the Kishon River. To the Israelites atop Mount Tabor, the amassing of chariots and men resembled ants converging on a fallen log.

"Look how many there are," Yehoshua said, awestruck.

"I didn't know there were that many Canaanites," wondered Peresh, of Manasseh. The Israelites had waited at the summit of the mountain for three days. Barak had organized the men into companies of five hundred, and appointed a captain over each company. Now they patiently ran through military drills and bided their time. Some of the captains included Ishmar the Kenite, Ulam of Manasseh, Malcam the Benjamite, Elon of Zebulun, Guni of Naphtali, Lappidot the Ephramite, and a recent volunteer from Judah who had shown himself to be exceedingly loyal and courageous: Shimon, son of Kasha, the Beershevite.

Yehoshua and Peresh, the two youngest members of the company, had become fast friends and bunked together in one of the many tents. Now Peresh experienced a thrill of fear as he crouched on a rock and observed the massive assembling of the enemy. "It's a good thing God is on our side," he muttered under his breath.

"I heard that," Yehoshua said from his perch. "He is, too."

Just then a shofar blast reverberated mournfully throughout the camp. The two youth looked at each other wide-eyed. It was starting! They scrambled down and raced over to the rest of the company.

To their disappointment, it was not yet time for battle. Rather, the shofar had been a call to pray to the Lord for His favor against this awesome and seemingly impenetrable foe. No one had failed to notice of the vastness of Sisra's army. Barak guessed they had at least fifty thousand men. All of those metal chariots reflected thousands of points of sunlight as they rolled into position. It took everything the men had to hold onto their faith.

Seventy bulls lay strapped to makeshift stone altars, preparing to die as a burnt offering before the Lord. After they were killed and the choice pieces offered up to God, the Levites carved the bulls' flesh and roasted it over the fires to feed the men. Worship and singing, praise and thanks went up to Adonai. A sense of the presence of the Lord descended upon the company and they looked to heaven with reverent awe.

"I believe the Lord has a word for Barak," Devorah said quietly to her husband.

Lappidot nodded in his direction. "Tell him."

Devorah walked over to the place where Barak knelt on the ground. His head was bowed and his hands were stretched out in front of him. With due reverence for his time before God, she tapped him lightly on the shoulder.

He opened his eyes. "Yes, Devorah?"

"I have a word for you from Adonai."

He looked expectantly at her.

Devorah closed her eyes. "Go! This is the day the Lord has given Sisra into your hands. Has not the Lord gone ahead of you?"

Barak stared at her for a moment, then his face broke into a tremendous smile. "*Baruch ha Shem*," he exclaimed. Years of waiting, watching, training, raiding, seeking and praying all came together in a single expression. Tears formed in his eyes. "*Baruch ha Shem*," he murmured again, overcome with emotion now that the time of redemption was at hand.

Almost instantaneously, word spread throughout the company. *It's time, it's time,* the men said, one to another. *The waiting is over. It's time to throw the Canaanites out of our land and to take back the possession given to us by the Lord.*

"Dawn," Barak shouted. "We meet the enemy at dawn. Go to sleep." And he went through the ranks one last time to encourage, console, advise, and instruct. The men reluctantly left each other's company and made ill-fated attempts at sleep. Minds raced, eyes stared into the blackness, and hearts beat with fearful expectation of what the next day would bring to them all.

At the end of a restless night, in the cold gray of pre-dawn, the troops arose. Men everywhere strapped on bow and arrows, concealed daggers, and tied swords around their waists. A heavy, somber mood settled like fog over the camp. Quickly, too quickly, Barak raised the shout and ten thousand men rallied to his side, preparing to follow him down the treacherous slopes of Mount Tabor.

It had already been decided that Devorah and Lappidot would stay back with two thousand men who would pray, intercede, and go in to battle later if needed. *The word from the Lord stressed ten thousand men*, Devorah had said emphatically. *I believe it would show a lack of faith to bring more men than Adonai specified.*

Barak had agreed, albeit not without his reservations. *This whole thing is a faith gamble anyway, isn't it?*

Devorah had stood firm. *We have to win, and we have to win on His terms*, she said. *The only reason we've had these foul Canaanites oppressing us is because we lost faith with Him. This is the only way.*

So the men left behind stirred restlessly, hearts joined to their brothers who would run first into battle. They knew their role was God-ordained and valuable, yet it remained hard to stay behind while the others plunged in.

As the morning progressed, the gray sky gave way to a blood-red color unlike any sunrise any of them had ever witnessed. The men looked at each other, their faces grave. *This is a bloody day. A sign from heaven*, they declared.

The red deepened, then faded as the sun came up over the horizon and struggled to pierce the heavy clouds. "Come!" Barak shouted. "Now is the day of deliverance, now is the day of salvation. The Lord Himself will fight for us. Those who are for Israel, follow me!"

With great whooping yells, ten thousand men in twenty companies swept after Barak and plunged down the mountain just as the first raindrops fell from heaven.

Devorah stood to the side, hands raised in blessing over the men as they rushed past her. *Victory, Lord. Grant us victory*, she prayed. *May our enemies fall by a sword that is not of man. Let their stronghold fall because of terror. May their commanders panic at the sight of our battle standard. Let them quail not before us, but before*

*You, O Lord. It is You whom they have treated with contempt all these years. Let them see Your awesome might. Let them know that there is one true God, and You are the One.*

After the last man descended down the mountain, she and an older Levite named Elkanah went to each of the captains of the four battalions who were left and encouraged them to pray as never before, for their very lives and the lives of their comrades. Then Elkanah bowed down in worship, and Devorah and those who were left on the mountain bowed down with him. They knew the battle would be won by prayer, and their watch was just beginning.

When Sisra's scouts saw the Israelites descend from Mount Tabor, they raced back to their leader with the news. "The Israelites are coming. They are heading toward us."

"Good," Sisra rubbed his hands together. "This will be satisfying."

He watched as the Israelites came into sight across the vast plain alongside the Kishon River. Then he strode confidently over to the group of officers at battle headquarters and raised his voice in a shout. "Who's ready to cut the heads off these miserable sons of Avraham?"

"We are!" came the bold and boisterous cries from the captains. They ran out and shouted to the western flank, which stood poised on a ridge overlooking the plain. "Who's ready to cut the heads off the miserable sons of Avraham?"

"We are!" the elite company of archers roared back.

"Who's ready to cut the heads off the miserable sons of Avraham?" the captains shouted again.

"We are!" the first-defense spear throwers yelled.

"Who else is ready to cut off the heads of the miserable sons of Avraham?" the captains screamed yet again.

"We are!" the sword carriers bellowed from behind the spear throwers. Man after man repeated Sisra's words until the whole vast multitude, tens of thousands of soldiers, roared back their approval. The clanging of spears and shields, swords and arrows combined with the neighing of horses tethered to hundreds of chariots caused a menacing cacophony. Abruptly, the noise ceased. Dark rain clouds moved in from the northeast until they covered the sky. The wind picked up and the temperature dropped.

Sisra's troops looked on in bewilderment as the clouds burst open and rain gushed, poured, flooded from the sky, blowing almost sideways right into their faces. The nine hundred iron chariots that had rolled into position behind the sword carriers began to sink. When the rains started, they slowed down considerably, wheels sinking into the wet earth.

"Hurry! Move those chariots now!" Sisra and his captains yelled. Frantically, the chariot drivers whipped their horses in a frenzy to move faster. As the ground beneath them turned into a mud pit, chariot wheels sunk down into the miry, gluey earth. Before their very eyes, their greatest military strength was turning them into an immobile target.

Angry officers ran up and down the lines of chariots, beating on men to dig the wheels out. Desperately, men dug with swords, spears, and bare hands, their skin soon ripped and bleeding. As quickly as they could free the chariot wheels, rain and mud poured back in. The heavy weight of the iron chariots caused them to sink deeper and deeper into the mud. More and more men cursed, strained, and sweated in the hopeless task to free the chariots. Sisra's greatest advantage was now a terrible liability.

The Israelites, led by Barak, advanced steadily across the plain.

"We should be rolling over those vile swine by now!" Sisra roared. His mind raced furiously as he surveyed his useless chariots and the thousands of men already worn out by the endless mud. The Israelites drew closer.

Sisra made up his mind. "Leave the chariots!" he ordered. "We have more weapons and we outnumber these upstarts. Let's fight them in the field. Every man to the plunder!"

He motioned for his frontline defense: the elite archers perched on a ridge slightly to the west and the spear carriers positioned in front of headquarters. As the archers fitted arrows to bows and the spear carriers raised their weapons, a phenomenon occurred that would be discussed for years afterward by all who witnessed it. Patches of blue sky and sun appeared to the east of the Israelites, the wind and rain at their backs, while the sky remained ominously dark over the Canaanites. As the Israelites progressed, the clear sky remained over them while the rain continued to deluge the Canaanites from a horizontal angle.

Under orders from Barak, Ulam of Manasseh led a contingent made up of renowned slingshot throwers from his tribe. They had crept far ahead of Barak and the rest of the company, on alert for Sisra's famed archers. When the archers came into view, Ulam prepared his men for action. The mighty gusts of wind and rain that blew directly into the archers' faces made it impossible to achieve a steady aim.

As the archers struggled to see their foe, Ulam gave his command.

"Now!"

Hundreds of stones were hurtled at lightning speed toward the archers, finding their marks in foreheads and sides of heads.

As the bodies of hundreds of archers toppled facedown off the ridge, great gusts of wind and rain continued to pour forth against the Canaanites and blinded them so that nary a man could see to aim his sword or spear against the advancing troops. And then, to Sisra's utter disbelief, the temperature dropped even further and hail the size of a man's fist began to fall. The Israelites watched in jubilation as hailstones felled the enemy left and right. Confusion and panic gripped the Canaanites. *The God of the Israelites is fighting against us*, they wailed, and their spirits shrank in fear as they retreated in self-defense, all thoughts of loot, plunder, and bloodlust forgotten.

As Barak rode up alongside the Kishon River and witnessed the routing of the Canaanite army before the Israelites had even reached them, he realized what was happening.

"Oh my Lord," he cried aloud. You are a great and mighty God. Thank You for this victory today!" His heart swelled within him and his courage grew until he felt as if angels carried him on their shoulders. "They're ours, men!" he yelled. "The Lord God is on our side. Don't leave a man alive!" And he ran, sword in his hand, howling wind at his back, to pay back all Israel had suffered at the hands of Yavin and Sisra.

Ten thousand men followed Barak, borne jubilantly along by the Presence of the Lord. They ran into the first line of Canaanites, swords flashing, and cut down the enemy like grain behind a reaper.

Metal clanged on metal as swords and spears struck shields. The Israelites fell on their enemies with great shouts, lopped off heads and disemboweled the enemy with their handmade swords. Blood and guts spilled out into the mud, and the stench rose such that men gasped for fresh air. As quickly as the Canaanites were killed, the Israelites would strip the fallen bodies and take ownership of their superior weapons. Soon Sisra's entire flank closest to battle headquarters collapsed.

Stunned at the slaughter of his troops, Sisra positioned himself further back in the ranks, desperate to put more men between himself and the Israelites. *This is going badly. Now is the time for me to save myself.* As he scrambled to escape, he quickly decided to follow the banks of the Kishon River east toward the Jordan River, where he would cross over and head north to Hazor. He moved swiftly among his men under the pretense of shouting commands, while secretly he awaited the opportunity to slip away unnoticed. As he sought to escape, Hadash, son of Hever, grabbed his arm.

Sisra stared angrily into the lad's terrified eyes."What is it, boy?" he growled.

"Please help me, sir," Hadash begged. "This isn't what you told me would happen. Keep me safe! Don't let them kill me!"

"Get away from me." Sisra shook off the lad's clutching fingers. "This is war. People die. Go fight like a man!" He shoved Hadash to the side and attempted to head down to the river when Hadash ran behind him and seized his arm again.

"You're leaving, aren't you?" Cunning mixed with the wild panic in his eyes. "You're running away. You're —"

Suddenly he stopped, eyes glazed in shock. He opened his mouth and blood poured forth. Sisra calmly pulled his dagger out of Hadash's heart and wiped it on the boy's tunic. "Stupid half-breed fool," he muttered scornfully. And he vanished into the underbrush alongside the river.

As Sisra escaped, the battle raged unchecked. The Israelites cut men down by the thousands, until the corpses so littered the field that men were forced to fight with writhing bodies beneath them. Slowly it dawned on Sisra's men that their commander was gone; whether dead or fled, they did not know. Helpless without their leader, the Canaanites began to divide and scatter.

Made desperate by fear and the comprehension that this was their day of destruction, the Canaanite hordes stampeded in retreat. They flung away weapons, cried out to their worthless gods, and ran blindly toward the river, heading west.

Barak and his troops gave chase and cut the Canaanites down all the way to Haroshet HaGoyim. Barak came upon Ishra the priest and two of his cohorts as they tried to escape and cut them down in mid-stride. And still the wind blew, the rain fell, and the hailstones pounded the earth.

Perched atop Mount Tabor, Devorah observed all these things and commanded the four remaining captains. "Go! The Lord has given us the victory. Now is the time to join your brothers and put to death the Canaanites. Do not leave one alive!" Filled with excitement, Lappidot and the other captains led their battalions down the mountain and across the plain to cut off the retreat to the river. Four hundred men stayed behind to guard the camp and prepare food for the return of the troops.

Down by the Kishon River, Ishmar the Kenite valiantly led his men from Naphtali. Sweating, bloodied, and filthy—yet exuberant by the tremendous victory the Lord had prepared for them—they swept after the fleeing Canaanites west along the Kishon River. Many of the Canaanites plunged into the river to escape the sword, only to be knocked down by the river's torrential current and drowned.

When they reached the river bank, Ishmar and his men continued to rout the retreating Canaanites. Suddenly, one of the enemies tripped and fell, blocking Ishmar's path. Ishmar grabbed the man by the hair and raised his sword to slit the fellow's throat, then stopped himself with a jolt. It was Hever.

All traces of smugness and pride had disappeared from Hever's eyes. His face was now smeared with dirt and blood almost beyond recognition. A pang of pity pierced Ishmar's heart for this man who had once been his friend. He hesitated. In that instant, Hever thrust with his sword to puncture Ishmar's side. Ishmar dodged the blow, escaping with a light surface wound. One of Ishmar's men came from behind and, with one powerful, bold stroke of his sword, severed Hever's head from his body.

Ishmar moved forward mechanically now, strands of black hair plastered to his face as sweat mixed with the blood of those whom his sword had devoured. His men waited for his direction. He knew they drew strength from his presence. "Keep going," he called above the din. "Pursue them to the last man!"

Pursue them they did. The destruction of Sisra's forces that day was enormous. Bodies of countless thousands of men lay rotting across the valley. Yet Lappidot and the brothers of Devorah continued forth from the mountaintop, not seeking to preserve their own lives but rather to destroy every enemy of the Lord Most High. Together, they led their troops to sever heads and pierce hearts until their hands were frozen to their swords. Relentlessly, they pushed themselves until every Canaanite for miles around lay dead on the ground.

With their last reserve of strength, the company dragged themselves up the slopes of Mount Tabor and back to their camp. Devorah and the four hundred men waited for them. Before she saw her husband and sons, Devorah greeted Barak. "Blessings, O Prince of Israel," she cried. "You have done great good today. The Lord God is mightily pleased with you. Israel is saved!" And she knelt down and kissed his hand.

"Arise, Devorah, judge of Israel," Barak answered. "If I am a prince, then you are a queen." He smiled graciously at her, and her heart filled with gladness for the salvation the day had wrought.

"Has not my lady a kiss for me?" Lappidot trudged up the hill from behind Barak.

"Lappidot," Devorah threw her arms around his neck and kissed him in full view of all the men. "I am so happy to see you, my husband."

"And I you," he said. "This day has been an historic one."

"What about our sons?"

"Still struggling up the mountain. All unscathed and filled with stories. But later. Now we must eat. We are weary beyond reason."

So they ate, and rested, and the Levites prepared thank offerings to the Lord.

"What of Sisra?" Barak said abruptly.

Ulam paused, his drink midway to his lips, and concern darkened his brow. "I have not seen him since the very start of the battle."

"Nor I," another captain murmured. Up and down the ranks, out of thousands of men, not one had put Sisra to the sword nor remembered seeing him since early in the day.

Barak jumped to his feet. "We have to hunt him down. If he is alive, trouble will rise from the ashes of today's defeat. He most certainly will head to Hazor to hide under what's left of Yavin's protection. Who will come with me?"

Every man there offered, and so in the end Barak handpicked twenty men, all valiant warriors, among them Ishmar the Kenite and Shimon the Beershevite. They headed to Hazor that very night in search of Sisra.

# TWENTY-FIVE

The camp of Hever the Kenite had altered drastically now that Hever and most of the men had left for war. Animals roamed wild and fields went untended. The hedonistic lifestyle of the pagans had created laziness throughout the camp, and few of the women left behind cared enough to maintain the camp. Yael tried to encourage people, but met with much resistance.

"Why should we bother?" one woman asked as she sat languidly at the entrance to her tent and peeled a pomegranate. She sucked noisily at the seeds. "When our men return, their arms will be filled with plunder and we will all be rich!" She smiled broadly, and the sticky red seeds covered her teeth like blood on the fangs of a young lion after a kill.

Most of the other women agreed. *Why should we work? Soon we'll have Hebrew slaves to do our work for us.*

Those faithful few who quietly trusted in Adonai gathered about Yael and formed a small enclave within the larger camp. Such a fear of Hever permeated the camp that even in his absence no one dared raise a hand against his first wife or those under her protection.

As the days crawled by and no news of the battle reached them, Yael grew more and more convinced that the Lord had lifted His hand against Sisra and his army. She was torn between jubilation for Israel and dread over the fate of her son. Over Hever's fate, she felt a sense of relief; it was over.

On the morning of the seventh day, Yael and the others in the camp awakened to a blood-red sky. Within hours, the red had dissipated to a leaden gray, accentuated by a light but persistent drizzle. Heaviness settled upon the camp. Yael tried to grind some of last year's wheat into flour, only to feel herself so pulled down by the weight of the air that she allowed her arms to drop limply at her sides. Getting up, she closed herself off in her tent and threw herself on her face before the Lord, not knowing how to pray. The Spirit of God helped her, interceding with groans that words cannot express. Sometime later, Yael pulled herself up and stood in the center of her tent, arms stretched up toward heaven.

"I am Yours, Lord," she said. "Everything I have is Yours. I exist to do Your will." As she bowed down in worship, a tremendous burden lifted from her spirit.

The next morning, before it was even light, the Lord woke Yael. *What is it, Lord?* she asked.

*Go outside*, the Lord commanded her spirit.

Obediently, Yael arose and threw a shawl around her shoulders. Quietly, she tiptoed out of the tent. All around her, people still slept. The air was very still, the sky dark. Stars twinkled in the sky overhead, soon to be obscured by the coming day. A sense of freedom came over Yael. She threw back her head and drank in the beauty of the heavens.

The whisper should have startled her, but somehow she expected it. "Yael."

She turned in the direction of the voice. "Who is it?" she whispered back.

"It's me. Sisra." Out of the gloom stepped the commander's familiar figure. Yael could just discern his outline in the dark. His eyes were those of a hunted animal fleeing for its life. As Yael looked at him, she knew without a doubt that he had lost the battle.

*What should I do, Lord?* she prayed silently.

*Take him into your tent*, came the response.

*Are you sure, Lord?*

*Do it*, He commanded.

"Come, Sisra." she beseeched him softly. "Come into my tent. Let me offer you refreshment and you can tell me what has happened."

Sisra hesitated. He glanced briefly over his shoulder.

Yael pulled open the flap to her tent. "Come, my lord. Come right in. Don't be afraid."

Mutely, he followed her inside. He was so tired he could barely stand. He shivered as he stood in the center of her tent.

"Come," Yael said. "Lie down in my bed and let me cover you with blankets."

So Sisra fell into the very bed where he had tried to seduce Yael so many years before. Now, however, he lay there like a complacent child, and not a powerful aggressor. Yael took the soft, fluffy sheepskin coverings and tucked them around his trembling form. His eyes followed her as she moved about the tent.

"I'm thirsty," he said. "I need water."

Yael had a skin of milk in her tent. She opened it up, and, on sudden impulse, pulled the bowl off its pedestal that her father Kasha had made for her as a wedding gift so many years ago. Pouring milk into the bowl, she brought it to Sisra, kneeled down, and held it to his lips. He drank greedily. "Thank you," he rasped.

"My lord," Yael said. "What of the battle?"

The last bit of strength drained from his countenance. "Not good."

Yael nodded. She already knew that but needed to hear Sisra confirm it himself. "What of the young man Hadash?"

Sisra shook his head. "I don't know," he lied as he closed his eyes.

Yael stared hard at him then, and realization hit her in the stomach. *He's dead*, she thought. But she said nothing aloud.

Sisra started to fall asleep, but roused himself. "Yael."

"Yes, my lord?"

"Stand in the doorway of the tent. If someone comes by and asks you, 'Is anyone here?' say 'no.'" Without waiting for an answer, he fell fast asleep, thoroughly exhausted.

Yael stood by the bed and looked at his face. He appeared to have aged twenty years overnight. The cruelty that characterized his life revealed itself in the ugly lines on his face. Years of overindulgence had marred his once handsome countenance so that his features seemed a mockery of their former glory.

*How could I ever have wanted him*, Yael wondered, sickened by the recollection. *How could I have ever sinned against my Lord God with this tool of the Enemy?*

*Destroy him, My daughter.* The voice of the Lord pressed in on her.

Yael's eyes opened wide and she swung around. A palpable presence of the Lord filled the tent. She knew He was here. Trembling, she knelt down.

*O Lord*, she prayed. *Who am I, Your maidservant, that you should bestow on me the honor of avenging Your people Israel?*

*You are My arrow*, He answered. *I have polished you since the day of your birth and hidden you in My quiver for just such a time as this. I have indeed beheld your misery and separation from your people, but it was My will that you should be prepared for this moment. Behold your enemy, My daughter!*

Yael turned her face then and looked upon Sisra, who snored softly under the sheepskin covers.

*He trusts you. His contempt for Me is such that he doesn't believe you would ever betray him to avenge My Name. But today is the day of his death. No longer will he mock My holy name. Destroy him now, My daughter.*

*How, Lord,* she asked. *How?*

*You have spent twenty years as a tent dweller,* came the enigmatic response.

A tent dweller? Yael scanned the tent, not sure what Adonai meant. In the corner, on the ground, something caught her attention. A tent peg! In that moment, she knew what to do. *Be with me, Lord,* she beseeched Him silently.

Stealthily, she crept over to the corner of the tent and picked up an extra tent peg. Quietly, she retrieved her hammer. Slowly, her heart in her throat, she walked over to the bed where Sisra lay, fast asleep. A moment of doubt assailed her. *Don't let him awaken, Lord. Help me,* she prayed. Then she carefully gripped the tent peg in her left hand and the hammer in her right. Her heart thumped so loudly her ears rang, as she placed the tent peg over Sisra's temple.

*Bam!* She pounded the hammer down on the peg with all of her strength. Again and again she hit the peg, driving it right through his head and into the ground. He never woke up.

Blood covered everything. Shattered pieces of bone, brains, hair and skin were smeared across her hands and down onto the pillow. Nauseated, Yael dropped the hammer as dizziness overwhelmed her. She took a few deep breaths before she realized she had better clean herself and hide Sisra until God showed her the next step. Her whole body trembled as she scrubbed her hands in the wash basin before she threw a clean cover over Sisra's mutilated form. She then changed her clothes, combed her hair, and positioned herself outside the entrance to her tent, standing guard.

Within the hour, Fatma approached Yael's tent, much as she did every morning. "May I tidy up for you, my lady?"

"No," Yael spoke too sharply, and blocked the doorway. She assumed a gentler tone and attempted a smile. "That will not be necessary today, thank you."

The servant was confused. "Well, how about food? Can I bring you something to eat?"

*Food? Ugh!* The thought was abhorrent right now. But it would look suspicious to refuse. Yael forced herself to speak calmly. "Yes, thank you. That would be fine." Relieved, she watched Fatma walk away, heading to a communal kitchen area.

Yael sat outside the entrance to her tent all morning. The Lord did not give her any more instructions, so she did not move from her seat. Members of the camp eyed her strangely, but no one dared question her.

About midday, a band of Israelites rode into the camp. They rode on horses and were dressed as warriors. Yael saw them approach and recognized Barak immediately. Her heart leapt within her. As they neared the center of the camp, the frightened people scattered.

Yael rose from her seat and came to meet them. She saw only Barak: the rest of the men were as a blur to her.

"My lord Barak!" She bowed low to the ground in front of him.

He jumped quickly down from his horse. "My lady Yael. Please arise." She arose and they studied each other.

*Still beautiful,* he thought. *How will she react when she learns of her husband's death?*

*A godly man,* she thought. *A man whom the Lord God loves.* Tenderly, she gazed upon his face and noted the fatigue, the battle stains, and the unmistakable hope in his eyes.

Suddenly, Barak remembered why he was there. "We're looking for Sisra. Have you seen him?"

An indecipherable look passed across her face. "Come with me. I will show you the man you're looking for."

So for the second time that day, a man not Yael's husband entered her tent. Barak followed her unquestioningly. His mouth dropped open in amazement when she led him to her bed and pulled the sheepskin cover off.

Barak's eyes grew wide and he stared at Yael in astonishment. "You did this?" he asked, as she pointed at Sisra's lifeless form.

Unable to speak, Yael simply nodded and looked down at the ground. Barak chuckled with delight as he cupped her face between his hands and kissed her full on the lips. Just as suddenly, he released her and stepped backward. "Forgive me for my boldness," he said when he saw the surprise in her eyes. "But you are an amazing woman."

She smiled shyly, her first real smile in a long while. "I am simply the Lord's maidservant."

"Come," Barak said. "Let's take care of this." Together they left the tent and Barak called to his men. When they came nearer, she spied a familiar face.

"Ishmar!"

"My good lady Yael." Ishmar, older, with the noble bearing of a prince, rushed over to her and she embraced him as she laughed and cried all at once.

He held her and stroked her hair while Barak looked on. "My lady," he said tenderly, "I am so pleased to see you well."

"And I you," she said through joyful tears. "What of Ria and the twins?"

"Very well, and more children besides. But later there will be time to speak of all these things." His face grew grave. "I bring sad news. Neither your husband nor your son survived the battle yesterday."

Yael's face crumpled. Of Hever she was not surprised. She had known he was a dead man the moment he left the camp. But she had held out a shred of hope that Hadash would be spared. Her son! Her own flesh and blood! Even though he had foolishly pitted himself against the Lord Almighty, she had prayed that somehow he would escape with his life. Tears flowed freely as Ishmar's words penetrated her soul and the last embers of hope were extinguished.

Ishmar held her while she sobbed. After a while he said, "I have other news that will lift your countenance some. One of our company knows you and greatly desires to see your face."

"Knows me?" She gazed up at him with eyes wet with tears. "Who?"

Shimon the Beershevite came up behind Ishmar. "It is good to see you, my sister."

Yael gasped. She had not seen her brother Shimon in twenty years— not since he was a youth of sixteen. Now he was a man in full strength. "Is that you, Shimon?"

"Yes, it is." He swept her into his arms and swung her around and around.

Suddenly, it was all too much for her. Again she sobbed uncontrollably. Tenderly, Shimon sat down and cradled her against his chest as one would hold a young child. After a while, her sobs abated and she was able to be still, her head upon his comforting shoulder.

Meanwhile, Barak motioned the rest of the warriors into Yael's tent. Great jubilation broke out among them as they realized the stunning work that the Lord had wrought this day. When Shimon heard the news, he touched his sister's cheek with reverence. "I bow to you, my sister," he said humbly. Then he spoke to her of all that had transpired in Beersheva since last she was there, and she listened with a glad heart to the news of people she had despaired of ever seeing again. In turn, Yael began to share some of what had happened in her life over the years, and of Hever's downfall into evil.

Shimon's face filled with compassion for Yael as she related these things. "I know that Hever is dead."

"Yes."

"Do you remember the last time we saw each other and I told you that you're not the slave woman, you're the free woman?"

"I have never forgotten that," she whispered hoarsely, and tears threatened to flow again.

He took her hands in his and looked into her eyes. "Do you know that you're the free woman now?"

Yael looked back at him, and her green eyes seemed fathomless. "I am free indeed."

Later that day, Barak took Yael aside. "My lady, it is imperative for your safety that I bring you and all those from this camp who are sympathetic to the Israelites back to Mount Tabor, where the rest of the army remains encamped. Will you come?"

Numbly, she shook her head *yes*. Was there no end to the changes in her life that today would bring? Dimly, she noticed the pleasure that sprang to Barak's eyes by her ready acquiescence.

"How many people would you say are loyal to you from this camp?"

"Including myself and Fatma, there are twelve."

"Can you be packed and ready to leave in two hours?"

Yael's eyes widened. "That's awfully fast. Must we leave so quickly?"

Barak looked grim. "I'm afraid so. Once I see you safely off with Shimon and Ishmar, the rest of us need to make sure no one from this camp wars against Israel again."

Yael put a hand over her mouth. "Do you mean to say...?"

His expression hardened. "Don't ask. The less you know, the better." His tone softened. "We've won the battle, but it's still not safe out there. We had better get moving." He cleared his throat. "I look forward to seeing you at Mount Tabor."

"As do I," she said simply, lifting her eyes to his.

Awkwardly, he touched her shoulder and then let his hand drop. "I'm sorry about your losses today, Yael. It is my prayer that the Lord God will richly reward you for your bravery." He paused. He longed to say more, but he knew it would be too much, too soon. "You deserve a life filled with much joy."

Yael's emotions felt raw to the point of bleeding. She understood the vista of possibilities that lay before her, but she needed time to recover. "Thank you, Barak. I know Adonai will take care of me."

Less than two hours later, Yael and those whom she handpicked doubled up on horses and galloped off into the fading dusk with Ishmar and Shimon leading the way back to Mount Tabor. Besides her clothes and jewelry, the only other thing Yael took was her father's bowl. *Don't worry about packing too much*, Barak had said. *We should be able to get these things after we relocate everyone.*

Then Barak and his men went through the camp and destroyed those who stood against the Lord God of Israel. Afterwards, they, too, rode off toward Mount Tabor. The camp of Hever the Kenite lay empty and desolate in the black night.

Ishmar, Shimon, and Yael reached Mount Tabor that evening. Shimon had told Yael during the course of their journey about Devorah, the prophetess and judge in Israel, and that she was currently at the mountain camp.

"Devorah!" Yael exclaimed. "I met her many years ago, outside of Ramah. She has had a profound influence on my relationship with Adonai. Is she really at this place we are going to?"

"She really is." Shimon tried to adjust mentally to the fact that this bold, godly woman was the volatile young girl he remembered from twenty years ago.

"I cannot wait to see her," Yael said quietly.

"Something tells me that she will want to see you as well."

After they arrived at the army camp, Ishmar went to Devorah and Lappidot and told them all that had transpired in Zaanannim. Devorah and Lappidot exchanged amazed glances. "The Lord said He would hand Sisra over to a woman," Devorah said. "He has done as He promised." And she went over to Yael, who stood shyly next to her horse, and hugged her, hard.

Yael looked at her in wonderment. "Do you remember me?"

"I have never forgotten you, Yael of Beersheva. I have prayed for you these last eighteen years, and I am thrilled with the woman of valor that you have become. Future generations will speak of your act of heroism and your name will never be forgotten. Now let me bless you."

Yael knelt obediently and Devorah placed her hand on Yael's head and prayed. "O Lord, thank You for this woman and how Your hand has upheld her throughout her life. I thank You that she has clung to You through many trials and temptations. I thank You that she is Your maidservant, obedient to Your voice. I ask that You hold her in Your arms as she grieves for her husband and son. I ask that You would grant her a new life, a life full of joy and promise. I thank You for Yael and ask Your blessings on her, in Your holy name. Amen."

"Amen," Yael repeated through her tears.

By the next morning, Barak and the rest of his warriors returned to the camp. A sacred assembly of thanksgiving to Adonai was scheduled for the following day, after which everyone would head back to their homes.

Barak immediately sought out Yael. He spoke haltingly. "My lady. I wonder…" He stopped, searching for words. "I wonder if you and those with you would desire to come back with me to Kedesh."

Yael didn't respond right away.

"Ishmar and Ria are there," he said in an awkward attempt to persuade her.

She laughed then—a beautiful sound. "I love Ishmar and Ria. But I don't believe they're the reason why you want me to come to Kedesh."

"No." Emboldened by her response, he took a deep breath and plunged in. "I want you to come for me." He took her hand and clasped it between his hands. "I want you to be my wife. Will you?"

He held his breath. Yael looked up at him. "Barak, son of Abinoam, I would be most honored to call you my husband. But I need time to mourn my dead. Will you wait for me?"

He exhaled and grinned broadly. "As long as it takes."

He bent down and kissed her willing lips. Yael sank into his embrace, finally experiencing a kiss that spoke of love, commitment, honor, dignity, and, yes, even passion.

# EPILOGUE

On that day Devorah and Barak son of Abinoam sang this song:

"When the princes in Israel take the lead,
when the people willingly offer themselves—
praise the Lord!

Hear this, you kings! Listen, you rulers!
I will sing to the Lord, I will sing;
I will make music to the Lord, the God of Israel.

O Lord, when You went out from Seir,
when You marched from the land of Edom,
the earth shook, the heavens poured,
the clouds poured down water.
The mountains quaked before the Lord, the One of Sinai,
before the Lord, the God of Israel.

In the days of Shamgar son of Anat,
in the days of Yael, the roads were abandoned;
travelers took to winding paths.
Village life in Israel ceased,
ceased until I, Devorah, arose,
arose a mother in Israel.
When they chose new gods,
war came to the city gates,
and not a shield or spear was seen
among forty thousand in Israel.
My heart is with Israel's princes,
with the willing volunteers among the people.
Praise the Lord!

You who ride on white donkeys
sitting on your saddle blankets,
and you who walk along the road,

consider the voice of the singers at the watering places.
They recite the righteous acts of the Lord,
the righteous acts of His warriors in Israel.

Then the people of the Lord went down to the city gates.
'Wake up, wake up, Devorah!
Wake up, wake up, break out in song!
Arise, O Barak!
Take captive your captives, O son of Abinoam.'

Then the men who were left came down to the nobles;
the people of the Lord came to me with the mighty.
Some came from Ephraim, whose roots were in Amalek;
Benjamin was with the people who followed you.
From Makir captains came down,
from Zebulun those who bear a commander's staff.
The princes of Issachar were with Devorah;
yes, Issachar was with Barak,
rushing after him into the valley.
In the districts of Reuben there was much searching of heart.
Why did you stay among the campfires
to hear the whistling of the flocks?
In the districts of Reuben there was much searching of heart.
Gilead stayed beyond the Jordan.
And Dan, why did he linger by the ships?
Asher remained on the coast and stayed in his coves.
The people of Zebulun risked their very lives;
so did Naphtali on the heights of the field.

Kings came, they fought; the kings of Canaan fought
at Taanach by the waters of Megiddo,
but they carried off no plunder.
From the heavens the stars fought,
from their courses they fought against Sisra.
The river Kishon swept them away,
the age-old river, the river Kishon.
March on, my soul; be strong!
Then thundered the horses' hoofs—
galloping, galloping go his mighty steeds.

'Curse Meroz,' said the Angel of the Lord.
'Curse its people bitterly,
because they did not come to help the Lord.
to help the Lord against the mighty.'

"Most blessed of women be Yael,
the wife of Hever the Kenite,
most blessed of tent-dwelling women.
He asked for water, and she gave him milk;
in a bowl fit for nobles she brought him curdled milk.
Her hand reached for the tent peg,
her right hand for the workman's hammer.
She struck Sisra, she crushed his head,
she shattered and pierced his temple.
At her feet he sank, he fell; there he lay.
At her feet he sank, he fell;
where he sank, there he fell—dead.

"Through the window peered Sisra's mother;
behind the lattice she cried out,
'Why is his chariot so long in coming?
Why is the clatter of his chariots delayed?'
The wisest of her ladies answer her;
indeed, she keeps saying to herself,
'Are they not finding and dividing the spoils:
a girl or two for each man,
colorful garments as plunder for Sisra,
colorful garments embroidered,
highly embroidered garments for my neck—
all this as plunder?'

"So may all your enemies perish, O Lord!
But may they who love You be like the sun
when it rises in its strength."

Then the land had peace forty years.

—Judges 5

# Glossary of Hebrew Terms

**Abba**—familiar term for father

**Adonai**—literally, "my lords." Used instead of speaking the Name of God aloud.

**Almah**—virgin

**Amen**—"so be it." Generally used at the end of a prayer.

**Anakim**—giants

**Avdah**—variant for the word *slave* or *servant*

**Avraham**—Abraham

**Avraham avinu**—Abraham our father

**Barak**—lightning

**Baruch Atah Adonai, Eloheinu Melech HaOlam**—Blessed are You, O Lord, Our God, King of the Universe. Traditional beginning to many Hebrew prayers.

**Baruch ha Shem**—literally, "bless the Name." The Hebrew way to say "praise God."

**Beeti**—my daughter

**Beit El**—literally, "house of God, "otherwise known as Bethel

**Beresheet**—Genesis

**Bimah**—platform

**Boker tov**—good morning

**Boobah**—doll

**Devorah**—Deborah, also means honey bee

**Dodi**—my beloved

**Elohim**—God

**Ema**—familiar term for "mother"

**Gamal**—camel

**Gehenna**—hell

**Hasatan**—literally, "the adversary; devil, satan"

**Ishra**—bad man

**Ketuvah**—marriage certificate

**Lappidot**—torch

**L'chaim**—literally, "to life!"; term of celebration

**Lilah tov**—good night

**Mazel tov**—literally, "good luck." Commonly used for "congratulations."

**Meshugga**—crazy

**Miryam**—Miriam

**Moshe**—Moses

**Motek**—term of endearment: darling, sweetheart

**Pesach**—Passover. Otherwise known as the Feast of Unleavened Bread. See Leviticus 23:4-8 and Deuteronomy 16:1-8.

**Rivkah**—Rebecca

**Saba**—Grandpa

**Savta**—Grandma

**Shabbat**—Sabbath. Here it refers to the seventh day of the week.

**Shabbat Shalom**—Sabbath peace. An expression used for greeting people on the Sabbath.

**Shalom**—literally, "peace"; can be used for hello or good-bye.

**Shimon**---Simon

**Shofar**—ram's horn. Used as a trumpet.

**Shuk**—market

**Sukkot**—plural of the word *sukkah,* or booth. Otherwise known as the Feast of Tabernacles. See Leviticus 23:33-44 and Deuteronomy16:13-17.

**Tamar**—date palm

**Tavita**—Tabitha

**Tomer Devorah**—palm of Deborah

**Torah**—Five Books of Moses; Pentateuch

**Yaakov**—Jacob

**Yael**—mountain goat or graceful woman

**Yafah**—pretty or nice, feminine

**Yaldah**—girl

**Yehoshua**—Joshua

**Yehuda**—Judah

**Yishai**—Jesse

**Yitzhak**—Isaac

**Yofee**—literally, beauty. Used to mean "wonderful."

**Yosef**—Joseph

# About the Author

**DEBORAH GALILEY** grew up in a conservative Jewish home on Long Island. After graduating from college, she moved to Los Angeles. There she became a believer in Yeshua (Jesus). Deborah and her husband, Steve, moved from L.A. to Central New York in the late 1980s and have been leading messianic Jewish congregations ever since. They have five children: Josh, Shimon, Yael, Noa, and Ellie.

"The Devorah in *Polished Arrows* is loosely based on myself," Deborah says. "My husband says that he is not surprised by the vitality of the Devorah character. Her willingness to take on new challenges and infuse energy into her roles of wife, mother, and an exhorter of God's people reminds him of me. But I assure you that the Yael in the book is quite different from Yael, my daughter! After choosing Yael's name when she was born, we soon realized that it was prophetically important as she would someday complete what I, the mother, had begun. In the same way, Yael in *Polished Arrows* completed what Devorah the prophetess began."

Over the years, Deborah has enjoyed her participation in activities as varied as bread baking, worship dance, playing clarinet, youth ministry, percussion, and teaching Hebrew. She has experienced the miraculous power of God in healing her of cancer three times!

How did *Polished Arrows* come about? "One day, while I was on a walk, the Lord gave me the concept for *Polished Arrows* and said, 'Start writing!' How can you say no to the Lord? So I plunged in." Since that time, she has completed a second novel, *Yohana*, and is currently at work on a third.

Deborah and Steve have also founded a messianic Jewish internet radio station: **www.soundsofshalom.com.**

For more information on Deborah, go to **www. capstonefiction. com.** You can contact her by writing to: Deborah Galiley, PO Box 1019, Utica, NY 13503.

Printed in the United States
81679LV00003B/4